Invitations to the Slaughterhouse

Once he had loved her totally, without question. Then she had betrayed that love and he had killed her—brutally, savagely . . .

They had caught and caged him like a crazed animal. They took him apart and put him back together again. They gave him a new name, a new identity . . . and told him to forget the past.

But someone was prodding his memory. First with a record whose songs brought back her screams . . . a pink sweat shirt that once ran red with blood . . . a news clipping that told a horrified world what he had done.

And with each reminder, his new grip on life weakened. Beneath the quiet surface, he was caught in an exitless maze, crazed by uncertainty . . . targeted by someone who wanted to kill him . . . or make him kill again!

SEVERED TIES

George E. Simpson
and
Neal R. Burger

A DELL BOOK

Published by
Dell Publishing Co., Inc.
1 Dag Hammarskjold Plaza
New York, New York 10017

Dell ® TM 681510, Dell Publishing Co., Inc.

ISBN: 0-440-17705-7

Printed in the United States of America
First printing—July 1983

Once again, to our wives,
Jean and Maureen,
and to our editor,
Jeanne F. Bernkopf

CHAPTER 1

Paul Mizzell got off the elevator and walked into the plush executive offices of Rok Records, the comp under his arm just finished, sprayed and covered. He headed for the marketing director's office, hoping for a quick approval. His worn cowboy boots clumped on the parquet floor. Tucking his shirt into his jeans and running a nervous hand through his beard, he went through the high-tech glass doors into Never-Never Land, so dubbed by the art staff because lately Tony Benedict's customary answer to a creative suggestion coming from anyone other than himself was "Hey—sorry, kids, but never."

From the moment Tony Benedict had come in as marketing director, Rok's homey atmosphere had vanished, replaced by air-conditioned sterility, efficiency checks, and stiffer deadlines.

Paul remembered coming through that door two years ago for his first meeting with the creative director, Linda Sharman, and being impressed by an air of vitality and fun. At that time in his life, after years of grim therapy and enforced soul-searching, the prospect of living normally and having work to enjoy and be absorbed in had seemed a godsend. But all that changed quickly when Tony Benedict arrived and, in a few short months, managed to completely turn around the company that Rocky Holt had founded with compassion and love.

Gone was the lobby display, the tacky collage of old record jackets pasted one on top of the other, making the wall bulge with cardboard—a warped monument to the company's achievements. Some of the staff had suggested having it bronzed and presented to Rocky, but Tony had personally supervised when it was cut up and carted away. The old didn't just make way for the new: at Rok it had to be systematically dismembered first. Now there was a cold brass plaque on the lobby wall—ROK spelled out in bold, slanted letters, trailing a short stream of gold discs. Like a lot of other jobs lately, the new company logo had been farmed out, and therefore found little appreciation among Rok's art staff.

Tony Benedict had been brought in to give the company a face-lift. Marketing Director was just a title—The Lone Re-arranger would have been more to the point.

Paul stopped in the outer office and nodded automatically at the secretary, dark-haired with eyes like ice—another stranger. He sat down to wait, propping his art work against the potted palm next to his chair. Another sign of indifference: Rok had become one of those places decorated with a lush abundance of greenery to display with-it extravagance. The plants were re-moved and replaced every Monday by a local exotic foliage service. The life expectancy of everything at Rok had grown depressingly short.

In the last eight months, Tony had created four new executive positions and had filled each of them with hotshots in their late twenties—his own age. Young fireballs full of ideas, and all of them *men*. Linda Sharman was thirty-seven and a woman. She had been Rocky Holt's first art designer years ago. He had promoted her to creative director, but where did she fit in now that Tony was in control?

And Rocky Holt, who should have been around to see that things ran smoothly and personalities didn't clash, was out of town most of the time—traveling, finding new acts, new talent, new music, and in Paul's opinion, abdicating his responsibility.

"Mizzell."

Paul looked up. Tony stood in the doorway to his office, wearing a sharply creased white tropical suit and a soft print shirt open at the collar, exposing a he-man thatch of chest fur and a heavy gold chain. He was macho down to his Gucci loafers, and his hair was styled in a fluffy mod wedge.

"Let's see what you've got," he said.

Paul closed the door and came in with his art work. There were other men in the room—Rok's sales director, Marvin Bensch; the Struts' producer, Steve Klemer; their attorney, Lou Eisen; and their manager, Jerry Madison.

"Shouldn't Linda be here?" Paul said, glancing at the men.

"I would have called her, but the fellas only have a minute. Come on, let's see. Put it down here." Tony pointed to a glass-topped coffee table.

Paul put the comp down and pulled back the cover sheet on his rendering of the Struts' first album cover. Everyone crowded around.

"What do you think?" Tony said without a trace of emotion. There were a few appreciative murmurs and a satisfied grunt from Marvin Bensch. Jerry Madison studied the work, reluctant to commit himself.

"Maybe I should explain it," Paul said to break the ice. When no one objected, he went on. "The background is the new Main Street in Venice. It's all illustration, to be finished in full-color airbrush. We'll strip in a stock crowd shot for people on the street, give it a one- or two-color tone, whatever works best. And over that we'll super the Struts wearing those turn-of-the-century band uniforms—a full-color photo we can do right here in the studio."

"Strutting, right?" Tony said.

"Of course."

The lawyer nodded and looked at Tony. "Sounds good," he said.

Tony smiled and sat down, pulled the art closer, and leaned over it, his fingers exploring the comp while he made a show of careful consideration.

"It's good," he said finally.

"I think it's terrific," said Steve Klemer.

Tony smiled encouragingly. "Fine work, Paul. You've done real well with the concept. I like the angle on the street there. Perfect depth. And with the Struts up front, I think we've got a solid eye-catcher. Now, Jerry, this is the Struts' first album, and I hope you understand we have your interest at heart."

"Sure, Tony."

"Good. Because I've got a way to make this better."

Why the hell isn't Linda here? Paul thought to himself.

"It'll raise the cost, though."

Jerry looked blankly at the art. "What could make it better?"

Tony got up and paced, eyeing Marvin Bensch, who stared back, ready to support anything. Tony patted his midriff in a studied gesture, then looked at Paul and said, "No airbrush, no art work. We do it live. The whole concept, one photograph."

Jerry was puzzled.

"The crowd and everything?" Paul asked.

"Everything. We take a crew out to Main Street, close it off for a few hours—"

"Close it off?" The lawyer was seeing dollar signs.

"Hire a crowd—got lots of folks down in Venice dying to be on an album cover. It's like the movies, only better, because the jacket sits in the stores forever. They can point it out to their friends, start word-of-mouth. We'll do the rest—schedule a Struts concert down there, create a whole cult in Venice, make this a Venice-based group. Local boys with new sound!"

"They're from Watts," Jerry said dully.

"Not anymore. They just moved to the beach. I got another idea!" His eyes flashed with the beauty of it. "The crowd in the street—we'll have them *all* strutting, like this!"

Tony struck a pose that was too practiced to be off the top of his head. He locked one leg out in front, set his arms rigidly at his sides and flared his fingers. Marvin Bensch laughed and applauded. Steve Klemer grinned and said, "All *right!*"

Paul stared at Tony. How long had he spent rehearsing this? Nothing wrong with it actually. Good commercial razzmatazz. But why hadn't he brought it up before?

Tony grinned at Jerry. "Get a hundred people out there, put the Struts in the foreground, shoot low, see everyone through their legs. Paul, this is going to be great."

"Hey," Paul said flatly, "whatever you want."

"I like it," Jerry finally admitted. "I think the boys will, too."

"Sure they will. We'll do a whole promotional thing on the day of the shoot—press, TV . . ."

"What about cost?" Lou Eisen said quietly. "You're going from a hundred percent illo to a hundred percent live photo. We're on a budget."

Jerry looked at Tony, concerned.

"Not anymore," Tony snapped. "This is too big. Right, Jerry? We want to get your boys launched. We need a zippy

cover and publicity on the shoot. I did it for the Gaudies and look
where they went—big.''

Paul swallowed hard. The design for the Gaudies' album was
his.

"We'll do the same with the Struts. Okay, Jerry?''

Jerry nodded. "Fine with me. Listen, the boys always told me
they wanted to go with Rok because it's first class. Now I see
why.''

"You're beautiful, Tony,'' said Marvin, the quintessential
yes-man. Around the company he was known as Oui-Oui.

"You bet your ass,'' Tony said, laying a strong, firm hand on
Jerry's shoulder and rocking him back and forth. Then he picked
up the comp, flipped the cover back, and gave it to Paul. "Finish
that up. We'll use it as the model for the shoot, okay? Thanks.''

Paul turned at the door and said, "Who explains the change to
Linda?''

"You do,'' Tony said nicely, and shut the door.

"Well, the son of a bitch has done it again.'' Linda sank into
her chair and pushed Paul Mizzell's comp across the desk. He
watched her stare out the window, drained.

Linda Sharman's office was still small, even after sixteen years
with the company. She kept it neat and uncluttered, with wall
unit counters and shelves lining every available space. Design
trophies and awards were prominently displayed, but there were
no other mementos—no photographs, no favorite record jackets,
no autographed publicity stills. The shelves were stacked with
back issues of *Cue*, *Rolling Stone*, and recording industry trade
publications. Her desk was a broad slab of oak on chrome legs
with no drawers. Three chairs were placed neatly around a single
small coffee table before it. There was a picture window that
looked out on Sunset Boulevard, a view she could have done
without. Hollywood was not home to her—just a place to work.

She stared at the Russian restaurant across the street, fashioned
after the country house at Varykino in *Doctor Zhivago*. She had
never been inside it; one of these days she really ought to give it
a chance. She started to rub tired eyes but stopped, recalling her
teenaged daughter's warning—rub your eyes and you get crow's-
feet. Terrific advice from a kid majoring in body sculpture or

beauty techniques, or whatever the hell it was. What was the difference? At thirty-seven, you either had crow's-feet or you didn't. Linda had them. It was getting harder to hide skin blemishes, but she was about ready to give up the battle anyway. She was still fresh-looking and careful about wardrobe, staying with skirts and soft pastel sweaters or tailored suits. No jeans—they made her look too thick. She wore her blond hair long and limited herself to one piece of jewelry, a jingly gold bracelet given to her by Rocky Holt on her tenth anniversary with the company.

Linda sighed heavily and smiled at Paul. He looked back sympathetically. "It's not your fault," she said. "He's just playing genius."

"I think he planned it ahead of time. He knew exactly what he was going to do."

"Probably. He's right, though. That cover should be photo. I thought so all along. But on the budget he gave us . . . Oh, Christ, I can't get around him. He makes the rules and he breaks them. Nobody else in this company can do that.

"Why don't you have it out with Rocky?" Paul suggested.

"Rocky loves Tony."

Paul frowned. "Why?"

"Because he gets results. You don't see what happens at the other end, just what passes through art. He's got every department head in the company on a short leash. He pulls, we jump."

Paul shrugged and picked up his comp. "Back to the drawing board?"

Linda nodded.

Paul went out without another word. When he was gone, Linda stared at the phone, anger washing over her so completely that her teeth clenched and she balled one hand into a fist. She couldn't understand Rocky anymore. What the hell was he doing gallivanting all over the world looking for new acts? Couldn't he see what was happening right under his own nose?

Tony had been marketing director at Capitol and RCA, so he knew how to manage volume, and how to handle a talent list as long as his arm. But Rok's success depended on the personal nurturing of a limited roster of quality acts. What had made Rocky think that Tony was equipped to deal with that? So far, his concept of management consisted of radical change and little else. His approach to employee relations was to fire people and farm out the work. Album packaging for half of Rok's artists was now done outside, and the results were good, which frustrated Linda. There was getting to be less and less work for Paul Mizzell and the few artists who remained.

She picked up the phone and punched Tony Benedict's extension. The secretary answered. "This is Linda," she snapped. "Put him on."

The secretary asked her to wait, then went off the line. Long seconds passed, Linda's anger building. She rehearsed a speech in her mind—

"Hi, Linda." Tony sounded cheery. "Hey, I loved your presentation on the Struts. We can really make something out of that."

"It wasn't a presentation, Tony. It was a comp. It was exactly what we agreed on at board, on the budget you approved—"

"Hey, I said I liked it. I just think photo will work better than illo. Don't you?"

"Look, I'm getting really tired of this."

"Tired of what, Linda?"

"Interference. Am I running creative or not?"

"I bought the layout."

"No, you changed it—to make yourself look good."

Tony sighed. "Can't we stop fighting?"

"Sure, but from now on, why don't we budget after you see the layout? Then we can all be geniuses."

Tony laughed. "I'll take it up with Rocky. I can't stay on the phone, sweetie. Got two producers and an artist in here— It's my creative director, fellas. She's on the warpath."

Linda bristled. "You condescending bastard—"

"Listen," he said. "I've got somebody waiting—a reporter from the L.A. *Times* wants an interview. Do me a favor and take him to lunch, okay? I'm really swamped."

"What are you talking about?"

"I'll send him right up." The line clicked off.

Linda stared at the phone in her hand then slammed it down. It's a man's world, she reminded herself. Especially in the

recording industry. She was one of a tiny handful of female
executives in the business, and she had a hunch that their number
was soon to be diminished by one.

Linda spotted the man throwing down his tip and was off to
grab his table before any of the twelve other people waiting
noticed. Brian Hawthorn was startled but hurried after her. She
sat down and waved him to the other chair. Tibbits' was crowded
but fast; Linda hated lingering over lunch. She passed a menu to
the reporter and studied him. He was somewhere in his midthirties
and running to seed. His suit was awful, straight off the rack
from a downtown discount house, ill-fitting and not helped by a
ten-year-old tie. He was sort of handsome but looked like he
never slept. He put his briefcase under his chair and his portable
tape recorder on the table.

Brian smiled and said, "What's good here?"

"Salads."

"Too healthy. They got a nice greasy hamburger?"

"Probably."

Brian smiled at the waiter too. "Cheeseburger, medium—extra
tomato, french fries, and coffee."

Linda winced and ordered. "Fruit salad, extra cottage cheese,
and a glass of Chablis."

"You on a diet?" Brian asked after the waiter left.

"No. Are you?"

He grinned. "Well, Miss Sharman—"

"Mrs."

"Excuse me. You're married?"

"Divorced."

"Oh. Me, too. Heather couldn't live with my hours." He
glanced at her breasts as she unbuttoned her jacket and smoothed
her sweater. She caught him looking.

"Is that going to be in your article? My divorce?"

"No. I'm doing a piece on mob influence in the recording
industry." He stood the tape deck up, directing the mike toward
her. "If this makes you uncomfortable, I'll just take notes."

"Either way, you won't get much. I don't know anything
about mob influence in the recording industry."

The waiter served her wine and his coffee. When he was gone again, Brian said, "You mean Rok Records is clean?"

"Can I ask you a question?"

"Sure."

"What on earth would make you do a story like that? Is that how you stir up news? Couldn't you go out and cover a murder or something?"

"I've done that." Brian sugared his coffee heavily.

"Then try the men's room at the Bijou. Ask the fags what they think about gay lib. That ought to sell papers."

"Sure. Reporter's head found floating in public toilet. I'll stick with the mob, thank you."

Linda raised her glass. "Your choice."

"Look, Mrs. Sharman," Brian said quietly, "I didn't ask to cover this story. It was assigned to me." Linda sipped her wine, eyeing him over the rim of the glass. "If you don't know anything," he continued, "it's cool. Okay?"

He looked away while stirring his coffee. Linda put down her glass and thought before speaking. "I know of a lot of things wrong with the recording industry. I could probably fill that tape. But nothing on mob influence. You're interviewing the wrong person."

"Not your department, huh?"

"Come on, Mr. Hawthorn, who are you kidding? You just want some poop on Rocky Holt. The *Times* would love to nail a big fish like that."

"Wrong. The *Times* doesn't crucify people. I'm on the level. I tried to see Rocky Holt, but I got funneled down to you. That makes me suspicious."

"Really? You'd laugh if you knew the truth."

"Tell me."

"You were palmed off because Tony Benedict didn't want to be bothered and he thought it would be a nice way to annoy me."

Brian arched an eyebrow. "Oh."

"How long have you been a reporter?"

"Thirteen years."

"I guess after all that time digging up dirt, you tend to see it everywhere."

"What have you got against reporters, Mrs. Sharman?"

"I was married to one." She paused. "And call me Linda."

The waiter returned with their food. They started eating in silence, then Linda spoke: "He worked for *The Star* for five years, then went straight to the top—the *National Enquirer*. Then the divorce. Now I don't know—or care."

"Any kids?" Brian asked.

"One daughter away at college."

"Who got custody?"

"Me. You need to know this?"

"No, but if we can't talk about the Mafia, how about some chitchat?"

Linda smiled. "How's the hamburger?"

"Greasy. What do you think I should write about?"

"No comment."

"Oh, come on. You must know something worth telling."

She sipped more wine. "You know what made Rocky Holt great?"

"Not his singing," Brian said. "I remember his first record—couldn't get it off the radio even by embedding emotion.."

" 'One and One Is Heart,' 1960."

"That's it. He bought the deejays."

"He did not. Rocky was straight."

"And I'm Ernest Hemingway. Come on—how did a third-rate vocalist come to head his own label?"

"He was a great businessman, and he had—still has—the best ear for talent in the industry." She ate sparingly and said, "Most record entrepreneurs build up their artists by giving them nothing up front, promising them a future down the line. Rocky gives them everything now and warns them there is no later. Unless you become a mammoth hit. Musicians respect him. He doesn't lie. He's been where they are."

"Very touching." He had saved the french fries; now he was shoveling them down, one after another.

Linda's anger rose. "I'm telling you this so you'll see why he doesn't need the Mafia. They have nothing to offer him."

"Well, that seems to put the lid on it."

"It does? Good." She pushed her plate away, drained the wine, and dabbed at her lips with her napkin.

"How about dessert?"

"Enjoy yourself." She picked up her handbag.

"I can't tell you how much help you've been."

"Ah—a nice backhanded compliment."

Brian laughed. "You're sharp for—" He broke off.

"For a woman?" she finished.

"Ah—a nice liberated feminist."

"Just a working girl, Mr. Hawthorn. Are we through?"

"I seem to have run out of grease."

"Oh, no. Not you." She stood up.

"Look, if I need anything more, can I get in touch with you? Maybe dinner some night?"

She sat down again, amazed. "I told you I used to be married to a reporter."

"It might be fun if you'd forget that."

She stared at him, amazed at his gall. Finally, she shook her head and picked up the check.

"Oh, that's very kind of you," he said. "I'm not on an expense account."

"Neither am I."

"Then you *will* let me return the treat."

"Treat?" she said narrowly, getting up again.

He stood up too. "Oh, one thing, Mrs. Sharman—uh, Linda. That fellow you spoke to when we were leaving the art department. What was his name?"

"Paul Mizzell."

Brian's face crinkled in thought a moment, then he shook his head. "Doesn't sound right. I know him from somewhere."

"It'll come to you. Good-bye, Mr. Hawthorn."

"Later, Linda."

She hurried to the cash register, and only after signing the check did she dare to look back. He was still at the table. He had ordered apple pie a la mode. Something about him made her uncomfortable, and it wasn't his eating habits.

Paul Mizzell never left the building for lunch. Every day he brought a fresh brown bag containing sandwich, fruit, and cheese, and ate alone at his desk while everyone else went out. They knew his routine and no one questioned it. He did it so he could be at the phone around one P.M. when his live-in girl friend, Judith Berg, took her lunch break at the bookstore and made her daily call to his office. They would talk quietly for a few minutes, their brief mutual strokings punctuated by long silences that Paul perceived as tender communication. If for any reason he missed her call, or if she got too busy to make it, he would try to reach her at exactly five after one. If he couldn't connect then, he would keep trying. If they failed to connect completely, he would be in a depression the rest of the day, almost unable to function. No one in the department suspected this clockwork dependence, because no one else was around often enough to see it happen. So Paul's occasional afternoon funk was usually attributed to moodiness or "bad brown bag."

Back in the pre–Tony Benedict days, when there was more work and overtime was permitted, Paul would often stay late. Judith would bring him dinner and sit with him while he finished his layouts. Sometimes she would go off alone and roam the building, then come back and ask him questions about the operation. He liked those evenings because it was the only time she showed any real interest in what he did. He even made her a duplicate of his back-door key, so she could come and go at will. On occasion, when everyone else had gone home and they were alone together, he would wrap up work and turn to find Judith watching him expectantly. There was an old sofa in the shooting studio. They got a lot of use out of it until Tony clamped down on the overtime. Now he couldn't work nights anymore unless he filled out a form ahead of time.

He finished the apple and glanced at the clock. A minute after one. Already his face was getting warm. In a couple of minutes he wouldn't be able to sit still. His eyes locked on the phone. *What was she doing?* he wondered. *Stocking the shelves? Dealing with a customer? Manning the register?* So much to do in a little neighborhood bookshop. Always busy. One would think that books just sat on the shelves and moved when a customer bought them. But no, there was so much rearranging to do. And returns. Special ordering. She had explained it all to him once so he would understand that if she called a little late now and then, it wasn't deliberate, nor was it forgetfulness.

The phone rang.

Paul snatched it up and waited.

"Paul," she said.

He relaxed. "Hi. How's it going?"

"So-so," she said. "I had a customer. You finished lunch?"

"Um-hm."

"How was the sandwich?"

"Good. Thanks." He heard a bag rustling: her lunch.

"How about a bike ride tonight?" she asked.

"Yeah—that sounds good."

"Then maybe a little fun."

"You're on."

A silence. Paul smiled to himself, tapping a felt pen on the drawing board. He heard her teeth crunch into an apple and felt good. He could listen to her eat all day, which was fine because he'd already run out of conversation.

"Shit!"

Paul looked up. Jimmy Otner, the one remaining staff photographer, stormed in.

"That cunt did it again!"

Jimmy was short and scruffy, with long stringy hair—a throwback to the sixties. Nobody had told him the revolution was over.

C. L. Clarke was right behind him—a transplanted Canadian: tall, lean, weathered, handsome, with sun-bleached hair and bad teeth, as relaxed as Jimmy was nervous. C. L. Clarke was one of the top free-lance shooters in the record business.

Paul excused himself to Judith and cupped the phone, a wave of anger knifing through him at being interrupted. In a cold voice he asked Jimmy what was wrong.

"That bitch—Candy Lee. Strung out!"

Paul forgot his anger. "The model?" he said. "She's not coming?"

"Oh, I'll bet she's doing plenty of that." Jimmy lit a cigarette and offered one to C.L., who declined. While Jimmy paced, C.L. perched on Paul's flat file with an inscrutable grin. "Banging some guy in Santa Barbara since yesterday lunch," Jimmy went on. "She just called and fed me her bullshit—I mean, who do these chicks think they are, anyway, man?"

"Just a second." Paul turned back to the phone. "Judith, something's come up. I have to go. See you tonight." He heard her bite the apple again, then mumble a reply. He hung up and turned to Jimmy and C.L. "Can we get anybody else? We need that shot today. Linda is supposed to show something to Crunchy Harris by tonight."

Jimmy shrugged. "I'll call the agency."

"No good," said C.L. "You know what happens when you ask for big tits and lush hips. You get everything *butt*." He winked at Paul.

"Then what do we do?" wailed Jimmy. "Use Tisa?"

The others groaned. Tisa Stimmel was overweight, plain, and generally regarded as unappealing, but she was a good artist, well-adjusted and uninterested in men. Jimmy was convinced she was a lesbian.

"I think we can do better than that," C.L. said.

Linda walked in.

"No naked. I don't do naked."

"Nobody's asking you to."

"We've got a swell leotard here, Linda. Never know the difference." C. L. Clarke dangled it temptingly.

Linda looked at Paul Mizzell for support. They were all standing in the studio, waiting for her decision. C.L. had his lights and drops ready, and the bulky two-and-a-quarter was on a tripod. Paul stood leaning against the door, hands stuffed in his pockets.

Linda pointed to the prop box, a large wooden bin by the door, and said, "Haven't we got some falsies in there? One of you guys could do it."

No one laughed. Paul finally took the leotard from C.L. and said, "If she doesn't want to, she doesn't have to. She's the boss."

"Oh, crap, I'll do it." Linda grabbed the leotard from him and stalked off to the changing room.

By the time C.L. had Linda posed, legs straight and spread slightly, hips swung to one side, tummy tucked in and breasts thrust forward, everything straining against the tight mesh, people had gathered from all over the floor to watch. Some exchanged whispered comments; most just looked on with mild interest. C.L. crouched over his finder—he'd lowered the camera to Linda's crotch level. They weren't selling her face.

Linda glanced down at her legs, wondering desperately how they looked. C.L. brushed by with his light meter and whispered, "You're in frame from the thighs up." He winked and moved back to the camera. Was that reassurance or a mercy gesture? His voice went deep with authority. "Okay, folks—circus is over. Everybody out but art people."

A few groans and protests but they left quietly. Only Jimmy, Tisa, and Paul remained. C.L. started shooting, coaxing Linda into tougher positions, working as fast as possible, Jimmy exchanging roll-backs rapidly behind him.

Linda glanced at Tisa. She was standing very still, like a slack-jawed statue, mesmerized by Linda's body.

Oh, God, Linda thought, *of all the people in here I have to turn her on?*

"To the right a little, Linda," said C.L. "That arm is falling too close again. That's it. Good . . ."

Paul Mizzell watched her, too, glancing away each time their eyes met. Linda had wondered about him, why he seemed so shy. When he had started dating Judith, Linda had invited them as a couple to dinner, parties, promotional gigs—they only showed up once. Maybe Paul never told Judith about the invitations. Maybe Judith felt Linda was a threat. Linda wasn't sure and she had long since stopped caring.

"Okay, Linda, that's it. Thanks very much." C.L. snapped off the lights.

Linda collapsed onto a stool. Tisa put a sweater around her shoulders and massaged her neck muscles. Linda cringed at her touch. "Thanks," she said, "but what I need is a drink."

Tisa stepped back. C.L. took over the massage. Linda rolled her eyes. "Don't do that," she said. "I don't need to be stroked. Just get me a drink."

"Scotch?" asked Tisa.

"Water!"

Tisa ran. Jimmy lit another cigarette and said, "You were great, boss. Do this more often. Give the hired help a kick."

"As soon as I get my boots on, I'll do just that. Suppose you get on the phone to the agency and tell them I don't want to see or hear from Candy Lee again. And tell them the next time one of their bimbos fails to show, they can take our number off their Rolodex."

"Right." Jimmy hurried away, eager to give someone else hell.

Tisa returned with a glass of water. Linda drank it down and stood up. She winced at a pain. *Muscles need exercise*, she told herself. *Get in shape, you lazy broad*. She padded across to the changing room, shut the door, and struggled to strip off the leotard. She finally held it up and couldn't believe how she'd ever squeezed into it. She dropped onto the bench, naked, and just sat for a minute, rubbing her tortured midriff. She caught her reflection in the full-length mirror and stared at the elastic marks left around her thighs. She studied her body critically, and decided she didn't like the color of her skin anymore. Too much white. Where was the pink flush of her youth? The great summer tan? She never got out anymore. She never did anything. She just worked and went to industry functions.

"Hell, you *are* an industry function," she said aloud.

"Good looking one, too," C.L. called back. He was on the other side of the wall, in the darkroom, unloading his roll-backs.

Linda sighed and stood up, reaching for her clothes. *What you need is a man. A nice, sexy, athletic man who'll go out and play tennis all day, work up a real rank libido, then come back and spend it all on you.*

"When was the last time you got laid, Linda?" C.L. called out.

"Last March," she called back. "By an entire Canadian hockey team. Not one of them even knew what a camera was. Best bang of my life."

C.L. didn't say a word.

"How did I look? Tell me the truth."

"Fine."

Linda walked back up the hall to the art department with Paul. "Think I should wear that leotard around the office?"

Paul laughed.

"Getting married, Paul?"

"I don't know."

"Getting along?"

He nodded.

"Why don't you bring Judith around someday?" she said.

"She works all the time."

"I mean around to my place. Dinner."

"You've asked before . . ."

"And nobody ever turns up. Is she afraid of me, Paul?"

"No," he said quickly.

"Jealous?"

"We're still getting to know each other. We like to be alone in the evenings. Is that wrong?"

"If you can stand each other's company that regularly, great. My ex-husband never came home at all, except the night we made my daughter."

Paul stopped at the door, half smiling, waiting to be let off the hook.

"Okay, don't come to dinner if you don't want to," Linda said. "It's not in your contract."

"Hey, we'll do it real soon."

He went in. She was about to follow when she heard Jimmy calling from down the hall, "Linda! They want you downstairs!"

Her eyes closed; she held her breath a moment then expelled it. *The Lord High Marketing Director summons you for an audience.* She turned and headed for the elevator. Jimmy was coming toward her, agitated.

"Something's happened to Rocky," he said. Linda stopped, then walked faster. "Car accident—somewhere in France—"

She punched the down button and felt a chill slice through her from head to toe. Her voice quavered. "Is he all right?"

Jimmy spread his hands uncertainly.

"Oh, shit," she said, stumbling into the elevator, remembering as the doors closed to stab the first-floor button.

The afternoon mail was in. Paul dropped into his chair and opened the letters first. One was from Chrysalis Records, inviting him to a promo party for the new Blondie release. He chucked it in the can. He never went to those things. The other was from his accountant, a bill for last year's tax preparation that he hadn't got around to paying. He stuffed that into his back pocket, then slit

open the package that was about the size of a record album. He
was surprised to pull out an old, battered copy of the Beatles'
Revolver.

Paul's brow furrowed and he stared at it, uncomprehending.
Then his heart began to thump and, with a premonition bordering
on dread, he flipped the album over and looked at the back. He
found it right where he expected to, in the upper left corner—
Lori Cornell's scrawled signature.

Paul froze in his chair. For a brief eternity, he was once again
in a small, dingy apartment off campus, alone in a dark, over-
heated room with shades drawn, incense burning, rock concert
posters plastered to the walls, *Revolver* blaring from a cheap
hi-fi . . . alone but for the girl sprawled over the edge of a sagging,
squeaky bed, her legs apart, naked and damp, her body jumping
with his as he hammered into her with long, measured strokes.
He stopped. They shared some dope and changed position, then
started again. She gasped as he went rigid. Her legs thrashed,
then quivered. . . . She moaned and he felt himself subside. . . .
His weight dropped on her. . . . Lori Cornell . . .

Sweating, Paul stared down at the album on his desk. It
couldn't be hers. He snatched up the wrapping and looked for a
return address. None. There was a Los Angeles postmark over
the stamps. His name and the address of Rok Records were neatly
typed on a gummed label. But there was no indication of who it
was from.

His mouth dry and sour, Paul glanced out of his cubicle to see
who was around. Tisa walked by, glanced at him, then disappeared into her cubicle. Pierre Carette was working at his drawing board, absorbed. Pierre was the epitome of the egotistical
foreigner, smug and condescending, temperamental and opinionated.
He delighted in conquering American women. Linda tolerated him
because he was superb at a certain kind of design innuendo. He
could make anything look sexy.

But would he play a gag like this? Somebody else in the office?
Impossible. Nobody here knows about Lori. Somebody outside
then?

Paul shoved the album back into the packing and slipped out of
his cubicle, trying to think where to get rid of it. He went to the
hallway. Somebody he knew from audio came out of a recording

room and headed for the elevator, then changed his mind and turned down the stairs. Paul slipped out of the art department and went down the hall, the package tucked under his arm. His boots clumped on the linoleum and echoed back at him noisily.

Take it easy. Take it easy. Who gives a damn about a beat-up copy of Revolver? *Who else would know the significance?*

Someone does.

Whoever sent it knows plenty.

The elevator opened. Paul stepped in and punched *one*. It started to close. He heard running feet, then a shoe kicked back the sensor panel. The doors opened and C. L. Clarke came in, carrying his camera cases. Paul managed a weak smile. C.L. would be going to the parking lot too. The doors closed and they started down.

"Can I ask you a personal question?" said C.L.

"Sure."

"You ever make it with Linda?"

"No."

"Anybody ever made it with Linda?"

Paul didn't answer. The doors opened and C.L. stepped out, struggling with his cases. Paul saw an opportunity to make his little trip seem natural. He snatched up one of the cases. "You need help," he said.

"Thanks."

C.L. led the way down the hall, away from the receptionist, who didn't even look up, and away from the executive wing. Paul looked back. He could see people standing outside Tony Benedict's office. He put them out of his mind and concentrated on what he had to do.

C.L. pushed open the side exit, and they walked out to the parking lot. "I'm over there." C.L. pointed to a flashy Pontiac Trans Am, a kid's car with custom striping and a hood-mounted air scoop. They walked over. C.L. popped the trunk and dumped in his cameras. Paul handed him the other case. C.L. put it in and shut the lid. Paul waited for him to leave, the package still under his arm. C.L. glanced at it, then got into the car, started the engine, and gunned it a few times, grinning at Paul. Over the roar of his idle he said, "How's Linda feel about fast cars?"

"I wouldn't know."

"Find out. Call me."

He took off with squealing tires. As soon as he was down the street and gone, Paul looked around to be sure he was alone. Satisfied, he walked across the lot to the big trash dumpster. The lid creaked as he opened it and propped it up. The garbage smell washed over him. With quick, shaking fingers, he took the album out. The wrapper dropped at his feet. He ripped the jacket open, broke the record in two against the steel dumpster, then threw the pieces into the trash. He shredded the cover and scattered the bits into holes in the piled garbage so they would filter to the bottom. He picked up the packing and ripped out the address label, tore that up, and shoved everything deep into the bin. He hit the prop with the heel of his hand; the lid clanged shut.

His pulse racing, still looking around to make sure he wasn't seen, Paul Mizzell went back to work.

CHAPTER 2

Linda sat on one of the sofas, squeezed between the sales director and the talent coordinator. The office was heavy with smoke and concerned faces. Tony Benedict played field marshal, relaxed in his executive swivel chair, coat removed, sleeves rolled up, hands clasped behind his head. There was a look of inscrutable authority on his face as he eyed the telephone, positioned in the center of the desk like the President's hot line. Linda watched some of the younger department heads drifting in and out, glancing at Tony for news, getting an imperceptible nod or shrug. The older faces—the ones she had worked with for so many years, the ones who knew Rocky Holt and loved him—were drawn, deep in thought, sifting through memories, searching out warm moments from the past so that if the worst was confirmed they would have something to hold on to.

Linda eyed Tony with open displeasure. He had made an announcement over the intercom a short while ago, letting everyone know what had happened and inviting people to gather in his office to await further word. She was convinced it wasn't done out of kindness: it was to confirm who was in charge, so that if Rocky Holt didn't survive the accident, everyone would already have gotten it fixed in their minds that Tony Benedict was the new father figure.

Linda had already made up her mind that if the news was the worst, she would resign. She couldn't work under that smarmy son of a bitch no matter how much he offered. *Who are you kidding?* she said to herself. *The first thing he'll offer you is the door.* She looked down at her hands. *What am I sweating over? My job or the man's life? Oh, Rocky, for Chrissakes, why couldn't you learn to use a driver?* Everywhere he went, no matter where it was in the world, Rocky Holt insisted on taking the wheel himself. Even the insurance company got stomach cramps whenever they learned he was out of the country.

So far, all they knew was that he had been in a car accident outside Marseilles. He was hurt, but no one knew how badly. The driver of the other car had been killed. Linda watched Miller, the chief attorney and an old crony of Rocky's, quietly discussing options with Tony, who probably wanted to know if the company was liable for the dead man.

The phone rang. Tony grabbed it and said, "Benedict." His eyes shot about the room as he listened, then his mouth clamped shut and Linda saw his features tighten and relax. . . .

"What about the other guy?" Tony asked, then listened again. "Okay, thanks." He hung up and looked around at the expectant faces. Finally, he smiled slightly and said, "Broken leg."

The concerned ones—those who were braced for the worst, sagged in relief. The newer group put on smug smiles that said "See? Nothing to worry about." Miller closed his eyes and turned to the window.

"Where is he?" Linda asked.

"Hospital in Marseilles. They're setting the leg, putting it in a cast, and he's screaming bloody murder. They haven't told him yet that the other driver is dead. Trying to figure out what they can charge him with."

"Was it his fault?" asked Marvin Bensch.

"Don't know yet." Tony glanced at Miller. "We'll need a company position on that."

"How long before he can return?" Linda asked.

Tony's eyes met hers. He hesitated. "That all depends."

"On what?"

"French doctors, French authorities, French airlines—they're going on strike."

There were moans.

"Come on, people. The ship is still afloat. Okay, everyone back to work. Linda, have one of your gang do up a nice big get-well card that everybody can sign."

Gradually they filed out, relieving the tension with jokes about Rocky's driving. Finally, there was only Tony, Miller, and Bensch. Linda smirked. Tony must have been rooting for a broken neck

and was disappointed at getting only a leg. She got up and
headed for the door. Tony called her back. She came to his desk
like an obedient servant. He smiled. "I want you to be at
Crunchy's tonight. Can you make it?"

"I guess so."

"Good. I'll pick you up at eight."

She stared at him. She didn't want to go anywhere or be seen
anywhere with Tony Benedict, but he'd maneuvered her perfectly. "Okay," she said. "You're the boss."

She left, hurrying down the hall nearly blind with anger.

Paul's Mustang inched along with the rush hour traffic up
Laurel Canyon. Cars crept by on his right, heading toward
Mulholland, the San Fernando Valley, and home. What the hell
was he going home to? Another something he couldn't tell
Judith. What if whoever sent the album cover got in touch with
her? Eight months of happiness could be ended with a letter, a
phone call, or another package that he would have to explain.

A car horn blared. Without realizing it, Paul had rolled into the
intersection, blocking another car. He waved sheepishly at the
driver then made his turn.

He swung left at the Wonderland School playground and continued up Lookout Mountain, past a bohemian collection of
houses that ranged from old to older, set with no apparent design
from right on the curb to high up the hillside. Each wore its
individuality like a badge—from a seedy I-don't-give-a-damn to
Don't-I-look-pretty, all painted and slicked up.

Paul's rented house fell into the first category. He pulled into
the street-level carport expecting to see Judith's blue VW bug already
there. But it wasn't. Disappointed, he locked his car, then trudged
up the fifty-two steps to the patio. The path crossed under a
balcony overlooking a rock garden, then meandered up to an
entry on the far side.

He unlocked the door and walked into the living room.

A light snapped on over the stairway above the dining room.
Rubbing sleep from her eyes, Judith Berg stretched, yawned, and
said "Hi," all in one fluid motion. She was wearing a blue
denim shirt with the tails knotted in front, tight over a hard, flat

tummy. Beneath that, shorts set off golden skin. Dark brown hair framed her face in soft, bouncing waves.

"Donna's car is on the blink," she said, coming downstairs barefoot. "She had to be in Riverside at five to bid on a book collection, so I loaned her the VW and we closed early." She smiled enticingly. "I've had a bath, a nap, and washed my hair." She came into Paul's arms, pressing her body to his. "New perfume. Like it?"

"Nice," Paul said, feeling a rush of gratitude.

Judith stepped back and scratched his cheek. "Wash up. I'll get some food."

Paul picked at his tuna salad and looked across at Judith, aching to tell her about *Revolver* and a lot of other things. He wanted desperately to unburden himself, but he had waited too long to make her his confidante. Now he feared he could never do it.

They ate quietly. He was subdued, so she didn't force conversation. She didn't like to talk much anyway. He remembered the day they met, the day he turned down her challenge to ride along the San Vicente Boulevard hike path. A perfect stranger, a chance encounter on his usual Sunday morning ride. He remembered being struck by her smile, suggestive but guarded. Her eyes were green and piercing, her breasts cupped in a sheer nylon tanktop. The lilt in her voice. His own dismay when he heard himself turning her down. Watching as she pulled away from him. Strong, tanned, shapely legs pumping the pedals effortlessly. She shot away from him and looked back. Another smile. Then the following Sunday, stationing himself at San Vicente and Twenty-sixth, hoping, then surprised and delighted when she rolled up next to him and spoke her name. Judith. Life had been a lot less complicated then.

The sun slipped over the hillside across the street as Paul settled into a chaise longue on his balcony. Judith was finishing the dishes. A dog barked somewhere up the street. Paul sipped wine, ignoring the dog and concentrating on the golden-red glow limning the trees across the road. His confusion and fear this afternoon already seemed part of the dim past. It was easy to relax with Judith. She seemed to go out of her way to avoid putting pressure on him—of any kind.

"What about our bike ride?"

Paul swung around. She was standing in the doorway, changed into a jogging suit.

"Oh," he said. He swirled the wine and offered it to her.

She came over and took a sip, cupping the glass in both hands.

"Not tonight?" she said.

"I don't feel up to it."

"That's okay."

"If you want to go—?"

"Not without you. So what'll we do?"

Paul sank back into the cushion, at a loss. He let her lead: she usually did.

"Want to talk?"

"No."

"Want to come inside?"

"It's nice out here." He closed his eyes and let the warm breeze brush his face. When he looked up again, expecting to find her gone, she was still there, smiling, unzipping her jogging jacket, shrugging out of it. Her breasts bounced as she kicked off her sneakers, then skinned down her pants and stepped out of them.

She stood before him naked, her flesh deeply colored in the last rays of daylight. His gaze drifted over her, amazed at the solid contours he found, drawn down her belly to the mound between her legs. The soft clean smell of her drifted over on the breeze and he felt eagerness stirring deep in the center of his body. He glanced over the balcony at the street below. A car rolled by.

"People can see," he said hoarsely.

"Let them." Judith placed her foot on his chest and gently but forcefully pressed him back.

"What are you doing?" he laughed. He knew exactly what she was doing and where it would lead. She stiffened the leg and her toes gripped his flesh. She raised her arms and locked both hands behind her head, stretched and thrust out her breasts. He saw her hips move. She was contracting rhythmically, undulating at him. He stared as her pelvis moved back and forth, still a bit bewildered by her brazen exhibitionism. She loved sensual risk. On their second bike ride together, she had taken him down to a canyon schoolyard and cornered him on the handball court. She had made love to him standing up, with a cold, matter-of-fact determination that left him stunned and spent. She had caught him completely by surprise, and he had never understood how or why. He had been interested and attracted, but he certainly hadn't flashed any signals. He never ceased wondering why she had singled him out, or how she had coaxed his long-repressed sexuality into full bloom.

He felt the weight removed from his chest and looked up. She dropped one knee on the chaise and fumbled at his belt. "Whoa. Now wait. Now, Judith—" She was too quick for him. Her fingers slid down into him and clutched, kneading gently. He felt himself springing to life.

"I want to go for a ride," she said, bending over to lick his lips. "You need the exercise." She flicked the tip and he quivered. She knew exactly what to do. Her fingers closed around him and squeezed. He felt his bottom contract and thrust. Her tongue darted over his mouth. She let go of him and pulled his hands down, then threw a leg over and straddled him.

She covered his lips with hers and worked her tongue in. Paul's hips undulated. He reached around her and pressed his hard penis against her buttocks, then his hands groped for her breasts. He tried to roll onto his side, but she locked her legs, pinning him to the cushion. They struggled silently for a minute before Paul, amazed at her strength, gave up.

Judith's nipples had become rock hard, his flicking thumbs bringing jerks of pleasure from her. Her legs relaxed their pressure. She rose slightly and guided him into her, making a guttural sound as she pushed down, grinding against his pelvis. Her hands circled his waist. She locked her arms and started to pump. Paul stared at where they connected. She was taking the lead once again. She slid up and down on him mechanically, watching him for reaction. No tenderness. No quiet buildup, just relentless motion. He winced from the pressure of her hands on his stomach. Her breath came in ragged bursts. Her face contorted with the effort of reaching for his orgasm. A tingling welled up from his groin. He lifted her, arching his body upward, meeting her thrusts with his own hard, rapid strokes.

Judith bent forward and nipped his ear. "Hurt me," she moaned. *"Hurt meeee . . ."*

Paul felt release swelling up and held her close, gripping her buttocks as he exploded inside her. She groaned and clutched and went rigid, then shuddered. Her breathing subsided and she lowered herself to lie on him. They lay entwined for a moment, then Paul eased her weight off him. Judith rose shakily and stood by the side of the chaise. "Change of pace," she said in a low voice.

Paul stared at her body in the dim light. She looked down at him, watching him grow small. "So much power," she said. He wasn't sure if she meant hers or his.

She stepped back, stooped to pick up her clothes, then went into the house. Paul reached down and pulled up his pants. No doubt about it, he decided. I've just been raped again.

Linda sat out on her balcony, sipping a gin and tonic, listening to music and waiting for Tony Benedict to show up. He was already fashionably late, but she figured he would deliberately stretch that to out-and-out rudeness. He might not show up at all. She smiled hopefully, then heard the roar of his Porsche 911S and saw him whip off Barrington Avenue and into the condo driveway. He zipped into a visitor's spot and gunned the engine once before shutting it off. The door popped open but he sat there awhile, finishing a cigarette and staring into space. She watched him, fascinated that he would keep up his macho image even when there was no one around to appreciate it. His legs came out first. He dusted off his trousers, dropped the cigarette on the blacktop, and crushed it with his heel. Then he rose from the car, reached into the back, and yanked out his jacket. He slipped into it, then spread open his shirt collar. He was wearing gray tapered slacks, powder-blue shirt, dark-blue blazer, and a handcrafted silver belt buckle. The only break in his smoothness came when he had to struggle with a stubborn door lock. He turned and came toward the building.

Linda rose and went inside, dumping the rest of her drink and grabbing her purse. She had deliberately chosen a severe black outfit. She went out the front door and locked it, then marched quickly to the elevator. He came off and stopped in surprise. "I thought we could have a drink first. I'm terribly thirsty."

She smiled. "My place is a mess. Let's get going." She stepped into the elevator. Disappointed, he followed.

They drove without speaking, as Tony went through the gears and tore among the cars on Sunset Boulevard. Quad stereo blared around Linda. Her legs bracketed a huge case of cassette tapes on the floor. Tony never let a cut finish. Before the fade, he would pop the tape out, reach between Linda's legs and exchange it for another—this without taking his eyes off the road. Once, as he reached down there, she breathed, "This is so exciting."

His hand jerked away and he glanced at her, surprised.

"You're some driver," she clarified with a smile.

"Oh, yeah. Got a hot car, drive it hot. Right?"

"Right. Me, I like my Honda."

"You should sell that thing. I got a guy'll give you a deal on one of these. You like Porsche?" He made it sound as if it were something to eat. He swerved to miss a truck, leaned on the horn and swore at the driver, then hunned around an old Dodge and threw it into third. The car surged ahead and Linda held on.

"I prefer living," she said over the roar.

He grinned and reached for another tape.

"Leave the last one on," Linda said firmly.

"Okay, you're the boss."

Like hell I am, Linda said to herself.

Crunchy Harris's house was way up Coldwater Canyon, at the end of a private drive lined with expensive iron. A boy in a red coat came running up to take Tony's car. Linda got out and watched Tony whisper something to the kid, whose eager look vanished as he slid cautiously behind the wheel. Tony took Linda's arm but stayed to watch the kid park his car.

"See?" she said. "If you had a Honda . . ."

The house was immense, sprawling over two and a half acres of prime hillside real estate, the whole package worth maybe a million or a million and a half, depending on which high-stakes broker sold it. Linda spotted two of them standing on the front lawn, nursing drinks and openly discussing the property's potential. She wondered if Crunchy knew they were casing the joint.

Tony led her in and flipped the high sign to some friends. They passed into a sunken living room crowded with people, spotted with long sofas, and lit from above through a stained-glass ceiling. Music seemed to pound from the walls—the new romantic rock sound that had replaced disco, reggae, and new wave. The English Beat, The Specials, Tom Petty and the Heart-breakers, Blondie, Adam and the Ants, and all the imitations they had spawned were stamped from a mold that had been reshaped by every Major Sound since Bill Haley and the Comets. Rock music had become endlessly regenerating variations on a theme, a living pastiche of sound and beat. Unlikely combinations like speed rock, popsoul, power pop and rockabilly. Everything came from somewhere, but it was always New, Newer, Newest. Nothing was old until it was on sale in the discount houses for half of list.

The bar was active. Through huge sliding glass doors she watched guests on the patio outside, a few already in the pool. Crunchy Harris, one of Hollywood's kingpin record producers, regularly played host to a mixed bag of agents, artists, attorneys, and managers. Linda glimpsed superstars wherever she looked. Several of Rok's singers drifted by and said hello.

Tony got her a drink, then she managed to get free of him. She sat down on a piano bench in a corner and eyed the crowd, wishing she had stayed home. She didn't like these parties. Too much food, drink, and aimless chitchat. It always ended with her ear being bent by some eager entrepreneur who wanted to use her to get to Rocky Holt.

"Linda." She looked up. Crunchy Harris stood on the other side of the piano, a small, beefy man with a thick face that seemed sculpted from a pumpkin. He grinned a jack-o'-lantern smile and came around with hand extended and gold bracelet nearly falling off. "Glad you could make it," he said.

He slipped an arm around her waist and touched hips. "You give terrific party, Crunchy," Linda shouted over the music.

"Let's go somewhere private and I'll tell you what I thought of that picture you sent over. That's some leotard!" He leered at her. "Christ, what boobs."

"Nice, huh?"

"Hey, you can test covers for me anytime. I'll put you under contract."

"Fine. Where's your casting couch?"

He laughed, then his expression changed. His eyes softened and he smiled pleasantly. Linda was surprised. She'd always seen him as nothing more than a lecherous asshole.

"What is it, Crunchy?" she said.

"I was just thinking . . ."

"What?"

"Oh, nothing. Once a jerk, always a jerk. I'll be chasing nineteen-year-olds the rest of my life, I guess. I was born chasing them."

"At least you're honest." Linda felt a twinge of sympathy.

"Buddy Dyal's in the smoking room," said Crunchy, his moment of reflection over. "Look him up. Anybody I can introduce you to, just let me know. And Linda, I liked the shot. My art guy will send it back marked tomorrow. Get the right girl, put your boobs on her and shoot it. Okay? See you."

He patted her cheek and left. Linda guessed that Tony had not spread the word about Rocky's accident, so she decided not to cross him. It would just be another thing he could hang her with. She saw him at the bar, sucking up to a lead vocalist RCA had managed to lure away from Rok that Tony would give his right arm to lure back.

After an hour of dodging other creative directors who wanted to talk shop, she managed to get out to the patio. A couple of singers from White Fuzz, a defunct British ska group, were lolling on a huge raft in the pool, getting their egos stroked by a pair of bare-breasted groupies.

Linda went looking for Buddy Dyal. He had been vice-president of marketing for Rok before Tony, but he'd had a falling-out with Rocky over drugs. He'd been supplying cocaine to one of Rok's groups. Rocky found out and gave him the ax. After ten years of close friendship they cut off all ties. Buddy quickly found a job as sales director for another label. Last she had seen him, he had claimed to be happy and not bitter.

She found the smoking room at the end of the house. She had to knock several times and give her name before they unlocked

the door. She was almost done in by the pungent aroma of dope.
The door closed behind her and she peered through a smoky
haze. Several men were sprawled on the floor watching a porno
movie on Crunchy's projection TV. Two couples were hunched
over a coffee table, snorting coke. Most of the marijuana was in
a corner group, Buddy Dyal among them. She was amazed at the
change. He had gone to pot—literally. A dissipated thirty-four-
year-old human wreck, hollow-eyed, prematurely gray, and flab-
by. He was molded into an easy chair, regarding the room
distantly, like the mandarin emperor of sin. His eyes focused on
Linda. A smile crooked his lips oddly. He patted the chair arm
and motioned her over. She perched on it and leaned over to kiss
his forehead.

"Are we still in love?" he asked hopefully.

"Not any more than before."

"Good. I hate change."

"How are you doing?"

He looked at his diminished weed. "Ready for more."

"Jesus, Buddy. What are you smoking—a pack a day?"

"Funny." He sucked the joint and his eyes rolled. He snorted
air through his nose and held it, nodding at her vacantly.

She wanted to leave. Maybe she would give him a couple of
minutes for old time's sake then clear out. No one in Hollywood
smoked more dope than Buddy Dyal. Maybe in the old days he
wouldn't have held that record, but today grass had become
passé. Only the diehards still toked up regularly. Everybody else
had either dropped it and gone on to something more potent or
had left drugs completely. But not Buddy. His dope kept him so
laid back she wondered how he could still function, particularly
in the high pressure go-get-'em world of sales.

"I hear things aren't so great over at Rok anymore," Buddy
said.

"Passable."

"Anybody get along with Tony Benedict?"

"Tony Benedict does."

"And Rocky. I never understood that. They're not alike at all.
Maybe Rocky needed somebody totally opposite."

"Maybe."

"He doesn't speak to me anymore, Linda. I'm just that shithead

who used to work with him. Can't complain, though. He made
sure I got a job. He looked after me."

"I didn't know that."

"Oh, yeah." Buddy took another hit. "How is the son of a
bitch?"

"He was in a car accident today, in France."

"Really? Anybody killed?" he joked.

*Yes, he killed someone, Buddy. A Frenchman died in that
accident. Rocky's leg was broken. He could have been killed too.
Why couldn't you have asked, Was my old friend Rocky hurt?*

She wanted to say these things, but she ended up saying
nothing. Buddy blew out the smoke, hiccuped and stared at the
roach in his fingers.

"You wouldn't have a clip?" he asked.

"Why don't you just eat it?"

Buddy nodded, crushed out the lit end, then hunched over the
butt, carefully removed the ash, and popped the residue into his
mouth.

"Ah, Linda," he said heavily, "everything is beautiful, huh?
The world is a nice place."

The porno finished and the videotape shut itself off. A switch
behind the closet door clicked over and music from the party
came over a speaker, loud and pulsating. Linda winced. The men
on the floor were still staring at the dark screen.

"I'm not enjoying myself anymore." Buddy was looking at
her, head nodding to the beat. "It's a disease called corporation.
The higher up you go, the less human you feel. Right now, I feel
only ten percent human."

"Which part of you is that?"

"My thing." He pointed to his crotch and laughed. "How
come we never got it on, Linda?"

"You were too busy becoming corporate."

"Too late now?"

"Probably."

He nodded and reached into his belt pouch, producing another
joint. "How's your work?" he asked.

"Fine."

"Still feel creative?"

"Sometimes."

"Never short of ideas?"

"Occasionally." He was looking up at her, genuinely interested, she thought. "It's hard to make things feel fresh, you know?" He nodded sagely and she went on: "Seems like every time there's a new trend, for me it's just plowing old ground and planting the same crop. So many new people tumble into the business, and you have to educate them from scratch. Artists, producers . . . so damned young—"

"How's Mizzell?"

He wasn't interested in her problems at all. She felt stupid bringing them up. "Paul is working out great. Thanks for bringing him to me."

"Don't mention it." He lit the new joint and dragged deeply, savored it, and grinned at Linda. She forced herself to smile back. "Want to know something about him—?" he said, then checked himself. His face clouded over and he drooped in the chair. "Too much grass," he said. "Is Paul okay? I mean no problems, huh?"

"No."

As a matter of fact, there had never been any problems with Paul Mizzell. She couldn't have been happier from the beginning. Two years ago, when Buddy was still vice-president of marketing, he heard that Linda needed another artist right away. He swept her off to lunch and spent two hours promoting Paul Mizzell for the job. They had been friends at UCLA. Mizzell had trained at Dickson Art Center and had a thorough grounding in graphic design. He had worked the last few years free-lancing record jackets, but now he wanted a permanent job. "Look at his portfolio," Buddy had said. "I'm not going to insist—just look at it."

Mizzell had shown up for the interview with all the right samples and qualifications. He had everything but personality; not that it was needed, but she would have expected a little chest-thumping from someone who desperately wanted the job. She told Paul she'd let him know and went back up to see Buddy, who was delighted the interview had gone well. Actually, not so much delighted as relieved.

Then he admitted there was something she should know about Paul Mizzell. He had spent time at Camarillo under psychiatric care, committed for something he did a long time ago. "I don't want to go into details," Buddy had said, "because I might unfairly influence your consideration of his talent."

"Are you asking me to hire a nut?" Linda said.

"Oh, no. He's completely rehabilitated. I know the doctor in charge of his case." He begged Linda to give Paul a chance. "We did undergraduate school together, then he went into art and I took chemistry. It was drugs. He got mixed up on acid. Don't ask me what he did. Just trust me: he's okay now. And help him, will you? He can't get ahead as a free-lancer. He needs this job."

Linda had hired Paul Mizzell with Buddy Dyal's assurance that if Paul showed any signs of emotional stress, she could call him right away and he would handle it.

But Paul had worked out. Linda forgot about his background and accepted him as a more-than-competent artist. Within four months she made him her assistant, giving him broader responsibility. She took an active interest in him and made him feel he was part of a big family. He was shy and restrained, didn't like to mix, and didn't make friends easily. She coaxed him to a couple of promotional parties, then lured him home one night, got a little drunk, and made a pass. He politely finished his drink then bolted for the door. He couldn't get out fast enough. Hurt and angry, Linda couldn't understand him. She was sure he wasn't gay. The next morning she had it figured out: he didn't want to jeopardize his job by making love to the boss. That she could understand: she never approached him again.

A few months later, he had met Judith Berg. From then on, he shut himself off socially, refusing to go to parties, openings, gigs, anything. Except once. The one time Linda met Judith. She and Paul came to a charity show and stayed for less than an hour, both of them so uncomfortable they couldn't wait to get out. Linda's impression of Judith—a clingy, quietly dominating brunette who was expertly manipulating Paul. If that was what he wanted, Linda had told herself, he was welcome to it.

With the stub of his last joint wedged between his lips, Buddy slumped in his chair, running down like a spring-wound watch. He was stoned, with a Cheshire cat grin fixed on his face. Poor

Buddy, Linda thought. Poor dumb bastard. Because of his appetite for weed and his reckless disregard of Rocky Holt's moral
stance, everybody at Rok was suffering today. But he was out—
what did he care? He was out and Tony Benedict was in.

She leaned over and whispered in his ear. "Why don't you get
married again and straighten yourself out?" He didn't reply. He
couldn't. She left the room, thinking that was such good advice
she should follow it herself.

She found Tony in the pool, naked along with a dozen other
guests, having a not-so-innocent game of volleyball, highlighted
by much leaping out of the water for display of breasts and
genitals. Nobody seemed to care who was winning: they were
all having such a good time playing tag underwater. Tony spotted
Linda and hollered for her to come in. She shook her head and
perched on a low brick wall to watch. Most of the party had
drifted outside for the show and the players were getting cheers
and whoops for springing entirely out of the water and showing
all.

"Here I come, babies!" a girl yelled from the living room.
She ran out in her underwear and hit the water in an ungainly
cannonball, disappeared for a moment, then came up flinging her
panties to the patio. She stretched out on the surface and floated
happily, thrusting her hips up so her black thatch was washed by
the ripples.

A man gave a whoop and jumped in next to her, fully clothed.
She screeched and giggled when he came up underneath her but
offered no resistance when he swept her into his arms and carried
her out of the pool. They disappeared into a cabana.

Linda looked up, surprised to find Tony Benedict naked and
dripping nearby. "My towel," he said softly. She glanced around,
found she was sitting on it, and passed it to him. Roughly he
dried his hair then his torso, eyeing Linda without expression.

"Want to go?" he said.

"That would be a good idea, Tony." Three more men jumped
into the pool, fully clothed and yelling, and went after the
women. "This party is getting dull."

"You're right. Come with me a second."

Wrapping the towel around his waist, he led her to Crunchy's
guest house, a cottage as warm and homey as the house was big

and imposing. He closed the door and padded past her to his clothes, spread on a table. She noted that a woman's dress and underthings were next to his.

"Where's your friend?" she said.

"Still in the pool." He pulled a comb out of his jacket and went into the bathroom. Leaving the door open so she could see, he removed the towel and finished drying. Linda felt mixed emotions. She hated his open display but knew as well as he did that he had little else to offer but his body. He was in superb shape, tanned and muscular, with a great carpet of hair that swelled at his chest and blanketed his back. It thinned down his belly then mushroomed out again between his legs. She found interest stirring despite her determination to keep him at a distance. She was fascinated. He was tantalizing her with visual stimulation, saving the attack for later.

He came out and plucked his shorts from the table, facing her as he drew them on. Then he sat down and stretched his legs. "So what do you think, Linda?"

"Of what, Tony? Your body?"

He shrugged.

"Marvelous. I think a little air-brush might cover your sins. Why don't you let me put Tisa on it?"

His smile froze, then he gave her a reproachful look. "That's cruel."

"I know. I'm terrible, aren't I. What do you want me to say, Tony? You have a magnificent prick and I'd like to play with it?"

"Really?"

He doesn't know you're kidding, she told herself. "Look, why don't you take me home? Get your mermaid friend to come with us if you need to be stroked. Thanks for the free look, but Tony, you're just not my type."

"How do you know? Don't be so choosy."

Linda bristled. He meant, How can you afford to be choosy? "All right, Tony, cards on the table," she said. "Give me one good reason why I should let you fuck me."

"Hey, come on, Linda. Lighten up . . ." He drew his legs together, cringing at the word, surprised at her directness. "I was in the pool and you were watching, so who's interested in who? Be honest.''

She sighed. ''Okay, so I watched. How often do I get to see a bunch of post-adolescents play bare-assed volleyball? It's a treat, really. I'm terribly grateful. But I hope it doesn't mean I'm expected to drop *my* pants too?''

''Forget it.'' He reached for his trousers.

''Oh, no. You don't get off that easily.'' She snatched his pants away and pushed him back into the chair. ''You really believe that every woman who comes in contact with you is supposed to fall down and leak with desire?''

''Hey, Linda—''

''I must be going weak in the head. How did I let you talk me into coming here tonight? Rocky's in a hospital, and I don't feel like celebrating. You seem to be enjoying yourself, so why don't you stick around? I'll take a cab home.''

She threw open the door and stalked out, only discovering she still had his pants as she passed the pool. She threw them in.

CHAPTER 3

When the Weapons of Mass Destruction showed up for their cover photo session, Paul Mizzell was kept hopping. Their manager, a skinny, pasty-faced cream puff named Van De Carlo, fluttered around complaining about everything. To placate him, Paul sent out for coffee and pastry, and tried to calm down Jimmy Otner, to whom the shoot had fallen by default: the photographer Paul had hired was behind on another job and couldn't make it. Jimmy had the bedside manner of a career schoolroom monitor; he couldn't get an ounce of cooperation from the Weapons.

They were no bargain, either—a quintet of ill-matched personalities, all heavily into a small arms trip. They packed real .38s and real .45s, and they were scaring the hell out of Jimmy.

"I can't deal with this, man," he told Paul. "That short-ass over there thinks he's Wyatt Earp. He just bought this Buntline Special and he wants his picture taken with the muzzle up his nose. You gotta straighten him out, man. I can't do shit. I can't even light."

The Weapons were scattered on the floor in front of a shocking pink backdrop, fishing doughnuts out of a box and dipping them into their coffee. They needed a collective shave and bath. They laughed and eyed Paul with contempt. The manager drifted by and tapped his watch.

"Mr. Mizzell," he said, "my boys are not used to waiting. Would you rather we went to another label?"

Jimmy flared. "You can go straight to hell, you little pain in the ass."

Van De Carlo tipped his tinted glasses forward. "Such a mouth," he said.

One of the Weapons rose and towered over Jimmy, fondling the automatic at his hip. "Hey, camera boy. Either you get shootin' or *we* do."

Jimmy's mouth clamped shut and he sat down hard.

"All right, all right," said Paul. "Let's just calm down and do what we're here to do. Okay? Come on, Jimmy. Get set up and let's go. And you"—he jabbed a finger at De Carlo—"get your musicians on their feet and up against that drop."

De Carlo erupted in outrage. Paul listened politely then said, "If we don't get the shot, it's on you, okay? We're ready and willing."

Tempers finally subsided. Somehow, they got the Weapons of Mass Destruction lined up against the drop. Jimmy worked with the pose a long time, fussing over chin angle and hand business, and balking at the Weapons' seamier attempts at humor—sticking gun barrels up their asses, out of their zippers, and so forth. Finally they struck a pose Jimmy could live with. He started shooting, then De Carlo stopped everything.

"It's not right," he said.

"What's the matter?" Paul asked.

"It needs something . . . dangerous."

Paul's eyes rolled. Sighing, he walked to the prop box and started fishing through it. De Carlo came over, sniffing.

"You won't find anything in there."

"How do you know?"

"The Weapons of Mass Destruction are unique. They need a unique prop."

"How about this?" Paul held up a two-foot circular target, painted in rainbow colors and decorated with tassels.

De Carlo shrieked. "That's funny!"

"No fucking way, man," said the lead Weapon.

Paul fumbled some more and came up with a large prop passport about three feet tall. He held it out to De Carlo. "Change the title," he said. "We'll call it the Weapons of Mass Destruction: *Passport to Danger*."

The Weapons liked that. Relieved, Jimmy spent another ten minutes lining up the new prop, grouping the Weapons around it with drawn guns and fierce expressions. Paul put the props away, grateful for Jimmy's foresight in stocking crazy bits and pieces from other jacket shots. He shoved the target deep into the bin, then dislodged something on top. A bit of cloth—costume. Costume didn't belong in here. It should go in the closet. He reached for the cloth and pulled. It came loose and he drew it out of the bin, stopping when he saw what it was.

A pink sweat shirt. Old and faded from washing but still retaining some color. He turned it over. On the front were the letters UCLA in white outline.

Paul stared at it, the way he had stared yesterday at the Beatles album that came in the mail. Could it be the same one Lori wore that night? Lori filling the sweat shirt, breasts jutting beneath the letters. Pulling the sweat shirt over her head. Coming toward him in a haze. The room that wasn't a room. Small, dark, dirty . . . metallic walls. The smell of gasoline and body heat. His own hands picking up the sweat shirt, crushing it, kneading it, reacting to sticky dampness. The pink running red . . .

Paul quivered. Remembering where he was, he stuffed the garment inside his shirt then turned and rushed to the door. He was out and moving up the hall with Jimmy calling after him. He made it to the art department and swept past Pierre and into his own cubicle. He fumbled minute his supplies for a huge manila envelope. With shaking hands he jammed the sweat shirt in and sealed it shut. Then he shoved the package deep into his wastebin, and dropped some sketch papers and trimmings over it. He stared down at the basket for a long moment, then turned to leave, almost colliding with Jimmy.

"What's the matter with you? Why'd you run out?"

Paul's anger rose. He wanted to ask Jimmy how the sweat shirt had gotten in the prop bin, but the question stuck in his throat.

"Come on, Paul. I can't control those assholes," Jimmy was saying. "You walk out and they start laughing at me. I can't get them to do anything. Now they want to smile. Jesus Christ, can you believe it? The Weapons of Mass Destruction smiling? I didn't know they *could*."

He followed Paul back to the studio. De Carlo was waiting, stamping his foot. "We are not used to this kind of treatment, Mr. Mizzell," he said. "This is our third album for Rok. We've made you a lot of money. We pay your salary—!"

Paul couldn't hold back anymore. He lashed out with a shout.

"You miserable jerk! Get out of here and let us make the shot! And the rest of you guys shape up or there won't be a third album!"

"You're threatening us!" De Carlo shrieked.

"Right!"

"You can't do that!"

Paul grabbed him and rushed him out the door, slamming it in his face. He turned back and faced the Weapons angrily. "Anyone else?" he said.

Surprised, they began to shuffle back into pose. Jimmy's hands shook as he checked his focus and resumed shooting. Paul leaned against the door and felt his adrenaline subside. All he could think about was the sweat shirt. Somebody had planted it, but who? And how long had it been there, waiting for him?

"It's not like you," Linda said, searching Paul's blank face for an explanation. They were sitting alone in her office. She had smoothed things over with De Carlo. Now she had to deal with Paul. She opened her office fridge and threw him a Tab. He nodded gratefully, snapped the pop-top and sipped.

Linda frowned and leaned forward, clasping her hands on the desktop. "Look, Paul, we're on the line with everything we do. If we start brutalizing the talent, we'll end up on the street. Is that what you want?"

He shook his head.

"Well, speak to me."

"I was wrong. I'm sorry."

There was something lurking in his face. Fear? Guilt? She had pressed her point enough. He wasn't given to angry outbursts. Of course, De Carlo could provoke violence in anyone, but Tony Benedict would never see it that way. She had been obliged to promise De Carlo that Paul would no longer be involved in anything concerning the Weapons of Mass Destruction.

"I have to take you off that job," she said. "Does that bother you?"

"No, I guess it's for the best."

"Turn everything over to Pierre. And in the future, keep your cool."

"I will," he said flatly, then went out.
She didn't know if he meant it.

"What sweat shirt, man? I'm standing there trying to shoot a bunch of trigger-happy assholes and I'm supposed to worry about what's in the prop box?" Jimmy walked over to the box and looked into it. "Where is it? Come on, show me."

"I took it," Paul said. "You sure you've never seen it before?"

"No, man. Is it important?"

Paul paused then shook his head. "Forget it."

Jimmy snorted in amazement, then disappeared into his lab. Paul peered into the prop bin again, then rubbed his palms against his trousers, wiping off the sweat.

Back in his cubicle a few moments later, he sat staring at the envelope in his wastebin. He debated taking it home tonight and was thinking of various ways to smuggle it out when he noticed Pierre looking at him from the coffee urn. Looking at him and sipping coffee. Paul's stomach crawled. Did Pierre know something about this? Is that why he was looking . . . ? Looking not at him but past him at the wall clock. Paul glanced up. It was 3:20 P.M. The phone in Pierre's cubicle rang. He grinned and dashed off to get it. Paul heard him answer: "Margit? *Ah, ma petite chérie.*"

Like clockwork, Pierre's phone rang at precise intervals during the day. He had his women completely under control. If he could manipulate them, Paul rationalized, he could do it to me. Maybe *he* put that sweat shirt in the prop bin. But why? Paul forced his imagination to stop playing detective. What did he know of Pierre, and what could Pierre know of him? It was ridiculous.

A few minutes later, Linda called Paul in and put him on a rush job. He forgot all about the package in his wastebin and left the building at five P.M. without it.

He didn't remember it until he was halfway through dinner; then he stopped eating abruptly and caught a look from Judith.

"Bad?" she said, waving a fork at his steak.

"No, it's fine. I'm not hungry."

She brought him a drink later and he sat staring at the TV, worried that someone would go through his wastebin and find that package, but even more worried that someone he worked with might have planted the sweat shirt in the first place. He slept badly that night, dreaming of metal walls closing in on him, echoing his choked screams, his hands crushing the sweat shirt, which ran red again. . . .

He woke abruptly and looked down at Judith. She was asleep, breathing softly, her bare back to him. He crept out of bed, his skin clammy with sweat.

He sat bundled up in the big chair in the living room, planning what he would do in the morning. Go to the office, dig that thing out of the wastebin and take it out to the rubbish, just as he had done with *Revolver*. Neat and clean, and it wouldn't be there to haunt him anymore.

When Paul entered his office the next morning, everything was clean and tidy, the wastebin empty. He had forgotten about the janitor. Quickly, before anyone else got in, he hurried down the elevator and out the side door. Cars were starting to fill the parking lot. He stood as if waiting for someone, furtively eyeing the rubbish bin. Finally, he got his chance. He hurried over and lifted the lid, hoping to find the package on top or at least within poking distance. He stared at the empty bin.

Of course. Today was pickup day.

Then there was nothing to worry about. The janitor had dumped it and the rubbish men had picked it up. Now it could never be traced. Everything was fine. He lowered the lid and went back into the building.

"The Struts? Paul Mizzell will do the logo. Right. Yes, I've got a photographer. C. L. Clarke. I've been on the phone to Venice all morning, Tony. We have approval from the arts council, the merchants' association, and we should have a police permit by tomorrow." Linda sat back and tucked the phone under her ear, reached for her coffee, and listened patiently to Tony Benedict on the other end of the line, going over details that were none of his business.

"No, Tony. It has to be early Sunday morning. The merchants will squawk if it's during business hours."

"Christ, Linda, everybody's in church on Sunday."

"In Venice?"

"Well, what about the media?"

"That's your department, dear boy. I do not arrange coverage."

"Okay, okay . . ." He went quiet a moment, then said, "Hey, Linda, I'm sorry about the other night."

"That's okay."

"I just want to know something. Were you tempted?"

Linda bared her teeth and mouthed a curse, then said aloud, "Tony, it's not the body that counts. It's what's in your heart. In your case, I recommend a transplant."

"You're a tough broad."

"Any word on Rocky?"

"I had to fly his analyst over to France this morning. He's all bent out of shape over that dead guy." He said it as if it were an imposition for Rocky Holt to be suffering any guilt at all.

"When is he coming back?" Linda asked.

"Who knows?" It sounded more like "Who cares?" She wanted to put the phone down, but he started in again about the Struts.

"Look, Tony, just leave it to me. We'll have it set up for next Sunday with no problem. Just tell Jerry Madison to keep them out of trouble till then."

A UPS messenger rapped on the door and stuck his head in. He held up a package. She motioned him over and signed for it. "Tony, I've got to go," she said. "Talk to you later, okay?" She hung up and looked at the package, puzzled. She wasn't expecting anything. She reached for it—

Jimmy Otner burst through the door and held up a large board. Grinning, he said, "May I have the honor of presenting you with a genuine, one of a kind, Museum of Modern Art quality original!" He flipped the board over.

It was a dry-mounted sixteen-by-twenty color blowup of Linda's leotard test. "Suitable for framing," Jimmy added.

Her first impulse was to order him out, then she looked closer and smiled. "Hey, that's pretty good," she said.

"Personally printed by C. L. Clarke and accompanied by the following shitty little ditty." He handed Linda the photo then opened a piece of paper and read dramatically: "To the girl with the golden hair—Roses are red, violets are blue, the picture is good, but not really you. Too bad it's a sin, exposing more skin, but how about posing for me anyway?''

Linda arched an eyebrow. "He calls that poetry?"

"I call it a come-on." Jimmy handed her the note and took the photo. "What do you want me to do with this?"

She shrugged.

"Good. I've got just the place for it."

"Not the men's room, Jimmy."

"Don't worry." He was half out the door. "Oh—any reply?"

"I'll call him. Have to talk to him anyway."

Jimmy left, and Linda stared at the note. *Good photographer but bad to get involved with.* The stories about C. L. Clarke were all true: he was great at wining, dining, and coaxing, a real seduction artist. But after the first success, a woman was just something to drape on the arm, a bit of decor that looked good at a party. *No thank you, Mr. Clarke.* But she wondered what it would be like to pose for him. Not for him specifically, but to pose, period. That leotard shot was as close to nude as she had ever done. *My God, you could see right through the material!* She glanced at her reflection in the glass partition. *You still turn them on, Mrs. Sharman. Career woman, married and divorced, thirty-seven years old with a teenaged daughter. . . . Why not preserve a piece of what's left? Have some shots done—front and profile, full body, "museum quality."* She chuckled, then regarded herself grimly. *Why not? By God, you won't have it much longer.*

She thrust out her bust and looked down, admiring the way it swelled, blocking her view of her knees. She felt a delicious tingle somewhere below and swore to herself. *This is ridiculous: I'm getting excited over me!*

Glancing through the partition, she saw a man standing in the aisle between the cubicles, looking back at her. A man in a rumpled suit with a tape recorder slung over his shoulder. That guy from the *Times.*

He came up and knocked on her door. She walked around the desk and opened it.

"How are you, Linda?" he said. "Brian Hawthorn. Remember me?"

"I never forget a reporter."

"May I come in?"

"Certainly, if you'll tell me how you got in the building."

He smiled. "I stroked your lovely receptionist under the chin and told her I was the lead singer for *The Morning Times*. She believed me."

"I'll bet she thought that tape recorder was a guitar. Look, Mr. Hawthorn—"

"Brian."

"Sit down." He dropped into a chair and she perched on the desk. "Brian, I don't know whether this is business or pleasure, but I really don't want you sneaking in here. Be straight or I'll have to ask you to leave."

"Straight," he echoed, putting on a dumb look.

"Tell the lovely receptionist who you are and who you want to see and wait till you're let in."

"Now?"

She sighed. "Next time."

"I see. Just like in the real world." He pulled out pad and pencil and made a note.

She stared at him. "What do you want? I can't believe you're going to ask me more about the Mafia."

He smiled again and tucked the pad away. "What are you doing for lunch?"

"Dieting."

"Me, too. Shall we do it together?"

She looked at him suspiciously. Why was he pursuing this? She wasn't giving him any encouragement.

"I tried to reach you for dinner," he said. "Nobody home."

"I don't recall giving you my home number."

"I'm taking a course in how to use the phone book," he said drily.

Her mouth clamped shut. She studied him again. He wasn't all bad. A reporter, yes, but he couldn't help that. One nice thing about him—he didn't seem as filled with himself as the other men who drifted in and out of her life.

"Okay. Lunch," she said.

"Good. Cheese, crackers, and salad. Very healthy. I know just the place."

"You'll have to wait a minute." She went around her desk

and reached for the package. She slit open the wrapping and ripped it off in chunks.

Brian got up and looked through the partition at the cubicles outside. He gestured. "So this is all yours."

"Oh, yes. I am the empress of all you see. And my subjects are loyal, hard-working and . . ." She frowned. Inside, there was a second package wrapped in plain brown paper, with a name written in felt-pen lettering, neat and undistinguished. It said *Paul Mizzell*.

Linda picked up the outer wrapping and found the chunk with her name and address on it, and the UPS sticker dated yesterday, mailed from Los Angeles. She was tempted to open the package but hesitated. Why would someone send a package to her that was meant for Paul? She looked up and saw Brian watching her—uninterested or engrossed, she couldn't be sure.

"Let's go," she said. She snatched up her jacket and the package and led the way out. Brian grabbed his tape recorder and followed.

"I'll bet you keep very busy," he said, walking behind her.

"Yes." She swung into Paul's cubicle. He was sitting at his drawing board. She put the package down and handed him the chunk of wrapper with the address on it. "This came addressed to me," she told him, "but it's for you."

Paul looked at the package, startled, momentarily helpless.

"If it's something I should know about, I'm sure you'll tell me," she said. "And Paul, try to straighten out whoever sent it, will you?"

"Sure, Linda."

She turned and came out, past Brian, whose gaze was riveted on Paul. Their eyes met. Paul turned away slowly.

"Coming, Brian?" Linda called from the door.

"Oh, yeah." He trotted after her.

Paul recognized the neat felt-pen lettering right away—the same as on the *Revolver* package.

By twelve thirty the department was empty. Paul was alone, facing the package across his drawing board, fear dancing inside his stomach.

It wasn't very big. Just a small flat box, about the size of a department store shirt shipper. Using his Exacto blade, he slit the paper and pulled it all away. It *was* a shirt box. But there was no shirt inside. There was only a folded, yellowed copy of the UCLA student newspaper, the *Daily Bruin*. Paul's heart began to pound. The date was October 21, 1968, and the headline read:

COED MURDERED ON CAMPUS

He dropped the paper back in the box and covered it over. He got up quickly and rushed to the bathroom. Leaning over the toilet, he threw up in great heaves that he thought would never end. Exhausted, he sank to his knees, flushed the toilet, and pulled down the seat. He rested his head on the cool plastic and didn't want to move, feeling momentarily safe, as if he had puked out the devil and washed him down the Styx.

Finally, he struggled to his feet and stared at his haggard reflection in the mirror. His eyes looked hollow and pained. The lids drooped heavily, a pair of wrinkled curtains trying to shut out all the horror he had discovered in life. The black beard streaked with gray dragged his face down even further, making him look older and wearier. Paul couldn't look anymore. He hated mirrors. That's why he had grown the beard—so he wouldn't have to look at his face every morning when he shaved. He lowered his head, peered into the sink, and cried. His body shook with sobs.

Ten minutes later, he returned to his cubicle, opened the box and stared again at the headline's block letters:

COED MURDERED ON CAMPUS
POLICE ARREST STUDENT

First the record album, then the sweat shirt, now this. But why was it sent to Linda? Would she know what it meant? When she hired me two years ago, how much did Buddy Dyal tell her? Whoever sent the newspaper—were they hoping Linda would open the package? Or had they just intended to draw her attention to my reaction? Oh, Christ, if that's it, it's working. If this continues, what's going to show up next? And who will it go to?

Paul snatched up the paper angrily and returned to the bathroom, ripping off the whole front page article, tearing it into pieces and dropping it down the toilet. He had to flush twice to get it all down. Then, still in a rage, he tore the rest of the paper to shreds and flung it into the wastebin.

When he came out, the phone was ringing in his cubicle. He started for it then stopped, checking his watch. Just after one P.M.

Judith.

He couldn't talk to her now: she would hear the terror in his voice. He let it ring till it stopped, then he went back to the cubicle, grabbed his jacket, and ran out.

Brian put down his fork and sighed. "Sorry," he apologized to Linda. "I can't help myself. I start with the right intention, but for me a salad is not lunch. That was a terrific steak."

Linda smirked and packed away the last of her cottage cheese and fruit. She leaned back against the hardwood wall of the booth and looked around Musso's. They were surrounded by people she knew. All through lunch she had been smiling and waving and exchanging comments with producers, agents, and record company executives. Brian was impressed; she was annoyed.

"It hasn't been a real getting-to-know-you lunch," she told him.

"No, but it's been an education. Tell you what—you order coffee, I'll have dessert, and we'll ignore everybody else."

She nodded. He caught the waiter going by and ordered ice cream. "I have a real sweet tooth," he explained to Linda, pointing to the one in front. "This one. Had it filled three weeks ago."

"I suppose you have lung cancer and smoke a pack a day too."

"No, but I like a cigar or a pipe now and then. How about you? Any vices?"

"Workaholic."

"Oh, that's bad. Now see, I shouldn't even be here. I'm supposed to be covering a liquor store holdup two blocks from your office. Happened yesterday, so they sent me out to do a follow-up on the nice old mom and pop who run the place, but they didn't come in today. Probably home cowering under the bed. So I should have checked in and taken another assignment, but I said no, I'm not going to kill myself for the L.A. *Times*."

"How ignoble."

"Besides, I couldn't pass up the chance to look in on you."

"Well, I *am* flattered." She batted her eyes.

He snorted a laugh. "You really are a sarcastic one. Where'd you pick that up?"

"School of hard knocks."

"You treat everybody this way, or just guys who like you?"

She held her breath a moment and thought, then blew it out. "I guess I respond badly to . . . possibilities."

"Now we're getting somewhere. Lie down on my couch and tell me all about it."

"I tried analysis. The doctor was crazier than I was. Besides, I like my neuroses. I'd feel lost without them."

"Boyfriend?"

"No."

"Want one?"

She sipped her coffee. "Don't press your luck,"

"Just trying to determine some parameters here.

Linda watched a shiny wave of black hair droop over his forehead as his grin spread wider. "Eat your ice cream," she said, "or you'll need a straw."

"Listen, don't build a wall between us. It's not necessary. We can be friends."

"You have female friends?"

"Sure. I get along fine with women. I work with some."

"I see." Her calm eyes held his. "It must be nice to be in a business where the men don't perceive the women as a threat."

He shrugged. "You're used to dealing with insecure assholes who think you're after their job. They pick on you but you can't pick on them. Not exactly tit for tat. Pardon my metaphor."

"That's okay. In the record business, tits do not help. You have to be egocentric, full of ideas, and constantly tooting your own horn. He who barks loudest gets the biggest job. At least, most companies are that way. Until recently, Rok was free of that crap."

"Uh-huh." Brian spooned up ice cream. Some of it dribbled down his chin. "Until Herr Benedict, right?"

Linda's eyes narrowed. "You aren't by chance doing an article on *him*, are you?"

"No. But I am interested in the company—generically speaking, *a* record company, yours by chance."

"Why?"

"Might make a good Sunday feature. Tell me about the people who work for you, the artists."

"I used to have more."

"Tell me about . . . let's see . . . the guy we saw on the way out, the one you gave the package to. I met him last time . . ."

"Paul Mizzell."

Brian snapped his fingers. "That's the one. Artist, right?"

"Yes."

"How long with the company?"

"Two years."

"Happy?"

"I think so."

"What's it like down at his end?"

Linda sat back again, frowning. "Why do I have the feeling I'm being pumped?"

"Ooo. Another bad metaphor. Look, if you don't want to talk business, we won't."

"Now I'm curious. Why do you want to know about Mizzell?"

"I'm not singling him out. He's the only one of your staff I've met."

"You're after something, Brian."

He put down his spoon and pushed the ice cream across, offering her some. She shook her head and looked away. He bit his lip. "I'm writing a book," he said finally. She looked back. "A novel. Nothing to do with you or your work or anything like that. I just . . . gather material where I can. Character traits. For instance, I was going to make the female lead in this story a sort of sweet, innocent career type, but in talking to you, I've decided that's unrealistic. Christ, how could anyone survive in business by being sweet and innocent? Only the secretaries, and that's all an act. So you'll have to forgive me. It never stops, I guess. I'm always after something."

She nodded knowingly. "Don't do it again."

He threw her a sheepish look. "How about dinner?"

58 GEORGE E. SIMPSON & NEAL R. BURGER

She laughed. "This is ludicrous. You'll just keep trying to pump me."

He grinned. "I have been known to do that, but not always for information."

She winced. He called for the check and dug out his wallet while she looked him over, much the way he had already looked her over. "Do you get *any* exercise?" she asked.

He thought a moment. "I do a lot of walking. And typing."

Well, he wasn't the athletic specimen she had been daydreaming about lately. For a moment, she tried to imagine him in bed and saw only the tape recorder, his pad and pencil, and felt fingers callused from typing roaming her body. She laughed out loud.

Brian thanked her at the door outside Rok. He gave her a respectful peck on the cheek and said, "Stay home some night and answer your telephone, will you?" He watched her go, pleased with his progress and admiring her legs. When she disappeared into the building, his smile faded.

Linda walked into turmoil. Pierre was searching Paul's cubicle for the finished layouts on the Struts' cover, in a panic because Tony Benedict wanted to show it to the group. *Oiseau de merdel!*" Pierre wailed. "They are all downstairs waiting. The Struts, their manager, and some girls. Paul is not here—I can't find it—what do I do?"

Linda edged Pierre aside and went through Paul's flat files. She found the comp along with some of his notes and other sketches.

Pierre slapped his forehead and sputtered in French. *"Mon cul, c'est une salade!"*

"It's okay," Linda said. "I'll take it down. You get C. L. Clarke on the phone and tell him to hold next Sunday open. Sunday *morning*."

"Oui."

"And where the hell is Paul?"

"Qui sait?"

Linda hurried to the elevator, smoothing her skirt and dodging her hair into place, angrily wondering what had made Paul Mizzell suddenly unreliable.

*   *   *

"Paul?"

"Up here."

He didn't move, just stretched a little while lying on the bed, his shoes off, head propped on a pillow, staring out the bedroom window. He tried to look tired as Judith walked in. She gazed at him quizzically.

"I called at one o'clock," she said. "Didn't get any answer, so I thought you might have come home. How long have you been here?"

"An hour."

"I telephoned here too. Why didn't you answer?"

"I switched it off. Had to get some sleep."

She sat down on the bed. "Anything wrong?"

"No, just tired."

"Did you have lunch?"

"No."

"I'll fix you something."

"I'm not hungry."

She frowned, then went out. He heard glasses clinking downstairs. He lay still, wondering if he should tell her, if he *could* tell her. Tell her what? That somebody was playing a gag and it was getting to him? He'd have to go into the whole story. She'd have to be *prepared* for that.

She returned with a bottle of sherry and two glasses. She poured him one, then sat down beside him and raised hers in a toast. "To us," she said. He clinked and drank. It was good sherry, a gift from one of Rok's more contented rock groups.

He managed a smile and stroked her arm. "You rushed home to check on me?"

She nodded and put her glass down. Arms on either side of him, she propped herself above and looked down into his eyes. A small knowing smile played on her lips. "It occurred to me that an afternoon off is not to be wasted."

"I feel lousy . . ."

"I can make you feel better."

She eased down, muscles taut along her arms. She kissed him, then rose up again. She was strong and liked showing it. His fingers traced the delicate bulge of her bicep and her lips parted. She ran the tip of her tongue along her teeth and closed her eyes suggestively. He felt her knees straddle his, then she straightened both legs and fitted her hips against him. Her back arched and she pressed her pelvis into his groin.

He tried to pull her down. She resisted, still smiling, still looming over him. She brushed a breast against his lips and moaned softly. He felt himself hardening under her pelvic ridge. She felt it, too, and pressed harder. Desire surged through him. He rolled her over and grappled her down.

She submitted for a moment, looking up at him, her smile disappearing, replaced by an urgent pout.

"Judith," he breathed, darting his hand to her thighs and pulling them apart.

Her palms slid over his chest, then she was pushing upwards slowly and steadily, holding him above her. He caught a flash of pride or pleasure or something he couldn't be sure of as she held him suspended in the air. Then she threw him over and flung herself on top. She spread open his shirt then licked his nipples. She rose and pulled off her sweater, freeing her breasts then pressing them into his face. Fingers tugged at his belt. He groaned and raised his hips. She pulled off his trousers and shorts, then her head moved lower and sucked him in.

He wanted to take control but she wouldn't let him. She moved her hips into his reach and undulated slightly, her signal for him to touch. His fingers slid into her jeans and pulled. They came down and hung around her knees. She opened her legs to let him explore, allowing him long minutes of play, until she drew her lips off him in a slow, agonizing stroke. Then she whirled around and dropped onto her back, kicking off the jeans.

Their bodies met, violently thrashing. She shoved him into her then worked him with rapid, desperate strokes. She clawed and moaned and rose on top of him, battering, holding him deep then battering some more. She worked harder than any woman he'd ever known, and he was overwhelmed by her, finally exploding in a deep, helpless shudder.

She groaned "Ahhh . . ." in triumph.

She squeezed everything out of him and didn't stop until he was exhausted and limp.

"What about you?" he said hoarsely.

Her fingernail scratched his cheek. She gripped his hand and pushed it down to cup the hot wet center of her. She pressed his middle finger in, then began rubbing against it. He fell into the rhythm she wanted and stroked rapidly. He wondered where she had learned to like *this*. Her eyes flicked over his face. She seemed completely lost. Her breath came faster, then she stiffened and lunged against his hand, squeezing it and quivering.

Her groan turned to a sob and she rolled away. Soon she was quiet, staring at her reflection in a full-length mirror attached to the closet door. She shut her eyes and Paul thought, *She's ashamed.*

"What's wrong?" he said.

"Nothing."

She lay contemplating the mirror a long time, one finger playing with her lip. He gazed along her body and felt drained. Now he was really exhausted. And bewildered. Sometimes she got like this after sex—strange and withdrawn. Sex was the ultimate communication between them, their only real common ground. Sex, meals, and physical activity brought them together. In everything else, they were solitary. Paul frowned. He didn't know Judith Berg very well—they were living in a dream. *But maybe that's how she wants it,* he thought. That's why he couldn't tell her about today, about any of his past. They weren't close enough.

She got up and pulled down the covers, then slid into bed and huddled for warmth. Her eyes closed. She never even looked at him again.

The phone rang. Paul picked it up. It was Linda, wanting to know why he had left work without saying anything. "Didn't feel well," he said.

"Well, how do you feel now?"

"Better."

"Good. I'm so glad. Look, Paul, next time leave a note. Understand?" She was angry or frustrated; he wasn't sure which.

"Something going on?"

She sighed. "Nothing much. Tony wanted to show the Struts their cover art, so I rushed down there with the comp and he complained that it wasn't finished. I said it wasn't supposed to be. Not if we were going photo, which was the way I understood it. He said he wanted a full representation so the Struts could see exactly what we had in mind. Can you believe that son of a bitch? I said I would be happy to explain it and answer questions. He said that wouldn't give anybody a clear idea of—'' She stopped, choking on the words.

Paul bit his lip. ''You want me to come in and finish the art, Linda? I can work all night.''

''No.'' She calmed down. ''I apologized until I was sick to my stomach. I got the goddamned Struts to okay the concept without seeing any more. The shoot is set for Sunday. I want you to be there.''

''Sure. Linda, I'm sorry . . .''

''It's okay. He's after *my* ass, not yours. I'll see you in the morning.''

The line clicked off. Paul hung up and frowned. He went to the bedroom window and looked out. Somebody *was* after *his* ass, and he stood to lose a lot more than his job. It could mean his future, his sanity, maybe even his life.

CHAPTER 4

Paul swung his Mustang onto Laurel Canyon, still guilty over yesterday. Getting in early this morning wouldn't change anything, but he felt he should make the gesture. He rolled the steering wheel with the curves and tapped his brakes, surprised as his foot thumped the floorboard. He held it there, expecting something to happen. The car kept going. The brakes didn't grab. He grunted then twisted the wheel and pumped the pedal rapidly. The car picked up speed.

Fear stabbed at him, fogging his brain. Narrowly missing a parked car, he fought panic. Instinct took over. He grabbed the gear shift and dropped down into second. The abrupt engine roar gave him a brief flicker of hope. He was still going too fast. He struggled to stay on his side of the narrow road. Even though no cars had passed him going the other way, the curves were too sharp to see around. If he could get past the signal at the market, the road would straighten out. He could edge over—let the wheels run along the curb—friction would stop him—

Tires screamed as he whipped through another curve. Paul went with the skid, barely missing a white pickup truck. He glimpsed a startled face and a fist raised in anger. He glanced at the speedometer. The needle was up to 35. If he hit anything now—

The Mustang fishtailed through the last curve. Paul's left foot jabbed the emergency brake. Metal shrieked, sparks flew, and a cloud of smoke erupted from his rear wheels. The car slowed but not enough. A red light at the intersection glinted at him, mocking his efforts, and the lone car waiting for it to change loomed in the road like a dark green wall.

Paul forced the shift lever into first. The transmission screamed

as the car shuddered and he was jerked forward. He crossed his
arms and flattened his head on the steering wheel to brace for the
impact.

A sickening crunch lifted him and slammed his legs into the
bottom of the steering wheel. Glass tinkled. The car bounced and
settled. Through the roaring in his ears, he half-heard something
rolling away. He looked up and saw a hubcap bouncing down the
street. He watched it spin to a rattling stop. Other sounds pierced
the roaring. Cars stopping, voices shouting, footsteps scuffling.
A squeaking sound next to him, then a hand on his shoulder and
a voice—"Hey, man, you okay?"

Paul did a quick mental inventory and, when he was sure he
was still in one piece, nodded. The man helped him climb out
and he stood shakily next to his car, wondering what everybody
was looking at, surprised when he realized they were staring at
him.

"What happened?" he asked, rubbing his legs.

A man shoved through the group around Paul. "You tell *me*,
buddy," he said. "That's my car you hit. I hope you have
insurance."

Paul took a few steps, looking for fire hydrant, debris, and tires.
The man spun to the debris in the street, spotted his bumper
guard, and picked it up, swearing loudly.

Paul came to him. "I'm sorry. I couldn't help it. You're not
hurt, are you?"

"Maybe I am, maybe I'm not. Why didn't you stop? Jesus—
look at my trunk!"

The lid was sprung. The bumper beneath was twisted at an
angle and hanging loose on the right side. Paul looked at his
Mustang. The grill was smashed and his hood was buckled.
Fluids leaked between the tires and ran down the street in a dirty
trickle.

The other man swore again and stuck out his jaw. "So let's
have it—what's your story?"

"Lost my brakes."

"Just like that? No fade?"

Paul nodded.

"Shit."

The man didn't believe him. Paul turned away, aware of the

traffic creeping around them, gawkers eyeing the accident. He began to wonder how it had happened. He'd never had brake trouble before. He moved to the Mustang and forced open the hood. He ran his eyes over the engine. His hand moved shakily to the brake fluid reservoir and he unscrewed the cap, stuck a finger in and pulled it out. Bone dry. The other driver looked over his shoulder. Paul ignored him and peered along the brake line to a dirt-streaked smudge running down the inside wall. His finger probed the hose and found a jagged split. "Line's been cut," he said.

The other driver backed away, eyes narrowing. "That's it," he said, reaching for his wallet. "Next you'll tell me I did it. Now, look, I don't give a shit what you're trying to pull. You hit me and you're at fault. Let's see your license."

Paul wasn't listening. His mind had locked onto one thing. Somebody wanted him dead. No more sneaking around with not-so-subtle reminders of the past. It was out in the open now. Somebody had cut his brake line, deliberately tried to kill him—

"That's not cut," said a voice. Paul turned. Another man was hunched over the Mustang's engine, feeling along the line. "It's worn," he said. "If it was cut, the break would be clean. Just a bad hose, mister."

Paul stared at him, knowing better. "It's easy to make a thing like that *look* worn," he said.

"A smartass like you could make it look like anything," said the other driver. "That's between you and your insurance company. And by the way, who are they?"

Paul didn't speak again, except to exchange information with the driver. The world seemed to be closing in on him, squeezing him into a corner, toying with him. He felt helpless and frightened. He hadn't a clue who might be after him, but he knew why. And he knew he couldn't go to the police because then it would all come out, and everything he had worked to build up would come crashing down. How could he fight it? Who could he talk it over with? There was no one.

"Can I see you for a minute?"

Linda glanced up from the sketches, shuffled them into a neat pile, and pushed them to the side of her desk. "Leave these here, Pierre. I'll get back to them later."

Pierre gave Paul a low warning whistle on the way out. Paul hesitantly took a chair.

"You're an hour and a half late," Linda said, masking her anger. She watched Paul clench and unclench his hands.

"Sorry," he said. "I was in a car accident." He paused. "It's made a lot of things clear to me."

Linda frowned, disturbed by the look on his face—if things were so clear, why did he look scared? "I'm listening, Paul."

"Somebody's trying to kill me."

He said it in such a flat, matter-of-fact way that it was several seconds before the impact sank in. Linda waited for him to continue.

"My brake line was cut. I lost control going down Laurel Canyon. It would have looked like an accident."

Linda eyed him gravely.

"I had the car towed to a gas station, and I went over it with a mechanic. He didn't believe the line was cut, but I know it was. Somebody went to a lot of trouble to make it look worn and didn't think I'd notice. The record jacket and the sweat shirt were morning. So was the package you got the one addressed to me. But I didn't catch on until this morning—"

"Wait a minute!" Linda held up a hand to stop his verbal assault. "What are you talking about? Who's trying to kill you?"

He told her about getting the *Revolver* album and the newspaper, and finding the sweat shirt, but he stopped short of explaining what they meant. He looked down at his feet, deeply disturbed.

"I'm waiting," she said.

"Look . . . it goes back to something that happened a long time ago." His jaw worked. He seemed about to blurt something out, then his muscles relaxed and he said, "I can't talk about it."

There was a long silence. Linda wondered if he was heading for a breakdown. He certainly sounded paranoid. "Somebody in the office is out to get you?" she said. "Is that what you want me to believe?"

He shook his head uncertainly. "I didn't think anyone here . . . I just don't understand why they would bring it up . . ."

"Bring what up?"

He couldn't answer.

"Where is all this stuff you're talking about? The sweat shirt and the—"

"I got rid of it."

"Then you don't have anything to show the police, do you?" Paul looked up abruptly. "The police?"

"Naturally, if you're being threatened, you'd want to get in touch with them."

"I don't know . . ." His hands shook. "You're the only one I've told."

Linda smiled wanly. "Very flattering, Paul. Look, if you have any more trouble, come straight to me. Between the two of us, we'll take care of it. Okay?"

Paul nodded, realizing he'd gone too far. "I don't want to drag you into this, Linda. Dumping my troubles all over you isn't . . . I guess the accident really shook me up."

They both knew what he was saying sounded hollow. "I'm not going to repeat this conversation," Linda said.

Paul mumbled his thanks, then got up and left the office.

Linda sat motionless, collecting her thoughts. Finally, she picked up the phone and called Buddy Dyal.

He looked even worse during the day. Buddy had taken up the disco uniform three years too late—Hawaiian shirt, pleated pants, plastic shoes—not the usual ensemble for a sales director, but at Timely Records, anything went. Linda found him in a recording studio. She stepped into the control booth and watched through the glass as Buddy commiserated with the lead guitarist of the Baba-Rums, a trendy New Romantic group just beginning to hit the charts. Buddy had one arm draped on the kid's shoulder and a cigarette wedged in his mouth as he tried to make sense of whatever this inarticulate artist had in mind. Finally, he nodded and whispered something to the kid, who smiled and showed a faceful of bad teeth.

"Jesus Christ," said the engineer. "Where do we find them?" He shook his head at Linda. She said nothing. She waited for Buddy to come through the baffled door, then wiggled her fingers at him.

"Linda," he said happily. He opened his arms and hugged her.

"Feeling better today?" she asked.

"Hey, I always feel fine. I feel really good about myself. Okay, Len, they're yours."

Len nodded and hit his mike button. "Go for a take?"

Their voices came over the speaker, a mumble of agreement. They shuffled into place.

"How come the sales director is supervising a session?" Linda asked.

"These kids are friends of mine," Buddy said. "The one with the teeth is my second cousin twice removed. Some days I'd like to remove him completely." Buddy smiled encouragement at the musicians.

"Okay," said Len. "Here we go." He started the tape. "Speed," he said. He called out some numbers, gave the boys a hand signal, then said, "You're on."

Four headsets picked up the beat, then the music crashed in, fast and pumpy. The kid with the teeth opened his mouth and poured out a falsetto howl that descended beat by beat into a basso profundo.

"Can we go somewhere and talk, Buddy?"

"Sure. Len, you handle things. We'll be down the hall."

They sat down in a filthy windowless coffee room, the Baba-Rums' music coming through the walls, muffled. Buddy sugared his coffee. Linda took it black and watched him rub tired eyes. "So what's the deal?" he said. "Does Rocky want me back?"

"No. Sorry."

"Hey, don't be. I wouldn't come back. Not even if the boy genius died suddenly. Benedict, I mean. So what is it, Linda?"

"Paul Mizzell."

"Oh." He sipped his coffee and looked up expectantly.

"You said to get in touch with you if he ever started acting funny."

"Funny?"

Carefully, she described the story Paul had come in with. The car problem, the packages he'd received, the fact that he had destroyed everything, and her uncertainty of how to deal with it. "You'd better tell me, Buddy. Is he headed for a breakdown?"

"A breakdown?" Buddy echoed hollowly.

"You never told me what he did to end up in Camarillo. Maybe now I should know."

He reached into his shirt pocket for his cigarettes, lit up, and drew deeply, double-inhaling through his nose.

"Buddy," she said, "don't turn this into a ceremony. Just give me some straight answers. What I don't need to know, don't tell me. But remember one thing: you got me to hire him. Now he's my responsibility. Just tell me if I have anything to worry about."

Buddy smiled. "I don't think so."

"Am I supposed to take your word for it?"

He squinted at her through the smoke. "You saw one of the packages?"

"Yes."

"Then he could be telling the truth. Somebody could be sending him things."

"He could be sending them himself. Is he likely to do that?"

"Beats the shit out of me." He shrugged.

She leaned over and snatched the cigarette away before it got to his lips again. She rolled it between her fingers and held it just out of reach, waiting for his eyes to meet hers. "Buddy, what the hell is wrong with him?"

"Nothing. He's completely rehabilitated."

"From what?"

Buddy bit his lip. "Is he doing drugs?"

"I've never even seen him high."

"Then you've got nothing to worry about."

Linda punched the cigarette out in an ashtray and moved to the table, sitting close to Buddy. She swung one leg back and forth, inches from his face. He watched it, fascinated. "Buddy, we're going to sit here all day unless you get on with it."

Buddy sighed. "Ever hear the name Gary Michael Steen?"

"No."

"I went to school with him."

She stopped swinging her leg. "Buddy, I'm on lunch. I have work stacked up. I'm not here for This Is Your Life!"

"Just listen." Deliberately choosing his words, Buddy outlined his friendship with Gary Michael Steen. "We were both at UCLA in the late sixties. Took a lot of classes together. He got

A's; I got C's. I didn't know where the hell I was going, and nobody was studying much then anyway. Nineteen sixty-eight—the Democratic convention, Johnson folding up his tent, Hubert pleased as punch, and Nixon. Oh—and Bobby Kennedy—'' He shook a finger significantly. "Everybody went crazy. Fuck classes, fuck school, fuck everything. Country was coming apart and we were sitting there trying to make grades. Seemed stupid and useless. Vietnam protests all the time. Couldn't turn around without running into one. Get to class, find it's been called on account of some political rally. We were all doing drugs. I changed my major to chemistry, thought I'd be a scientist or something important—I don't know. Anyway, I was convinced there wasn't gonna be a future. It was all going down the drain. So, I got really loose. Gary, he was still up there plugging away in the art department, but it got to him too.''

He stopped a minute and pulled out another cigarette. "You mind?'' he asked.

"Not if you get to the point.''

He lit up and went on. "So anyway, Gary met this girl—well, actually, I met her first.'' His flashed a lecherous smirk.

"Okay, so you took her to bed. Go on,'' said Linda.

"Bed?'' He snorted. "That chick didn't need a bed. She could do it anywhere. Young, but she knew a lot, you know?'' Linda nodded. "So I was with her a little while and the next I know she turns up with Gary. Lori Cornell was her name. He moved in with her. She was sort of an artist too. A little pottery and some collages. Real half-assed. We talked about it and couldn't figure out how she was gonna make it through school, she was so horny all the time. Anyway, she really got him going. Drugs—grass, bennies, hash—cheap stuff in sixty-eight. Then LSD. Acid was the big campus drug then. You sat around, dropped a little acid, got a big hoo-hoo. But it affected some people really strange, you know? Ever do any of that, Linda?''

Linda shifted on the table. "No. I missed out.''

"You learn a lot about yourself on acid. I had a friend couldn't make it with women. He came to the chem department and dropped acid under a controlled experiment. Really found out about himself, discovered he was a fag. From that day on, he was happy as a pig in shit. Got himself a mess of boyfriends and became queen of the north campus.'' Buddy laughed.

''Come on, Buddy. Don't waste my time.''

''It's a little involved, okay?'' He was getting agitated. Something was bothering him, she wasn't sure what. ''Anyway, LSD sort of brings out things that lie just below the surface, sort of hidden personality quirks. And I guess Gary had a lot of them.''

Buddy slumped in the chair and smoked as he continued. ''He was getting it on pretty hot and heavy with this Lori Cornell. Every chance they got—off someplace going at it like rabbits. She got to be an obsession with him, like the acid. If he wasn't on one, he was on top of the other. So one night—the fall of sixty-eight—he was tripped out on acid. He took Lori off to a movie at Royce Hall—big old barn at UCLA where they used to have all the public screenings. It was some old German flick . . .'' He stopped, trying to remember. ''It was about this girl,'' he said quietly. ''Really beautiful, really loose, doesn't give a shit. Goes around destroying guys, one after the other. Eventually, she becomes a hooker and picks up Jack the Ripper. . . . Guess how it ends.''

Linda's stomach growled, but not from hunger. ''She dies?''

''Uh-huh.''

Linda slid off the table and dropped back into the chair. ''Look, Buddy, I don't want to hear a movie review. I asked you about Paul Mizzell and you've given me a long story about someone else.''

''I'm getting to Mizzell.'' He paused to collect his thoughts and after that superhuman effort went on. ''So Gary was watching this movie, see? Tripped out. You have to have dropped acid to know what it feels like. You watch a movie, it's like everything's heightened. He must have hallucinated. So anyway, they left and went back to the parking lot where he had this van they were using, one of those psychedelic jobs. On the side it said *Love* in seventy-two different colors. Gary was a hell of an artist. Now, I never knew *exactly* what happened, but the combination of things—the drug, the movie, this girl's sexual whatever, and some problem I guess Gary had over his mother—it all sort of came to a boil, you know?''

Linda wanted to move away from him. She had already guessed what was coming.

"He killed her."

He said it flatly, as if it were the logical conclusion to everything he'd described.

"With a knife. Very messy." Buddy winced at the memory, then sat back and dragged on his cigarette. Finally, he said something that made the breath constrict in Linda's throat.

"Paul Mizzell is Gary Michael Steen."

CHAPTER 5

Linda sat in stunned silence while Buddy took a phone call in the recording booth. Buddy had to be wrong. Paul Mizzell couldn't be the same man who had gone crazy on drugs and sliced up his girl friend. It didn't fit. There had to be some mistake. But if there wasn't . . .

He came back, hands shoved in his pockets, avoiding her gaze.

"Buddy," she said, "why did you keep this from me?"

"Would you have hired him?"

"That's not the point. I should have known!"

Buddy shrugged. "Okay, I was wrong."

"Wait a minute." She got up and circled, questions beginning to tumble in her mind. "You knew what he did. Why was it important for you to help him?"

"I told you. We were friends."

"Loyalty?"

"Yeah. Look, Linda, he went crazy, but that was *then*—now he's cured. He's a good artist; he deserves a chance."

"He killed somebody! And he's walking through life as though it never happened."

"What would you do? Put a sign outside his office—Caution, Killer Earning a Living?"

"No, but I—" She choked and swore. "Damn it, I accepted the responsibility of hiring him! I should have been told everything! He's having a problem right now. I can handle a little paranoia, but if it's deep-seated and he needs to be watched, I don't know if I can deal with it! And I'm a little pissed at you for sticking me this way! Paul thinks somebody is trying to kill him.

Coming from anyone, that's serious. Coming from him—!" She broke off and paced rapidly, confused and upset.

Buddy bit his lip again, tried to light a cigarette, and couldn't. "You think he's flipped his cork?"

"Buddy! You're making me nervous! Now I'm afraid if he looks at me cockeyed, I'm going to get sick!"

"That'll pass—"

"How do you know!?" she shouted, fed up with his idiotic replies. *"How do you fucking know?"* She flew to the door and closed it, then whirled to face him. "You irresponsible son of a bitch! You didn't feel like taking him on yourself, so you palmed him off on me—"

Buddy shook his head. "You're wrong. I owed him."

"Oh, come on—"

"I was in charge of marketing—what was I going to do with an artist? Giving him to you was logical."

"Only in your fucked-up head!"

He looked down at the floor. Linda watched him, sensing something wrong. Why hadn't she seen it before? Buddy had never been known for his charity. He was hiding something.

"Why don't you give his doctor a call?" Buddy said.

Me?

"Yeah. Gene Dahlke. Psychiatrist. Has his own practice in Beverly Hills. He supervised Gary Steen's treatment at Camarillo and turned him into Paul Mizzell."

"Turned him?" Linda gaped at Buddy. "What do you mean? He's been brainwashed? He doesn't remember what he did?"

"No," said Buddy. "He remembers. But they got him to a point where he can live with it. I can't explain it. I'll call your office and leave Dahlke's number. You can discuss Paul openly with him—he'll hear anything you have to say. I don't think he sees Paul much anymore, but he's still responsible for him."

"I'm glad somebody is."

"Just don't fly off the handle. Believe me, the guy is not going to do it again." Buddy stood looking at Linda a moment. When he put a hand to her cheek and gave her a smile, she almost believed he was genuinely sorry. "We all destroy ourselves," he said sagely. "But there are fun ways to do it and not such fun ways. Worry and stress . . .'' He shook his head as if they were the ultimate no-no. "Be cool.''

She wanted to hit him but let the moment pass. He walked out the door and went back to recording. Linda picked up her handbag and hurried out of the building, not surprised that his advice was dopey and outdated.

She returned to her office and closed the door, sat down heavily, and stared through the glass partition. Pierre walked by. Tisa shuffled to the coffee urn for a refill. Paul was nowhere to be seen. In his cubicle, she guessed. She had avoided looking in when she came back.

She stared at the messages on her desk. Tony Benedict, C. L. Clarke, and Brian Hawthorn. She picked up the phone.

"Brian? This is Linda.'' He seemed delighted to hear from her. She sat back and listened to him chatter about some assignment he was on that meant a weekend trip to San Diego. Before she knew it, he was asking if she would like to go along.

"Separate hotel rooms, of course," he said. "But be my guest.''

"I can't, Brian. We're doing a shoot Sunday morning.''

"Then come down Saturday. I'll send you back by plane.''

"No. I've got too much preparation. But thanks for thinking of me.''

"What about dinner tonight?''

She frowned, beginning to be sorry she had called. She didn't want to talk with anyone right now. The other phone rang. "I've got to go, Brian.''

"Oh . . .''

On the other hand, she *did* want to see *him*. "Pick me up at eight,'' she said.

"Terrific!''

She gave him her address and hung up, wondering if she was making a mistake. She wouldn't be in any better mood tonight— probably worse. She snatched up the other phone. It was C. L. Clarke.

"Hey, babe. I've been trying to get you all day. This gig with the Struts on Sunday. I need details.''

"Paul Mizzell is handling that.''

"Can't reach him. What do you say you and me put our heads together tonight and sort of work everything out?"

"I'm busy. I'll find Paul and get back to you."

She hung up and stared through the partition again. So Paul wasn't here. For a moment she entertained the notion of firing him for cause. The phone rang again. It was Buddy Dyal's secretary with Dr. Dahlke's phone number. She scribbled it on a pad, tore off the sheet and folded it. Then she held on to it, not sure what to do. She got up and went down the aisle to Paul's cubicle.

He was there after all, sitting at his drawing board, his back to her, hands draped in his lap, staring at the wall. He didn't hear her come in. She stood looking at him a long time, the telephone number still cupped in her hand. The phone rang but Paul didn't move to get it. It rang five times and he never even flinched. Finally, his head swung and he appeared to stare at the phone but still didn't pick it up.

Linda's anger rose. She reached over his shoulder and snatched up the phone. "Hello," she growled.

Paul looked up, startled.

"Sure, Judith. He's right here." Linda held the phone out to him with a tight expression. Paul took it and waited for her to leave. She whirled and stormed out.

Back in her office, Linda shut the door, went to the window, and stared out, calming herself. Why was he sitting there like that, almost catatonic, not answering the phone? How many calls had he missed? How much work had he screwed up? How long had this been going on? Again she considered firing him and a voice inside told her, *Do it now! Do it while you're angry!* She opened the paper and stared at Dahlke's number. If she called him, what would she say?

Hi, this is Linda Sharman and I've got one of your nuts working for me.

And what would she get out of this doctor? More of Buddy Dyal's phony reassurance?

Oh, he's okay. Completely rehabilitated. Wouldn't hurt a fly. Now and then likes to sharpen his knife, but don't worry about that. . . .

She reached for the phone and saw Paul standing just outside her door, looking through the glass. Their eyes met, and she was certain he could see, even feel, her terror. He knocked on the door, then opened it and leaned over the threshold.

"You okay, Linda?"

She choked back an involuntary laugh. "Yes, fine."

"Sorry about this morning. I must have sounded really—"

"Forget it." She took a deep breath. "Listen, Paul, C. L. Clarke is trying to reach you for the rundown on Sunday's shoot. Would you call him, please?"

"Oh, sure."

"Then coordinate with publicity so we get the people there on time. And Paul—make sure I have all the information."

"Right."

He closed the door and walked back to his cubicle. She watched him go, then sat down and tried to relax, glancing once more at the folded note.

She wouldn't call Dahlke just yet. She needed time to think, time to consider what was involved. If she got in touch with him now, she might end up totally roped in, a go-between, reporting to Dahlke on Paul's behavior and following his suggestions for dealing with it. She didn't know if she could handle that. At the moment, she just wanted out. Maybe after the weekend she would know what to do. She closed her eyes and dreamed about tall fruit drinks laced with rum.

"Jesus, I haven't been here in years," Brian said as the maître d' guided them through Trader Vic's. They took a table at the window overlooking the pond and the little red bridge. Linda grabbed the bar menu and ran her finger down the list of rum drinks. Her other hand gripped the waiter's arm. She ordered a mai tai and sat back happily.

"You're in a good mood," Brian said.

"It's Friday. I may get drunk."

"Great news. Front page tomorrow."

She laughed and listened to the waterfall outside. "I used to come here when I was a kid. My sister and I drank Shirley Temples and ate a lot of pressed duck. We loved it."

"You were brought up here?"

"Santa Monica. Had a house on Georgina."

"Nice area."

"Today. Back then it wasn't so chic. In fact, it got so expensive around ten years ago that my folks finally sold out at a huge profit and moved up to Oregon. Now they live in perpetual wet. My mother hates it."

Brian held out his hand and ticked off on his fingers: "Raised in Santa Monica, went to Samo High then Art Center—"

"I never told you that."

He spread his hands and grinned. "Research."

"You do that with all your dates?"

"Don't date that much. I sort of zero in on someone I like and—go for it."

"Go for it, eh?" Linda crossed her legs, making a show of being demure.

His eyes caught the movement. "I didn't mean it quite that way."

"That's all right." She laughed.

After two mai tais, Linda got very loose and chatty. They talked about common experiences. He was born and lived locally, too, and had gone to work at the *Times* as a copy boy one summer between semesters. "I never finished college," he admitted. "My old man thought I was stupid. He was convinced that if I turned my back on education, I would grow up with narrow attitudes about everything."

"And did you?"

"Probably. But so did he. And he graduated from Yale."

"Everybody's narrow-minded about something." She tried to keep her voice from slurring. She felt light-headed and knew her movements were getting sloppy.

"I agree with you," Brian said. "Narrow thinking . . . My ex-wife suffered a lingering case of it. She didn't like my *work*. She liked the glamor of being married to a *Times* reporter, but that wore thin pretty fast, and we were left with a mock marriage. That was five years ago. I'm thirty-four now, and I'm not sure how I feel about taking the plunge again." He paused, smiled halfheartedly, and changed the subject.

But Linda had caught a twinge of uncertainty, a momentary lapse in his façade, as if he were tentatively feeling his way.

Dinner arrived. Linda had ordered two portions of pressed

duck, which she attacked vigorously. Brian ate a steak and watched her.

She almost made it through the meal and off to complete light-headedness, but after the food the drinks wore off and she sank into a depression. She couldn't touch dessert.

"What's wrong?" Brian finally asked. "One minute all the defenses are down and the next you're hiding behind the Great Wall of China."

"Nothing. . . . It's business."

"Oh? Can't even pack it in for one night out with Prince Charming?"

She looked at Brian and did what Buddy Dyal had done to her for reassurance, only she meant it. She put her hand on his cheek. He stared at her, excited by the warmth and boldness of her touch.

"Christ, Linda," he muttered. "Have you got any idea what I'd like to do to you right now?"

"Yes." Slowly, she drew her hand away. "But let's not," she said finally.

He searched her eyes and saw that she meant it, so he changed the subject quickly, telling her more about his job at the *Times:* who he worked for and what he liked and didn't like about it. He told her it was stimulating to get on new stories all the time, but he resented not having enough time to himself.

"I'd like to finish this novel I'm doing," he explained, "but I'm too pooped when I get home. I manage about two pages a night, but I have to rewrite ten for every two. Nothing ever comes out the way I want it. Maybe I just can't do fiction: I'm drowning in *fact*. And I get scared thinking, Gee, if this book is good and successful, then I'd quit my job and write full time, but then I'd be working for myself with no security." He paused. "What's it like being able to hire and fire people?"

She looked at him blankly. Suddenly, he wasn't there. Suddenly, she was across another table a long time ago, meeting Paul Mizzell for the first time, trying to decide whether Buddy Dyal was pushing a loser at her or what.

Brian asked the question again

"It's . . . not my favorite part of the job," she said

At that moment, she knew she would not be able to fire Paul

and cast him out on the street. If he was going crazy again, he might just fix on her as the root of his problem. She had no desire to make herself a target. Monday she would contact Dahlke and get it straightened out.

Brian drove her home slowly, taking the far right lane on Wilshire Boulevard, letting the Friday night maniacs hog the road. He suggested a side trip into Westwood—maybe a movie or a late cappuccino. She turned him down.

He parked in the visitors' space and walked Linda upstairs. She had trouble with the key; he opened the door for her.

"This thing you have to do Sunday," he said. "What is it? Recording?"

"Photo session. Big setup down on Main Street. Album cover for one of our groups. Sorry, Brian. I can't get out of it."

"That's okay. I'll call again."

"Thanks." She looked at him, then leaned forward. They came together in a kiss. Her hands rested on his shoulder. He looped an arm around her back and held her close, gently stroking her hair. They stood in the hallway kissing, both knowing it would go no further tonight, but neither willing to be the first to break it off. Finally, Linda pulled back and gasped for air. She went into her apartment quickly and shut the door. Brian stared after her a long time, then walked away.

"Right now, strutting is a local phenomenon here in Venice, but very soon you're going to see it spread across the country and catch on like wildfire." Tony Benedict faced a phalanx of microphones and cameras outside his base of operations, the Pelican Café on Main Street.

"Isn't this just another rock group?" a reporter asked.

"No, sir," Tony said quickly. "It's four very talented musicians who exemplify a way of being and thinking, an attitude expressed in a physical movement as old as the oldest rooster. It's a walk that telegraphs pride. It says, I feel great and I want everyone to know it! Strutting will be the focal image of the eighties, as the Beatles were to the sixties! We've got Bobby DiPreto, one of the foremost experts on disco, developing a dance called The Strut, based around the lead selection in our new album."

Linda watched Tony's performance from a bank of director's chairs set up on the sidewalk where Main Street was cordoned off. Uniformed police shunted traffic down side streets. It was 11 A.M., and C. L. Clarke was still directing five studio electricians from Warner Bros., who were trying to get ten arc lamps to do what the sun could not. Tony had approved the hiring of two Hollywood assistant directors to wrangle the crowd, but they were not enough to cope with the horde of nonpros who had been hastily assembled from among the denizens of Venice. Through newspaper ads and radio appeals on Saturday, rock music fans had been notified of a "spontaneous happening" arranged by Rok Records on behalf of their sensational new rock group, the Struts. The hype had been enough to drag out more people than Tony could ever hope to want in a crowd shot, and they had arrived in some of the strangest costumes—from full-length granny dresses that probably hadn't been washed since the sixties, to shorts cut so high that pubic hair was on full display. It looked like an ersatz Hallowe'en party, with an eclectic assortment of pirate outfits, ruffled shirts, clown faces, and weird hats, all part of the New Romantic image.

The assistants, under the harassed direction of Steve Klemer, the Struts' producer, were trying to get the crowd to pose in the established Strut mode, with very little success. Everybody thought it was a put-on and they were just here to get their picture taken.

Klemer brushed past Linda, growling "I wish to Christ we had stuck with art work."

Marvin Bensch, Rok's sales director, was in a head-to-head with Pepe Morasta, business affairs, both glancing uncertainly at Tony, wondering which of them should inform the marketing director he was over budget.

Linda relished the chaos. Her smile broadened when C. L. Clarke came by, yelling at two kids to get off his Trans Am.

Paul Mizzell arrived late. He sat down next to Linda, a sweater draped over his shoulders. "Warmer than I thought it would be," he said. He watched the confusion with quiet detachment.

Linda found it hard to sit next to him calmly. She forced herself to pretend that everything was all right.

Tony led the press in a mob parade to the Struts' camper. Jerry Madison, the manager, ran ahead, urging them to douse their weed. They straightened and put on their coolest looks as Tony introduced them to the reporters.

"And baby makes three," said a voice behind Linda. She turned to see Brian Hawthorn standing behind her with a photographer. "Mrs. Sharman, meet Larry Hilbrick. His idol was Animal on *Lou Grant*."

Linda got up and shook hands with a skinny, ragged young man badly in need of a shave. "What are you doing here?" she asked Brian.

"Got another assignment. Bye-bye San Diego, hello Main Street."

"You switched so you could be here?"

"Ah-ah. I said assignment. Right, Larry?" Larry nodded and held up his camera. "The *Times* has to cover this too. What's good for the networks is good enough for people who read."

"Why do I think you finagled this?"

Brian crossed himself. "Scout's honor I didn't." He rubbed his hands and looked around. "Now, what's going on here? Looks like an underground circus. These people all refugees from *Zap Comics!* Hey, hello there—Paul Miggell, right?" Brian stuck his hand out at Paul. "We've passed each other in the office a couple of times."

"Nice to meet you," Paul said stiffly.

"Hey, Linda, I've got a great idea: How about a picture of you for the article?" Brian said.

"I don't think so." She nodded in Tony's direction. "He's the showpiece today."

"No way. That guy's so transparent he wouldn't even show up on film. But you're an interesting subject. Woman in the industry in a responsible position, enviable—you're news today. How about a nice shot of you down by the whatchamacallit building, the one with all the phony windows painted on the side?"

"Man, that'd be great," echoed Larry. "One of those windows is painted sideways. Knocks your eye out."

"Sorry." Linda shook her head. "I have to stay here."

"Aw, look, just one. A two-shot. You and Paul."

Linda glanced at Paul and saw him go rigid.

"Just the right height," Brian continued. "You'd look great together."

"No pictures," Paul said.

"Come on—it won't hurt—"

"No pictures," he repeated, backing away.

"Suppose we pose you with the Struts—"

"No!"

"Leave him alone," Linda said firmly.

"Okay, okay—" Brian stopped and listened.

Everybody listened. Music had started from somewhere, loud, overmodulated, a big sound trying to come through a small speaker. An East Indian beat, a sitar that segued into a whining, chanting voice that Linda recognized immediately. The Beatles. John Lennon. She knew the song but couldn't remember the title. She looked around, trying to determine the source. It was coming from up the street, in the direction of the crowd. Tony stepped away from the newsmen, annoyed.

Linda caught a frightened look on Paul's face as Brian said, "Isn't that from *Revolver*?"

Paul glanced at him sharply.

At a gesture from Tony, one of the assistants darted into the crowd and shouldered through, hands over his head, clapping for attention. "All right, all right," he shouted. "Whoever has that radio, would you mind turning it down?"

The music growled back at him, getting wilder, doing acoustic gyrations that echoed up and down the street, threatening to turn a minor nuisance into a major problem as the crowd picked up on it and joined the chant. Tony swore out loud, puffed himself up, and bulled through the crowd.

The assistant hollered back, "Who the hell owns a piss yellow Porsche?!"

Tony stopped, then started to run, yelling at the kids to get out of his way.

Linda wondered what Tony was getting excited about, then remembered that *his* Porsche was piss yellow. She laughed and turned to tell Paul. She saw his face contorted in terror, hands tightly pressed against his ears to blot out the sound. He stared right through her, panic-stricken. Behind him, the photographer raised his camera and nodded. Brian tapped Paul's shoulder.

Paul whirled and the photographer snapped three pictures.

Linda saw it all and stared at Brian, puzzled.

The music cut off abruptly and a cheer rose from the crowd, followed by derisive laughter.

Paul dropped his hands and stood very still, staring at the camera. The photographer lowered it slowly, glancing uncertainly at Brian. "I was shooting the crowd," he mumbled.

Linda took a step forward, but Paul was faster. His hand shot out and ripped the camera out of Larry Hilbrick's hand.

"Hey, man, what are you—?"

Paul backed away, fumbling with the release.

"Wait a minute," said Brian. "I just wanted you out of the way—"

Paul ripped out the film with a grunt of rage. Then he returned the camera to Hilbrick.

Brian scowled. "Was that necessary?"

"Yes," Paul replied coldly, then walked away.

Linda stared after him, all her doubts about him heightened. He didn't want his picture taken, and only she knew why. He was worried about his past coming out. If those shots ended up in the newspaper, somebody might spot him as Gary Steen, and that could start trouble.

She looked at Brian. Had Brian deliberately provoked this? She was about to ask him when Tony's voice boomed over a bullhorn. "Now listen to me," he exhorted the crowd. "If we don't get this shot soon, there won't be any concert this afternoon. I don't care what was promised."

There were hoots from the crowd, and somebody hollered, "Beatles, man—sure beat the fucking Struts!"

Tony waited for the laughter to subside. "All right, you've had your fun. Now settle down and let's get this over with."

He came back toward Linda and tossed her a cassette tape. It was a commercial copy of the Beatles' *Revolver*. "Goddamned kids," he said. "I'd like to find out who put that in my car." He stalked off.

When he was gone, Brian edged closer to Linda and regarded the tape coldly. "Hell of a thing to frighten a guy, isn't it?"

"What were you trying to pull with that camera?"

"Nothing."

"Like hell. You heard him say he didn't want his picture taken."

Brian shrugged. "Larry got carried away."

"Sorry," Larry said.

Linda was no longer listening. Tony Benedict might assume that some kid had planted the tape to disrupt the shooting. But suppose it was meant to scare Paul Mizzell. Wasn't it *Revolver* he said he had gotten in the mail? She slipped the tape into a pocket and decided she shouldn't waste any more time.

Get hold of Dahlke—fast.

CHAPTER 6

Gene Dahlke's office was on one of those fashionable medical side streets in Beverly Hills—two-story, old on the outside, beautifully furnished and decorated inside. The waiting room was spacious, with two long comfortable sofas flanked by expensive bonsai plants. Dahlke shared the office with an associate, Hugo Bass. Linda had phoned Dahlke in the morning, trying to get him to see Paul, but he insisted on seeing her first. "He's the one who needs help," she had said.

"Let me decide that after I talk with you."

Smiling, Dr. Bass came out while she was waiting and introduced himself. He was about fifty, short and balding with cold, dry hands. In a tiny nasal voice he asked if she had ever been in analysis.

"I don't mean to be rude," said Linda, "but I'm really here to talk about someone else."

"I know. Paul Mizzell. Dr. Dahlke and I worked together on his case for quite some time."

Linda looked back at him blankly, wondering if Dahlke had sent him out here to shortstop her.

"You haven't answered my question," Bass said.

"I've had some analysis, yes."

"Good. May I inquire the nature of the problem?"

"Husband. I had a lot of guilt feelings when our marriage fell apart."

"And who was your doctor?"

"Herman Obendiner."

"Are you still seeing him?"

"No." She gave Bass a pert smile. "I'm fine now." She

wasn't sure if he believed her. "Listen, Dr. Bass, is this necessary?"

"Your past analysis experience and your present state of mind directly influence what you're going to tell us about Paul."

"I see." Of course he was right, but she was starting to dislike him. "Why can't I go through this with Dr. Dahlke?"

"He'll ask different questions, then we'll compare notes."

"How clever."

He smiled and picked up his clipboard. "Now then, if you will step into my office . . . Believe me, Mrs. Sharman, it will help you to go through it twice. That way we'll pick up discrepancies." He smiled and held the door open for her.

A half hour later, Bass stopped writing and slipped papers off the clipboard and into a folder. She couldn't read anything on his face as he motioned her over to a connecting door. He knocked. A voice inside said, "Come in."

Gene Dahlke stood up as Linda entered. He was tall and handsome, with steel gray hair and dark green eyes. He reminded Linda of the "older man" in a daytime soap, mysterious and cautiously sensual.

The two men held a brief whispered conference, then Bass excused himself, handed Dahlke the folder, and went out. Dahlke smiled at Linda and sat down opposite her in a big leather chair. He crossed his legs and rested his head on spread forefinger and thumb. "I hope our procedure is not too wearing, Linda. May I call you Linda?"

"You may." She eyed him just long enough to let him know she had no intention of playing the subservient-patient role.

"I gather you've heard a lot of detail from Mr. Dyal," said Dahlke. "You know, he was the only one who visited Paul in the hospital. Quite frequently too . . ."

"Somehow I can't see Buddy making weekly trips with flowers and candy," Linda said. "Why did he do it?"

"Mr. Dyal was a little bit driven. By what I'm not sure. He asked that we not question his motives as long as he did some good. He did a lot of good."

"But he and Paul aren't friends today."

"No," said Dahlke. "Mr. Dyal moved rather rapidly into management and could no longer devote any time to Paul."

"Is that so?" Linda said with a touch of sarcasm.

"Now, suppose you tell me exactly how much you know of Paul's background."

Linda repeated what she had learned from Buddy, ending with Lori Cornell's murder.

"How do you feel about that?" said Dahlke.

"I should have been told before."

He put her through a barrage of questions, trying to establish her state of mind over the whole business, explaining that he had to determine if she was going to color her information about Paul. Bass was wrong: Dahlke was asking the same questions. She felt it was an awfully roundabout way of getting a few facts.

"Now," he said with a fatherly smile, "tell me what Paul Mizzell has been doing that upsets you."

She stared at him, then said, "Apart from that, Mrs. Lincoln, how did you like the play?"

Dahlke permitted himself a small chuckle, then said sagely, "You have to accept his rehabilitation, Linda. It's as much a fact as the event that got him into treatment."

"I don't have to accept anything."

"No." Dahlke smiled patiently. "But Paul's well-being is at stake."

"What about mine? I didn't get much sleep last night."

"If we hash this out together, you'll sleep fine. Now do you understand why I wanted to see *you* first?"

She sighed out loud, but she gave him what he wanted, detailing as best she could Paul's two years as her employee, how he had proved himself a solid artist, how she had developed enough confidence in him to make him an assistant, and what that meant. Dahlke lapped it up like a beaming daddy. She described Paul's reluctance to socialize and Dahlke nodded knowingly.

"Understandable," he said. "Paul has a reasonable fear of recognition and discovery. He feels comfortable working because there's plenty of privacy, but he gets nervous in crowds—afraid he'll let something slip. We were never able to clean that out of him—one very good reason for changing his identity. Does he have friends at work?"

"Not really. He never sees any of us after hours."

"Go on, then."

Linda described the events of the last week. The package that came addressed to her but was for Paul, his emotional tiff with Van De Carlo, leaving work without telling anyone, his story about things being mailed to him or planted for him to find, the car accident and his belief that someone was trying to kill him, and the incident on Main Street involving the tape of *Revolver*.

"And when a reporter tried to take his picture, he freaked. Tore the film out of the camera, then ran off."

Dahlke pursed his lips. "Again, fear of recognition."

"But the other things . . . ?"

"Well, if they really have been mailed to him . . . Perhaps I should take a look—"

"He got rid of everything. There was the one package addressed to me, but I never saw what was inside."

Dahlke studied his knee, and Linda got the feeling he didn't believe *her*. She wanted to laugh. What a twist.

"You think he's paranoid?" she suggested.

"Perhaps," Dahlke replied. "He could be manufacturing a persecution complex out of residual guilt. It's hard to say."

"Think you can nip it in the bud?" Linda said with a trace of sarcasm. When Dahlke didn't respond, she continued, "Look, Doctor, I have a tough job. I need people I can depend on. If Paul's problems are going to interfere with his work, then I have to do something about it. But if I let him go, if I fire him, will I be making an enemy?"

"Please, Mrs. Sharman, it's not that serious."

"No?" She got up, her lips working angrily.

"Paul Mizzell is *not* homicidal," Dahlke said with firm professional conviction. "In order to believe that, you need a better understanding of his case." He glanced at his clock. "It's five thirty. I have to catch up on some paperwork. Could you stay and listen to some tapes?"

Linda regarded him suspiciously.

Dahlke made Linda comfortable in Bass's office, gave her coffee, and loaded the first tape into a cassette player. "Ethically speaking," he said, "I am violating the patient-doctor relation-

ship. But I believe you have a vital interest." He smiled. "Just
so we understand one another."

She understood. He was being cooperative but cautious.

"This is an interview I had with Gary Michael Steen shortly
after he was committed for psychiatric care. It was recorded at
Camarillo in the spring of 1969, about six months after the
murder. Listen all the way through and then we can discuss it.
All right?"

Linda nodded and gazed apprehensively at the machine. He
showed her how to work it, then left her alone. She sipped the
coffee first, feeling uncomfortable in Bass's cold leather chaise.
She moved to a hardback chair and turned on the tape.

Paul's voice came out of the speaker, sounding flat and lifeless. Linda listened in silence, her arms hugged beneath her
breasts.

". . . We'd been makin' it most of that term. She'd moved
into my place on Strathmore and both of us really got into each
other. It was really heavy. She wasn't doin' well in classes and
didn't really care, with all the politics going down and everything. We just wanted to be together . . . like, you know,
makin' it all the time."

"Did you attend any classes at all?" Dahlke's voice.

"Oh, sure. She'd go to mine and I'd go to hers. But nobody
was paying any attention. The war, man. Everybody was out
protesting. That's where it was at."

Dahlke's voice paused. "Tell me about the movie you went to
at Royce Hall."

"*Pandora's Box?*"

"That's the one. What do you remember about it?"

"It was part of a series—I think they called it Psychological
Masterpieces."

"Had you seen *Pandora's Box* before?"

"No."

"Had you wanted to see it? Is that why you went?"

"No, it was sort of a regular thing. We'd get stoned together
and go to these old movies at Royce."

"Were you stoned when you went to *Pandora's Box*?"

"I had a little grass . . . but it was the acid . . ."

"Did Lori get stoned?"

"Yeah. She always started that."

"She turned *you* on?"

"Yeah. She had charge of the grass."

"So you started the evening by getting stoned. Before dinner?"

"What? Oh, yeah . . . gives you an appetite."

"You smoked dope, then you ate. What did you eat?"

"Whatever was around. . . . Some soup and cheese, I think. We smoked some dope and ate, then I dropped the acid."

"Did you do anything else?"

"Like what?"

"Did you have sex?"

"We goofed around a bit."

"Explain."

"Like tickling. Touching."

"Don't be delicate. How did you touch?"

"We just touched. We were always *touching* each other."

"Where?"

"Face . . . you know, like legs . . ."

"Genitals?"

"Yeah, there was a little of that."

"Did you have an orgasm?"

"No, man . . ."

"So you just played with each other."

"Yeah . . . sort of teasing. . . . We do it—did it all the time."

"But neither of you had a climax."

"No."

"Did you get excited?"

"She did—a little."

"And you didn't?"

"A little."

"But no climax."

"Nope. Sorry."

"Did you urinate before leaving for the movie?"

A sharp laugh from Gary Steen. Linda twitched.

"Answer the question, please."

"No, I didn't urinate."

"So, you smoked some grass, ate some soup and cheese,

masturbated a little, dropped acid, and didn't urinate. And then you went to a movie.''

"Yeah.''

"It's possible, then, that while you were sitting in the theater, you were experiencing pressure from a full bladder and from swollen, unrelieved genitals. Yes?''

"I don't remember.''

"Sometimes, Gary, sexual tension will directly affect the trip you get from acid. Would you describe your condition that night as sexually tense?''

"I guess so.''

"All right. . . . Now I want you to relax, Gary. Relax and take yourself back to when you pulled into the parking lot at UCLA. Who was driving?''

"She was.''

"Lori was driving the van, and you were high on acid. Remember any details?''

"I . . .''

"Think back. Take your time and concentrate. She was driving. You parked where?''

"The big structure outside Royce.''

"What was she wearing?''

"A T-shirt. Then she put on her other thing . . .''

"Her what?''

"The pink sweat shirt . . . UCLA.''

"Pardon?''

"It had UCLA across the front. I remember because the letters . . . the letters really stood out   like, they leaped out at me . . . they were so white . . .''

"That's fine, Gary. Go on. You left the van, then what?''

"She gave me a big candy bar.   . I was hungry.''

"You shared it?''

"No. I ate the whole thing. So what?''

"I'm not accusing you. Just relax and let's go on. What were you wearing? Describe your clothing.''

"Jeans.''

"What else?'

"Oh, shit . . . sandals, a shirt, and my vest   leather, with a fringe. . . . She kissed me.''

"Pardon?"

"On the way into Royce, she stopped and kissed me."

"That's all?"

"Yeah. . . . Then we went into the hall."

"Where did you sit?"

"We always sat in the balcony. . . . I remember one thing. . . . I was sort of tripping out on the pipes, the organ pipes, above the stage. . . . Then . . . Then the old man came out, the guy who plays the organ. . . . Then the movie."

"You remember much about the film?"

"A little hazy. I remember the girl. She was . . . beautiful. Black hair . . . I guess I missed a lot of it."

"You don't recall what it was about?"

"Not exactly."

"The heroine is a whore, Gary. The film is about whoring."

"You've seen it?"

"I ran it last night. The girl destroys everyone she comes in contact with. And throughout, she remains blindly ignorant of the consequences. It seemed to me that she had a knack for sin. How did it seem to you?"

"I guess that's right."

Linda heard distinct shifting sounds on the tape. There was a momentary silence.

"Would you say she lacked a conscience, Gary?"

"Uh . . . yes."

"And for her, remorse was as easy as going to the toilet, right?"

"I guess so."

"How do you feel about that?"

"What?"

"That lack of genuine remorse. Do you identify with it?"

"You mean . . . am I . . . am I sorry about what I did?"

"Are you?"

Long, long silence. Linda could almost see the two of them in the darkened office. She could feel Gary Steen struggling with the answer, and she realized she didn't want to hear him say yes, because she would never believe it.

"I don't know."

"That's good. That's very good, Gary. It gives us room to grow, something to work toward."

"It does?"

"The girl in the film couldn't help herself. It was in her nature to let these things happen, to take advantage of men and to tear them apart in the process. Did she remind you of anyone?"

"No."

"Now you seem sure."

More silence. Linda almost broke out in applause. Dahlke was mousetrapping him.

"My . . . My mother . . ."

"Go on."

"She . . . My mother used to . . . She had boyfriends."

"After your father left?"

"He didn't *leave*. That's not the way it happened. She . . . When I was twelve, she drove him out. She wanted to get rid of him so she could see other guys. She cried a lot when he left . . . but she didn't mean it. She found somebody else right away . . . then another and another. A parade of them in and out. It was like she was eating them up alive, then spitting them out. Just so much garbage."

"What do you mean? She was cruel to them?"

"After she got what she wanted, she'd turn really bitchy. They wouldn't understand what hit them. First she'd raise their hopes, make them think she loved them, then all of a sudden, wham! The hammer dropped and they were out. And she'd be off with the next one."

"And how did that make you feel?"

"Like any day she'd do the same to me."

"Explain."

"You know, like throw me out too."

"You didn't think she loved you?"

"How the hell was I supposed to know? She never told anybody the truth! Maybe she never meant it when she said— Oh, shit."

"When she said what, Gary?"

"She used to say . . . like, with the tears . . . 'I'll never leave you, Gary. I promise I'll never leave you.' Bull *shit*! I knew she'd leave. I knew it, and so did she. She took advantage of everybody. She sucked us all dry! Women are like that . . ."

Linda took a deep breath to relieve the pressure building in her chest. God, what a childhood he must have had.

"Do you believe all women are like that, Gary?"

"I don't know."

"Did you meet other women—girls—who were like your mother?"

"Yeah . . . some. They'd lead you on, maybe even go to bed with you, then all of a sudden . . . Maybe it's just the way things are today. Everybody's so loose . . ."

"And you're not. You weren't."

"No. I guess not."

"You wanted what?"

"I don't know . . . Just *somebody*."

"After your mother left, you went to live with your aunt. What was she like?"

"Old. She couldn't pick up on what I was going through."

"What's the matter?"

"Nothing . . . I guess . . . I'm sorry I hurt her."

There was another long silence. Linda rolled her head back and closed her eyes, picturing Gary's kindly old aunt getting the phone call telling her that her nephew had just carved up his girl friend.

"Let's go back to the movie, Gary. What stands out in your mind about it? Anything?"

"Maybe . . . the gray man."

"Which one is that?"

"The guy at the end."

"The one with the knife?"

"Yeah. See, I was sitting there and Lori had fallen asleep, sort of slumped over my lap. Her head was down here . . . and her breath . . . I could feel her breath, hot all over my . . ."

"Your lap."

"And I started feeling really . . . I—I wanted her. You know what I mean? It just came over me. I wanted her so much, and then I was looking at the screen, and the girl up there was in the arms of this . . ."

"The gray man."

"Yeah, and she wanted him, just like I wanted Lori. But he couldn't help himself. Her back—it was so white and beautiful. And I remember he picked up the knife that was on her table . . ."

Linda hit the stop button. She didn't want to hear any more of that. She skipped ahead and came in as Gary was describing leaving the hall, looking up at the twin towers at the front of Royce, making his way back to the parking lot with Lori helping him.

". . . There was a crowd and she was sort of propping me up and moving me along. . . . When we got to the structure, the cars were starting up and moving, and I remember lights stabbing my eyes, hurting, and the squealing brakes. . . . Then I got scared and left Lori and got lost in the cars. I think she was calling me, but I couldn't fix on where she was. . . . I remember her saying that if I didn't come back, she would leave. Don't leave! Don't leave! that's what I hollered back. I must have yelled that over and over . . ."

"You believed she was running out on you?"

"That's it, exactly. When I found the van, she was sitting on the back bumper with the doors open   she helped me in and she was sort of cooing at me."

"Cooing?"

"Really really nice."

"Not threatening to leave you anymore?"

"No."

"You seem uncertain."

"Well . . . no, she didn't say it anymore, but . . ."

"But you still felt she might go?"

"I—I don't . . ."

"What did she tell you?"

"That it was . . . that I was having a bad trip. . . . I fell on the floor in the back of the van. There were blankets and the tool box and the metal walls. . . . She was saying, 'Don't worry, I'll take care of you. Mommy knows what to do . . .' "

"She said that?"

"Yeah. . . . Then we went at it."

"You had sex?"

"Yeah."

"Who initiated it?"

"She did. Took off her clothes and was sort of teasing me."

"How?"

"Sticking her tits in my face. . . . She still had the sweat shirt on, just sort of draped over her shoulders, and she was rubbing me. . . . She took it off . . ."

"The sweat shirt?"

"Yeah. . . . And she put it under my head like a pillow. Then she said . . . First she sort of got over me and like, straddled, and then she moved her hips up to my face, and she said, 'Trip out on this.' "

"She was naked, except for the sweatshirt?"

"Yeah . . ."

"And you?"

"Oh, yeah. She'd already pulled everything off me. Then she was saying like, 'I'll never leave you, Gary. I'll never . . .' Oh, Christ . . ."

"What?"

"My mother said that."

Linda couldn't help herself. A moan escaped. Her hand went to her mouth.

"What did you do then, Gary?"

Another silence.

"Gary?"

"We . . . went at it . . . like we always did. . . . It was fierce. But I kept flashing on the movie, the girl in the movie . . ."

"And your mother?"

"Yeah. I saw her too. Then I had my hands on her neck and I was squeezing, really hard. Then I banged her head on the floor. I banged it and banged it—She was lying there naked and sort of limp, and I knew she was leaving me."

"Leaving you?"

"She was going away. She would never come back, and I wanted to stop her. I was shouting at her to come back, but she wouldn't. I got mad, and I remember looking around for something to stop her with, and there was the toolbox right beside me. And there was my knife, the hunting knife my Dad gave me . . ."

"Go on."

"I . . . I used it."

"You stabbed her with it?"

"Yes."

"More than once?"

"Yes. Then, I suddenly felt this anger . . . something I couldn't stop. . . . I shoved the knife . . ."

"Between her legs."

"Yes. Between her . . . her legs. And left it there. There was so much blood. . . . The sweatshirt . . . I was wiping my hands on it. . . . She was lying there. . . . I got my pants on but nothing else, and I ran."

"You left her? You didn't go back?"

"How could I?"

"Of course."

"I just ran back into Royce. Somehow, I got up to the third floor and I found a door, and then I was out on the roof. . . . I cut my feet on the gravel, but I kept running. There were all these vents with steam coming out. . . . And I went through a window into an office. There was a hallway over some library, and I found these rungs that went up, a sort of ladder, up to a little tiny room. And then there was another ladder that went up to another room, and then another after that. . . . It was really freaky, and finally I was in the tower."

"The tower at Royce? One of the two towers you mentioned before?"

"Yeah. When we came out of the theater, I'd been looking at them, and I guess they stuck in my mind. I must have known right where I was going. Isn't that . . . isn't that weird?"

"You stayed up there?"

"Yeah, in the top room. I felt really sort of safe. I could look out through the open arches and see the stars. . . . And the chimes across the plaza went off every hour. . . . I remember being cold. . . . I don't . . . I didn't think about Lori much. . . . I just waited . . ."

Linda shut off the recorder and leaned back, drained and horrified She'd had enough psychiatry for a lifetime.

She got up and knocked on Dahlke's door. "Come in," she heard him mumble. She walked in and laid the tapes on his desk. He looked up from his papers and stared her full in the face He seemed relaxed and less imposing, his coat off, sleeves rolled up, and a pipe in the corner of his mouth. He waited for her to speak.

"Do you like Paul?" she asked.

Dahlke continued to stare at her, then appeared to consider the question. "I don't know," he said finally. "Basically, he's a reconstructed personality. A lot of the life has been burned out of him."

"A clockwork orange?" she said aloud.

Dahlke smiled. "An extreme way of putting it. We didn't perform any progressive experiments on him. And we certainly did not attempt to make violence repulsive to him. That was not his problem."

"What was?" Linda sat down across the desk.

Dahlke repacked his pipe. "Drugs," he said flatly.

"No. That was a symptom. There's something in what he was trying to say about his mother. Buddy Dyal mentioned it too."

"I see we've awakened an interest in psychiatry."

"I could hardly have slept through those tapes," Linda snapped back.

Dahlke relit the pipe and a cloud of smoke obscured his eyes. "Yes, he had a strong mother fixation. He was raised by a single parent. He believed that she loved him, but she was always leaving him with somebody or other. She couldn't cope with him, or with money, jobs, boyfriends, with life itself. Finally, she left him with a rather old and inflexible aunt, after promising she would *never* leave him. He was ten years old at the time, and it was something he never got over. He never saw her again and in his mind developed this love-hate relationship with her, which he tried to sublimate. Drugs, particularly LSD, brought it all to the surface. Somehow, in his hallucination, he associated Lori Cornell with his mother—and got his revenge."

They sat looking at each other a long time, then Dahlke offered Linda a drink. She accepted with a curt "Thank you," and he went to a cabinet. She took straight bourbon and sipped it sparingly. He made himself a scotch and soda and sat down again, his eyes flicking furtively over Linda's body.

She ignored his glances and said finally, "Doctor, why wasn't he sorry?"

"He couldn't feel anything when we did that interview. He

wouldn't allow himself to. He was in shock all through the trial, still in shock when he came to Camarillo and for most of the first year under my care. He was hiding from himself, afraid to admit that he was this Gary Michael Steen who had done something so unspeakable. Hugo—Dr. Bass—finally hit on the idea of providing him with a new identity just so he could gain some distance from the part of his personality that he couldn't live with. It worked quite well, actually. In a sense, we turned him schizoid. He became Paul Mizzell; we encouraged his art training and continued to treat him. And in the sessions, he was finally able to separate who he was from who he had been. He could think of Gary Steen as another human being entirely. Getting him to be that objective about himself took nearly two years. Then we had to turn him around and make him accept the fact that Paul Mizzell had once been Gary Steen. In other words, remove the schizophrenia. Very complicated case, and it took much longer than usual. Then, of course, there was a continuing effort on the part of the dead girl's family to see that he was never released. Paul is not a violent man; neither was Gary. That one act, brought about by drugs, released all the violence there had ever been inside Gary Steen.''

Linda wasn't so sure. Throwing Van De Carlo out of a shooting session was not the act of a milquetoast. She lifted her drink and was surprised to find she had already finished it. "What made you sure he was rehabilitated?" she asked. "How did you know when to let him out?"

"When I was sufficiently convinced he had a stable personality and could function in society. Sometimes mistakes are made, you see, but Paul's crime resulted from dropping acid. When we were finished with him, there was no reason to believe he would ever again experiment with drugs. Consequently, no danger of a repeat offense."

She looked him in the eye. "You've done a pretty good job clarifying things for me, Doctor, but I want to know if you're going to see *him*."

Dahlke drummed his fingers on the desk. "Mrs. Sharman, if I did go to him, and he was suffering from some unjustified paranoid delusion, I think it would just tend to solidify that belief. I think he would clam up, and it would become impossible to get anything out of him. He would then have to come back in for treatment; you would probably fire him; he would feel rejection and failure; and we would end up doing more damage than good. Now, is that what we want?''

Linda gave him a thin smile. ''I don't know that *we* want any of the responsibility, Doctor.''

Dahlke frowned. ''Look, if he really is imagining things, it will come to a head; he will realize that he can't cope with it alone, and then he'll come to me. I find in these situations that it's best to let some of the steam off before you open the boiler. On the other hand, if his persecution is genuine, and someone really is playing games with him, then it's a matter for the police.''

Linda stared at him in disbelief. ''How will it come to a head, Doctor?''

Dahlke stared back. ''He won't kill again. That's not in him.''

''I'll quote you in my will.''

''Mrs. Sharman—''

''He murdered a girl once, Dr. Dahlke. I may not be a girl anymore, but I am a woman, and that's close enough to make me very nervous! He also *lives* with a woman. Now, don't you think she might be in some danger and ought to be warned? Because frankly, I think he's too close-mouthed and scared to have told *her* about his past. And if she doesn't know, and he suddenly explodes around her—'' She stopped.

Dahlke was looking back, frowning deeply. ''I didn't know about this girl friend,'' he said. ''That's a different matter.''

''When did you last see him?''

''About six months ago.''

''He's been living with Judith for eight months.''

''Well . . . You're quite right, then. He should have told me.''

Linda got up. ''And what would you have done?''

''I would have insisted he tell the girl everything.'' He leaned back and sucked on his pipe. ''You know, it's possible that this whole paranoia—if that's what it is—could be growing out of his fear of the girl's finding out about him.''

He got up, too, and walked Linda to the door. ''Naturally, under these circumstances, I will get in touch with him. Mrs.

Sharman, thanks for your help and your concern. I'm sure your first inclination was to get rid of him, but if you're willing to cope a little bit, I'm certain we can get Paul back on the track quickly.''

He smiled and shook her hand warmly, lingering over the contact. She thanked him for his time and was very polite but walked out disgusted. Dahlke's whole approach seemed haphazard. She wondered if instead of curing the patient he hadn't created a time bomb.

CHAPTER 7

Linda dropped the proof sheets back into the folder, closed the flap, and drummed angry fingers on her desk. "Why didn't you tell me about this sooner?"

Jimmy Otner blew a stream of smoke from the corner of his mouth, crushed his cigarette in the ashtray, and looked over at spidery-thin Red Richards, sitting in the other chair. "Because we figured you already knew. That's the way Benedict made it sound."

Red nodded agreement. "That's the impression I got, boss lady. Just count yourself lucky you didn't have to be at that zoo they call a house at five-o-goddamn clock in the morning."

Linda searched their faces. "*Freebase* doesn't record for another month. Or has that been changed too?"

Jimmy rubbed his tired eyes. "You'll have to take that up with Tony. He didn't tell us anything. But I got a feeling nothing's been set—he was just fishing for ideas."

Linda masked her anger. Changing a jacket concept was one of the realities of the business—something she could accept. But going behind her back, assigning *her* people to a project without *her* knowledge? That was a direct challenge to *her* authority. Did Tony think she would ignore it? The knot of anger in her stomach expanded. "Leave the proofs with me, Red. I don't want you or Jimmy to do any work on this until I've had a chance to talk with Tony. If he asks, tell him those are my direct orders. Understood?"

Red studied her, one hand tugging at an earlobe. Jimmy gave a knowing smile and heaved himself up. "It was wheel-spinning time this morning. No way anybody's going to get those assholes to stand still long enough for photos. It's got to be illo Maybe that's what Benedict was trying to find out."

"Could be," Linda said coolly. "Personally, I don't give a shit." She watched them leave, then swung her chair around and looked out the window at the smog blanket covering Hollywood. The dirty brown air matched her mood. So Tony was escalating their little war. The bastard was uncanny: he always knew exactly where to put the knife. Of course Red had no way of knowing it, but he could have called her at five A.M. It wouldn't have mattered: she had been up all night, haunted by what she had heard in Dahlke's office yesterday. Gary Steen's words had buzzed around in her head like a malevolent bee, keeping her awake.

"You busy?"

Linda swung around. Tony stood in the doorway, smiling strangely. "Somebody to see you downstairs."

Linda bristled. "Another interview?"

"No."

Linda wanted to smash the grin off his face. "I'm not in the mood for games, Tony, unless you want to talk about your little stunt this morning with *Freebase*."

"That? Just a whim. Look, Rocky isn't going to hang around here much longer, but he wanted to see you before he left."

She stared at him. "I thought he had to stay in France."

"I can tell you all about it, but I know you'd rather hear it from him. Or we can talk about *Freebase*. Your choice."

His smug tone grated. She reached behind her for her purse. When she looked up, Tony was gone. She glared at the open door, groped around for her compact, and popped it open. Bleary red eyes stared back at her from the small mirror. Not much she could do about that. But now, Mr. Benedict was about to get some of his own back. It was time Rocky found out what he had spawned.

Rocky Holt pivoted his wheelchair, and his craggy face broke into a lopsided grin. Half Hungarian and half Irish, he had strong features and plenty of charm. "Are you just going to stand there?" He waved Linda in.

She crossed quickly, with a frozen smile. She was prepared for the cast on his leg but not the puffiness and discoloration on his face. She bent down and pecked his cheek. Rocky snaked an arm around her neck. "You call that a kiss?" he said. She bent lower and embraced him. "That's more like it. How do I look?"

"Terrible," she said, rubbing a smudge of lipstick from his mouth.

His grin widened. "You're the only one who's honest."

She matched his smile. "Sorry, Rocky. I didn't mean to be so blunt, but you look like you were in a fight—and lost."

"Looks a helluva lot worse than it feels."

"Why did you come home so soon? Didn't you like the French nurses?"

"Hah!" He hit a button on the arm of his wheelchair, backed up and began roaming the office, his leg propped out in front of him like a plaster battering ram. "Goddamned frogs were always waking me up, giving me pills to make me go back to sleep. Had to get out of there."

Linda watched him buzz back and forth like a kid with a new toy. Rocky was home; now everything would get back to normal.

He glanced at the cast. "I was pretty shook up over that accident. Did you know the other driver died?" She nodded. "So I sent for Haskell, my shrink, figuring I'd need a psychological boost. Before he arrived, I found out the other driver had been higher than a flute, and not on booze. So suddenly I didn't feel responsible anymore. Haskell showed up; I told him he could go home. Jesus—did he get mad! Here I am, my leg in traction, wrapped like a mummy, and he wants to talk about when I was six years old. So while he was sitting on the end of my bed, I wrote him a check and told him to get out. He wouldn't. Finally, I wormed the truth out of him. He'd brought along his girl friend—not his wife—and he was all set for two weeks of bliss. I looked at him like this"—he dropped his chin and arched his eye—"and told him to screw on his own time and money, not mine. He said 'Fuck you' and went to Vienna. Vienna he can write off. He's probably still there, kissing the sheets in Sigmund Freud's house."

Linda laughed.

Rocky grinned, then rolled to a stop in front of her. "I listened to a lot of music on French radio. Most of it imported British ska and that New Romantic shit. Nothing for us. And I began to think,

Maybe you're just not hearing it anymore, Rocky. Maybe it's all around you, but you're not sensitive to it. I began to get worried."

"You were depressed," Linda offered.

"Of course I was. But you know, for the whole trip—even before the accident—I wasn't hearing anything. Stuff came to my attention, but I couldn't get interested." He paused, reflecting distantly. "Anyway, they took a lot of X rays after the accident. I glowed in the dark for days. They found something at the base of my spine, sort of a growth."

Linda stopped smiling.

"Actually I've been back two days. Been over at UCLA for tests. Now they're telling me it's malignant."

The color drained from Linda's face. She didn't know what to say.

"In fact, I'm not staying. I'm leaving right away for the Eisenhower Medical Center down in Rancho Mirage. I'll be staying at my condo in the desert, but it's going to take time."

"How long?"

"Nine months—a year."

They both fell silent, looking at each other. Linda blinked back tears and swore to herself, then reached out blindly and embraced him. He held her.

"I know they'll take care of you," she said. "But you've got to take care of yourself too." She didn't know if she was making sense. She couldn't find the right words.

He patted her back. "I know things will run smoothly without me, so I'm only making one change. I hope you agree it's the right one. I want someone I can trust running Rok while I'm away."

"Don't worry about that—"

"I don't intend to. This treatment is going to knock me on my ass. I won't be in any condition to make decisions. So, I've just promoted Tony Benedict to vice-president."

She stiffened.

"I hope that meets with your approval."

Too stunned to speak, Linda looked at his cast.

"I know sometimes he's rough, but he knows the business. I'm lucky to have him, and right now I really think he's the only one who can fill my shoes."

Fill them? she thought. Tony would steal the shoes off his feet and fill them with cement. She stared at Rocky.

He cupped an ear. "Why don't I hear applause?"

She took a deep breath and smiled. "Don't worry about anything. I'll work with Tony."

"Hah! I told him you'd say that."

"Did you?"

"And he said he'd work with you."

I'll bet, she thought. Work me right out of a job. She couldn't really blame Rocky. He had to do what made *him* breathe easier. She leaned over and kissed him again. "Get well, Rocky."

She left him chatting on the phone, telling a producer from Capitol about the unfortunate Dr. Haskell. Tony's actions were clear to her now. Knowing about his promotion, he'd already made his first move. The *Freebase* assignment? Was that how he would do it? Take every opportunity to go around her? She wondered how long she could fight back—or, given Rocky's surprising lack of support, whether it was worth it.

Linda drove home in a daze. She felt tired, gritty, and used. She wanted a hot bath and a cold drink.

She parked and trudged up to her condo, unlocked the door, and went in. She snapped on the living room light and paused, spotting an envelope on the carpet. Somebody had slipped a note under the door. It was from Brian, an invitation to dinner at Peppone's, a restaurant just up the street. She crumpled the note and tossed it on the coffee table, closed her door, and walked into the bathroom. She didn't want to see Brian tonight—she didn't want to see anyone. She ran water for the bath, stripped off her clothing, and walked naked into the kitchen. She poured a straight bourbon on the rocks and drained it immediately, then grabbed the bottle and headed for the bathroom.

She lay soaking in the tub for a half hour, sipping bourbon and idly watching the bubbles evaporate over her skin. Her head lolled lazily, and the water lapped at her breasts. They glistened in front of her and she studied them critically. "Poor old tits," she said. "Nobody loves you." She broke up in inebriated laughter, swallowed water, and choked. Sitting up, she coughed it out, then began to cry. Deep sobs racked her body and she swore out loud. "Son of a bitch, you're letting them run your life!"

That's right, talk to yourself. Go bananas, then you can sign up with Dahlke, become his patient, maybe go away for a while, take a nice little rest . . .

She took a deep breath and heaved herself upright. She stood, weaving uncertainly, the liquor and the damp heat making her woozy. She listened to the water drip from her body, then reached for a towel.

Snuggled in an oversize white terry robe, Linda padded barefoot back to the kitchen and opened the refrigerator, hunger bringing her back to reality. The doorbell rang. She went to it and called through the door, "Yes?"

"It's Brian," said the voice. "Get my note?"

She fumbled with the chain and opened the door. "Yes," she said. "I'm sorry . . ." He looked the same. Didn't he ever change that suit? "I tried to call," she lied, "but I couldn't get through."

"That's okay. Came down to pick you up. Can I come in?"

"Sure." She backed and stumbled. He caught her hand and pulled her up. She bobbed in front of him with a stupid smile. "Guess I'm a little bombed," she said.

He held onto her while closing the door, then looked into her eyes. "Want to get dressed?" he said. "They'll hold the table another twenty minutes."

"No."

"You're not hungry?"

"I was."

"But not now."

"No."

"Want me to go?"

"No." She felt a rush of heat and knew it flowed from where their fingers touched. A sob welled up and she fought it. It got as far as a damp glow in the corner of one eye, then she released Brian's hand and touched the belt of her robe. His eyes followed the movement. She pulled the belt apart slowly. Then she threw herself at him. She buried her face in his chest and kissed him. He reached for her hips and pulled her close. As his hands moved over her, she stiffened and bit her lip.

They fell on the sofa and he pulled the robe off her shoulders. He stood up and stripped quickly, then he fell on her, kissing her breasts and reaching down between her legs. In a moment, he was inside and moving rapidly. With a groan, she clutched him with arms and legs. Her head whipped back and forth as long-dormant nerves began to send pulses of pleasure through her body. Sensations grew until her breath caught and so did his, and they both cried out in release. She quivered, then fell back.

He collapsed, sprawling at an odd angle, his legs off the sofa, feet under the coffee table. His face rested on her breast. Lazily, her hand stroked his cheek.

"Brian," she said.

"Hmm?"

"This doesn't mean . . ."

"Doesn't mean what?"

"That we're having an affair."

"No?"

She shook her head. "It's just sex."

"I *know* what it is," he growled. "Just tell me when we're going to do it again."

"After we eat."

She made a quick spaghetti, with butter and mushrooms, and they sat down to it, smiling at each other. "Boy, am I lucky," Brian said. "You realize I could have sat in that restaurant all night waiting for you, gotten pissed, finally called you and told you what a rat you were. Instead, I listened to a little voice inside that said 'Go pick her up, jerk,' and here we are. This is page one, let me tell you."

"Brian," she said solemnly, "I hope to God you don't write about things like this."

"Things like what? Spaghetti? Terrific. You've got a lot of talents, Linda. Pass the Parmesan." He rattled on, full of compliments and jokes. She listened raptly, grateful that he had come by. She, too, could have sat around getting pissed, a different kind of pissed, and what good would it have done? It was sex she had needed, not drink.

"What brought on this attack, by the way?" he asked. "Not that I object—I'm just curious."

"Pressure," she said.

"I see. The job. What are they doing to you now?"

"Getting ready to cut my head off."

"That bad?" She nodded. "Then let me ask a very tough question. Do you deserve it?"

"Are you kidding?"

"No. Maybe you're in the wrong place. I had an editor like that once. Couldn't understand why everybody wanted him out—"

"You no-good bastard." Linda put down her fork. "I throw myself at you because I need somebody desperately—the whole world is closing in on me—and you—"

"You need *somebody*," he said loudly, over her words. She stopped. He waved his wine glass in mock toast. "Not me in particular."

Linda's anger faded. He was right. She had used him.

"I'm just suggesting a possibility," Brian went on. "I'm not siding against you. Persecution is quite common in business, real or imagined."

Suddenly she thought of Paul Mizzell.

She looked at Brian as if she were about to tell him something. When she didn't, he said, "What's the matter?"

"Nothing. Forget it. I shouldn't confide in you. You're a newspaper reporter."

"What's that—first cousin to a leper?"

"You know what I mean."

"Oh, well, if you're going to lump me in with your ex-husband, then of course I don't stand a chance. Listen, Linda"—he gripped her hand—"I liked tonight. I've never been seduced like that before. It was fun. You can do that to me anytime. But if I really need it, I can get that. Friendship, however, is hard to find. When it's offered, take it."

"Thank you," she said flatly.

"Now, if you want to confide in me, go right ahead. I'm a great listener. Come on, what's happening in that office of yours? What's making everybody uptight? What about this Paul Mizzell character? Why does he jump like a rabbit when someone tries to take his picture?"

She stared at him, wanting to tell him, wanting his advice But he *was* a reporter. Paul Mizzell was a story he would be obliged to go after. She saw it in his eyes as plainly as his desire to help.

She relaxed and smiled and held his hand. "I don't need you for that," she lied. "Not right now. If it gets really bad and I can't cope with it, I *will* come to you. I promise. But you've already helped. I haven't had a screw like that in years."

He stared at her a long moment then rose slowly. He picked her up and carried her into the bedroom, kicking the door shut.

When Linda came to work in the morning, somebody was already down the hall in Never-Never Land, adding "Vice-President" over Tony Benedict's name. Linda flashed a curt smile at the secretary and rapped on Tony's door.

"Just a minute," said the secretary.

"Sit down," Linda snapped, opening the door and walking in.

Tony was behind his desk, reading the sports section. He looked up in surprise.

"Congratulations," Linda said, sitting on the edge of his desk. "Rocky tells me you've gone all the way to the top. I just thought I'd let you know how pleased I am to hear it." She batted her eyes.

"Oh. Well, thanks, Linda. Awfully sweet of you."

"Don't mention it, Tony. If there's anything I can do to make your new responsibility a little easier to handle, just let me know. We also serve who only stand around and work."

He eyed her curiously. "Then I can expect your full co-operation?"

"When have you ever had less from me?"

"No hard feelings?"

"About what?"

"You've been here a lot longer than I have. Maybe you thought . . ."

"What? That I'd become a vice-president? Please, Tony. I'm only a woman." She got up and went to the door.

"Damned attractive too," he said to her back.

She whirled and forced a thin smile. "Naturally. That's how I got to be creative director. Right?"

His jaw dropped. It wasn't much but, as she rode the elevator up to the third floor, she felt smugly satisfied. If nothing else, she had put him on notice that his campaign of intimidation was not working. He would have to get much tougher to force her out.

The phone on Paul's desk rang. It was Judith. "Aren't you going to work?" he said.

"I was just on my way out the door." She seemed agitated. "Do you know a psychiatrist named Dahlke?"

Paul put down his pencil. "I don't think so."

"He just called. He wants you to come in and see him today."

His throat tightened. He felt a wild urge to drop the phone and run. "Uh . . . I can't. I'm too busy."

"I thought you said you didn't know him."

"Well . . . maybe I do."

"I see. Why don't you make up your mind?" Her tone became impatient. "What's going on, Paul? He asked me all sorts of questions."

"Like what?"

"How long have I known you? Were we living together? Private things. You've never told me anything about a psychiatrist."

"I'll handle it," he mumbled.

"Are you going to see him?"

"I don't know."

"I'd rather you didn't."

"Why?"

"If we have a problem, we should discuss it. I don't want anyone outside prying into our lives." She hung up.

He sat with the phone buzzing in his hand, anger building. After six months of silence, Dahlke calls out of the blue and gets Judith. *Of course he wants to see you. He's going to shit all over you for breaking trust, and he'll insist on seeing Judith. Why? To tell her who she's been living with.* Paul put down the phone, his anger turning to panic. He couldn't let that happen. If Judith left him, his whole world would come crashing down.

"You what?" Linda stared at him over a desk full of photographs, prints of the *Freebase* job.

Paul repeated quietly, "I think I'd better quit."

He means it! Her mind raced frantically. If she let him go, she would no longer have to deal with the problem he presented. But in the face of her coming war with Tony Benedict, wouldn't it appear as a black mark against her if one of her "loyal workers" walked out with no explanation? She leaned back and stared at him. "What brought this on?"

He thought for a moment, then said, "I thought I better do it before you fire me."

"Paul, what are you talking about?"

"Because I probably won't be able to work full time for a while."

"Why not?"

"I have to see a doctor."

She paused a moment, realizing that Dahlke must have reached him. She decided to tread carefully: she wasn't supposed to know this. "Are you ill?" she asked.

"Sort of . . . I don't know."

"What kind of answer is that? You are or you aren't."

"He's a psychiatrist." He sat down heavily, then tears formed in his eyes. "I don't want to see him at all because, if I do, it's going to be bad."

"What do you mean?"

"I can't explain, but it's related to what I was getting in the mail."

Linda kept a poker face. "Look, Paul—if you're still disturbed about that, I think you *should* see this doctor. Maybe he can help."

Paul looked at her miserably. "You really think so?"

Linda nodded. "Go see him. And let's not hear any more about quitting."

Paul sat still for a moment, then rose. He started for the door and turned back. "I don't want to hurt Judith."

"What do you mean?"

"Well . . . I've actually known Dr. Dahlke for a long time. And she doesn't . . . doesn't know him or about him." He looked helplessly at her.

Linda realized her guess had been right. Judith didn't know anything about Paul's past. "Why don't you ask the doctor how to handle that?" she said.

His mouth set in a grim line. "Can't. I know what he'll say. Thanks, anyway." He went out.

At five thirty Gene Dahlke's receptionist stuck her head in and said, "Dr. Bass won't be back. He's with a patient at UCLA. Will you be leaving soon?"

"No," Dahlke said, rubbing his eyes. "I have to stick around for a while."

"If you have somebody coming in, I can wait."

"No. No, that's okay. You go ahead."

She smiled and went out. He watched her close his inner door and listened to the jingle of the front entrance as she went out. He sat back behind his desk and closed his eyes. He would wait till six. If Mizzell didn't show up by then, he would go home. Tomorrow he was due at Camarillo. Paul would have to wait till the next day. That wouldn't make Mrs. Sharman too happy, but Paul could not be rushed. If he didn't want to come, he shouldn't be made to. Even so, keeping his live-in girl friend a secret was a breach of trust. Dahlke had made it a rule that any intimate relation ship Paul developed had to be treated with complete and forthright honesty if it went beyond casual sex. If he was too scared to tell his doctor about the girl, it was probably because he was too scared to tell the girl.

At six o'clock he got up, put on his coat and straightened his tie, then picked up his briefcase and started out. He heard the jingle of the front entry again. That had to be Paul. He opened the door and stopped, surprised.

"Well," he said, "it's been a long time."

He saw the flash of the knife. Then it was in his chest and a powerful hand plunged it deeper. Dahlke gasped and dropped his briefcase. He clawed for the blade and felt it jerked out of his chest, then thrust in again, into his side, twisting. He saw it—a big blade—a hunting knife. He gasped as it whipped back out, then seemed to plunge from every direction, over and over, slamming into his stomach, his thigh, his neck. He threw his hands up to cover his face, then felt it cut into his groin. With a loud groan, he collapsed to the floor.

CHAPTER 8

It was the lead story on the eleven o'clock news. Linda stood in front of her TV, a sandwich crushed in her hand, switching through the channels to catch all the reports. She hadn't realized till now just how prominent Dahlke was in the medical community. She heard him described variously as an innovator, a champion of patients' rights, a spokesman for the state mental health program, and a noted expert on the psychology of the criminally insane. Over the years, Dahlke had treated many psychopaths through both his private practice and his position at Camarillo. On ABC they had Dr. Bass, looking ashen, his voice quivering with emotion as he described what a good man his partner was, how in twenty-five years of practice no one had ever threatened either one of them. He couldn't understand who would do such a horrible thing.

Linda shook as he spoke. Bits of chicken salad dropped on the carpet at her feet. Instinctively, she bent to pick them up, then realized she was still clutching the sandwich. She tossed it into an ashtray and sat down abruptly, covering her mouth with her hand.

Dahlke's body had been discovered in his outer office by a cleaning lady shortly after seven P.M. His briefcase was found beneath the body, indicating he had probably been surprised on his way out for the night. The police had the murder weapon but no apparent motive. Nothing had been taken. The receptionist had left at five thirty and reported that Dahlke had not been expecting anybody. The police were going to search Dahlke's records and carefully check out his patients to try and establish a motivational link.

Linda paid particular attention when they reported that Dahlke's appointment book had been clear for the afternoon. What about Paul? she wondered. Hadn't he gone there when he had left work? Of course he had. Who else could have done this? Suddenly she hated him—hated them both—Paul for being vicious and crazy and Dahlke for being complacent and stupid. She stared at the phone. Should she call the police and tell them what she knew, or wait to see what developed? If Paul didn't show up tomorrow, the police would get onto him quickly. He was too dangerous to be running around loose. She thought of everything she should be doing: calling the police, warning Dr. Bass, Judith—

What if Paul went home? What if he was starting on a rampage and Judith was next? And who after that?

Me?

She couldn't move. She stared at the front door. Was it locked? Had she put up the chain when she had come home? She forced herself to get up and cross to the front door, her mind racing with fears—for herself, for Dahlke and Judith and Bass.

She reached the door and her fingers scrabbled at the locks. Everything was in place. The door was secure. She leaned against it and bit her lip. She saw Paul's face, blank and scared, a bloody knife in his hand, her own words—"No, no"—on his lips.

The phone rang and she jumped.

She huddled against the door, each ring resounding in her ears. It had to be Paul. He was going to lie, tell her some story she'd be tempted to believe, putting her off guard so he could get in here and kill her the way he'd killed that girl in the van. All she could think of as the phone kept ringing was where he had left the knife.

The caller was persistent. She went over, intending to rip the cord out of the wall. But if she did that, then he would know for certain she was home. She hesitated, her hand hovering over the phone. She could tell him she had already spoken with the police, that they were watching her house . . .

It stopped ringing.

She stared at it, suddenly thinking she had made a mistake. Now he would assume she *wasn't* home. Now he would come right over, break in, and wait for her return. But she wasn't out. She was here. He would find her.

Terrified, she flung herself on the sofa. *Ring again, damn you!*

Ring again and I'll send you straight to hell! She kept her eye on the phone till after the news finished and a game show came on. Gradually, she was lulled back to the safe, warm fantasy of television. If they could still ask contestants those stupid questions while the world came apart, then life wasn't real—television was. She watched the show blankly, emptying her mind, getting recharged on mundane entertainment. After an hour of stupefaction, she was able to get up and make a drink. Time was all she needed, time to clear her head of silly fears and sort out what had to be done.

The phone rang again. She felt a surge of indignation. It *is* him, she told herself. *Don't let him get to you.* She picked up the receiver.

"Hello?"

"Linda! Hey, thank God you're there!" She heard a thin-lipped sucking sound then a snort of caught breath. "Seen the news?"

"Yes, Buddy, I've seen it."

"Christ. Wow, I mean, you were right! He's gone screwy. How the fuck could he do that?"

"You mean Paul, Buddy?"

"No. Ronald Reagan. Come on, Linda, we gotta talk."

Buddy wanted to come right over. She wouldn't allow that. She agreed to meet him at Central Park West, a restaurant down the street from her. She hung up, doubting that he would make it. He'd be so stoned by the time he got into his car, he would probably pass out and spend the night in his garage. So she didn't hurry and was surprised when she walked into the restaurant to find him already there, motioning to her from a table near the front window.

Central Park West was a small, high-ceilinged, noisy eating palace that had once been a bar haunted by rummies from the Veterans' Hospital across the street. Now it was a chic Brentwood night spot, with small round tables and creaky chairs. There was a thick carpet of sawdust on the floor, scattered plants, and people crowded around a polished central bar.

Buddy's eyes were wide and dilated. He sipped Perrier and ordered a bourbon and soda for Linda. He chain-smoked cigarettes and went through the angst of betrayal, several times patting his chest. Linda wasn't sure why: to show the wounded animal or to prove he had a heart?

"How could he do this to *us*?" was Buddy's cry. "After all we've done for him."

"Maybe *we* didn't do enough," Linda replied quietly.

"Did you get in touch with D—?" He stopped short of mentioning Dahlke's name and looked around furtively.

"Yes, I went to see him. I got the full treatment." She recounted the gist of her meeting with Dahlke. Buddy listened, nodding frequently and straining to hear her over the conversation bouncing off the walls.

"I had a hard time convincing him he should see Paul," she said, "but he called this morning finally, and I had to coax Paul to go to him. I had no idea—" She choked and stopped.

"It's not your fault," Buddy said. "Jesus, what are you going to do?" He looked at her expectantly.

She stared back and wondered why he wanted to meet tonight. "Call the police, I guess," she said. "But I don't even know where he is right now."

"If you tell them who to look for, they'll find him."

"If *I* tell them . . . Buddy, he's *your* friend."

"Hey, come on, babe. Don't get me involved."

She stared at him. "That's why you wanted to see me?"

"Listen, honey, I did my good deed. I got him the job. He blew it. I don't owe him anymore."

"Is that so?"

"I don't see *you* jumping to his defense. You should have broomed him out already—!" His voice rose excitedly.

"Buddy, shut up."

He lapsed into silence and speared a piece of fruit from the salad she had ordered.

"You really are a son of a bitch," she said.

"That's not what you used to think."

She glowered at him. "I always thought so. Maybe once a long time ago I considered sleeping with you. Don't look so shocked. Yes, I did consider it. I told myself, Go ahead and sleep with the bastard. He's a vice-president and you don't want to be in design the rest of your life. He's your ticket to an executive chair. Go ahead and do it."

"Why didn't you?"

"Because every time I thought about it, I wanted to throw up."

His face flushed with anger. The couple at the next table ate in silence but were glancing over uncomfortably. Buddy snapped at Linda, "You wouldn't open your mouth if you still worked for me, so don't get all wound up with false courage."

She laughed. "It doesn't take courage to see through you. And as for your liberal conscience—giving Paul Mizzell a job—"

He leaped up and stared at her, shaking with anger. Then he dug frantically for his wallet, ripped out money, and slapped it on the table. He stalked out.

Linda caught up with him in the parking lot, grabbed his arm, and pulled him around. "Your poor old schoolmate who stuck a knife in some girl's twat because he didn't have the sense to stay away from drugs! You felt sorry for *him*! What about the girl he killed? You told me you knew both of them—you even *slept with her*! You didn't help Paul because of your conscience, Buddy. You don't have one! You felt guilty—Why?"

Buddy's anger was blown away by her attack. He sagged against his car. His gaze hit the ground and stayed there. "It was my acid," he said finally. "He got it from me."

Linda stared at him. "Oh, for God's sake. . . . Of course. That's why you hung around the hospital while he was being treated. You made a deal with him not to blow the whistle on you—the big supplier at UCLA! What were you doing—brewing it in the chem lab?"

Buddy laughed uneasily. "A bunch of us—"

"Spare me. So he agreed not to say anything about you, but if and when he got out on the street again, you agreed to help him—somehow."

Buddy nodded.

"By getting him a job, right?"

"Yeah."

"Well, what are you worried about now, Buddy? That this time he *will* talk and get your tailfeathers dirty? Oh, come on—that was a long time ago. You can always say you were young and stupid." She leaned closer. "But what if he's nuts, Buddy, and he blames you for all of it?"

She turned and walked to her car, looked back once and called, "Better keep your door locked. He might come looking for you."

She saw him jerk upright, then reach shakily for his car keys. Her heels clicked on the pavement, and in the darkness she too looked around uncertainly.

When she got back, the phone was ringing again. This time Linda didn't care who it was, she wasn't going to answer. She sat in front of the television and watched whatever was on, trying not to think about Paul, Buddy, or Dahlke.

The phone rang again, loud and insistent. Whoever it was wouldn't give up. It rang for five minutes. She fidgeted in a chair, trying to ignore it. Finally, it stopped, and her pulse slowed accordingly.

Don't think about who it is. Paul? Buddy? Brian? Jennifer . . .?

Jennifer. She hadn't called her daughter in two weeks. She reached for the phone. If she could keep it occupied, then it wouldn't ring. She dialed the number in Berkeley and waited. Jennifer had two roommates—surely one of them had to be in.

"Hello?" It was a sleepy voice, not Jennifer's.

"Susan? Is this Susan or Nita?"

"It's Susan."

"Is Jennifer there, Susan? This is her mother."

"Oh, hi, Mrs. Sharman. Uh—she's out . . . right now. Any message?"

Out for the night, you mean. "That's all right, Susan. I was just calling to see if she's okay. We haven't talked in a while." *Don't get off the phone: it'll ring again.* "How is she?"

"Fine. She's been busy."

"Studying?"

"Uh, yeah."

"New boyfriend?"

"No. I mean yes, sort of. She sees somebody now and then."

"How are you getting along?"

"Oh, gee, Mrs. Sharman, I don't know if I can keep up—"

Linda relaxed and listened to Susan ramble, frequently clucking in sympathy and asking questions that prompted more me-

me-me. As long as she could keep Susan talking about herself, she wouldn't shut up.

This went on for fifteen minutes. By then Linda was sure that her phantom caller would have gotten the message—she wasn't going to answer: she had her own calls to make.

"Anyway, Mrs. Sharman, I gotta go. It's awful late and I got an eight o'clock. You want Jennifer to call?"

"Yes, please. At home or at the office, when she can." They said good-bye and hung up.

Linda waited apprehensively for the ringing to start again. It didn't. Gratefully, she rose and went to the bedroom, undressed, and got into her terry robe. She couldn't sleep. Maybe if she read for a while . . . She found a book she had started three months ago and padded back to the living room, poured a little brandy, and curled up on the sofa. It was quiet, peaceful, and secure with the TV off. She should do this more often.

She got into a chapter about a mother whose daughter is kidnaped. She stopped cold.

Jennifer.

What have you done? You've used your own daughter as a weapon to fight fear. You didn't even listen to what her roommate was saying, nor did you care. Jennifer is so far away and you're so preoccupied—What have you been using for a heart, Linda?

She slammed the book shut and ran to her desk, sat down, and pulled out her stationery and a pen. She started a letter but didn't know what to say.

You should go up there. Fly up to Berkeley next weekend and see the little monster. Pay some attention to her. It'll take your mind off all this—There you go again, using her—

The doorbell rang.

She sat up, startled, at first thinking it couldn't be hers. It rang again. It was hers.

It's him. This time of night? Don't be silly.

She looked at the phone.

Of course it's him. You're dumb. You were using the phone, so the line was busy when he called again. He knew you were home. So now he's here—

"Linda?" The voice was muffled but she knew right away it was Paul. She didn't answer. She sat perfectly still and waited.

"Linda?"

The phone. Call the police. Don't try to deal with him yourself. She got up too fast and knocked the chair over.

"Linda!"

She stared across the room at the double locks and the chain, wondering if he could get through. She crossed slowly on tiptoe.

"Linda, please."

His voice sounded slushy. He was just outside, leaning against the door. She heard the thump of his arm against the wood.

"Linda? Please . . . I didn't do it."

She caught her breath and stared at the chain.

"Please let me in . . ."

She stood to one side of the door, feeling stupid and helpless. "Is that you, Paul?"

"Yes. Please let me in."

"What do you want?"

"You've got to believe me—I didn't do it . . ."

"Do what?"

His voice broke. "Dahlke!"

She jumped.

You can stand out in the hall and scream "Dahlke!" at the top of your lungs. You're not getting in. I shouldn't even be talking with you. I should be on the phone to the police. So why am I standing here?

Because I want a look at you. Just one look. If I can see your face, I'll know what to do.

She opened the door cautiously, keeping it on the chain.

He backed off about a foot, thinking she was going to let him in. They stood there—Linda staring at him, Paul looking back wildly. He was rumpled, unsteady, probably drunk. She had never seen him like this.

"It wasn't me," he said, shaking his head, then weaving with the effort. "I swear to God, Linda, I never went there. I never saw him."

"Yes you did."

"No! I couldn't face him! You've got to believe me. I didn't kill Dahlke!"

She flinched as he leaned against the doorjamb for support.

What if he gets angry and kicks the door? Will the chain hold? If he gets loud and upset, will one of my neighbors call the police?

She hardly listened as he babbled about his afternoon, telling her he hadn't been able to work up the nerve to see Dahlke, so he had gone to a bar instead: Sabato's, on Sunset.

"I couldn't go home or come back to work. I must have passed out. When I woke up, it was eleven. I stayed to watch the news . . ." He broke into sobs. "Oh, God, Linda, I didn't do it. I couldn't have." He flung himself against the door. She jerked back involuntarily. His eyes pleaded for understanding.

He's lying. I know he's lying. He slept in a bar? What a crock! Then who was on the phone trying to get me all evening? Jack the Ripper? And what the hell is he doing here? Did he just come by to borrow my knife sharpener?

She wanted to scream at him to go away, but she struggled to remain calm. In a quavering voice, she said, "Have you spoken with Judith?"

He looked right through her.

"Judith, Paul. Have you talked to her? Have you seen her?"

"I . . . I called her. After I saw it on the news, I called . . . she didn't even know. I told her . . . I don't know what I said . . . So woozy . . ." He blinked and collected his thoughts. "Told her not to be scared, to believe I didn't do it. Told her I didn't go to see him. I couldn't . . ." He was sobbing again. "She doesn't know anything about me. . . . I told her I didn't even know Dahlke. . . . I *lied* to her, Linda!" He sank down against the door.

Oh, boy, are you in trouble. Lying, lying, lying. You did kill Dahlke and now you want to get in here.

"Why did you come here, Paul?"

"You're the only one I can trust. You knew I was going to see him."

Of course! He has to kill you too! You're the only one who knew he was going directly to Dahlke's office. Make him admit it.

"Why did he want to see you, Paul?"

He turned and sat with his back to the door. "If I tell you, you'll only want to turn me over to the police. It's that bad."

That sounded rational enough. Encouraging. She decided to level with him. "I already know the story, Paul. I know all about Gary Michael Steen. Your friend Buddy Dyal sent *me* to Dahlke. He got in touch with you because I told him to, because of all the things you were telling me. Now, what else have you got to tell me, Paul?"

Come on, confess.

Paul was motionless for a long moment, then his head dropped to his hands and he began to weep. "Please help me, Linda. I don't know what to do! Don't make me stay out here and shout. Please. Look, you can search me. I've never done anything to hurt you, Linda—you know I wouldn't. You've got to believe me. Let me come in and we'll talk. I just need to talk. I need somebody."

Linda watched him uneasily, embarrassed, worried that someone—

A light appeared a few doors down. A sliver in a doorway. Paul was still talking, getting louder. She slid the chain off the hook and opened the door. Paul whirled and looked up. She was immediately sorry.

CHAPTER 9

Stupid, stupid, stupid. You've let the monster in your house.

Linda banged around in the kitchen to let him know she felt perfectly at ease—or to convince herself—she wasn't sure which. She put up water for coffee, ignoring the insistent voice telling her to call the police even before she heard his story.

At least let someone know he's here. What about Judith?

She reached for her address book and flipped it open. The rings snapped apart and pages flew out. She jumped to catch them, grabbed them off the floor and threw them back on the counter, fishing nervously through them till she found an "M" . . . She found the number and picked up the kitchen phone. She stopped, another fear welling up.

What if he's lied about Judith? What if he's already killed her and I'm next on the hit parade?

She glanced into the living room. He was right where she had left him, slumped on the sofa. He appeared to have passed out.

She dialed. Judith answered quickly. Linda was glad to know someone else was up late worrying. "If you're wondering about Paul," she said quietly, "he's here, drunk. I'm going to sober him up, then . . ." She paused.

What am I going to do? Send him home? Drive him? Get the police?

"If he's too far gone, I'll just let him sleep on my couch till morning."

"No," Judith said quickly. And coldly, Linda sensed. "I'll come and get him."

"Don't be silly. I'm telling you he's drunk. In fact, I think he's just passed out. You won't be able to move him."

"I don't like this," Judith said, an edge of suspicion in her voice. "He called me from Sabato's a while ago, babbling something about a murder. A psychiatrist who called him today—"

"Dahlke."

Judith hesitated then said, "Paul had nothing to do with that."

Isn't that sweet? Rushes right to his defense.

"Did you hear me? Paul wouldn't hurt anybody. What are you making him think?"

"Me?"

"What's going on over there? Why is he with you? Why is it he's fine when he leaves home in the morning but when he comes back from work, there's always something wrong! And why should he have to see a psychiatrist? *What are you doing to him?*"

What am I doing to him? Oh, lady, have you got it twisted. She cursed Paul under her breath. *Why couldn't he be honest with his goddamned girl friend? Why am I in the middle?*

"Look," Linda said firmly, "you sort it out with him tomorrow, when he's sober. Don't come over here tonight—I don't need any more visitors. As for this doctor getting killed, you bettri have Paul didn't have anything to do with it!"

Linda hung up. The kettle was whistling. Shaking with anger, she made coffee and stood very still, watching the water drip through the grounds and smelling the nutty aroma. She checked the clock—almost 1 A.M. How was she going to function tomorrow? And why was she making coffee? The man had already passed out.

Let him alone. Get yourself together. Start thinking. He insists he's innocent, but he sure looks guilty. Yet you let him in—why? Because you're stupid, stupid, stupid.

She snatched the filter holder off the pot and dumped it in the sink, then poured two cups. She decided to wake him up and chase him out. She turned with one of the cups—

And dropped it. Paul was standing in the kitchen doorway, a wild look on his face.

A frozen moment—neither of them could move. Then she realized that his look wasn't wild: it was startled. His eyes went to the smashed cup on the floor, and the pool of coffee spreading toward his shoes. Linda dropped to her knees and began picking up the shattered china.

"I'm so goddamned clumsy," she said. "I'll have this cleaned up in a sec—" She glanced over. He was down on his knees with a towel, wiping all the liquid into a coordinated puddle. She stared at him, mesmerized. He seemed completely involved in sopping up coffee . . .

Linda backed away, wondering how Paul Mizzell could have killed somebody this evening and be here on the floor right now, wiping up spilled coffee. The two images just did not go together.

They sat down across from each other in the living room, Linda with her legs tucked under her bottom on the sofa, Paul in the straight-backed chair, a cup balanced on his knee. They didn't speak for a long time. Finally, Paul took a deep breath and said, "So you know about Gary Steen."

"Yes."

"You took a chance letting me in here. Is that why you called Judith?"

"I didn't want her to worry. It's bad enough I do."

Anguish contorted his features. "I said I wouldn't hurt you, Linda."

She desperately wanted to believe him. "What are we going to do about you? Was there anyone at Sabato's who could vouch you were there around six o'clock."

He shook his head uncertainly. "I got really drunk. The whole afternoon is a blur."

"Do you want to go to the police?"

Paul thought that over carefully. "I can't," he said. "What would I tell them? I had an appointment with Dahlke but I didn't go? I got bombed instead, and I'm sorry he got killed?" He shook his head. "If any of that Gary Steen business comes out now, and they find out I was supposed to see Dahlke today, they'll lock me up for good. I didn't kill him. Let the police find what they can—it won't lead to me, and I don't want to help them. I've been through that before."

Linda saw his point. "Okay," she said.

He raised his cup in gratitude. "I think I can make it home now."

Her first instinct was to grab the cup from his hand and push him out the door, but she felt she had to warn him. "If you do," she said, "you'll only have to explain to Judith. I don't think you're up to it." She saw his eyes fill with panic.

She made him comfortable on the sofa with an extra pillow and blanket, then walked quickly to her bedroom and closed the door.

Then locked it.

She stood staring at the lock a long time.

Do you believe him now or not?

She kept a loaded pistol in a bureau drawer. For the first time since she had bought it, she dug it out and stuck it under her pillow. She washed her face and brushed her teeth, then climbed into bed. She tried to go to sleep but couldn't. She wanted a drink, but that meant going out to the living room again. She heard sounds from the other side of the door and sat up to listen. The sounds stopped. She felt for the gun under the pillow. Her fingers closed on the cold butt.

What if you have a nightmare and shoot yourself in the head? Now that would be really dumb. Why did you get that gun, anyway? Because Tisa kept repeating that story about her mother getting beaten and robbed one night in her own apartment.

Linda let go of the gun, closed her eyes and forced herself to think about something pleasant. Brian. An irritating realization went through her. All those calls she hadn't answered tonight—they probably weren't from Paul—they were probably poor old Brian. Thinking of ways to make it up to him, Linda finally drifted off to sleep.

The alarm went off at seven. Linda woke with a start and her dream faded. She struggled to hold onto the details, but they eluded her. She could only recall something about a man in her living room, sitting upright on her sofa, holding a knife like it was a sceptre . . . Paul. She threw off the covers and rolled out of bed. She sat looking at the locked bedroom door, wondering what to do about him. Finally, routine prevailed. First, she would have a shower.

Hot water stung her skin. She closed her eyes and waved her head under the spray, thinking about all the things Paul claimed he had received in the mail. They meant nothing to her. He had

destroyed them; she had never seen them. The brakes going out
in his car—an accident. And his fear—just a paranoid reaction.
But the tape of *Revolver* that popped up in Tony's car on Main
Street was real. That and the murder of Dahlke somehow pulled
things together. Either somebody was trying to scare Paul, or he
was doing these things to himself—

She stopped weaving under the spray. Her eyes popped open
and she followed the thought. *If he's doing it to himself but
doesn't know . . . What do they call it? Paranoid schizophrenic?
Double personality?*

*That means he could stand here and tell you he didn't kill
anybody and believe it. And in the next moment he could turn
around and do it again.*

She turned off the shower and snatched a towel. She dried and
dressed quickly, then cautiously unlocked her door, placing the
gun within reach on a bureau. She peered into the living room.
He wasn't there. The sofa was rumpled and the blanket tossed
carelessly aside, but there was no sign of Paul.

Where is he?

She went in on tiptoe, glancing into the kitchen, checking the
closets, pausing at the front door. The chain was off.

He must have gone during the night.

She opened the door and leaned out, looking both ways along
the hall. Relieved, she picked up the morning paper, closed the
door, and locked it.

She made breakfast—coffee, toast, and fruit—then sat down.
Dahlke's murder got coverage on the bottom of page one, along
with a picture—a posed portrait taken before his hair had gone
gray. There was the same confident look she remembered, and
the youthful charisma. He still looked like something out of an
afternoon soap.

The police were still theorizing that the killer was one of the
doctor's patients, and they were setting out to interview them,
one by one.

*Paul wasn't Dahlke's only patient. Should the finger necessar-
ily point to him? Besides, why would he kill Dahlke anyway?
Fear of exposure? Dahlke certainly wouldn't expose him. What
could Paul have gained?*

Confused, Linda looked at Dahlke's picture again, then noticed something that made a weight drop in the pit of her stomach. The byline over the article: Brian Hawthorn.

Judith had hardly slept at all. She came downstairs early, surprised to find Paul curled up on the couch, fully clothed except for his shoes, which were under the coffee table. She came over quietly and looked down at him. He was snoring peacefully. She picked up his shoes and took them over to the stairs, leaving them on the third step. Then she went into the kitchen and brewed coffee.

She sat alone at the breakfast table, smoking a cigarette and waiting for him to wake up. She thought about how to handle him, what questions to ask. At seven fifteen she looked into the living room. He was sitting up, rubbing his hair.

"Come in and have breakfast," she called.

He looked up, startled. He rose and stumbled to the kitchen, sat down obediently, and dug into half a grapefruit. She ate sparingly, hardly looking at him.

Paul wondered if she was giving him the cold treatment. No, this was normal: they hardly ever spoke in the morning. But there was tension in her silence. He felt that she was waiting for an explanation.

"Judith," he began, "about yesterday—"

"I only want to know one thing," she said, her eyes boring into his. "Why did you go to Linda Sharman?"

He stared back. "She was closer . . ."

Judith shook her head.

"I knew she would understand—"

"And I wouldn't?"

"No . . ."

"Did you want to hurt me, Paul?"

"Hurt you?"

"By going to her."

"No."

"Then why did you do it?"

He rubbed his throat.

"Why, Paul?"

"I don't know."

She paused and sat back. "There's something wrong, isn't there? What about Dr. Dahlke?"

"I—I didn't see him—"

"He wanted to see you. Why?"

"I didn't kill him."

"I'm not saying you did. Is that what you're afraid of? That I think you killed him?"

Paul nodded.

"Paul, I don't think you could kill anyone."

He flinched.

"But he called here yesterday morning, looking for you. Then he was murdered. What am I supposed to think? And what did a psychiatrist want with you?"

"I—I was in therapy . . . a long time ago . . ."

"For what?"

He wouldn't answer.

"Don't you want to tell me?"

"Yes."

"But you can't. Why? Is it me? Is it our relationship?"

"No . . ."

"Then what?"

Paul jumped up and paced. "I can't talk about it!"

She looked up at him sharply. "It must have been serious, this therapy."

His mouth worked and his eyes darted about painfully. Then he fell to his knees in front of her and threw his arms around her waist. "Judith, please," he cried. "Trust me. Please trust me. When I can talk about it, I will."

His head dropped in her lap. She let him stay there a moment, then put a comforting hand on his back. She leaned over and whispered in his ear, "You see, Paul? You need me. I'm the only one who cares. I'm the only one who can help you." She lifted his face up in her hands and smiled. "You know that, don't you?"

He nodded.

"You don't need a doctor. You don't need anyone but me. I know you'll tell me everything. I want to hear it, Paul. Whatever it is, I want to hear it. Understand?"

He nodded. "Yes."

She kissed him softly on the forehead. "You're mine. We belong to each other. We don't need anyone else." She kissed him on the lips. Then her fingers dug into his pants. Suddenly, she had hold of him and was gripping him tightly, her thumb flicking along the tip, then her nail . . .

His eyes flew open. She grinned at him. Her eyes fluttered and her tongue thrust between his lips. She pulled him down to the kitchen floor and spread her robe, arching herself up against him. He threw his arms around her and lunged ferociously. He was caught up in her, wild with desire. She was right. He didn't need anyone else—for anything.

Linda came in to face a pile of work on her desk, along with messages from Tony, Buddy Dyal, C. L. Clarke, and Jennifer. She called Jennifer first.

"Hi, Mom."

"Hello, sprout. How are you getting along?"

"Real good. I could use some more money . . ."

"How much?"

"About two hundred."

"May I ask what it's for?"

"Oh, books, club dues, movies . . . the usual."

"Still have your job?"

"Got a better one. Part-time at a boutique. Pays three fifty an hour. Isn't that great?"

"Sure is."

"But it's still not enough, Mom. I hope you can send something . . ."

"Doing any studying?"

"Uh-huh."

"And how's your new boyfriend?"

Silence. Then an audible intake of breath. "Did Susan open her big mouth?"

"No, I'm psychic."

"Well, he's really nice, Mom. He's in journalism—"

"Oh, shit."

"He's not like Daddy at all."

"How could there be two?" Linda sighed. "Listen, my innocent little lamb, how would you like a visit from your mother? What if I fly up to Berkeley on Friday?"

"This weekend?"

"Yes. We'll do the town. You can watch your mother eat and I can watch you attract boys."

"That's great . . . but I had plans."

"Oh?"

"Yeah, I've got studying to catch up on, and there's this party Saturday—"

"And you're shacked up with Citizen Kane, and you don't want me to horn in, right?"

"Mom, I'm sorry. It means a lot to me. Please come next weekend."

"Oh, all right." She paused. "Jennifer, I miss you. I know I'm bad about writing and I don't call often, but I do think of you. And if you need anything—"

"Just the check, Mom."

Oh, shit. They turn eighteen and suddenly you're nothing but a bankbook. Oh, well, let the kid have her fun while she's young.

She promised to send the check and they made plans for the following weekend, then hung up.

Tony had sent down an envelope of prints from the Struts' job last Sunday. He was unhappy with the color and wanted to know if anything could be done in the lab. Of course, that was what C. L. Clarke had called about. Tony had complained to him and Clarke was mad. Linda calmed him down and said she would send the prints back with suggestions for filtering.

"Just keep that asshole off my back," C.L. said. "I can't deal with him. He thinks I'm a fucking employee."

Linda held the phone away and made a face at it.

Buddy Dyal's secretary kept her waiting on the phone a full five minutes. Finally, Buddy got on and spoke hurriedly. He only had a few minutes. He wanted to know if anything had happened with Paul yet.

"Yes, I've seen him," said Linda. "He says he had nothing to do with Dahlke."

Buddy spoke through his teeth. "You mean that's all you did? You just *asked* him? You didn't contact the police?"

"Buddy, leave it alone. If there's evidence against him—"

"I don't want to hear any *ifs*! You turn that son of a bitch in and keep me out of it!"

"If you're so concerned, *you* turn him in."

"Linda!" He choked on his rage. "This is serious. Is he at work today?"

"Yes. You want to speak with him?"

"No! Look, from here on it's your neck. I'm out. You want my advice—turn the bastard in!"

"Thanks. I'll quote you."

Buddy hung up. Linda picked up her desk calendar and slammed it down, swearing out loud. Paul Mizzell was taking too much of her time. She went looking for him and found him in the studio, staring at the photo of her that C.L. had done the day that model failed to show up. Jimmy had tacked it up on the wall.

Linda sat on a table and looked at him. "Almost as good as the real thing, isn't it?"

He glanced over, startled. Embarrassed, he shoved his hands in his pockets. "Nice picture," he said.

"Thank you."

He had trouble looking at her. "Listen," he said, "I'm real sorry about last night and—and skipping out without a word, but I felt better after we talked, and I just didn't want to involve you anymore. Hope I didn't scare you—too much."

She managed a wan smile.

"See, I haven't had anybody to talk with since I got out of Camarillo. The doctors . . . Bass used to listen, but Dahlke was the one I usually saw . . . and he always seemed to be off in space. My relatives didn't want anything to do with me after the . . . after sixty-eight. Now they're all gone. I'm really alone. It felt so good when I was driving home from your place . . . that somebody finally knew . . . and wasn't, you know . . . afraid . . ."

He looked at her and tears formed in his eyes.

She said nothing for a moment then, "Paul, you know it's only a matter of time before the police will want to see you."

He nodded. "Do you want me to quit?"

"I don't know. I guess I can try to believe you awhile longer. But Paul, I can't take any more of your personal problems. So please, no more nonsense about mysterious packages in the mail. If you can't deal with these things yourself, then get professional help from someone else. I can't handle this anymore. Do you understand?"

The tears had dried..His empty look was back. He nodded.

"As for who killed Dr. Dahlke, I'll leave that to the police. If it turns out you're involved—" She shrugged.

"It's okay, Linda."

Don't look at me like that. I already feel lousy. "There's one other thing I want you to do," she said. "Tell Judith everything."

He hesitated. "I'm going to . . . tonight."

"Okay." She slid off the table and gave him an uncertain smile, then she headed for the door.

"Linda," he called after her, "If the police talk to you, what are you going to tell them?"

"The truth."

She walked out, wondering if it was wise to be so blunt.

"Hi. I was trying to reach you last night."

"Oh, Brian, I'm sorry. I was out. Had to see a client." Linda went on her guard the moment she recognized his voice on the phone. He was covering the Dahlke story and that meant a change in their relationship. She sensed that he knew it too—not why there was a change, just that there was.

"Did I do something wrong?" he said.

"No, I'm just up to my neck. . . . Don't you ever get busy?"

"Yeah, I'm busy now. This Beverly Hills psychiatrist who got himself murdered. Did you see my story?"

"Uh-huh."

"He's the big thing today. Did you know him?"

"Why should I know him?"

"No reason. How about dinner?"

"I'd like to, Brian, but I have to work late tonight."

"Maybe on the weekend?"

"Can't. I'm going to visit my daughter."

"Before the weekend."

He kept pressing, so she made a tentative agreement to see him, then hung up, angry with herself, angry with Paul Mizzell—now his life was interfering with hers.

CHAPTER 10

The Captain's Cabin was one of the newer restaurants on the ocean side of Pacific Coast Highway. Predictably, its decor was old nautical, with glass-encased models of square riggers jammed between ship's wheels, harpoons, brass lanterns, and faded prints—an eclectic effort to recreate the age of sail.

Paul and Judith took a booth facing a window that looked out on a rocky floodlit beach. He sat trying to figure how he was going to tell Judith about Lori Cornell.

"You haven't said a word to me since we came in." He swung around. Judith sipped her wine and frowned. "What are you thinking?" she said.

"I had something to . . . tell you."

"I'm listening."

Resolve deserted him. He just couldn't think of the right way to tell her he'd killed someone. "Let's forget it," he said.

She picked bread crumbs off the tablecloth and dropped them on her plate. "Does it concern us?"

"Yes," he muttered, turning away, unable to look at her.

Judith waited for a burst of loud laughter from another table to die down. "Then I want to hear about it," she said quietly.

Paul almost bolted. His voice broke. "It happened a long time ago. I don't want to talk about it."

"How long ago?"

"When I was at UCLA. Look, it'll keep. Let's eat and go home. I'll tell you later."

"Tell me now."

Paul swallowed. "It's a . . . It's a girl I knew there. I—"

"You can stop." Judith snapped. "I think I know the rest."

"You do?" he croaked, surprised at the look on her face.

Tears welled up in her eyes and streamed down her cheeks. "Oh, sure," she said. "You haven't seen her in years. You thought you'd forgotten her, but then you happened to meet her again and the two of you realized you were still in love, so now you're going to leave me . . ." She covered her face and cried softly into her hands.

Paul sat stunned, unable to move. Then he reached across the table and pried her hands open. "That's not it," he said. "You couldn't be more wrong."

She sniffled. "Are you sure?"

"Yes." He slid over and threw an arm around her, hugging her close. Judith buried her head in his shoulder. She took his napkin and dabbed at her eyes.

"Do I look awful?"

He kissed her lightly on the lips. "No, you look great."

"You're not seeing someone else?"

"What gave you that idea?"

Her head went back to his shoulder. "You've been acting so strangely, I thought . . . Am I being silly?"

"Very." His voice cracked with emotion. He would have to save the Lori Cornell story for some other time. Right now he was filled with love and a sense of well-being, something he hadn't felt for years. "Why don't we think about going home?" he said. "We can eat there."

Her reply was muffled. "I'm not hungry. Could we go for a ride?"

She clung to him in the parking lot, nibbling on his ear, oblivious to the other people waiting for cars, glancing at them.

Paul pointed the Mustang north, leaving the lights of the Malibu Colony behind them. Judith was cuddled next to him, her eyes closed. He took his right hand off the steering wheel and let it drop into her lap. She shifted and her legs opened slightly. His hand slid down, cupping her crotch. He stroked gently, feeling her body heat through the thin material of her skirt.

Judith moaned, her breath coming in short gasps. Paul felt his own passion rising. He tried to pull her skirt up and was surprised when she gripped his wrist and placed his hand back on the steering wheel. "Don't," she murmured.

"Why not?"

"I'd rather talk."

"About what?"

She sat up, moved away from him and put her back against the car door. "The girl from UCLA you were going to tell me about. Were you in love with her?"

"No," he lied, feeling control slip away in the dark.

"Tell me about her."

"She was just a girl."

"Was she your first?"

"First what?" Approaching headlights lit up Judith's face and he caught a glimpse of her pained expression. "What are you getting at?"

"I read someplace that a man never forgets the first time he's had sex with a woman. Was she your first?"

A flash of panic shot through Paul. He didn't want to get into this now. He couldn't. "Forget about it," he said. "The only thing that matters is us." He glanced down and saw the speedometer needle hovering at 70. He took his foot off the gas and the Mustang slowed.

Judith tucked up her legs and stared straight ahead. "Find a place to park by the ocean," she said, not at him. "I want to talk this out."

They drove in silence, winding through a curvy stretch of the highway, each mile making Paul more confused. Fear of Judith's reaction twisted inside him like a burning knife blade, a feeling he always got when he was pressed to think about Lori. . . . He shuddered.

"Slow down," Judith said. "I know a place up ahead."

Paul's eyes found the spot and he blanched. A dark mass loomed on his left—an enormous rock, a mountainous lump of eroded stone overlooking the beach. There was a sign carved in redwood: "Big Rock."

Paul knew it. He'd been here years ago with Lori. It was a well-known coastal lover's lane.

The Mustang crunched over gravel, rolling to a stop against a low retaining wall. He turned off the headlights and sat in the darkness, his eyes gradually adjusting. He lowered his window. Down below, the surf pounded. A flood of memories threatened to engulf him. He fought them and said hoarsely, "Can't we go someplace else?"

Judith sat with her hands up, picking at her nails. "Why?" she said. "I thought we could go for a little walk."

Beads of sweat popped out on Paul's forehead. "It's too dark."

"There's no one else around. What are you afraid of?"

He saw the flash of her teeth. Was she smiling at him? Mocking him? Teasing? "It's not safe at night anymore," he said. "Other people. We could be seen. I mean, there's been some murders—" He choked.

"Oh, for God's sake, Paul." She opened the door and stepped out, looking at the way the moonlight fell on the water. "I think it's romantic, don't you?"

"No."

That brought her down. "Well, that's a nice short answer. See what I mean? We never talk."

"Okay. Get in. What do you want to talk about?"

She climbed back in and shut the door. There was a glint in her eye. "Did you ever make it in a car?"

"Yeah."

"Want to make it now? In this car?"

He shook his head. "Please, I really don't like it here. We're grown up. We've got a home and a bed for that. Let's go." He started the Mustang and backed up sharply, his rear wheels scattering gravel.

As the car jerked out onto the road, she said, "I made it here once." She gave him a broad, lustful smile. "It's true," she went on. "Several times. I think everybody's made it at Big Rock."

The car roared south. Paul couldn't get home fast enough. She wouldn't let up needling him. She continued asking strange questions. Had he ever fucked on drugs? Did it help or inhibit? Had he ever had two girls at the same time? Had he ever made it with a guy? Finally, struggling to keep his voice under control, Paul asked what brought this on.

"Nothing," she said lightly. She lapsed into silence, and as they wound up the canyon toward home, he noticed she was frowning unhappily. "Now what's the matter?" he asked.

She remained silent until he turned onto their street. As his lights picked out darkened homes up and down the road, she said, "I've changed my mind. We can't talk, so let's make a pact not to tell each other anything—ever again—that would make either of us unhappy. Okay?"

He swallowed hard before nodding.

"Linda, these people don't want to hear excuses. They want to see results. Now why do you think I sent Jimmy Otner out to that house to get shots of Freebase—because I wanted them for my scrapbook?" Tony made a gesture he had picked up from *The Godfather*. "Come on, honey. You were supposed to come up with a concept! Look, this fellow sitting here on the end of the sofa with a lovely smile—he's the producer. Mr. Dibella there is the agent. Now, I didn't get them up here just for a slug of tomato juice. Where's the concept?"

Linda shifted from one foot to the other. "It's not done," she said quietly.

"Is it started?"

"Yes," she lied.

"Can't we see what you've got?"

"No."

Tony threw up his hands, exasperated. "Sweetie, we have deadlines. Now, unless you want me to send this job out, I suggest you go back to your office and dig something up. Anything. So we know where we stand."

"Now?"

"Well, not tomorrow!"

Linda's ears burned as she ran out the door, colliding with Tony's secretary.

"Excuse me. . . . Oh, Linda, there are two detectives to see you. I told them you were in a meeting. They went up to wait in your office."

"Detectives?" Tony said, coming up behind her. "What's with the police?"

"Search me," she said.

"Look. Get rid of them. Just bring what you've got on Freebase down here *now*. We'll wait."

She whirled and ran to the elevator.

*   *   *

They were plainclothes officers. One wore a slick gray suit, the other a tan raincoat. Both had pasty faces and blank expressions. She closed the door to her office, introduced herself, and asked how she could help.

"Mr. Benedict's office sent us up here, Mrs. Sharman. We're looking for Paul Mizzell."

She stared at them grimly, not volunteering anything.

"We'd like to ask him some questions. Purely routine."

His whole speech was routine. She could have quoted it from *Dragnet, Kojak,* or *Streets of San Francisco.* "If you'd like, you can use my office," she said. "I have to get back to a meeting."

"That'll be fine, thank you. Could you point out Mr. Mizzell?"

"Certainly."

Paul looked up from his drawing board as they walked in. He knew immediately who they were. His mouth went slack, but he managed to stand up and keep his cool.

Linda introduced everyone politely and took them back to her office. She left them and went straight to the ladies' room. She sat on a bench and dropped her head between her knees, breathing deeply to calm her nerves. She was getting it from all sides today and her nights weren't helping: lack of sleep, heavy drinking—she was turning into an emotional punching bag. If Paul didn't give the right answers in there, her job might hang in the balance. She suddenly realized what she'd overlooked till now: once Tony Benedict got wind of what was going on with Paul, he could use that as a weapon to get rid of her.

After a while, she remembered the concept they were waiting for. What concept? The Freebase job had been slipped right past her. She had never talked with Tony after he had sent Jimmy and Red out for the pictures. It had been very preliminary—nobody had told her to go ahead and work up a concept. Maybe Tony had forgotten, too, and now he was trying to stick her with the responsibility.

She hurried back down to his office. The secretary caught her at the door and triumphantly explained, "They couldn't wait. Tony took them to lunch and said to tell you to forget about Freebase. He's going to have it done outside."

Linda left, choking back tears. She ran out the back door to the parking lot, stepped into her car, sat behind the wheel, and cried. She wanted to quit. Her strength was going. Her resolve, her fight, everything was being pummeled out of her.

Can't you see—you're reverting to type: helpless woman. I don't care. I've had it. Chuck it all. Go up to Berkeley, get an apartment with Jennifer and go back to school. Learn to play the flute. Do something where nobody gets hurt.

She wiped away the tears, blew her nose, and looked into the rearview mirror. *Passable. Touch up the makeup a little—nobody will know. As long as they don't look at your eyes.*

When she returned to her office, the police were just wrapping it up with Paul. They saw her waiting and got up, then one of them paused to ask him another question. Through the glass partition, Linda saw Paul go stiff then shake his head. The detective said something else. Paul fidgeted a moment, then bumbled a reply. Linda saw them stare at him a long moment, then the tension broke. They smiled at him and opened the door—

"—for your cooperation, Mr. Mizzell. If we need you again, we'll be in touch."

They passed by Linda and thanked her, too, then went out. Linda entered her office, closed the door, and watched Paul drop into a chair.

"They know everything," he said. "Got it all from Dahlke's files."

"What did they ask?"

"A lot of stuff about Dahlke, when I last saw him. . . . They were really nice about it. Polite."

"Did you tell them that Dahlke wanted to see you?"

"No. I couldn't. But right before they left, one of them asked me if the doctor had been in touch with me the day he died. I said no. And that's true. I never talked to him. So then he said, 'Well, we know he tried.' I thought they were going to nail me there. Then he said they got it from phone records that he called my home. So I said that was true, but I didn't go in to see him. I said that when I heard on the news that he'd been murdered and they were looking up old patients, I just wanted to stay out of it." He paused. "I think they believed me, but that doesn't stop them from coming back." His eyes went dull and he sat staring at the floor. "That's how they were the last time. Real polite, then they started digging." He looked up at her, anguished. "I hate the police. I know what's going to happen."

Shortly after eleven that night, Judith padded downstairs. Paul was still curled on the sofa, watching the news on TV.

"Aren't you coming to bed?"

"Later."

She moved to the end of the sofa, and looking down at him, she leaned over and smiled. He didn't smile back. Her hand dropped to his thigh and stroked gently. He squeezed his legs shut. Surprised, she removed her hand and stood up. "I'll . . . I'll be upstairs."

He nodded. She went up alone.

At three in the morning, she woke up. He still hadn't come to bed. She got up, stumbled out to the landing, and looked down. He was still sprawled on the sofa, sound asleep. There was electronic snow and a high-pitched buzzing from the TV set. She went down and switched it off, then stood over him, wondering if she should wake him. She decided not to and went back upstairs, into the bathroom.

She shut the door, turned on the light, and stood looking at her face in the mirror. She took off her nightdress and studied her body, looking for changes, signs of wear. She leaned closer to the mirror and examined her eyes. She saw it there—the look in which everything was written—past, present, future.

She wept.

Linda glanced up from Tony Benedict's memo. Paul stood in the doorway, the two detectives flanking him. "I'm going to have to go with them," he said miserably.

"Where?"

One of the detectives leaned in. "Just another chat, Mrs. Sharman. We'll try not to keep him long."

"Can't you talk to him here?" She could see Pierre and Tisa staring at them from the coffee machine.

"We'll have him back soon as we can."

She felt a flash of annoyance. "I hope you're not going to make this a habit. We have work to do around here."

The detective smiled thinly. "We're all busy," he said, turning on his heel and taking Paul by the arm. Paul stiffened at his touch. For a second, Linda thought he was going to run. He struggled for control, shrugging out of the cop's grasp.

He looked back at Linda and said painfully, "I'll make up the time."

An hour later she was going over cost sheets from the Struts' shooting session, trying to make sense of the figures. The phone rang. She picked it up, grateful for the interruption.

Judith Berg's hysterical voice crackled in her ear. "They've arrested him! They're saying he murdered that Dr. Dahlke."

"Calm down," Linda said. "They didn't arrest him. They took him in for questioning."

"He just called me," she snapped. "They're holding him as a suspect! I don't understand—" She went on.

Linda hardly listened. Two things became clear. The police thought they had enough to hold Paul, and he had not followed through with his promise to tell Judith about his past.

She managed to get Judith under control then said, "If you want to help him, the first thing is to get him a lawyer."

"I—I . . . I don't know any."

"Never mind. I'll take care of it. Where are you?"

"Home."

"Stay there. Don't talk to anybody. Do you know where they're holding him?" She took down the information and reassured Judith. She hung up, flipped her Rolodex, and dialed a number.

Isaac Grodman was a successful criminal lawyer Linda had met years ago when he was carrying on a torrid romance with her husband's sister, Dana. Dana had been trying to pressure Isaac into marriage and had come to Linda for moral support. Linda had advised her to go slowly and let nature take its course. Dana had ignored her and had kept hounding Isaac, until one day she surprised everyone. She simply gave up and, the same weekend, met and married an elderly judge from Reno, then cut all ties with friends and family.

Isaac Grodman's ego had been shattered, and Linda had been forced to spend a lot of time commiserating with him. As a result, they had become good friends. Over the years they had bumped into each other regularly and were forever making plans to get together, plans that never came off.

"Sharman, are we finally going to have that dinner?" Grodman asked.

"No," she told him, explaining that this was a professional call. When she was finished telling him about Paul Mizzell's arrest, he only wanted to know one thing: Did she think he was guilty?

"I don't know, Isaac. There's more to the story, but why don't you find out what's going on, then we'll talk about it."

"Late lunch?"

She checked her desk calendar. "Sure."

"Two o'clock at the Lamplighter, Western and Sixth. I'll see what I can dig up."

Isaac was waiting for her at the bar. He bent his tall frame, flashed an uncomfortable smile, and gave her a peck on the cheek. "Listen, I'm not so sure about lunch. How squeamish are you?" he said as they were led to a table.

"Don't keep anything from me, Isaac."

"Okay. They ordered drinks. When the waiter left Isaac said, "How much do you know about Paul Mizzell?"

"Everything."

"And about Gary Michael Steen?"

"Everything."

She told Isaac of her meeting with Dahlke and the contents of his tapes. Isaac listened patiently then said, "And you don't know whether this man is guilty? The police think so. They're saying that the killer left a little signal—the murder weapon, a rather large hunting knife, buried up to the hilt in Dahlke's crotch. Gary Steen did the same thing to Lori Cornell—"

"Oh, no—"

"The NCIC computer picked up the connection when they fed in some details from Dahlke's files. They just walked Mizzell out of an interrogation room and booked him as a suspect."

Linda sighed. "That's it, then. Why are you shaking your head?"

"This may sound ridiculous, but they can't hold him."

"Why not? My God, isn't it obvious?"

"Not at all. The evidence is too slim and circumstantial. And when I saw him, he wasn't talking. I convinced him to keep quiet until I could determine how to handle it. Frankly, they can only hold him seventy-two hours."

"Why?"

"What do they have to go on? Nobody can place him at Dahlke's office. No witnesses, no fingerprints on the knife, nothing. Unless my sources are holding out on me, the D.A.'s office won't even ask for an indictment. Any judge would toss them out on their asses. Believe me, they have nothing."

"Don't try to reassure me, Isaac. And I wouldn't blame you if you didn't want to get involved."

"Wait a minute. This could be a very interesting case. Don't you know lawyers never lose? Good publicity either way. It so happens, I am *very* interested. Now, I've managed to get one thing accomplished," he said as lunch arrived. "The police are within their rights to announce they have a suspect. That'll attract the press. They'll want to know more. Since their case is so shaky, I got them to agree not to mention the Steen business, unless they get better evidence. Let's just say I called in a favor."

Linda frowned. "But that's public record, isn't it? Anyone could dredge it up."

"So let them work for it. But if it comes out of the police and Mizzell turns out to be innocent, I'll make them look like idiots. Now, the best thing we can do is get Paul out, as fast as possible. That is, if you still want me to get him out. The question is, who am I working for?"

Linda glanced at her watch. "You better talk with Paul's girl friend," she said. "And I think I should come along."

"No need."

"You don't understand," she said bitterly. "Paul hasn't told her about his past."

Isaac winced.

Judith let them in warily, stiffly greeting the lawyer, barely polite to Linda.

Linda had never been inside Paul's house. Expecting to find it a private art gallery containing the best of Mizzell, she was surprised to discover there wasn't a single painting on any of the walls. They were bare. Not a sketch or a print, not even a poster. Nor were there any mirrors downstairs, just functional furniture, a TV and a hi-fi. Most of the free-lance artists she knew worked out of home studios. And most of the staff artists had at least a cubbyhole at home for their personal work. She had never met one before who had nothing. There wasn't even a pencil in sight. While Judith was making coffee, Linda asked if Paul stored his work upstairs.

"He doesn't keep anything," Judith said. "Art is just a job to him."

Really. For a man with his problems, I would have thought it would be therapeutic as well.

They sat down in the living room. Grodman listened patiently as Linda explained everything to Judith, everything that Paul should have explained. She didn't spare any feelings either, as she graphically recounted what she had heard on Dahlke's tape, and detailed Paul's erratic behavior over the last couple of weeks.

Judith sat stonily through it all, consuming the news like a machine and, when Linda was finished, regarding her with a dead silence.

"Where's your liquor?" Linda asked. Judith pointed to a cabinet. Linda went over and poured a brandy. She brought it back and held it out to Judith, who took it and mouthed her thanks.

She sipped and finally said, "He couldn't have done it."

Linda sensed a need for diplomacy. Judith wasn't facing the truth. "I can understand that you don't want to believe it," she told Judith. "I only found out about him just before he . . . before Dahlke was killed. Can you imagine what I've been going through?"

"He didn't do it!" Judith snapped.

"How do you know?"

"Because I was with him at Sabato's when Dahlke was killed!"

Linda stared at her in shock. It was a bald-faced lie. Paul went alone to that bar, and then came to her apartment and told her he'd been alone. Nothing about Judith being with him. In fact, Paul had said he called Judith from the bar, and when Linda spoke to her later—

"He called me from Sabato's."

Grodman was hearing this for the first time. Whether he believed it or not didn't seem to matter. Paul hadn't told him anything different. He regarded Judith flatly and said, "Would you sign a statement to that effect, Miss Berg?"

"Of course." Judith couldn't meet Linda's gaze.

Linda sat on the edge of her chair, troubled. The reason for the lie was obvious: Judith was trying to protect Paul by providing an alibi. A nice loyal thing to do, but a lie nevertheless.

"Fine, perfect," said Grodman, getting up and thrusting his hands into his pockets. He paced, thinking it out. "That's all we need. Unless they can prove she's lying, they can't hold Paul. They need physical evidence placing him at the murder scene— and that they haven't got. With your statement, we're in great shape. Just one thing, though, Miss Berg—if later on they prove he did go to Dahlke's office, they can charge you with perjury."

"He wasn't there!"

"I believe you." Grodman smiled disarmingly. "I just like my witnesses to know they're accountable for what they say. Just be sure you can live with it."

Judith got up. "I'm not lying."

"Fine. Then let's do it."

Judith went upstairs to get her purse.

Linda looked at Grodman helplessly. "You mean they really haven't got a case?"

Grodman smiled. "Oh, they'll come up with one. You can be sure of that. But I'm not going to make it easy for them."

"Don't you believe he's innocent?"

Grodman shrugged. "*She* does. And she's willing to back it up. We have to let her do it."

Linda wanted to tell him it was a lie, to get him out of this, but Isaac was a big boy. And it was Judith's lie, not hers. Besides, Isaac was right: the evidence against Paul was circumstantial. Why let appearances prevail? One small lie wasn't so much if it prevented a greater injustice. . . . But no matter how she rationalized it, it still felt wrong.

"We have to let her do it," she echoed. "Even if it puts him back on the streets?"

"It all evens out in the end," said Isaac. "You gotta have faith in the system."

"I see," Linda said weakly, not liking his point of view either.

Judith came down and locked the house. As Grodman went to his car, Linda stopped her and demanded an explanation. "Are you sure you know what you're doing, Judith?"

"Perfectly."

"Do you expect me to back you up?"

Judith eyed her coldly. "Do what you want."

"Okay," Linda agreed. "But when Paul gets out, keep him home for a while. I don't want to see him at work."

"Are you firing him?"

"No. He'll stay on the payroll, but I'd feel better if he wasn't around until this gets straightened out."

"Whatever you say."

Linda felt a surge of anger as she watched them drive off. After everything she had done to help Paul—listening to him, taking the time to see his doctor, giving him a place to sleep on the night he might have murdered Dahlke—to have his goddamned girl friend treat her like dirt was the last straw. And to expect her to corroborate perjury on top of that—

She got into her car and sat behind the wheel, wondering what Judith was doing. Just being loyal? If her alibi backfired, it would look a lot worse for Paul. And what would happen if Judith discovered she was wrong about him?

CHAPTER 11

The art department was filled with reporters. As Linda walked in, she saw them scattered in little knots, pinning her people to the wall. There was Jimmy at the door to the lab, smoking a cigarette and trying to look cool; Red stretching a full head over two newsmen scribbling in little books; Tisa and Pierre back to back, speaking into microphones. One of the department heads stopped her in the doorway and whispered breathlessly, "You hear about Mizzell?"

Linda's jaw set, and she walked through the department quickly, heading right for her office. They swarmed over her, buzzing with questions. She tried to tune them out as she turned to close the door. Two feet were in her way. "I think you'd all better leave," she said, immediately drowned out by louder questions. "Look!" she shouted, "I've got nothing to say!"

"Can we quote you?" someone shouted back.

"Oh, shit." She whirled and went to her desk. They poured in like locusts, crowding the office and leaning against whatever was available—desk, chairs, glass partitions. Bulbs snapped and the photographers caught Linda's angry pout.

Mizzell. They wanted to know everything about him and all at once.

"He's a fine artist," she said.

"Carving out a name for himself?" somebody cracked.

"A fine artist! An asset to this company. And I expect him to be back at work very shortly."

"After what he did?"

"I don't know that he did anything!" Linda snapped back.

"Then why did they pick him up?"

"I can't answer that. Now, you'll have to go. I don't have time for this."

They kept pressing her, but Grodman was right. The police had not yet released any information about Mizzell's past as Gary Steen. And none of these ace reporters had happened on it independently yet. She gave them a short history of Paul's background with Rok, then she advised them not to make a big deal over him, as the police had the wrong man and he was about to be released anyway.

"How do you know that?"

"I've spoken with his lawyer. Now will you please go?"

"What's the attorney's name, please?"

"Isaac Grodman."

The room cleared out. Presumably, they were off to hassle Grodman. At least he was better equipped to deal with this sort of thing. Linda looked out to be sure they were all gone and spotted one man still standing in the far doorway, huddled with Pierre and Tisa. He turned. It was Brian Hawthorn.

Linda came out and called to him. He smiled and hurried over, stopping to kiss her on the cheek, then he waved a hand at her office. "Can we talk?"

"I suppose we have to."

She led him in and shut the door. He regarded her sheepishly. "I doubt you're here for pleasure," she said.

"Business."

"Just one of the herd today? Out for a little blood?"

"Linda, it's a story."

"An assignment?"

Brian shrugged. "I asked to cover it."

"Did you think you'd be doing me a favor?"

"I thought maybe you'd like the truth told."

"Sorry to disappoint you, Brian. But I don't want to talk about Paul Mizzell to you or anyone else. If you want to take me to lunch or to dinner or up to my apartment, that's okay. But I don't want to get on a professional basis with you. Now, can you go back to the *Times* and ask them to put somebody else on this story? Believe me, there's not much in it. It won't make your career."

"No?" He gave her a look that said "I know better." And that look put Linda on her guard.

Wait a minute. Something's wrong here. Go easy.

Without being invited, Brian sat down. "I can't drop the story, Linda. I've got a personal stake in it."

"What stake? Me?"

He shook his head. "Mizzell, or shall we call him Gary Michael Steen?"

Linda sat down. "I should have known you'd be the first to figure that out."

"I'm not taking any bows. It didn't come to me in a blinding flash, either. I've known it for quite a while."

She stared at him. "How long?"

"Probably since the first time I saw him in here." He smiled wanly. "I have a terrific memory."

"What are you talking about?"

"Nineteen sixty-eight. Gary Michael Steen. UCLA. Lori Cornell. Chop chop chop."

"Don't joke," she said tightly.

"Sorry. But thank God we don't have to do the dance of 'What are you talking about, Brian?—I never heard of any Gary Michael Steen.' Of course you've heard of him. You spent an afternoon in Dahlke's office getting the full story."

"How do you know that?"

"I have a friend at Parker Center who could pass for a detective. You're in Dahlke's appointment book the Friday before he was murdered."

Linda glared at him. "What the hell are you up to, Brian?"

Trying to imitate Humphrey Bogart, he said, "I'm laying my cards on the table, sweetheart. It's time we were honest with each other."

"I don't have anything to hide."

"And I'm not the police. I'm not going to persecute you, but I don't want to masquerade anymore."

"Anymore?"

"I confess. I've been playing a part. Innocent, dumb, affectionate, flatfooted newsman, in hot pursuit of a lady and a story."

"I see. Which were you chasing first?"

Brian smiled. "That's tough to answer."

"I think you just did. It was an accident that you were sent to me. I did everything I could to put you off. But the minute you spotted Paul Mizzell, you smelled a story. Okay, that's fair. I can understand the slimy way you work, but I don't understand how you knew about him from the beginning."

Brian leaned forward. "I covered the Cornell murder, and Steen's trial, back in sixty-eight, sixty-nine. My first homicide. I had just come up to metro from feature news. Threw myself into that case. Nasty business. On one side I had crazy Gary Steen hollering 'The acid did it! The acid did it!' On the other side, the Cornell family, everybody providing testimonials to Lori's character. I don't think they even knew their own daughter. Then the jury finds Gary nuts, and he goes to Camarillo and falls into the hands of the eminent Dr. Gene Dahlke. A few years later he's out. Free. I wrote a story on that, too. They stuck it away on page twenty-seven because he wasn't news anymore. Then he turns up here, and I spot him, and I can see right away the guy is scared. Why? Now, that's an interesting question, which I ponder while I'm being nice to you. As I see more of you, I see more of him too. And each time he looks worried, like he's about to crack. So I figure that's what's happening—he's going to do it again. The son of a bitch is going to kill somebody. And who turns up dead? The great Dr. Dahlke. Now, doesn't that make neat sense?" He held up both hands and spread his fingers to make a frame. "Psycho rebels against radical treatment—kills doctor."

"Is that your headline?"

"In the L.A. *Times*? Are you kidding?"

Linda sat back and glared at him, numb, unable to feel anger, but feeling used.

That makes twice in your life, dumbo. Twice by reporters. First your husband, now this twerp.

"So," she said.

"Yes?"

"So you wined me and dined me and slept with me, just to keep tabs on Mizzell. You carried on an affair for the sake of a story. How noble and self-sacrificing!"

"Wait a minute, Linda."

"No. No, I'm not waiting. I'm calling security. If you're not out of here in ten seconds—" She reached for the phone. His hand clamped down on hers. She looked at him and saw firmness, determination, control.

"There are two people sitting in front of you, Mrs. Sharman. There's Brian Hawthorn, reporter, who has to file a story by seven tonight in order to beat the other baboons who were here. And there's Brian Hawthorn, your friend, who never intended to take advantage of you. It just worked out that way. Both of us are sorry."

Linda said nothing. She stared at his hand on hers. After a moment, he relaxed the pressure and she pulled away. "What story are you going to file?" she said.

"Just the truth. Paul Mizzell held as a suspect. A rehash of his past as Gary Steen. And if they release him, I'll put that in too." He paused and looked at her sadly. "I know what's going through your mind. If all this hits the news, it'll make your problems with your boss even tougher."

"I wasn't thinking of that, though I probably should. If that concerned me so much, I never would have kept Paul on."

"Why did you?"

"I wasn't sure about him," she said, her eyes tightening with worry. "I didn't want to condemn him. And I was a little afraid of him." Expecting sympathy, she looked up—and saw his mind working. She had seen that before: cornering his interviews, her ex-husband had been exactly like that. She jumped up. "What the hell am I doing? I'm letting you pump me again! You're looking for a human interest angle—a drama you can hang over all this! You're going to *use* whatever I tell you!"

He shook his head. She was saved a lying reply: the phone rang. She snatched it up and growled, "Linda Sharman." It was Tony Benedict. He wanted to see her right away, and he sounded icy. She hung up and snapped at Brian, "I have to go."

"Wait a minute. I want to talk this out."

"Some other time—"

"I told you, I've only got till seven."

"You don't understand, do you? I'm not giving you any more, Brian—ever!"

"Linda—listen to me—" He followed her out the door, running after her. "Linda, I won't file the story, okay? I'll hold it off, but you and I have got to talk."

"About what?"

"Us!"

"I'm not going to help you, Brian."

"You've got it turned around. I can help you."

"I don't *need* your help."

He rode down the elevator with her. "You're being really stubborn. This story's going to come out, whether I get it first or somebody else does. But your side of it—what you knew about Mizzell being Steen, and what you didn't say—"

"Makes no difference."

"Makes a lot of difference. Don't you understand? You'll *have* to explain! You met with Dahlke the Friday before he was killed! He told you all about Gary Steen. Dr. Bass has already made a statement to the police. Now, don't you think they're going to ask why you didn't come forward after the murder?"

"Let them ask."

The elevator doors opened. Brian stepped out and called after her, "Why didn't you, Linda?"

She didn't answer. She went through the glass doors and down the hall quickly.

She sat still and calm, matching Tony's practiced cool, while he questioned her about why the police had picked up Paul Mizzell. Linda played innocent.

"Tony, it's a mistake. I'm sure of it."

"What makes you so sure? The place is swarming with reporters and they're all carrying on about murder!" Tony paced in front of her, hands on his hips, putting on a show of deep thought. "You know, Linda, you never did tell me the cops were here to question him before. I had to get that through the grapevine. I thought sure you'd get around to telling me yourself. But no—not a word. What's the matter, Linda? Don't you trust me?"

"What do you think?"

"I think you're cute." She stood up. "Cute meaning clever, shrewd. Watch out it doesn't backfire." She went to the door, and he called after her, "We haven't resolved this yet. I want to know one thing: are you standing behind that guy?"

Her eyes flashed. It was a challenge and she knew better than to accept it, and she wasn't at all sure when she said "Yes!" and stalked out.

She left early and was surprised to find Brian Hawthorn lurking in the hallway outside her condo. She walked past him to her door and unlocked it, muttering, "You'll never make that seven o'clock deadline."

"I can always phone it in."

"Not from here." She went in and turned to close the door; his foot was in the way. They stood eyeing each other—Linda sullenly, Brian with mounting impatience. Suddenly, he shoved the door out of her hand. It slammed open. He was in and the door was shut in an instant. He faced her. "Get out," she said.

"No." His arms swooped around her. She panicked, then felt his lips hard and insistent on hers. Surprised, she fought him. He wrestled her down to the floor. She pushed and kicked but he had her in a tight grip. He inched his body up until he was almost prone over her, then he grunted and sighed. "The floor's too hard. How about the bedroom?"

She broke out in laughter. He let go and sprawled backward, holding his tummy and grimacing. She spluttered and pulled herself up, finally asking, "What's the matter?"

"Late lunch. Chili dog. Oh . . . heartburn."

"Serves you right."

"I meant well."

"You meant rape."

"Call it what you want. Personally, I'd call it coitus interruptus." He burped. "By chili doggius. Oh God, Linda, I'm sorry."

She laughed again. "I almost wish you'd finished the job."

"I can, you know. Just get me some soda water or crackers . . ."

She waved a hand. "Forget it. I'm mad at you anyway."

"Right. May I sit?" She nodded. He pulled himself up and, gripping his stomach, moved to a chair. "I really could use that cracker—soaks up the stomach acid."

She shook her head in amazement, then got up and went to the kitchen. She returned with a plate of crackers, which he nibbled gratefully. She sat on the floor in front of him and studied his face as he munched.

He smiled with his mouth full. Then he said, "See? I'm still a nice guy. Now what are we going to do? You've got a story you don't want to tell, and I want to get you to tell it. But I don't want to jeopardize our—what'll we call it—friendship?"

Linda frowned. "It's not just you and me. There's a third person involved."

"Mizzell."

"That's right. He has a life and feelings and the right to a fair trial, if it comes to that. I'm not about to help convict him in the press."

Brian chewed up the last cracker and said, "Linda, he has no more right to anything than did the man who's just been murdered and the girl he killed thirteen years ago."

"But if he's innocent, why dredge up his past?"

"The public has a right to know."

"Oh, come on, Brian." Linda stood up. "Is that engraved on your desk?"

"No, it's engraved here." He tapped his head.

"Well, I don't agree."

"Your privilege."

"And I'm not going to help you."

"That's fine. At least it clarifies where we stand. But I think you should consider this: If you have some special information that rules Paul Mizzell out as Dahlke's killer, then don't you think you should come out with it? You'd only be helping him. I'm offering you an opportunity to do that."

She gazed at his shoes: brown loafers, scuffed and frayed. One sock was inside out.

"What do you say?"

"You're just looking for something you can rush into print."

"No." He got up. "No, I'll keep it out. I'll even guarantee that I won't use it until you agree with me."

"Am I supposed to trust you?"

"Please."

"You believe he's guilty."

Brian pursed his lips then nodded. "See, Linda, I don't know what information you've got, but I think it's coloring the way you look at that guy."

"Let's have a drink."

He followed her to the kitchen and watched her mix two bourbon and sodas. They sat down at her dining table across from each other.

"Thirteen years of reporting, Linda. I can't tell you how many homicides I've covered. But I have found one thing: this city is filled with people who lead double lives, who go properly about their business most of the time, but sometimes when the moon is full they become monsters. Just like in the old horror movies, except they don't sprout fangs. All they have to do is pick up a knife or a gun and they can play God. Cops and reporters see it all the time. Families and friends won't accept the truth—that Mom or Dad or Sonny or Sis is a homicidal maniac. 'Oh, he couldn't be like that! Not my Johnny!' You want to believe them, but then you find out yeah, Johnny really did do it. He sure did. He cut off that girl's head and—"

"Stop it."

Brian frowned. Linda drained her drink, put the glass down hard, and stared at her hand.

"So what's the explanation?" Brian continued. "Are we all blind to what the next guy is capable of? We just don't want to know? Are we unwilling to protect ourselves? Or are we afraid to admit the truth—that our principle of 'innocent till proven guilty' is outmoded."

Linda looked at him sharply.

"That's what you think," he said. "Isn't it? That he's innocent, despite everything you've found out. Don't bother answering." Brian snorted. "Maybe he's two personalities. That wouldn't surprise me. Look at the job Dahlke did on him. Here he is, folks. Gary Steen on the left, Paul Mizzell on the right. Which one is the real killer? Only his doctor knows for sure, and he's not talking—because he's dead! I'll bet Mizzell believes in his own innocence too. Has he got a girl friend?"

Linda nodded.

"I'll bet *she* doesn't believe he did it. And his lawyer will holler like hell that he didn't do it. And what will you do?"

Linda choked on her bourbon. *What will you do, stupid? Support the lie when Judith tells it?*

"And the rest of us? What are we supposed to do? Believe them? I'd rather be safe. Nail the rehabilitated son of a bitch!"

She bristled, and he held up his hands for peace.

"I don't want to fight with you, Linda. But you've got to think about protecting the poor innocent folks like you and me who could be his next victims."

Linda hurried into the kitchen and shakily made herself another drink. She leaned over the kitchen counter and sipped it. She looked through the opening and said, "I'm going to tell you a few things, Brian, but I don't want to see them in print. Agreed?"

He nodded. She came around the counter and went to the living room sofa. He joined her on the opposite end of it. Slowly, carefully, she told him about the last couple of weeks with Paul Mizzell: the things that came in the mail that she had never seen, the arguments, the car accident, his paranoia—everything that had become imbued into her memory.

Brian listened silently, clutching his drink.

She told him nothing about Paul visiting her the night of Dahlke's murder. She wasn't ready yet to expose Judith's alibi. She felt he would leap on that and all bets would be off. Finally, she summed up: "I don't know whether he was telling me the truth, whether it was all an act, or if it's really something strange like you're suggesting—two personalities in conflict. It's occurred to me that he could have been torturing *himself*. Maybe the murder is the end result. But there's something behind his behavior—that maybe only a woman would sense—"

Brian blinked in disbelief.

"He's still got the benefit of *my* doubt. I don't believe he killed Dahlke. Maybe another psychiatrist can figure him out. I'd like to see him go back for treatment, because I do believe he needs some sort of help. But if you print a lot of circumstantial hooey, you'll destroy him. He'll go right off the deep end."

"And if I don't print it," Brian said quietly, "the next guy will. Not what you're telling me, but for sure all the rest of it—his past, the obvious connections. It's inevitable. And if he's that thin-skinned, don't you think he *should* be back in Camarillo?''

Linda shrugged. ''Anyway, you'd look pretty foolish.''

''Why?''

''Paul's girl friend is telling the police that she was in a bar with him when Dahlke was murdered.''

There. That wasn't so hard. Rolled right off the tongue. Just like honey.

Brian was silent a moment. ''I'd like to talk with her.''

''Leave her alone.''

''I can do it without permission.''

''You can mark him for life too. Suppose they find some guy from El Monte who turns out to be the real killer—''

''Then I'll write his story. Meanwhile, I've got this one.''

She stood up, ready to throw him out.

''Take it easy, Linda. I promise I'll just follow the herd for a while. I won't try to be Scoop Scanlon. And you promise not to give your story to anyone else.''

''Okay.''

''Right.'' He looked at her a long moment then put down his drink and said, ''I better leave.'' He moved closer. ''I feel I should *ask* for a goodnight kiss.''

She offered him a cheek. He came over and kissed it warmly, then stroked her neck. She edged his hand away gently.

He smiled, then said, ''There's one thing. If he gets out, and there is another murder . . . all bets are off.''

He left quickly.

Even the drinking didn't help her sleep. She lay awake, staring at the ceiling until she couldn't stand it anymore. She got out of bed and padded naked into the living room. In the dark, she put on a Mozart symphony and curled up on the sofa under a blanket. Her thoughts wandered back to Brian. She was just at the point of chastising herself for not asking him to stay—sex would have been just the thing to knock her out tonight—when she was struck by a chilling prospect: Suppose Paul Mizzell really was getting threats by mail . . .

And suppose they were coming from Brian.

Linda sat up sharply, a whole plot unfolding in her mind. Brian spotting Paul somewhere in town, remembering him from 1968, tracing him to Rok Records, coming in on a pretext, inveigling her friendship—all to get closer to Paul. And doing it in such a way that he established a unique alibi—the reporter on the trail of a story—a man with an inalienable right to the facts. But why was he doing it? He'd revealed that himself: he had covered the Steen case in 1968.

Didn't he tell you he was a novelist? Facts, hell. He's got a vivid imagination. What possibilities! Latch onto a rehabilitated psychotic, drive him crazy, then commit a copycat murder to make it look like the psychotic's in action again. Then be first in with the blockbuster story. Who but a reporter on the original case would remember the details of Lori Cornell's murder? Hey. He didn't even have to remember it: he has access to the newspaper files!

The more she thought about it, the more frightening it became. So far, Paul's doctor had been killed. Who was the next logical victim?

You, Linda.

The record shut off and she felt the pressure of silence.

And you've let him into your home, let him invade your body!

She pulled the blanket tighter and sank down on the sofa, trying to make herself small. A sob caught in her throat. Once she began crying, she couldn't stop. The tears flowed in a relieving rush.

Oh, Brian, how could you . . . ?

She wiped her eyes on the blanket and felt a salty dryness on her cheeks. She told herself that she was the one going crazy. She was so overwrought she could only imagine the worst. Brian was a friend.

Are you sure?

He said so.

Then why is he so hot on Paul's trail?

For the story, as he said.

You need your head examined.

"Oh, shut up!" Her own shout surprised her. She threw off the blanket and stumbled to the kitchen, pulled down the bourbon and made another drink—a tall one.

And you're becoming an alcoholic too.

She growled at herself. Swirling the ice cubes in her glass, she made her way back to bed.

In the morning, it'll be better. In the morning, you won't believe anything.

CHAPTER 12

Next morning, Isaac Grodman was feeling pleased with himself. Obtaining Paul Mizzell's release had gone exactly the way he thought it would. At an eight A.M. hearing, the judge had skewered the assistant D.A. for lack of evidence. Paul had been picked up on probable cause, which the judge pronounced improbable.

The authorities reluctantly parted with Paul after Grodman pointed out that if they insisted on keeping him they ran the risk of screwing up their entire case on technicalities. Grodman was an expert on technicalities.

"Honest to Christ, Mizzell," he said in the car. "Those guys are so afraid of blowing a case, they'd do anything to avoid losing on a technicality. The whole system has the D.A. up the wall. They don't know whether they're coming or going. Makes it pretty tough when they've got the right guy, but who's to know that, eh? You're lucky, you know. So far the press hasn't gotten hold of your background. When they do, it could get ugly. Think you can handle that?"

Paul was silent. He didn't like Grodman, didn't like lawyers at all. He remembered the pair from the Cornell trial. The two Slick City types hired by his aunt. . . . Poor old woman, she couldn't believe what he had done until he told her it was true. He never saw her after that. The lawyers stayed with him: they were paid to. But the way they twisted things—sometimes he didn't know whether they were helping him or hurting him. But they always said, "Relax. Everything'll be fine." And when he was declared insane, they celebrated like kings while Paul went to Camarillo to have his head rearranged. He couldn't understand their delight until he realized attorneys cared more about winning than about the client. He had never questioned his need to pay for killing Lori Cornell, but he wasn't quite sure that he had paid.

"What would you do with a killer?" he asked Grodman.

"Huh?"

"If you knew someone had killed another person, what would you think should happen to him?"

Grodman shrugged. "I think he should be represented."

Paul stared at him, getting annoyed. "Forget you're a lawyer. Just some guy on the street. This killer is a stranger, not a meal ticket."

Grodman stiffened. "Look, Paul, if you want to confess something to me, I'll regard it as privileged communication. It won't have any bearing on what I can do for you."

"I'm not confessing, God damn it! I'm asking a question. Suppose *you* kill somebody and I find out about it. I'm society: what have I got a right to expect?"

"A fair trial."

"And the family of the victim?"

"I don't know what you're getting at."

"I killed Lori Cornell. I was out of my head on drugs when I did it, but I did it. She's dead. I took her life; they sent me to a hospital; I got my head shrunk, and here I am."

"Here you are what?"

"Again."

Grodman was silent, trying to fathom what Paul was telling him. Paul stared out the window, angrily watching cars roar down the freeway, rushing to a thousand urgent destinies. He was rushing, too, but to what? His head felt mushy from all the hours he'd spent staring blankly at the police in tiny little rooms—on Grodman's advice, refusing to answer—until Grodman had returned to take him home.

"Why did they let me go?" Paul asked quietly.

"Because among other things your girlfriend provided an alibi."

"Judith?"

Grodman nodded. "She said you couldn't have been with Dahlke at six o'clock the other night—you were with her at Sabato's."

Paul stared ahead stiffly. *With her? So that's how I got off. She lied for me.* He was grateful but wondered why she did it. Out of love, duty, belief in his innocence? Would she retract the story once she found out about his past? She must have told the police the truth as she wanted it to be. But it was a lie nevertheless. He couldn't blame her for that. It probably sounded better anyway. And she had managed to get him out. Again, he felt a twinge of guilt. Did he deserve to be free? What if he *did* kill Dahlke? He began to sweat. He had the strangest sensation of being pulled into a hole against his will. Even if he didn't do it, even if it wasn't his hand on the knife, he still knew he was somehow responsible. Maybe Gary Steen, the unfeeling, tortured ghost that still lurked inside him, was knocking on the doors of his mind, trying to get out, committing murder as a signal—

Paul groaned aloud, anguished. Grodman asked if anything was wrong.

"No." Paul shook his head, trying to banish the thoughts crowding in on him. He didn't know anymore. He just wanted it to end. *What's the matter with you?* he asked himself. *You were all right until the police took you in, then you fell apart. Everything collapsed. Nothing was real anymore, only the guilt. The world you built up so carefully—could it have been that flimsy? Did Dahlke fail? Was Paul Mizzell nothing more than a name?*

Reporters and local TV newsmen were camped out in front of the house on Laurel Canyon as Grodman drove up with Paul. Two police cars were also parked conspicuously nearby. "Don't say anything," Grodman urged. He got out, came around the passenger side, and opened the door. Reporters descended, photographing Paul's bewildered look. Paul quickly lowered his eyes and let Grodman pull him through the crush of microphones.

"Does this mean you're not a suspect in the Dahlke murder, Mr. Mizzell?"

"What was the bail?"

"How come they let you out, Mr. Steen?"

Paul froze. Evidently, the truth was out. Grodman grabbed the nearest microphone. "My client's legal name is Mizzell. He has not been charged with any crime, and he is no longer being held as a suspect. There is no case against him."

"How'd you get him off?"

"I didn't get him off. That implies legal process. There was none. We presented the police with the statement of a witness who could account for Mr. Mizzell's whereabouts. The police are unable to place him at the scene of the crime—therefore, no case. Thank you, gentlemen.''

He flipped the mike into the air and plowed through them, up the stone steps, followed by a crowd still demanding the answers to questions.

Judith opened the door. Paul paused on the front steps to stare at her. Grodman shoved him through, came in himself, and slammed the door shut. "Jesus, aren't they unbelievable?''

He glanced out the window. They were roaming around outside. Nobody was leaving. They were prepared to wait. He looked back and saw Paul move to embrace Judith. She let him put his arms around her, but she responded with the warmth of a brick wall.

Paul leaned back and looked into her eyes. He saw bitterness.

"Why didn't you tell me?'' Judith said in a quavering voice. "Why didn't you trust me?''

Paul opened his mouth but couldn't say anything. He knew what she meant. His past. She'd found out.

"Want me to wait outside?'' Grodman said.

"No,'' Judith replied. "You can stay. I'm the one who's leaving.''

Paul stared at her in shock. "Judith—Christ, I'm sorry—I meant to tell you. I tried!'' He paused. "How did you find out?''

"Linda.''

Paul collapsed into a chair. "Linda?'' he said, his voice choked with disbelief.

Judith backed away. "I can't stay, Paul. I'm sorry. I don't think you did what they're saying you've done, but I just can't stay.''

"Why not?''

"Because you didn't trust me.'' She whirled and headed for the stairs. Paul looked after her dully.

Grodman moved away from the door. "Miss Berg,'' he called, "you can't just take off! We may need you.''

Judith didn't answer him. Grodman frowned at Paul, shrunk into the chair, confusion filling his eyes.

"She'll change her mind," Grodman said, then added absently, "I wonder why she waited for you to come home."

Paul looked over at a large ceramic ashtray on the table next to him, a gift from Judith. He picked it up and threw it against the wall. It made a resounding crash.

"Hey, watch it," Grodman said, glancing through the window to see if the reporters had heard.

Paul leaped up, angry. "Linda—" he said.

Grodman touched his arm. "Calm down! She's upset! Believe me, she'll come round. I'll be happy to play peacemaker. I'm sure you feel like tearing the house apart—"

"How do you *know* what I feel?"

"All right, all right—I don't think you should stay here—"

Paul started pacing. "Why not? She's the one who's leaving."

"Too many reporters. You won't be able to make a move without them."

"Where am I going to go?" He continued pacing, glancing upstairs frequently, slamming one fist into the other hand. "Damn it! Why is this happening? Who's doing it?" He whirled on Grodman. "I didn't kill anybody! You understand?"

"Yes, sure."

"Paul Mizzell is innocent! That was Dahlke's whole theory. I have to believe that or they might as well throw me back in the hospital! Do you understand that? *I* haven't done anything wrong!"

Grodman's jaw worked. He didn't like the tone of this. "Now listen to me, Paul. Protesting your innocence at the top of your voice is no way to get anybody on your side. We have to start planning a defense in case they pick you up again."

Paul was shaking his head. "No, there's something wrong with me. I better go back to Camarillo. I'm insane. I really am."

He stopped, looking past Grodman at Judith coming down the stairs, carrying a suitcase. He ran to her. "Judith, please—Give me a chance. Let's sit and talk."

"There's nothing more to say."

Something in him snapped. "That's the problem, isn't it? That's always been our problem. No communication. Just sex."

Judith walked past him and put the suitcase down. She bent over and reached for her purse. Paul stared at the curve of her hips. He moved toward her.

"That's what you want, isn't it?" He grabbed her from behind and threw her on the sofa. She let out a scream.

"Paul—!" Grodman leaped to stop him.

Paul swept him aside and looked down at Judith. She pulled her legs together and held her skirt in place. "A good fuck," Paul said. "That always makes it better. Come on—" He plucked at her skirt.

Judith slapped him. Surprised, he backed away. Slowly, she got up. "Don't touch me," she said, barely controlled. "Just don't."

"I'm sorry—" He wheeled around and looked at Grodman staring back at him, white-faced.

Judith straightened her clothing and reached for the suitcase. Grodman scuttled ahead and picked it up. "I'll take it out for you."

Paul sensed Grodman's fear and knew what he was thinking. *I'm dangerous. I'm violent. I'm crazy.* "Get out," he said. "Both of you."

"Paul—"

"Go on, lawyer. You're afraid I'm going to do something to her? Then take her with you!"

Grodman glanced anxiously at the window. "Keep your voice down," he cautioned.

Paul lunged for the suitcase and flung open the door. The reporters outside looked up. He threw out the suitcase. "You want somebody to talk to?" he yelled. "Here!" He shoved Judith and Grodman out the door, and slammed it after them just as the first strobe lights went off.

Stunned, Judith threw up her hands and buried her face in Grodman's shoulder. He stumbled and picked up the suitcase, reddening. Shielding her from the photographers, he rushed her down to his car.

Paul locked the door and backed into the living room, shaking with rage. He had to get out. While they were busy in front, maybe he could slip away. . . . He ran for the back door, went through it and climbed the hill behind the house. Vaulting his back fence, he scrambled to the street above. Catching his breath, he walked quickly away.

* * *

Tony Benedict let Linda in, not for a second breaking his line of patter. He was busy telling Marvin Bensch how to hype the local deejays on the upcoming Struts' release. Linda walked in and took a seat. Marvin was gathering up his pressbooks and nodding at everything Tony said.

Tony walloped Marvin on the back and told him, "We're all counting on you, babe. Go to it." Marvin nodded again and left, closing the door timidly. Tony shuffled back to his desk, gesturing at a small, hawk-faced man in the corner reclining chair. "Nelson Carlisle, meet Linda Sharman. Linda's our creative director."

Linda and Carlisle met halfway, shook hands, and took their seats again. Tony dropped into his chair and rubbed his eyes.

"Nelson is our new chief attorney."

Linda's mouth opened slightly. Carlisle interlaced his fingers and regarded her through a haze of smoke from his long panatela. Tony coughed and asked if Linda wanted a drink.

"Yes, I could . . ." She caught his smile. She never drank during the day and he knew it. He was testing, trying to determine just how on-the-spot he had her. "What happened to Miller?" she asked.

"Who?"

"Our former chief attorney."

"Oh, Miller! Gone to the Springs with Rocky. I think they're drawing up papers having to do with a transition of management."

"What does that mean?"

"Search me. I said I only *think* that's what's going on. Won't change the situation here, of course. I'm still running things."

Into the ground, Tony, into the ground. She wanted to hit him. What the hell was she doing in a meeting with a new attorney? And then she realized—Paul Mizzell was out of custody—she'd heard it on the news.

"Nelson and I have been discussing our little situation, our Paul Mizzell problem. You know, Linda, I don't think you told me everything."

"No?"

"Such as this stuff on the news about his first murder, the one before he changed his name. You knew about Gary Michael Steen, didn't you?"

Linda nodded.

Tony leaned forward, relishing this. "College kid on drugs stabs his girl friend, leaves the knife in her twat—I mean, what kind of people are you hiring around here, Linda?"

Linda's lip quivered again. "They let him out. He has an alibi for the Dahlke murder."

"He has shit!" Tony's eyes flashed. "Nelson has been down at Parker Center, getting details. Tell her, Nelson."

Nelson Carlisle drew the panatela out of his mouth and picked a bit of wrapper off his lip. He tilted his head back and watched Linda through hooded lids. "His girl friend claims he was in a bar with her when that psychiatrist was killed."

"In a bar," Tony repeated with heavy significance. "When he should have been at work."

"I didn't know you were handing out demerits," Linda snapped back.

Tony's glare turned to a smile. He had her going now.

Nelson continued. "The police checked this place called Sabato's and couldn't find anybody who remembers seeing either Mizzell or his girl. They don't believe he was in there at all."

Linda felt a lump form in her throat. Of course. It was a crappy alibi. All they had to do was check. Nobody would recall Judith, because she was never there. And Paul? Maybe he had never been there either. She swallowed the lump and said halfheartedly, "That doesn't prove anything."

"Exactly," Tony agreed. "It doesn't help Mizzell, either."

"It's only a matter of time," Nelson said quietly. "Letting him go was a psychological move. The police don't believe Miss Berg's story, but they want Paul to think he's in the clear."

"Why?"

"They're watching him. They think he may try to kill her next."

"Oh, for God's sake—"

"He did it thirteen years ago," said Tony. "That's what it's all leading up to—*a goddamned rerun!*"

"You're not serious." Linda stared at Carlisle.

"I'm telling you what the police think."

"They let him go believing that?"

"I'm not giving you the official version, just a way of looking at it. Judith Berg provided him with an alibi. If it's the truth, then he's innocent. If it's not, and she becomes the next victim—poetic justice.''

Linda leaped up. ''Poetic murder, you mean!''

''Sit down!'' Tony shouted, his mouth tightening into a thin line. ''You're forgetting something, Linda. *You* were the one who kept a close friendship with that psychotic and failed to tell anybody what was going on! *You* went to see his doctor and still didn't say anything! *You* knew he was a nutcase! And *your* stupidity may be putting us all in danger!''

''What do you mean—us?''

Nelson spoke carefully. ''If Mizzell really is crazy, he might attack anyone he regards as a friend, or any friend he regards as an enemy.''

''And you and I fit in there somewhere,'' Tony added.

''I know exactly where you fit,'' Linda said, sitting down.

Tony glared at her. ''You better watch it, Sharman. You're really close.''

''To what?''

''Please—'' said Nelson, gesturing for restraint. ''What I'm telling you is all police speculation. They're looking for a break, which they won't get if Mizzell is locked up. They're not ready to charge him. They haven't got the evidence to make it stick.''

''So in the meantime,'' said Tony, ''we all walk around nervous and wait for the bomb to go off. I hope to Christ you told him not to come to work.''

Linda nodded.

''Good. 'Cause if he's going to pop his cork, I don't want it to happen around here. Now—'' Tony leaned back and gave Linda a relaxed smile. ''One more question, and I want the truth. How long have you known that Mizzell was this Steen character?''

Linda stared at him blankly, trying to guess his motive.

''Come on, Linda. Did you know it when you hired him?''

''No.''

''You sure?''

''I'm sure.''

''So you only found out recently?''

''Yes.''

''And you didn't think it was anything I needed to know.''

Linda couldn't answer. He had her at last. If he took this to
Rocky, how could she ever explain why she had kept quiet?
Brian Hawthorn was right. That question was going to destroy
her. "Tony," she said finally, "we don't know that Paul is
involved in murder. I don't want to prejudge him based on
something that happened a long time ago. Give him a chance."

Tony shook his head. "Linda, you're the one who wants a
chance, not him. Nelson?"

Nelson tried to keep up his calm façade, but he was uncomfortable with the thought that his first official duty with Rok was
turning into a hatchet job. "This puts the company in an awk-
ward spot," he said. "If it comes out that you knew about
Mizzell and said nothing, and he did kill again, we're going to
look very bad. I'm afraid you may have to bear the brunt of that,
Mrs. Sharman. We think you ought to be prepared."

Linda stood up, struggling to keep her lip still. "You want me
to resign?"

"A little early for that," said Nelson, glancing at Tony, who
rocked back and forth in his chair.

Of course it was early, Linda thought. Tony wanted the pleasure of firing her. Her voice quavered. "Won't it be too goddamned bad if it turns out Paul is innocent?" She waited for a
reply. There was none.

Tony got up slowly. He waved her toward the door, held it
open for her, and said, "Just in case, Linda, pick a new assistant
out of the group and make sure he knows your job."

"Sure, Tony."

Before she was out the waiting room door, he told his secretary, loud enough so Linda couldn't help hearing: "Get Buddy
Dyal on the phone."

Linda missed a step. Her eyes filled with tears as she made her
way back to the elevator. Buddy Dyal. The working girl's friend.
What would he tell Tony? Probably anything Tony wanted, so
long as his name was kept out of it. Tony would get him to say that
Linda knew everything about Paul Mizzell being Gary Steen
from the day she hired him, and then use that as his final wedge
to force her out.

She was finished.

*   *   *

Linda walked through the department like a zombie, her face slack and her eyes wounded. She went into her office and shut the door. She glanced at the glass partitions and wished she had installed those blinds she'd been planning to get for five years.

Five years? Christ, how the time has shot by. Sixteen years of my life in this place. Why the hell do I hang on?

The phone rang. She heard it distantly but was slow in responding. Tisa was standing down the aisle, making a hand gesture, like she'd be happy to answer it if—

Linda picked it up. It was Brian. He spoke urgently. "Mizzell has disappeared. The lawyer took him home this morning; there was a fight with the girl friend right in front of twenty reporters, then Mizzell split! The police were there, but he still got away. Now they're really pissed."

Linda couldn't work up any interest. "Were you one of the twenty?" she asked.

"No. I got it secondhand. But Linda, you can't keep out of this anymore. You've got to come forward and tell the police everything you know."

"I don't have to do a goddamned thing. Not for you or anybody else."

He was silent a moment. "Something wrong?"

"I'm tired . . . tired of being responsible for *everything*."

"You want to talk? I'll come right over."

"No."

"Well, what *do* you want?"

She couldn't answer. She didn't *have* an answer. Then suddenly she did. "I want my freedom. I want my life back. I've sold it for sixteen years. *I want it back.*"

Brian didn't know what to say. "I think we ought to get together—"

"No! I'm tired of being pumped, Brian. Pumped physically and mentally. Understand?"

"Yeah . . ."

"Good." She hung up, surprising herself.

The phone rang again almost immediately. Tisa popped out of her cubicle and gestured again. Linda gave her the finger. Tisa's eyes bulged in shocked disbelief. She scooted back out of sight. Linda snatched up the phone. "Yes?" she barked.

"Linda?"

It was Paul Mizzell, calling from a phone booth. She could hear the boxy sound and the cars going by. "What do you want?"

"You shouldn't have done it," he said ominously. "You were my friend. I thought you were on my side."

Her anger was abruptly crushed by a wave of fear. Her cheeks burned with it. She stumbled over words and found herself trying to placate him. "I—I am your friend, Paul. But you've got to face things. You can't hide anymore. It's all coming out."

"You told Judith."

"Would you rather she heard it on the news?"

"*I* could have told her!"

But you didn't—either because you're a coward, a murderer, or desperately in need of help.

"Where's Judith?" she said.

There was a long pause, then: "She's gone. I don't know what I'm going to do next."

"Paul—"

He hung up. His words rang in her ears. *My God*, Linda thought, *he's done something to Judith!* Her fingers missed the buttons as she punched out Paul's home number. There was no answer. Stumbling to her feet, she slammed down the phone, her head pounding with anxiety. She banged through the door and walked quickly out of the department. Tisa looked out from her cubicle as Linda flew past.

She hit the street and stopped. It was rush hour. Cars were bumper to bumper on Sunset Boulevard. Automatically, she turned and walked, looking for the nearest watering hole.

Isaac Grodman's initial shock over Paul's outburst gave way quickly to anger and self-justification. As he explained to Judith while they drove back to his office, he was not used to being manhandled by clients. He could understand ingratitude, which most often emerged as contempt: You got me off, but I'm really guilty, so you're no better than I am. But he didn't like clients who failed to realize when they were being helped. He intimated that if Mizzell didn't get the message quickly, he would be out one attorney. Having salved his ego by verbally putting Paul in his place, Isaac turned his attention back to Judith. What to do with her?

She seemed in a daze. No emotion there, no anger or rage or any of the things he was feeling. She simply sat quietly in his office, sipping coffee, her eyes lost in the skyline outside. Grodman sensed something beneath the surface, but whatever it was, she hid it well. She waited patiently while he went through a series of phone calls and some of his mail. More than once Grodman caught her studying him, and in turn, he found himself mentally undressing her. Attractive, damn it. How could she get mixed up with a screwball like Mizzell? Suddenly, he hit on what to do.

"Do you have any place to go?" he asked.

Judith shook her head.

"Well, then—" He explained that he had a large spare bedroom. She could stay there until she decided what she wanted to do. She wouldn't be in the way, and besides, he would be up and gone early in the morning and back late at night. "How about it?"

She thought for a moment, giving him a lost look, then a grateful one. Ten minutes later he was driving her through Beverly Hills, chatting amiably about a lawyer's lot in life: hard work, great financial rewards, but no free time. No matter where he went to relax—Ojai, Santa Barbara, the wine country—he was never without a satchel of work. He had lost more girl friends because of success than anything else.

Judith smiled and said little. On walking into his apartment, she marveled gratefully. It was spacious, full of expensive high-tech furniture and electronic gimmickry: stereo systems, projection TV, videotape decks, a computer, and a word processor. Impressive. Grodman made light of his toys but couldn't hide his enjoyment at being able to show them off. He led her into the spare bedroom and deposited her suitcase on a dresser. She looked at him expectantly. He wasn't quite sure what to do next—return to work or stay awhile to see that she was comfortable.

She smiled and sat demurely on the bed. He stood with his back to the window and dispensed advice, for want of any better line of gab, telling her she should stay away from Mizzell for a while, get her head straight about her feelings for him, and maybe in a day or so they could talk out what to do next . . .

She stared at him, and her smile slowly faded. He stopped talking, feeling heat well up from his loins. God, she was sending signals, right from her eyes. Sex flashed across the room at him, and he knew for an absolute certainty that they were going to make it.

Even before she slipped out of her sweater.

He stared at her breasts with their erect pink nipples and felt desire surge through his body. He wanted to fling himself across the empty space between them, but somehow he managed to make the move gracefully, with aplomb. He lost it as soon as she grabbed him.

He left her in the afternoon. They had made love twice, both times with equal vigor and delight, his delight. She had come on like a voracious animal, and Grodman realized that Paul Mizzell had good reason to be upset at her departure. Tough luck, Mizzell, Grodman chuckled to himself. He'd gotten even for this morning. Chalk that up as a first installment on the case. It wouldn't bother him in the least if he marched Mizzell through the legal process and all he got for payment was a steady balling from the girl friend. But he wondered why she was so cooperative. She wasn't doing this to help Paul. That's *my* fantasy, Grodman smirked. Is she loose? Crazy for sex? Trying to get back at Paul? The more Isaac Grodman thought about it, the more he questioned what was happening.

Why bother? he decided. Gift horse; don't look for the teeth or you'll get bitten. He decided to enjoy his good fortune. She was the perfect lover—all sex, no conversation. A man couldn't ask for more. He must remember to thank Linda for getting him involved. He tromped on the accelerator and laughed out loud as he flew down the freeway.

Judith sat in the dark, ignoring the lawyer's expensive toys, her frolic with him already forgotten. She never dwelled on those things. They just happened. Besides, she needed him. What she thought of him didn't matter, so she hardly thought of him at all. He was a convenient port in the storm, a respite from Paul— that's how she rationalized it. But she would have to get back with Paul soon. Where would he be now? She tried the house but there was no answer. She called his number at work. No answer there, either.

Okay. He took off. Where would he go? To Linda? No. Not during the day. Linda would be at work. She began to worry. What if her leaving had really upset him? What if he became totally unpredictable?

That would be bad. The worst.

What is he really capable of? That's something she hadn't considered yet.

If he was going berserk, what would he do next?

Linda. Wouldn't he make a try at Linda?

Linda sat alone in the darkest corner of the restaurant, relaxing under the air conditioning and the gentle mood music, nursing a bourbon and soda. She thought about nothing but the drink for a half hour, then began pulling herself together, contemplating what to do. First, she ought to return to her office: she was behind in paperwork, and if she went home, she might only keep drinking.

When they put the food down in front of her, she was surprised at having ordered such a big meal. Absently, she worked at the crab salad and nibbled a roll. The food stuck in her throat when she realized that Paul might have already done his worst. Suppose that tomorrow morning they find Judith all carved up like a Christmas turkey?

You can't stop him now: you don't know where he is.

That's no excuse. Can't you do something?

Isaac—call Isaac. Warn him that Paul might go after Judith. Or you.

She got up and made her way to a phone in the front of the restaurant. She had to call information for Grodman's home number, then wrote it down in her book. His answering machine picked up the call. She left word that she could be reached at her office until 9 P.M., or later at home, then she hung up.

On the way back to Rok, she considered calling the police, but the prospect of spending the evening answering a lot of unpleasant questions made her anxious again. She went back through the main entrance, using her key. She didn't like being alone in the building at night. There was no security guard anymore—another of Tony Benedict's economy moves. And the antiquated alarm system did not make her feel any safer.

The bottom floor was deserted. As she waited for the elevator, which seemed to be hung up on another floor, she had a growing feeling that she was being watched, that eyes were boring into her back. . . .

She turned and stared down the hall toward the rear exit. It was dark. The light that was supposed to be on at the far end was not. She continued gazing into the gloom until she was sure no one was there, then she looked back the other way, through the glass doors and into the executive corridor. The overhead lights were on but no others, and no sign of anyone. . . .

Nerves. Must be nerves.

The elevator arrived. She stepped in and went up to her floor.

Linda's footsteps echoed hollowly as she strode down the well-lit hall. She unlocked the door to the art department and stood in a cone of light, looking at the deserted cubicles. She thought about how lifeless this place was at night, like an animal in hibernation. Silent, dark, still smelling of people, ink, paint, and stale smoke. She glanced at the row of record jackets tacked along one wall. Some of those covers weren't more than three months old, yet they were already warped and faded, looking as though they had been there for years.

They fit in with everything else that's old—including you.

She entered her office, leaving the outer door open so she could see light in the hallway. She sat down at her desk and attacked a stack of papers, pushing from her mind everything not connected with Rok Records. She worked with a single-minded concentration: initialing bills, answering memos, approving requisitions. After an hour of silence, broken only by the scratch of her pen, the pile had shrunk by more than half. She was pleased with how much she'd accomplished. This was tedious work but so much easier than the creative infighting that had been her daily routine for months. . . . She opened another folder.

There was a far-off swish and metal clang. Linda stiffened and listened. Something was rolling down the corridor outside. Something heavy. She rose from her desk and walked cautiously down the aisle, glancing into the dark cubicles, then she stopped at the hall door. Peering out, she saw what was making the noise.

The old man shuffled behind his barrel, a large metal drum on rollers. He pushed it along the hallway with the broom handle sticking out of it, resting against his left shoulder.

Relieved, Linda called out, "Hey, Bill!"

The janitor brightened and stopped pushing. "Mrs. Sharman, long time no see. Working late?"

"Uh-huh."

"Well, don't let me interrupt."

"It's okay. How's your family?"

"Fine. My daughter, she's almost out of college. They sure grow fast."

Linda smiled. Bill was the only person other than Rocky and herself who had been here from the beginning. His daughter was the same age as Jennifer, and he was putting her through school with Rocky's help.

"Is it okay if I turn off the hall lights? I've got orders—conserve electricity. I can leave on this one light here by the elevator, though. Do you mind?"

"No. Go right ahead."

Whistling one of Rocky's early songs—the only tune he considered memorable in sixteen years with Rok—Bill took out a large ring of keys and inserted one into a wall socket. He turned it and the lights went out down the hall, plunging the corridor into shadowy darkness. Only the one by the freight elevator remained on.

Bill returned to his barrel, smiling and waving the keys. "Simple, huh?" he said, stripping off his jacket and placing it on the rim of the barrel. "How long you gonna be working, Mrs Sharman?" he asked, pulling down the sleeves of his sweatshirt

"About an hour. You want to get in here?"

"Later," he said, selecting a large plastic bag from the side of the barrel. "You go back to work—I got plenty to keep me busy."

Linda stood in the doorway and watched him push the button for the freight elevator. The doors clanged back and he stepped inside, waving at her, then waving the bag. She heard the whoosh as he was carried down a floor. He had left the barrel sitting in the hallway. She looked at it and smiled. The plastic bag was a habit—a cover. He was taking a break, and he didn't want her to think he was goofing off. She turned and went back to her office, musing on the fears of the common man, terrified he might lose it all just for being human. Of course that's not you, she thought grimly. Even so, she was glad for his company.

Ten minutes later, she wasn't so sure. The music burst out in a garbled roar, a driving beat pounding down the hall, echoing off the bare walls. Her brow furrowed and she listened a moment.

Beatles. "Got to Get You Into My Life."

Now, why would Bill play it that loud? Annoyed, she dropped the production folder, scattering proofs on her desk.

She stepped into the darkened hallway. Bill's cart was right where he'd left it. The corridor was still dark. She tried to fix where the sound was coming from and guessed the studio. She sighed and trudged down the hall, sorry to have to spoil his fun. She glanced at the barrel as she passed and wondered if it really was Bill playing the music. He didn't like that sixties stuff. She remembered him complaining all through those years. . . . Maybe it was a clock radio on automatic alarm. . . .

She pushed the door open and stepped in. The entry was dark. She shouted his name over the deafening music. "Bill! Bill!"

There was a backdrop in her way. She edged around it and pushed the black curtains aside, surprised to find a light on—a baby spot rigged over a large easel in the center of the room, facing away from her. At the base, leaning against one of the legs, was an album jacket. She glanced at it while crossing to the music system at the back of the room. She lifted the tone arm and the music stopped. She switched it off and moved back to the easel, staring at the album cover, feeling something start to churn inside. The Beatles. *Revolver*. She stood looking down at it, trying not to think about who might have put it there, who might have put the music on, and why. . . .

In the silence, she sensed another presence. Not Bill the janitor. Not anything human.

Her eyes rose up the easel and she moved around to see what the spot was illuminating. It was a photograph, drymounted on gray cardboard. She froze, remembering the day it was taken, the day the model failed to show up. She remembered C. L. Clarke sending over the sixteen-by-twenty blowup that Jimmy Otner had insisted be displayed here in the studio. But she didn't remember it looking like this, with slash marks crisscrossing the breasts—her breasts—and farther below, punctures mutilating the belly and crotch, the photo ripped from its backing. She'd seen the knife before, seen it in her dreams ever since Buddy Dyal admitted the truth about Paul Mizzell. Vividly, she'd seen it where Paul had left it, buried up to the hilt between Lori Cornell's legs, just as someone had left it here, buried up to the hilt in the photograph, in what was left of Linda's crotch.

Linda staggered back, shock giving way to a strangled scream. Blindly she whirled and ran for the door—and collided with Brian Hawthorn.

CHAPTER 13

She crashed into the backdrop and screamed again. Brian moved toward her and she shrank against the wall, deeper into the shadows, all her suspicions of him abruptly, vitally alive.

"What's wrong?" he said, startled.

For a moment, she couldn't speak. She stood rigidly in front of him. "What are you *doing* here?" she demanded finally.

"I—I came to see you—"

"Why?"

"You were upset when I called—"

She didn't let him finish. Grabbing his hand, she pulled him across the studio to the easel, jerked him around, thrust his head against the picture and made him look. His eyes went wide.

"To do this? Is that what you mean? To sneak in here and scare the hell out of me? Why?"

He stood still and took it all in, the vicious slash marks and the knife embedded in the cardboard. Only the blood was missing. His gaze narrowed. "Is that you?" he croaked.

"You know it is, you lying son of a bitch!"

He turned. She was circling away from him, keeping her distance.

"Linda, you don't believe—"

"Don't I! Why waste time, Brian? Why don't you just take the knife out and kill me? Here—" She moved quickly to the easel and reached for the knife.

"Don't touch it!"

She looked at him, expecting the maniac's glint to spring into his eyes. Nothing happened, except for the strong grip of his fingers on her wrist, gently forcing her hand down.

"The police," he said. "Don't touch anything. The police have to see this."

"Oh, what an act," she mumbled. "How did you get in the building?"

"The janitor. I showed him my press card."

"Bull—" Her voice broke and she felt the tears start. "Brian . . . Brian, please . . . If you're going to do it, go ahead. I don't want to be tortured anymore."

"Linda, for God's sake—!" He grabbed her and pulled her close. No anger, no hatred, nothing but compassion. She saw it finally and fell into his arms. He held her close and murmured in her hair, "You've got the wrong guy. I'm not out to hurt you."

She pulled back, still holding onto him, and looked into his eyes. "You knew about Paul from the start. You could have sent him those things, planted the Beatles tape at the Main Street session, killed Dahlke—Who else had access to his past—?"

"Linda—"

"You've been talking to Bass. You've followed every move . . ."

"Linda, why would I do this?"

"You're a journalist, and you're trying to create the best story of your career! And this picture is supposed to be a warning to me." She stopped and waited for his denial.

He sat on the edge of a table. "You really believe that?"

"I don't know. Prove me wrong."

"Look at the photograph."

She couldn't look at it again. Instead, she watched him.

"Come on, Linda. You know who it is. You're trying to lay it on someone else because you can't admit you were wrong about him in the first place. You still believe him. And *he's* the one with the murder record."

"Paul," she said hollowly.

"Gary Michael Steen."

She closed her mouth and frowned. Brian got up and hooked an arm through hers. She let him walk her back to the art department and make coffee, which she sipped gratefully. He leaned on the edge of her desk and regarded her silently.

"Two personalities," he said finally. "Steen and Mizzell, living in the same body, the product of Gene Dahlke's progressive therapy. Submerge one personality; replace it with another. Only he didn't realize the first one would come back.''

Linda took a deep breath. ''I think I heard the other one on the phone this afternoon. He called me.''

''From where?''

''I don't know. He was upset because I told his girl friend all about Gary Steen. 'She's gone,' he said. I don't know if that means she's gone left him or gone dead.'' Linda looked into her coffee and tried to recall the conversation. ''He blamed me,'' she went on. ''He said I'm not his friend anymore. I guess he must have slipped in here while I was out to dinner.'' She sat up abruptly. ''He could still be in the building.''

Brian thought about that then offered to go take a look.

''Don't,'' she said quickly, touching his hand.

He smiled. ''He's not still here, anyway. Like you said, that was done to scare you. If he'd meant to kill, you'd be dead now.''

''Then why warn me? He didn't warn Dahlke.''

Brian sighed. ''Listen, he's off his cork; there are no rational explanations for his behavior. He's capable of anything. Now—'' He picked up the phone and placed it in front of her. ''Call the police.''

Linda stared at the phone.

Brian caught her hesitation and moved closer, leaning over the desk and resting his weight on his arms. ''Isn't it strange, Linda? A nut is on the loose because there isn't a shred of real evidence to hold him. He has to be caught in the act of killing somebody— literally caught in the act! You know, you almost had me convinced he could be innocent. I was ready to let some other genius dredge up all that shit from thirteen years ago. Because *you* wanted to believe it, and I wanted to stay on your good side, I compromised *my* principles.'' He picked up the receiver and placed it in her hand. ''Call the police. And don't be afraid to slant your story. Your aim is to get him off the street.'' He went to the door.

''Where are you going?'' she asked, controlling a surge of panic.

''Down to my car to get a camera. I want a picture of that photo for the story I'm going to write.'' He called back as he went up the aisle, ''Tell the police about the girl friend!'' He stepped through the cone of light at the door and disappeared.

Linda held the phone and heard distantly the irregular beep of a disrupted dial tone. She pressed ''O'' and asked the operator to get the police. She waited for the connection, bitterly realizing Brian was right.

A voice came on the line. She started to introduce herself then realized she was talking to a recording. ''You have reached the Los Angeles Police Department, Hollywood Division. Please stay on the line. An officer will be with you in a moment.'' Her anxiety subsided. She waited. The recording repeated. She was growing disgusted when she heard a distant clang.

The freight elevator?

She stood up. ''You have reached the Los Angeles . . .'' Her hand shook as she lowered the receiver.

Goddamn you, Brian. You were wrong. It's Paul. He's still in the building. And I'm up here alone. . . .

The creak of something rolling across the linoleum, something heavy. The trash cart? The janitor, Bill, coming back to do her department?

Or Paul Mizzell. He's going to carry me away in it.

''You have reached the Los Angeles Police . . .'' She held the phone and waited.

I'm safe. I couldn't be safer. I'm on the phone to the police. On hold, idiot. . . .

The cart creaked under the cone of light, and the figure of a man stepped through. . . .

''Mrs. Sharman?''

He hit the wall switch. The whole department was instantly flooded with light.

Bill looked into Linda's office and waved. ''Okay if I come in now?''

''You have reached the Los Angeles—''

She plunged the phone down, cutting off the voice. Her hand went to her mouth. Ashamed of her fear, she nodded wildly and sat down, turning away from him.

''You okay, Mrs. Sharman?''

Yes, I'm fine. Please don't come over here. Just let me be.

"Did I scare you?" he called. "I'm sorry. Want me to come back later?"

"No!" she managed to blurt out. "No, please stay. It's all right. I get a little scared in the dark."

"Well, there's plenty of lights on now," he said. She heard the rattle of his long broom and turned to watch him chase the dust and scraps on the floor.

"That reporter find you okay?"

"Who? Oh, Brian . . . Yes, he's . . ." Her eyes settled on Bill.

And she leaped to her feet.

"Where did you get that?!"

Startled, Bill froze with both hands wrapped around the broom. Linda stumbled out of her office and came up to him. His eyes darted guiltily. "Get what?" he croaked. She pointed to the pink sweat shirt with UCLA spelled out across his chest. He plucked at it nervously. "This?" he said. "Uh . . . my kid got it for me."

"Your kid goes to Stanford, Bill."

"Look, Mrs. Sharman, I don't take things. Please—"

"Bill!"

Hurt, he looked away. "It was in one of the wastebaskets."

"Show me which one!"

Bill led her up the aisle, grumbling that he should have left it where he found it. He paused at the entrance to Paul Mizzell's cubicle and pointed. "In there. It was in a manila envelope." Linda stepped in and stared at the basket.

So Paul did find a sweat shirt.

"People around here don't usually throw out things they want," Bill said lamely. "Look, I'll give it back—"

"Did you get through to the police?"

They turned to see Brian standing behind them holding a camera. Bill's eyes went wide and he glanced from one to the other fearfully. Linda grabbed his arm and showed Brian the sweat shirt.

"Remember this?" she said. Brian looked blank. "The sweat shirt that Paul said was planted in our prop bin to scare him! He said he threw it out because he was upset—and I didn't believe him! But Bill fished it out of his trash. Now what does it mean to you?''

Brian shrugged.

"Paul was telling me the truth. Somebody *was* sending him things."

"Maybe he sent it to himself."

"Why? He'd have to be crazy—"

Brian nodded smugly. Linda's certainty faded.

How convenient! He's crazy; that explains everything.

Brian clapped Bill on the shoulder. "Thanks for letting me in, sport. You can go back to work and forget I was here, okay? Keep the sweat shirt: it looks great."

Bill glanced at him uncertainly.

Brian motioned to Linda. "Get your bag."

With a sigh, she returned to her office and closed up, retrieving her handbag from the back of her chair.

He's right. You're still clinging to this notion that Paul is innocent. Why?

On the way down the elevator, Brian guessed what she was thinking. "Two personalities," he said. "One wants to exploit the other's guilt, so he sends himself little reminders. It's classic."

"You're not a psychiatrist.

"I got that from Hugo Bass."

When they got to the ground floor, Linda started for the back exit to the parking lot. Brian grabbed her arm and pulled her toward the front. "What are you doing?" she demanded.

"You're going with me." He hit the locking bar on the front door and shoved it open, pulling her through and letting it slam shut behind them. She stopped and twisted free of his grip.

"I'm going home," she said.

"No. Not with Mizzell the Knife on the loose. It's not safe. And you're rattled anyway. You shouldn't drive. Come on." He started up the street. She stayed where she was. He came back and cupped her face in his hands. "Still afraid of me?"

"No."

"Then come on. I'll bring you back early in the morning."

She let him lead her to his car. He put his camera in the trunk, then opened the passenger door. She had to wait while he attacked the clutter piled on the seat. He threw some of it in the back, but the rest—food wrappers, soft drink cans, brown paper bags—he scooped out and dumped into the gutter.

"If I'd known I was having company," he muttered sheepishly, "I'd have had the car—"

"Fumigated," she finished. "Honest to God, Brian, I'd rather take the bus."

"It'll be fine. There." He stepped back with a flourish, then helped her in.

Linda sat quietly with one leg tucked under the other while Brian followed the cruisers on Sunset Boulevard. When he crossed into Beverly Hills, she frowned and said, "I thought you lived in Hollywood."

"I do."

"Aren't we going the wrong way?"

"I have an appointment. You mind?"

"Won't I be in the way?"

"No—Oh, Christ!" He slowed the car. "The police. We should have stayed."

Linda stared at him then swore. "Damn, Brian. I never got through to them. I got a recording, then Bill came in and I—"

"Shit." Brian's lips drew back over his teeth.

"Well, I *am* sorry—"

"It's not you. Guess who ran down to his car for a camera then forgot to take a picture?"

She burst out laughing. He burned for a moment then laughed with her.

"Promise you won't tell my editor?"

Linda stuck out her hand and they shook on it.

"What is this mysterious appointment?" she asked.

"Something Bass arranged for me. Has to do with the Mizzell story."

"Couldn't we skip it? I'm not in the mood."

"I think you'll find it interesting. Stimulating," he added with a private chuckle.

Linda rolled down her window and closed her eyes, letting the cool night air flow over her. "Why is Bass helping you?" she asked.

"Wants to avoid some of the mud settling on him."

"You're blackmailing him?"

"Please! I trade in facts. If people are afraid of the truth, they either clam up or sing like birds. Dr. Bass is hitting high C."

"Isn't it unethical for him to talk about a patient?"

Brian snorted. "His former associate, the eminent Gene Dahlke, sort of threw that out the window when he played you his tapes. Besides, Gary Steen—Paul Mizzell—was a state case. His treatment is public record. Bass couldn't hide anything if he wanted to. So, he'd rather have everything out in the open, or at least selected things that tend to exonerate *him*. And he's a little scared. Did you know what Mizzell—excuse me—what the killer did to Dahlke?"

Linda shrugged. "Other than stabbing him to death?"

"Yeah."

"No, what?"

"Tried to make a woman out of him. Instant sex change. Cut off his thing, turned it around, stuck it in the other way—"

"Stop." A wave of nausea churned in Linda's stomach. She gulped air and fought it down. "Oh, God," she said. "Paul wouldn't do that."

"Oh, wouldn't he?" Brian shook his head. "Did you know that he's been to a sex clinic?"

"A what?"

"Sex clinic. S-E-X. Dahlke sent him there."

"He did? Why?"

"After only six years of having Paul under observation, Dahlke convinced a medical board that Paul no longer had any violent tendencies. They had all been treated out of him. The neuroses released by the drug he took were all gone. How did Dahlke accomplish this? By turning him into a sexual neuter, a zippo in bed. Took away his drive. Well, that worked great in the hospital. There were no girls around, anyway. Stick a little saltpeter in his food and his libido is reduced to a whimper. But then he gets out on the street and goes to work as an artist, and suddenly there are women all around him. He works with women; he's bombarded with sex on TV and in movies and ads like all the rest of us. Back comes the drive, the need, the hunger. But the minute he gets near a woman, he wilts. Even if Mizzell had pinned hundred dollar bills to his shirt, he couldn't get laid. And he was frustrated."

"I can imagine."

"So could Bass. When he found out, he wanted to prescribe suppressants. Dahlke wanted to play God and give Paul back his sex life. But he couldn't do it at Camarillo, so—"

"So he sent Paul to this sex clinic."

"Right." Brian shot through a red light and over the San Diego Freeway into Brentwood. Linda saw her street coming up and wondered if he'd changed his mind and was taking her home. But he went past Barrington and kept talking. "Ever hear the name Klaus Von Lochen?"

Linda shook her head.

"The classic American success story. See a need and fill it. He started in Woodside, south of San Francisco, serving the jaded folks in the Bay Area, only his name wasn't Von Lochen then. He ran into a little trouble with the police and suddenly realized Southern California was much more fertile territory. He disappeared from there and popped up here. Has a hell of a clientele, but nobody will talk about him. Got a mania for secrecy—worse than the government."

"Is that who you're going to see?" Linda asked.

Brian nodded. "Bass set it up for me. Dahlke was very thick with Von Lochen, and Bass still has some clout, enough to convince the sex doctor that it might be smart to say a few words to a dumbshit reporter from the *Times* who only wants to be fair. . . . I'm probably the first newsman he's ever talked to. It's a journalistic breakthrough." He laughed.

Linda eyed him curiously. "What's so funny?"

"That's the name of the clinic—Breakthrough."

The unmarked entrance was set back off Old Topanga Road. Brian pulled up to a massive wrought-iron gate and looked into a security TV camera. A disembodied voice asked his name. He gave it. There was a long wait, then the gate swung open silently. Brian drove through, winding up a tree-flanked dirt road that curved gently with the contour of the land. They came around a bend, and in the distance Linda saw a sprawling U-shaped ranch house sitting in a cleared meadow. Behind it, dark hills rose dramatically, accentuating the isolation.

Brian crept into a parking area and got out. Linda opened her door and hesitated. There were a few cars nearby, and a large

motor home. Up close, the house seemed huge, with the front
porch stretching almost a hundred feet. The walls were white
textured plaster with dark green trim. Garden floodlights were
strategically planted to light up ghostly trees. Brian helped her
out, gesturing at the land around them. "Any idea what this
spread is worth?"

"No. Look, I'll probably get in your way. Why don't I just sit
in the car?"

He slammed the door and locked it. "Wouldn't hear of it," he
said, taking her arm and leading her toward the house. "Might
interest you to know that when Von Lochen bought all this, he
paid cash."

"How thrilling."

Klaus Von Lochen was waiting for them at the reception desk:
a big balding man with the start of a paunch, and a neatly
trimmed gray beard framing a thick tanned face. He had a
doctor's hands—large, manicured, and scrubbed clean. Linda
thought he was a bit Buddha-like with his serene great-white-
father manner. He shook hands and regarded them with a soft,
enigmatic smile, making no comment about the lateness of the
hour. Then he invited them into his office. As she passed, Linda
felt his eyes undressing her.

His office was spacious with a large picture window that faced
the main frontage, two Persian rugs on a glossy parquet floor,
thick oak paneling on the walls, and soft, comfortable furniture
everywhere. His blue eyes watched warily as they took seats
before his glass-topped desk. Von Lochen sat down, hiking up
his trouser legs and clasping his hands over his stomach, confirm-
ing Linda's impression of Oriental serenity.

He offered them drinks. Brian asked for coffee. Linda declined, though she was very thirsty. Von Lochen pressed an
intercom button and ordered a coffee, a large bottle of Perrier, and
two glasses. He smiled deliberately at Linda, as if to say he knew
what was best for her and he would see that she got it.

"So, Mr. Hawthorn, Dr. Bass wants me to cooperate with
you," Von Lochen said with a slight German accent. "Of course,
you understand, our clients require the utmost discretion, and I
can only respond to questions of a general nature."

"Oh, sure," Brian said, looking around the walls. Then he added bluntly, "So this is a sex clinic. How come I don't hear the sounds of an orgy?"

Von Lochen chuckled. "Orgies are not necessarily noisy, Mr. Hawthorn. But nothing like that goes on here. Our purpose is to cure sexual problems, not indulge them."

Brian's pencil moved. "What problems?"

A male attendant dressed like a hospital orderly knocked and came in with the drinks. Brian took the coffee. Von Lochen poured two Perriers and held one out to Linda. She took it without comment. As soon as the attendant left and Brian was done emptying the sugar bowl into his coffee, Von Lochen resumed in a quiet, serious tone.

"You were asking what sort of problems we handle, Mr. Hawthorn. We treat sexual dysfunctions: premature ejaculation, frigidity, impotence, fear of intercourse—"

"You mean, if for some reason I couldn't make it with my wife or girl friend or—let's say, Linda here—then you could fix that?"

Von Lochen nodded, his eyes going curiously to Linda. She looked deep into her Perrier, her ears burning.

"Depending on the nature of the problem," Von Lochen added, "which, of course, would have to be diagnosed by a licensed professional. Then you could be referred to us for treatment or come here voluntarily. But you would have to be aware of the cause of your condition."

"Well, let's say I'm real shy. I'm so shy I just go limp when I get near Linda, and it's frustrating me."

Von Lochen stroked his beard. "We would want to work with both partners," he said. "That's the ideal arrangement. Failing that, we would prescribe a surrogate."

"A what?"

"Surrogate. A partner from our staff."

"Really?"

"That shouldn't surprise you, Mr. Hawthorn. It's not a novel approach. In fact, with clinics like ours, it's getting to be common practice."

"Yes, but I can go down to Hollywood Boulevard and get

that.'' He watched Von Lochen stiffen. ''I don't mean to be crude, but how does Breakthrough differ?''

''Our personnel are highly trained professionals. They are interested in your emotional well-being. It is not their job to make you momentarily happy, but to give you a long-lasting sense of sexual worth.''

Brian scribbled, mouthing Von Lochen's last speech. ''Very good, Doctor. That's helpful.''

''I hope so.''

''In other words, I could lose all my shyness just by popping off with one of your surrogates.''

''There are limitations, Mr. Hawthorn.''

''Oh?''

''While we can have great success in treating the actual dysfunction, we are not equipped to deal with the source of it. In other words, if you're shy with women, we can remove that shyness from your bedroom technique but not from your ability to meet and seduce. We don't run a how-to-pick-up-girls school.''

Brian looked disappointed. ''You mean, when I'd step up to the bar to try and introduce myself to some girl, I'd still be tongue-tied?'' Von Lochen nodded. ''But if I could get her into bed, I'd be fantastic! Right?''

''More or less.'' Von Lochen sighed.

''Well, that takes care of me, but what can you offer Linda here?''

Von Lochen smiled. ''We have male surrogates too.''

''I'll be damned,'' said Brian.

''Surely you don't believe that sexual problems are endemic to one gender only,'' Von Lochen said thickly. ''It may interest you to know that we also work with homosexuals and lesbians.''

''Let's get back to shy single guy. What does he do when he leaves here? Go out and find an aggressive single girl?''

''We deal with that on an individual basis.''

''You do, huh?'' Brian tapped the pencil and looked amiably at Von Lochen, then said, ''Dr. Bass was of the opinion that you might answer a few specific questions.''

Von Lochen shook his head. ''If you're going to inquire about my clients, the answer is no.''

''Not clients, Doctor. Just one. Paul Mizzell.''

Von Lochen displayed no reaction. His swivel chair squeaked slightly as he rocked in it.

"You know the name?"

Von Lochen said nothing.

"Okay, how about Herb Schransky?"

He looked up sharply.

Brian flipped pages in his little notebook. Linda stared at him. *Who the hell was—?*

"Herb Schransky," Brian repeated, clearing his throat. "Of Akron, Ohio. A straight-arrow CPA until 1965, when he turned in his calculator for beads, beard, and sandals, leaving his wife and striking out for points west. Resided in San Francisco's Haight-Ashbury district in 1968. But the little love children he was guruing turned to drugs and the scene got ugly, so he split. Floated around a while, then dropped from sight. Resurfaced with a new name, new image, new profession. Sex doctor Michael Sage. Great name. Put together a big farmhouse clinic in the Bay Area and raked in dough for years, siphoning it off to various dummy corporations. Suddenly, problems with the law, and Dr. Sage split again. Enter Klaus Von Lochen, rumored to be the last surviving son of an Austrian duke, but in reality plain old Herb Schransky from Akron, Ohio, loving but long-missing husband of the ever-suffering Milla Schransky, still of Akron, Ohio. She sure would like to know where the fuck you are, Herb."

Linda sat still. The Perrier had gone warm in her hand. She watched Von Lochen's face drain of color and his hands go slack on his belly.

"I think you'd better leave."

Brian shook his notes. "If I leave, I print this."

"What do you want?"

"Ever swap baseball cards, Doc?"

"What?"

"A simple trade. My interest is Mizzell. I'll forget about Herb Schransky and Michael Sage and only raise what I feel are legitimate questions about Mizzell's involvement with Breakthrough—if you cooperate."

Von Lochen's stomach swelled. He let air out through pursed lips.

"Don't take too long deciding, Herb. I'm sure Mrs. Schransky and her attorney could find a use for all this land."

"You've made your point!" Von Lochen barked venomously. "How do I know you'll keep your word?"

"I've never broken it yet."

Von Lochen snorted, then spread his hands helplessly. He even managed a smile. "Once a Schransky, always a Schransky," he said without a trace of the German accent.

Brian gave him a patronizing chuckle.

"I think . . ." Von Lochen got serious again, as if this had suddenly acquired great importance. "I think you should speak with Paul Mizzell's surrogate."

CHAPTER 14

Von Lochen led them down a long corridor to a small room in the back. He opened the door and stood aside. Linda looked in and hesitated. There was a large bed, a low bench, a single straight-back chair, a music system on a built-in shelf, and a small adjoining bathroom. The single window was heavily curtained. Von Lochen asked them to wait, then disappeared back up the hall, leaving them alone.

Linda stared at the bed before sitting on it. "Do I have to stick around?" she asked.

"I think you should."

They heard footsteps coming down the hall. A woman paused at the door and looked in at them. She was tall, shapely, in her early thirties, dressed in jeans and a light sweater. Her hair was short, black, and styleless. "I'm Norma," she said.

Brian made the introductions. Linda shook hands with Norma and noticed she had large, heavy hands with stubby fingers. Norma took the chair and sat with her legs straight out, knees apart. She lit a cigarette with a silver lighter, inhaled deeply, and blew the smoke over her shoulder. She wore no bra and had large, pendulous breasts, which she hid with hunched shoulders. Her eyes seemed as heavy as her hands, dark pools that hid her thoughts and feelings.

Brian sat on the edge of the bed and took out his pad and the pencil he had borrowed from Von Lochen.

Linda sat against the headboard and tucked up her legs.

"Norma," said Brian, "how long have you worked here?"

"Four years."

"Like it?"

She nodded. "I get a salary, living quarters, bonuses—"

"Commissions?"

"No. Satisfaction."

Brian smiled back. Linda caught Norma's eyes roaming to her legs, just like Von Lochen. Was everybody up here leg-happy?

"How are you qualified for your work?" Brian asked.

"I've been trained."

"By Von Lochen?"

"Yes, and others."

"You've been to bed with Von Lochen?"

"Yes."

"Is that required of all the surrogates?"

"Where else can we go to learn our work—Caltech?"

"Does Von Lochen train the male surrogates too?"

"Ask him." She paused. "I was told you'd want to know about Paul Mizzell."

"You were his surrogate."

"Yes."

"Okay, tell me about him."

Norma shifted in her chair and looked hard at Linda. "Are you Mizzell's wife?"

Linda stiffened in surprise. She gave Norma a firm, drawn-out "No."

Norma flicked ashes into a tray in her hand and smiled to herself. "That was three years ago," she said. "He was a nice-enough guy. Quiet, anxious, couldn't get an erection. I fixed that." She looked at them both, inviting contradiction, projecting pride.

"How?" said Brian.

Norma chuckled. "You want a demonstration?"

"He must have made quite an impression for you to remember him so well."

"He was here a lot."

Brian nodded. "So Von Lochen taught you such great technique that you were able to get Mizzell aroused again? Come on, Norma, any woman worth her salt is capable of that. Just what did you do to him that could be called scientific treatment?"

"Sex is treatment. The more you do it, the better you get. If you don't do it, you're hung up. Then you can't do it. Start doing it again, and pretty soon the problem disappears."

"I see," said Brian. "Medicine triumphs again."

Linda got up to walk around and was conscious of Norma's eyes following her everywhere. Her skin crawled.

"So you had it easy with Mizzell," Brian said.

"Not exactly. I had to spend a lot of time with him, talking—he didn't like to talk—and touching."

"How did you go about that?"

"We did it in stages, getting partially undressed at first, then more at each session. When he was comfortable with nudity, we'd do more intense touching. We'd take showers, soap each other, explore. I gave him confidence. Then, when *he* was ready, we really got into it."

"Was Gene Dahlke around for any of those sessions?"

"No. He checked the tapes once every few weeks."

"Tapes?"

Norma pointed to the air duct behind her.

Brian got up and went over to it. There was a video camera behind the grill. "Wow," he said. "Instant porn."

"Strictly in-house and for only one purpose," Norma replied.

"Yeah. Staff smokers. You all sit around and get your jollies watching each other's *technique*. Is that it?"

Norma looked at the ceiling and shook her head. "Klaus said you were an asshole. What an understatement."

Linda interrupted. "Do you play music?" She was standing by the cassette deck. She had been going through the tapes while they were talking, and she had found something. "Do you play music?" she repeated. "I mean, when you're with a *patient*."

"Sometimes," Norma replied. "If they request it. Or if I think they need it."

"Did you play music for Paul?"

"A few times."

Linda felt the eyes on her legs again and turned quickly, catching her. Norma glanced away and Linda suddenly remembered where she'd seen that look before—at work, in the art department, constantly from Tisa, the lesbian. She turned back to the tapes and pulled one out, showing it to Norma. It was the Beatles' *Revolver*.

"Did you ever play this for Paul?"

Brian frowned.

Norma stared at it, then looked at Linda, puzzled. "Once," she said. "He freaked."

"What do you mean?"

"He went wild. Ranting, raving, pleading with me to turn it off. He went into that corner over there and couldn't move. I said if he didn't like it, he was welcome to turn it off himself. He said he couldn't touch it. So I did."

Linda's gaze met Brian's. He turned back to Norma.

"Did you ever get it on with Gene Dahlke?"

"What kind of question is that?"

"A straightforward one, like the answer you're going to give me. Did you fuck Gene Dahlke?"

Norma hesitated. Linda had had enough. She said, "I'll wait for you outside," and walked out, turning back at the door. "Maybe you'll get lucky, Brian, and she'll demonstrate her technique for you."

"Maybe you're the one who needs help," Norma shot back.

Brian finally emerged twenty minutes later, coming out of the house with Von Lochen and a burly attendant. Leaning against the car, Linda watched Brian turn to say good-bye to Von Lochen, then cross the parking lot.

"I don't see any bruises," she said. "Did you sample Norma's work?"

"For Chrissake, she's a dyke." He unlocked the car and let her in.

"Oh, you noticed."

"Real man hater. I don't know how she does it."

"I do."

He got behind the wheel, stuck the key in the ignition, and turned to her. "Okay. I'm listening."

"Easy. She's a switch-hitter, paid to make love—"

"To have *intercourse*. There's a distinction. I know because I asked."

"All right, to have intercourse, but obviously with as many females as males, and under controlled conditions. She doesn't have to get involved with anyone. There are no strings, no heartbreaks, no nasty scenes, and she doesn't have to cruise to get what she wants. And if she has to take on an occasional male, that's all right, too, because it's on her terms. She dominates every sexual contact."

Brian smiled. "Very good, Sherlock."

"And Paul Mizzell did *not* slash that picture tonight," she said firmly. "Because whoever did it put on a Beatles record, and Paul Mizzell freaks when he hears the Beatles!"

"Does Gary Steen?"

"Oh, Christ, Brian!"

"Oh, Christ, Linda." He started the car, backed up, and drove slowly down the road to the gate, which opened as if by magic as he approached.

"You're really stubborn," Linda said.

"So are you."

"I hope you got what you wanted up here."

"Tip of the iceberg. I'll have a talk with Bass tomorrow. He's coming down to the paper. Von Lochen is really running nothing more than a glorified whorehouse. Can you imagine Norma on a witness stand, trying to sound clinical?"

"Did she help Paul or didn't she?"

"I doubt it."

"But you don't know. Truth is, Von Lochen accomplishes exactly what he says he does. No more, no less. And I don't think you could show that he damaged Paul."

"You got any idea what Dahlke was doing up here every few weeks?"

"I don't care. I think you're an insensitive bastard and you'd do anything for a story."

Brian glanced at her, surprised, then concentrated on the road. Topanga was dead-dark at night. He thought for a while, then said, "You know, you're probably right. I do step on toes, sometimes the wrong ones. I've done some dumb things in the name of good journalism."

She looked at him without commenting.

"Back in sixty-eight when I covered the Cornell case, maybe I was just too young to know what I was doing. I saw the way the trial was going—the defense pushing for diminished capacity, temporary insanity—and I felt it wasn't right. I felt that the Cornell family was going to be cheated out of justice. I wanted to help. So, in nosing around among Lori Cornell's friends at

UCLA, I found out she was something of a swinger. Before she and Gary Steen moved in together, she'd balled a lot of other guys. Heavily into sex, trying to get all kinds of experience. I got this idea in my head that maybe she should be painted in a different light to a jury—instead of this innocent, harmless little coed with a holy-holy background—that it should be brought out she was sleeping around. And that Gary Steen found out about it and went crazy with jealousy. Good-bye diminished capacity, hello gas chamber. I went to the Cornell family with it, thinking in my boneheaded way that they'd leap at the idea.'' He went silent a moment, remembering.

Linda asked, ''What happened?''

''They pleaded with me not to do anything to smear Lori's name. They were convinced that God would handle everything—except, that is, for one little teenaged cousin. She caught me out at my car, positive I was still going to print that stuff. She offered to sleep with me if I wouldn't.'' He looked at Linda, punctuating with a nod. ''I felt lower than snakeshit.''

''Deservedly.''

''Right. But since then, I've learned how to be insensitive and *not care* what people think.''

''That's redundant.''

''So is life.''

They rode back to the city in silence, with both windows open and cool air blowing around them. Linda thought about Buddy Dyal and what he'd told her about Lori Cornell, about his feeling that she'd learned sex from an expert. Who? Maybe someone like Norma. Thinking of Norma, she felt a hot flush on the back of her neck. Lesbians didn't bother her generally. She had no problem tolerating Tisa, who was sort of timid and pathetic, and whose sexuality never got in the way. But she'd always thought there was something threatening about *aggressive* lesbians. And somehow she knew what Norma would be like with a woman. An animal.

Brian drove straight to his apartment, a two-bedroom corner suite in a boxy complex in West Hollywood. He apologized for the state of it, joking that it should prove that his bachelorhood was total. Linda had to believe him: the only room anywhere near tidy was the hallway. "I don't spend much time in the hallway," he explained.

The living room was cluttered with bookshelves, the curtains threadbare and stained. Two mismatched and badly placed sofas sagged uninvitingly. The coffee table looked as if it had been swiped from a cheap motel. He wouldn't let her get near the kitchen, but through a swinging door she glimpsed stacks of dirty dishes and newspapers amid open boxes of rice, cereal, and crackers. Proudly he showed her his office—the corner bedroom, with large, streaked picture windows on two sides. More bookshelves crowded the walls. She couldn't even see his desk beneath all the papers. He had two typewriters—an office electric and a portable, both caked white with dried correction fluid. Maybe Paul Mizzell didn't take his work home at night, but from all appearances Brian Hawthorn *lived* in his.

He showed her his far-from-finished novel: several stacks of typed pages on a library table held down with chunks of brick. "Maybe sometime you'll read it," he said hopefully.

Linda searched for a polite answer. Brian's manuscript looked positively threatening. "Wouldn't you rather give it to someone who can really help?" she said. "One of your friends at the paper?"

Brian laughed. "Any idea how many reporters want to be novelists?"

"No."

"All except the ones who want to write movies."

"Oh."

Grinning, he led her to the bedroom. He stumbled around, picking up clothes and throwing them into a closet. He started to straighten the bed, then looked up. "I guess I ought to put fresh sheets on it."

"Don't go to any—" Too late. With a sweep of his arm, he stripped the bed, rolled up the sheets, and threw them in the closet too. She helped him remake it. They smiled at each other as they worked.

He left her to get undressed and went off to make a couple of hot toddies. She laid her clothes out neatly and found a bathrobe. Putting it on, she tied the belt and glanced at herself in the mirror. She looked tired; the robe looked exhausted. It did nothing for her body. She went into the bathroom and nearly walked right out again.

The man is unbelievable. How can anyone be such a slob?

She joined him in the living room ten minutes later. He offered her his only coaster and watched her sit demurely on one of the sofas. Sinking down a full foot, she said, "What have you got in these cushions—quicksand?"

Without a word, he dropped onto the other one. It creaked and groaned, and she thought she heard something snap. He sat regarding her proudly. "Man cannot live by furniture alone," he said, slowly sipping his toddy.

After a moment she snapped her fingers. "My God, we still haven't called the police about that photograph!"

Brian checked his watch. "That was hours ago. We'd sound awfully silly if we called now."

"The janitor—"

"Are you kidding?" Brian shook his head. "He's going to think it's just another record jacket. Let somebody else find it in the morning. It might ease the pressure on you around there."

"How?"

"If your kindly old nemesis, Mr. Big Shot Benedict, believes somebody's threatening your life, he might just call a truce until this is over."

"You don't know Tony."

"I've had editors like him. You learn to play by their rules and take any leg-up you can get."

Linda swirled the toddy and took a strong gulp. "What about Judith?"

Brian thought about that. "You want to warn the police that Paul may have done something to her?"

"If he hasn't, I'd like to warn *her.*"

"The lawyer," he said brightly, handing her the phone. "She and Paul fought this morning and she left with the lawyer. He'll know where she is."

Linda stared at him.

"What's the matter?"

"You never told me that," she said.

"Didn't I?"

"No—and I've been worried all evening that something happened to her."

"Well, let's call him and be sure."

Linda rummaged in her purse for her address book, found Isaac Grodman's home number, and dialed. The machine answered again. She left her name, the time, and Brian's number, and asked that Isaac call back any time during the night or early in the morning. She hung up and gave the phone back to Brian.

"More toddy?"

"No thanks."

"Look, I'd like to make it easier on you and say 'Don't worry,' but that would be asinine right now. I just hope you're beginning to see reality."

"What reality?"

He leaned back on the sofa and hooked his hands behind his head. "Presuming innocence while trying to prove guilt is stupid."

"That's in the Constitution."

"I don't care if it's in the Bible. It's okay for the law to be set up that way, but how does it help people trying to protect themselves from a maniac?"

"You'd rather shoot him now and learn the truth later?"

"No. But I'd feel better if he was in custody."

Linda sighed. "Oh, Brian, I don't want to argue with you anymore."

"You still believe he's innocent. Every chance you get, you're looking at the other side of the coin. Because he freaked when they played Beatles music at Breakthrough, he couldn't have put on the record at Rok tonight. Come on, Linda! The man is loony: he could do *anything!*"

She frowned at him. "I wonder why you don't give the police your ideas," she said. "You're so concerned with protecting the public. Are you saving all that for your book?"

His arms came down suddenly and his face contorted with anger.

"My book is not about Paul Mizzell."

"No? Then what?"

"Crime. The way people react to it."

"You're obsessed with facts—how can you get anything out of writing fiction?"

He calmed down. "Fiction is my therapy, my way of heightening reality. I can take a common, everyday crime and sit for hours thinking of alternate solutions. Sometimes I get a clearer view of the people I'm writing about by imagining how far they'll go to achieve what they want. I've covered a lot of homicides, so I'm not short of material. I take a little from this, a little from that. The result is an overview."

"A distortion."

"What's wrong with writing fiction, Linda?"

She regarded him quietly a moment. "Nothing, as long as you separate it from reporting."

"I do."

"I'm not so sure. Your theory about Paul is fiction until you can prove it, which you'd like to do at any cost. You're so goddamned cocksure of what's right. If I'm on one end of this seesaw, you're on the other—not in the middle, where you think you are."

Brian drained the rest of his toddy. "So what are we supposed to do? Sit around like lummies while Mizzell proves one of us right?"

"No . . ." She fell silent, not sure at all what they should do.

Brian looked at her darkly. "The trouble is, all you know of Mizzell is his work and what you got from Gene Dahlke, a clinical assessment of Gary Steen's state of mind. You know very little of the Cornell case, the emotions of the time, or the way the justice system worked. So, before firing off these grand statements, why not take the time to find out more?"

Linda mulled that over then replied, "All right, I'll go with you tomorrow morning to the *Times*. You can dig out the files for me."

Brian was surprised that she took up the challenge so readily. "Okay," he agreed. They glared at each other. After a few moments, hostility subsided. He shifted; the sofa creaked and snapped again. He hesitated a second, then moved and sat down next to her. Linda looked at him blankly.

"Are you thinking that if you make love to me, I'll agree with you?"

"No. Frankly, my sofa is about to collapse."

"Oh, come on—"

"Really. I never sit on it." He grinned. "I certainly wouldn't want to make love on it."

"Neither would I."

"Is that neither would I at all—or just on the sofa?"

She looked at him, trying to maintain her stern expression. "Oh, hell," she said finally, and got up. She started for the bedroom and looked back, surprised he wasn't following. "Well, come on!"

He grinned widely and tumbled off the sofa, swaggering after her.

"Don't look so smug," she said. "I'm only doing this to stimulate a little housecleaning . . . if you ever expect to see me here again."

"I'll hire a maid tomorrow."

The phone rang at eight o'clock. Linda rolled over and blinked at it across the room. It stopped ringing. She looked for Brian—saw the door was open—and smelled bacon frying. She pushed the covers down and looked at her body. Hardly a trace of last night's vigorous horseplay, except she felt about five pounds lighter and very hungry. She threw on the robe and hurried out.

Brian was mumbling in the kitchen. She peered over the swinging door and was astonished to see he had cleaned the place up. The only things out were the pans he was using to cook breakfast. Wearing only shorts, he stood turning the bacon, the phone crooked on his shoulder. He spotted Linda and said, "Just a minute," into the mouthpiece. He cupped it and turned to her. "It's the girl friend, Judith. Looking for you."

"Is she all right?"

"Yeah. She got your message."

Linda took the phone. "Judith, where are you?"

"I'm at Isaac Grodman's apartment." Her voice sounded calm and restrained, very much under control. "He put me up for the night."

Good old Isaac. Linda wondered if he'd made a pass—or a score. "Can I speak with him?"

"He's not here. He had to drive out to Glendale to see a

client." Judith hesitated. "I should be hearing from him later. Do you want to leave word?"

"Has he heard anything from Paul?" She paused. "Have you?"

"No."

Linda took a breath. "Judith, somebody threatened my life. I won't go into details, but Brian is convinced it was Paul."

"Who's Brian?"

"A friend of mine, a reporter. Judith, if Paul gets in touch with you, find out where he is but don't go near him. Okay?" She caught an approving look from Brian.

"Where will you be?"

"I'm going to the newspaper with Brian." She paused, then went on. "I'm going to dig back into the files on Gary Steen. I still think Paul is being railroaded."

"I see," said Judith. "What newspaper?—in case I have to reach you."

"The *Times*. What are you going to do?"

"Stay right here." Judith hesitated a moment, then her voice dropped. "I know I didn't sound grateful yesterday, but . . . I'm glad you told me."

"That's okay. I'm sorry it had to be me."

Judith went silent a moment then said, "I don't really believe he would ever hurt me . . . but then he already has . . ."

"Don't give up on him completely, Judith. He's going to need our help."

"Yes. . . . I appreciate everything you're doing, but I have to deal with this myself." She hung up abruptly, and Linda wondered what she meant.

Judith rewound Isaac Grodman's answering machine. She played back the second phone call one more time. It was Paul calling the lawyer, confused, his words tumbling out in half sentences and broken thoughts. He was desperate to talk to someone he could believe was a friend, and at the end of the message he begged to know where he could find Judith.

She listened to it again, then sat back in Grodman's thick leather chair, toyed with his letter opener, and thought about what to do. She had lied to Linda. She could call her back right

now and tell her the truth, but that might mean involving the
reporter. Linda would tell him everything. Somehow, she had to
get to Linda but avoid the reporter. And Paul—should she call
back the number he left or wait? She thought about logic—what
Grodman would have her do. No contact, he had insisted last
night at dinner. Keep away from him and keep cool. The hell
with Grodman, she decided. Act now. Don't wait. She stared at
the number she had copied down, an 825 exchange. West Los
Angeles. But where? She steeled herself and dialed. It was
picked up on the third ring.

   The voice said hesitantly, "Grodman?"

   "No, Paul. It's me."

   "Judith?" He sounded surprised, then there was silence.

   "I couldn't go back home last night, Paul."

   "Where are you?"

   "Grodman's place."

   "Is he with you?"

   "No. Where are you?"

   He hesitated. "UCLA."

   "Where exactly?"

   "A pay phone . . . at the Student Union."

   "Have you been there all night?"

   "I've . . . I've got a place. It's safe."

She thought about how safe it was. With his beard and peren-
nially shabby look, he probably fit in fine. If they didn't take him
for a student, they might easily believe he was a professor. "Still
there?" she said.

For a moment, she thought he'd hung up, then his voice came
back cupped and boxy. "Sorry about yesterday," he muttered.
"I just . . . I went a little crazy. I didn't mean to hurt you . . ."

   "I know."

   "Look, can you . . . can you find Grodman for me?"

   "I don't know where to reach him. Do you need help?"

   "I don't know what to do—" His voice broke. "Should I turn
myself in?"

   Judith bit her lip. "Paul, listen to me—"

   "I'll give up, tell them I killed Dahlke. I just can't stand it
anymore! It's Gary, Judith. He's trying to get out."

   "Paul—" She twisted the cord around her finger.

"I killed my doctor. I've got to be locked up!"

"Paul!" she shouted. "Stop it!" She leaned forward, afraid he would lose control and draw attention to himself. "Listen to me. You're not turning yourself in. You're not doing anything. Stay out of sight. Leave the Student Union: it's too crowded. Where is this place you were talking about?"

"I can't tell you. . . . Maybe if I got hold of Linda . . ."

"I don't know how much help she would be now, Paul," Judith said slowly. "Somebody threatened her life last night. She thinks it was you."

She heard an anguished groan, then his voice came back cracking with emotion. "It wasn't me. I swear it."

"I know. I believe you. Please, Paul, tell me where this place is."

"Oh God . . ." He trailed off incoherently, then came back and told her what she wanted to know.

CHAPTER 15

They rounded the corner at Spring Street and walked up First. Linda paused to look up at the façade of the old Times-Mirror Building and Brian stopped just ahead of her. "Nineteen thirty-five," he said. "Monumental modern. You can throw a stone from here and hit City Hall, the Music Center . . ." His pointing finger swept around in a circle.

"I should think you outgrew this building a long time ago."

"Oh, no. They just keep adding on." He opened the main entrance and led her into the rotunda. Her heels clicked on marble floors. There was an enormous world globe in the center, the *Times* foreign bureaus pinpointed around it and linked by dark thread.

Brian took her to the security guard's desk, flashed his i.d. and said, "Visitor, George. She'll be with me."

"Okay, Mr. Hawthorn." The guard pushed a clipboard over and asked Linda to sign in. She wrote down her name and time of entry. The guard thanked her and handed her a visitor's pass, which she pinned to her jacket. She followed Brian to the elevators just beyond the rotunda. They went up to the fourth floor and stepped into a hall.

"This part hasn't been redone yet," Brian said, tapping gray marble inlay that came to hip level. Above it was white textured wallpaper up to a blue ceiling; the floor was charcoal marbled linoleum. As he walked Linda down mysterious winding halls, he explained, "It's a big plant. Refurbishing and updating takes a long time. You finish and you've got to start all over again. We've only become computerized in the last few years. Reporters are beginning to get VDTs to replace their typewriters."

"VDTs?" asked Linda.

"Video display terminals. You type the story and it goes right into computerized composing. They've got it up in feature right now."

"Feature," she echoed.

"Non-news. Art, music, drama, et cetera. Where I work, we just use the old clickety-clacks. Manuals."

He opened a door and they went up a connecting ramp to another part of the building, through another door and into the news division. Linda looked across a sea of desks crammed together at odd angles. Reporters were already at work; the room was alive with the buzz of conversation and clicking typewriters. Along the right wall was a row of glassed-in offices.

"Editors," Brian explained. "Metropolitan, national, and foreign news are all in this one department. Set off a bomb in here and we wouldn't get out a newspaper tomorrow to tell about it." He indicated a large room to the left. "Wire room," he said, "though we don't really use the wire anymore. Pictures come in much cleaner by Laserphoto."

He led her through the maze to his "office," a small steel four-drawer desk with a low bulletin board attached to the back. He perched on the edge and gave her the only chair. She glanced around: a few men were eyeing her curiously.

"I'm what they call a general assignment reporter," Brian said. "I don't have a beat and I don't specialize. Keeps the job flexible, and full of fun and variety." He grinned weakly. "Want to see the presses?"

"No," she said.

"Good. You'd look silly covered with ink. Ready to do some research, or have I intimidated you enough?"

"Let's get started."

On their way out, he was stopped by an editor and got sidetracked for twenty minutes. Linda returned to his desk and thought about calling her office. She finally decided not to. By now, Tony Benedict would have found out about the slashed picture. She didn't feel like answering his questions. She sat back and waited for Brian.

He finally returned, wearing a scowl. Linda followed him down the hallway. He grumbled, "That guy has buttocks for blinders. Last week, I promised him an exclusive interview with

Mizzell; now he wants to know where it is. I had hoped *you* were going to help me get it." He stopped at a bend and turned to her. "What about a trade? I'm helping you. You help me."

"Come on, Brian. Even if I knew where to find Paul, would you want to be in the same room with him?"

"Just a thought. I told my editor I had something on Break-through. That'll hold him for a while."

The editorial library was a large room partitioned from the hall by floor-to-ceiling glass walls. Brian opened the door for Linda. She glanced at orange carpeting and paneling and white desks and walls. Along the far side were library racks containing rows of manila envelopes.

"There's twelve million clippings in here," said Brian. "Over a million and a half articles on microfilm or microfiche. We're in the process of converting all our paper files to film."

He took her around a counter to a wall on the right and showed her the Lektriever. "Here's what you want." He operated a panel of buttons, and she watched endless levels of drawers roll by. "Everything is alphabetical, filed by public figure, subject, and reporter's byline. Steen qualifies as a public figure, so there should be plenty under his name. You can also look under subject: Cornell murder, or byline: Hawthorn, Brian." He grinned, then pressed buttons again. The levels rolled by and stopped at "ST."

Brian pulled out a drawer, displaying a deep file of oblong manila envelopes. He thumbed through and found a set of six marked "Steen, G. M."

He took them over to the counter and spread them out. "You've got a lot of reading to do. Don't forget: everything is cross-filed. To make sure nobody slipped up and left anything out, be thorough."

Linda glared at him. "You're hoping it'll take me all day."

"You wanted to do it."

"Where will you be?"

He pointed through a window to another glass-walled room across the hall. "Photo lab. I'm going to have some pictures printed up for you. If you need me, just pick up a phone." He wrote down the lab number and his desk extension on a pad, gave her a peck on the cheek, then went out.

She sat down at the counter and watched him cross into the lab. She was feeling deserted and unsure of herself.

What the hell are you looking for? Aren't you just wasting your time trying to prove a point? Brian expects you to realize he's right. Well, if you read what he wrote in 1968, how can you think otherwise. Nuts.

The first envelope was stuffed with yellowed clippings. She unfolded each of them and laid them out, staring at the top one, with its photo of Gary Michael Steen on page one—

God, he looked different then. Scary.

Over the picture was the headline UCLA GIRL STABBED TO DEATH. The date was Saturday, October 19, 1968. And there was Brian's byline. She started to read.

Brian ordered up negatives from the Lektriever in the photo lab and checked the envelope labels carefully, pulling out only those taken during the trial or at the murder scene. He hesitated. Linda might take it the wrong way—she might think he was trying to rub her nose in it. Well, maybe he was. He found another packet under "Cornell," then took everything over to the assignment desk and rush-ordered eight-by-ten glossies. Leaving the lab, he paused to glance into the library. Linda was hunched over the back counter. Brian's smile faded. This was cruel, but she wouldn't be satisfied till the last dog was hung. He checked his watch. Just enough time for a snack before Bass showed up.

He took the biggest jelly doughnut he could find back to his desk and laid it out on a napkin. He ate slowly, thinking back over the years to that Saturday morning at UCLA when he went over to cover his first murder case. He remembered the battered psychedelic van in parking lot 5 outside Royce Hall, the coroner's boys removing something in a dark body bag, then the excitement as word got through they had found a suspect. A mob of reporters had stumbled all over each other finding the stairway exits. He recalled stampeding along with everyone else, the police holding them back outside the north entrance to Royce. Then they brought the kid out—shoeless, shirtless, with his jeans almost falling off, hair sticky and disheveled, and a wild, tortured look in his eye. Reporters begging to know where the police had found him. Somebody hollering back, "Towers at the other end." Brian remembered hurrying down the hall and out the other side to look up at the twin towers. Everybody confused—which one? Cameras snapping pictures. Then back to where they had the van cordoned off. Press briefing from the LAPD public relations guy. Details. Brian recalled listening, being stunned, then feeling sick.

He finished the doughnut and washed it down with coffee, licking his fingers, marveling at the thick skin he had developed in the intervening years. Murder didn't sicken him anymore: it didn't even surprise him. In the years since, he had seen almost everything. Reporters and cops lived in a different world, he told himself. To most people, death was a shock, a trauma. To him, it was an everyday occurrence, a part of life. But the Steen case had made a lasting impression. He remembered it as months of covering the trial and the legal manipulations, of watching the emerging portrait of an emotionally confused kid trying to give his life meaning with mind-expanding drugs, of seeing him finally committed to a hospital for psychiatric care, Dahlke's brand of it. He could understand how the Cornell family must have felt about the court's decision, how it must have rankled. Their public remarks had amounted to philosophical Bible quotations, indicating they had accepted the "will of God" and were prepared to live with it. He remembered that vividly, and the look on the father's face as the mother spoke for both of them: a drained look, heavy with regret, sorrow, and resignation. The mother had been tall, middle-aged, proud, and sure that God had not betrayed her. Just as sure as Brian was that He had.

Of all the homicides he had covered, that one had stayed with him. Over the years, he had never lost interest in Gary Michael Steen. Whenever his name had come up—usually in comparison to later murders—Brian had automatically called Camarillo to find out how Gary was doing. Several times he had spoken to Dahlke himself, who had always been determinedly uncooperative. That's how Brian had come to know Bass—by going around Dahlke. Bass had phoned him up six years ago to tell him of Gary's release from the facility, of his thorough rehabilitation. But he had stopped short of revealing Gary's new identity. Why else had they given him a new name if not to protect him from the curious? Newspaper reporters included.

So Brian had lost track of Gary Steen. It was hard letting go, like giving up a security blanket. Recognizing him at Rok Records a few weeks ago had been a shock, immediately reviving his old fascination along with a host of feelings he had thought long since buried, chief among them the conviction that drug-induced insanity was the most hypocritical defense of all. Who was responsible for taking the drugs in the first place? Brian had always perceived the Steen case as a miscarriage of justice. Nobody could change his mind about that, not even Linda.

She was repacking the fourth envelope when a researcher, a girl of about twenty-three, heard her groan and looked up. "Is everything all right?" the girl asked.

"Another pair of eyes would be great," Linda said, shifting on the stool and arching her back to fight the stiffness.

"How about some coffee?" offered the girl. Her Mickey Mouse T-shirt was distorted out of shape by a jutting bustline.

"That *would* help," Linda said. "Thank you."

Linda opened the next envelope and carefully spread out more clippings. The girl came over with a cup of coffee, a packet of sugar, and a tub of cream. She peered over Linda's shoulder to see what she was researching. "Are you a writer?" she asked.

"No. Actually, I'm in the music business."

"Really?" The girl brightened. "That's what I want to get into. I love pop music. Specially rockabilly." She wiggled and Mickey did a dance on her chest. "What company you work for?"

"Rok."

"Oh . . ." She looked blank. "Who's your biggest star?"

This is the public, Linda. The great mass market of working people and kids who make up your audience. They live, eat, and breathe pop music, and all they care about is the latest hit record, so don't say anything rude because—

"Biggest star . . ." She mulled. "Tony Benedict."

"Tony who? Bennett?"

"Benedict. You haven't heard of him?"

The girl looked worried. "Is he an album?"

"He's a slipped disc."

The girl regarded her suspiciously. "You're putting me on. There is no Tony Benedict."

"If you say so."

She flounced back to her desk and glared at Linda, who felt a twinge of guilt. She hadn't meant to be a wise-ass: it just came out that way.

What's wrong with you? Lately you go around antagonizing everybody.

She went back to the clippings and picked up one that contained an interview with Lori Cornell's mother, Lovita Cornell. It dated from the trial, and the writer—again Brian—was very sympathetic to the family's plight. In the article, Lovita Cornell stated that Gary Steen's punishment was ordained not to come from the courts but through his own inner torment, which would be far more devastating than any retribution meted out by society.

Linda thought about that. In a roundabout way Lori's mother had predicted the truth. Even though Paul might be innocent of Dahlke's murder, he was suffering emotionally.

But that only made Linda wonder if someone from Paul's past could be performing a ritual of revenge. For example, Lovita Cornell had a motive. A deeply religious woman, over the years dissatisifed with the snail's pace of divine retribution, couldn't she have stepped in to work "God's will" herself?

You're reaching.

Looking at a picture of her, Linda had a hard time visualizing Lovita Cornell as a monster, avenging her daughter by murdering the killer's psychiatrist. The idea was ridiculous.

More ridiculous than Paul doing it?

She opened the last envelope and thumbed through the clippings quickly. One caught her eye. It was a short piece, probably a filler from deep in the paper, dated 1975.

FATHER OF MURDERED GIRL DIES

PASADENA—Herbert Cornell, father of a UCLA coed brutally murdered in 1968, died yesterday at his home on Green Street.

Mr. Cornell had recently retired from his job as chief accountant for Thorpe & Son, a textile mill in Glendale.

> Survived by Lovita Cornell, his wife of 28 years, he was
> held in high regard as the financial consultant to three large
> church groups in the Pasadena community . . .

There wasn't much left after that piece, nothing more about
Lovita Cornell or anyone else in the family. Linda found one
article with a photograph taken outside the courtroom the day the
decision was rendered. There were the Cornells and behind them
other members of the family, both close and distant relatives
who, according to the article, had attended the trial from beginning to end. She could make out the faces of several older
people, all with that proud, devout look, and a few teenaged
children—cousins. She looked among the girls, trying to spot the
one who might have offered herself to Brian, but the faces were
indistinct. She glanced through the article and discovered that in
1968 most of the family had lived on the east coast. Lovita and
Herbert had been the only ones in the West.

*That doesn't mean anything. Today they could be scattered
across the continent. Besides, someone bent on getting revenge
could easily hop a plane and descend on Los Angeles.*

She rubbed her eyes and groaned again, not knowing what to
do. Finally, she packed up the Steen clippings and returned them
to the proper drawer, then followed Brian's advice to be thorough. She punched buttons and called up "H" for Hawthorn.

"Hugo Bass. Dr. Hugo Bass," he said to the guard at the
desk. "Mr. Hawthorn is expecting me."

"Just a moment, Doctor. Have a seat."

"Thank you."

Bass didn't sit. He walked around the rotunda, glancing into
the waiting area. Several families were clustered on the benches,
waiting for the daily scheduled tour. A woman with dark hair
was leaning against one of the marble pillars, her back to him.
She appeared to be studying the bust of Harry Chandler, her arm
weighted down with an oversized handbag. She had nice legs.
Bass circled the globe and went to the other side of the rotunda.
He looked back and saw that the guard was still on the phone. He
paused to inspect an old linotype machine on display.

"Dr. Bass," the guard called. He returned to the desk and signed in. The guard gave him a pass and asked him to wait. "Mr. Hawthorn will be right down."

Bass circled the globe again, glancing at the dark-haired woman's legs and sighing to himself. He had inherited Dahlke's practice but not the man's way with women. Gene would have been over there by now, talking softly, laying his groundwork. Incorrigible. Bass cursed him silently.

Brian stepped off the elevator and motioned to him. Bass hurried over. "I've got appointments starting at one," he said. "I hope this won't take all day."

"Not at all," said Brian. "I've been out to Breakthrough. I thought we should discuss it—"

They disappeared into the elevator, and the dark-haired woman came around the pillar, staring after them impassively. She watched the guard and thought some more about how to get past him.

"Have you ever been there?" Brian asked.

Bass shook his head. "Dahlke went out occasionally. He was sort of an unofficial consultant to Von Lochen. Sent over a lot of patients."

"Was that s.o.p. for sex problems?"

"Some cases required advanced treatment."

"Did Dahlke test the treatment himself?"

"Pardon? You mean did he—?"

"Did he go into a room with one of the surrogates and get it on?"

Bass stiffened. The elevator doors opened. "After you," Brian said. Bass hesitated, then stepped off. Brian led him to the news department the long way around, careful not to take him past the library. "I'd still like an answer to that, Hugo. Did Dahlke have the treatment himself?"

"Yes . . ."

"Did you?"

"None of your business."

"Did he do it more than once?"

"Yes."

"He went there a lot, didn't he, Hugo? And not for conferences. The surrogates had a little sideline going, providing sex for staff and consultants. Right?''

"I—I wouldn't know—"

Brian stopped him. "Come on, Hugo, how many times were *you* out there getting your ashes hauled?"

Bass reddened and started to protest, but a door opened nearby and two men in shirtsleeves came out. He looked for an escape route, muttering, "I don't have to stand for this."

"Of course not, Hugo. In fact, I'd prefer we sit down to talk about whether or not I'm going to print any of this."

Bass's mouth clamped shut. He followed Brian up the hall and into the newsroom, stopping inside the door, intimidated by the horde of people in front of him.

Brian led Bass over to his desk, giving him the chair and standing over him. Bass fidgeted, avoiding the looks of nearby reporters. "Can't we go somewhere private?" he whispered.

"Hugo, nobody'll be interested in what we have to say unless you raise your voice. Now then, how many times were you out to Breakthrough   in an unofficial capacity?

"Uh . . I think three . . maybe four."

"Were you offered sex?"

Bass nodded.

"How was it?"

He swallowed. "Very good. They know what they're doing."

"I'll bet. Okay, we're through the hard part, Hugo. See, I don't want to pin anything on you, but I think we both realize it's important to get Dahlke's position clear, if you know what I mean."

For a moment, Bass didn't. Then he began to see. Lay it all on his poor old murdered colleague. After all, Gene had been the contact with Breakthrough: Bass had never sent a patient over. And if the stink was rising from Von Lochen and his fabled technique, Bass would prefer *eau d'innocence*. Suddenly, he began talking about things he had only "suspected," as he put it. Dahlke had an arrangement with Von Lochen. Kickbacks—part of the payment in money, part in sexual favors from the surrogates. Bass had never seen a nickel—that was Dahlke's sideline— but he had been treated to a few "favors."

"I must say, I felt rather dirty afterwards. . . ."

"Oh, sure." Brian smirked. He reached for a pad and made some notes. Bass watched him, wondering what the hell he was writing. He felt warm, trickly sweat on his cheek and reached for a Kleenex to wipe his face.

"I'm curious about one thing, Hugo," said Brian. "If you thought Von Lochen was full of shit, and Dahlke certainly *knew* he was, then what was the purpose of sending Paul Mizzell there? Did Dahlke really believe they could cure his sex hangup?"

Bass pondered that a moment, then said lamely, "Breakthrough did help *some* of Gene's patients—"

Brian spoke through his teeth. "Paul Mizzell was a rehabilitated killer. What in hell was Breakthrough supposed to do for him?"

Bass glanced around furtively. A couple of reporters were watching him. He spoke quietly. "His sexual problem was an unforeseen result of Dahlke's treatment, and Breakthrough was the best way to handle it. Gene wanted to give back to Paul what he had been forced to remove—his sexual confidence."

"Did either of you stop to think that Von Lochen could be hurting him rather than helping?"

A runner tapped Brian on the shoulder and handed him a thick envelope. "From the photo lab," the boy said and hurried off.

Brian opened the envelope and drew out a sheaf of eight-by-ten glossies, the pictures he had ordered printed. "These ought to interest you, Hugo," he said, and spread them out on the desk, pulling out the Cornell murder scene pictures one by one.

Bass winced at some of them. Brian opened a drawer and drew out another photo: Dahlke's carved-up body.

Bass stared at the two pictures.

"That's the guy your partner rehabilitated, Hugo."

"Can I help you, miss?"

The dark-haired woman turned around and smiled at a short, pretty girl wearing a company badge. "Are you from public relations?" she asked.

"Yes."

"Oh, good. I wanted to get up to your clipping library and the guard said I should talk to someone in PR. I won't be long. I'm looking for something specific."

The girl thought a moment then said, "Sure. Just give the guard your name and he'll make out a pass, then you sign in."

"Oh, thank you."

The guard fumbled for his pen. "Name, miss?"

"Judith Berg."

Linda glanced up as the door opened and two women came into the library. Her mouth opened as she recognized the second one: Judith. Judith put a finger to her lips. Linda waited while Judith was instructed in using the Lektriever, wondering what she was doing here. Had something happened to Paul . . . ?

Judith finally said, "I've got the hang of it. Thanks very much. I can manage now."

"Oh," said the girl, uncertain whether she should leave.

Linda piped up, "If she has trouble, I can help her."

"Okay. Just don't wander in the building, please. I'll check back in twenty minutes."

The short girl left. Linda watched her go and caught Mickey Mouse T-shirt looking her way again, still miffed. Linda turned to Judith and spoke quietly. "What are you doing here?"

Judith put down the handbag and looked at the clippings, then she moved closer, whispering, "Paul wants to see us."

"What?"

"Shh. I spoke to him. We're the only two people in the world he trusts right now, and I think he wants to be talked into surrendering."

Linda stared at Judith, catching the nervous flutter of her hand. "You don't want to go alone, is that it?"

Judith nodded. "Paul asked for you. He's afraid."

The churning returned to Linda's stomach. "We can't go alone," she said.

"That's how he wants it."

"Let me get Brian."

"The reporter?"

Linda nodded.

"Paul would bolt if we brought anyone else." Tears sprang to

Judith's eyes as she lifted the handbag and showed Linda what was tucked into a pocket of it—a small revolver. "Isaac gave it to me," she said.

"He gave you a gun?"

"Yes. He said to keep it out of sight but . . . but ready, in case . . . Oh, Christ, Linda . . ." She caught her breath and looked away.

Linda glanced back. Mickey Mouse T-shirt was watching them out of the corner of her eye. "Put that away," Linda said. Judith closed the bag. "What else is in there?"

"Food, thermos of iced tea—"

"Why bring supplies if we're trying to persuade him to give up?"

"In case he doesn't—" She sobbed. "He's got to have something."

Linda put a hand on Judith's shoulder. "All right, I'll go with you." Her mind raced.

Should you leave word with Brian? No. He's on the wrong side in this. He wouldn't hesitate to call the police.

She packed up the envelopes, shoved them back into the drawer and closed it, then nodded for Judith to follow. She went first, flashing Mickey Mouse T-shirt a quick smile. Judith took a moment to regain her composure, then lifted the handbag and walked out of the room.

Bass had a headache listening to Brian hold forth on his pet subject, the responsibility of doctors for letting deranged criminals on the loose too soon. If Brian had his way, none of them would ever get out. Bass managed to get in a shot about reporters in general being too stubborn and fact-conscious to see the gray areas that psychiatrists have to deal with. Brian responded by assailing him with the psychiatrist's failure to see anything *but* gray areas. Bass gave up the argument and mentally turned him off.

A reporter hurried over from the wire room and poked Brian. "What is it?" Brian said.

"Police call. The lawyer who got Paul Mizzell out yesterday just turned up dead."

Brian stared at him. "The *lawyer?*"

"Couple of people from his office got worried when he didn't show up this morning. Sent someone out to check. Found him in his bathtub, ripped open like a watermelon." He drew his thumb up from his groin to his breastbone, then made a face.

Brian looked at Dr. Bass, who had gone ashen. "Your gray areas are getting blacker by the minute, Hugo."

CHAPTER 16

The ride from downtown unnerved Linda. Judith refused to talk. Staring straight ahead, she weaved the VW in and out of traffic at breakneck speed. Linda braced her feet on the floorboard and shrank back as they rushed toward the rear of a truck. At the last second, Judith swerved to the right, careened across three lanes and shot down the ramp onto the northbound San Diego Freeway, saluted by hornblasts from the cars she had cut off.

"We're not going to help Paul if you get us killed," Linda said.

Judith muttered an apology. The engine whine dropped half an octave as she eased up on the gas pedal.

Linda tried to relax. "Where are we going?"

"Didn't I tell you?"

"No. You haven't said a word since I set foot in this guided missile. Where?"

"UCLA."

Linda's mouth dropped open. "*That's* where he is?"

"Yes." Judith picked up speed again and Linda wondered what would make Paul go there. Then she realized it was probably the last place anyone would ever look for him.

Judith came off the freeway and headed east on Wilshire Boulevard.

"What time are we meeting him?"

"Around noon."

"Then slow down. We've got an hour."

Judith let up on the gas again. "Sorry. Guess I'm scared."

"Me, too. So let's take it easy. How did he sound on the phone?"

Judith shrugged. "Confused."

Linda stared out the window, then turned back abruptly. "Look, if you'd rather not go through with this—"

"I have to."

"Why? You're not responsible for him."

"Yes, I am." She nodded her head repeatedly and gripped the steering wheel tighter. "Don't you remember? I lied to the police about being with Paul at Sabato's."

Linda did not like being reminded she had gone along with that. "Did you tell Isaac?"

"He said I could make an amended statement to the police."

"And will you?"

Judith was quiet a long time, then she said tightly, "I don't know."

They parked in lot 5. Linda got out and waited for Judith to fish out the big handbag. "Exactly where is he going to be?"

"In front of Royce Hall."

"Oh, Christ, Whose idea was that?"

"Paul's. What's wrong?"

"He killed the Cornell girl in this parking lot! And he hid overnight in Royce! But Owl's safe. Judith he's reliving his past!"

Judith draped the bag over her shoulder. She seemed to gain determination. "Now do you see why he needs our help?"

"Yeah, but who's going to watch out for us?"

Judith started up the stairs. Linda followed reluctantly. They emerged on the drive that led down to Royce. Judith paused to look up at the massive Mediterranean-style building, then she led Linda down a hall that ran the length of the building. She walked quickly, her head bent forward, her flat shoes noiseless on the floor while Linda's heels clicked behind her. Linda glanced into classrooms filled with students and caught snatches of lecture: English lit, history, sociology. She checked a wall clock. It was shortly after eleven; classes had just begun.

They came out under the south portico, a long walkway fronted by pillared arches, facing Dickson Plaza. Students were perched on ledges, their backs to the pillars, studying. Dickson Plaza was a broad concrete walkway bordered with brick and patches of grass. Across the plaza was Powell Library, another Mediterranean behemoth. Royce and Powell dated from 1929 and were patterned after churches in Northern Italy. At the western end of the plaza was a brick terrace opening out on the Janss steps, which descended a steep meadow to the gyms below. The terrace was occupied by the usual tables devoted to radical politics.

Linda scanned faces, hoping to spot Paul. Judith walked the length of the portico looking for him and came back with a deep frown.

"Maybe he got hungry," Linda said.

"It's not noon yet. We'll wait."

They hung around under the portico, meandering into the Royce Hall foyer, Linda absently checking the posters for coming events: concerts, plays, films. Judith poked her head through doors and even went upstairs briefly, returning with her frown deepened.

"Let's wait outside," she said, and Linda followed obediently.

Judith stood at the edge of the steps fronting Royce and shifted back and forth on her feet, glancing around anxiously while they talked.

"Brian stumbled onto something I hadn't known about," Linda said. "Did you know Paul had been to a sex clinic?"

Judith forced a smile. "I think he mentioned it."

"I went there last night."

Judith stopped moving and cocked her head.

"Brian took me. It's up in Topanga Canyon, a place called Breakthrough—"

"Shit." Judith's face darkened with anger. "I suppose it'll be in tomorrow's *Times*. Doesn't your friend have any respect for privacy?"

Startled, Linda replied. "I don't know what he's going to print. We spoke to the head of the clinic, a man named Von Lochen, and a woman . . ." She paused, reluctant to anger Judith any further.

"What woman?"

"Well, it's the way they operate up there. Paul had a surrogate. I guess he didn't tell you that, either."

"No," she said, "he never said anything about his treatment."

"That's understandable. When Paul got out of Camarillo, they had taken away his sex drive. In order to restore it, he was sent to Breakthrough. Brian thinks that they screwed him up." She

paused. "I don't mean to pry, but did you and Paul . . . did you
ever have any . . . problems?"

Judith glared at her then turned away. "He was never the
aggressive one. Look, Linda, you're not doing Paul any favors by
running around with this reporter. He doesn't know what he's
getting into—" She stopped herself. "What did they tell you at
the clinic? Who was the woman you spoke to?"

"I don't think you have to worry about Norma," Linda said.
"Even though she works with men, it was obvious to me she's a
lesbian."

Judith stood very still.

"Was he seeing her while you were living with him?"

"I don't know. . . . What did she say?"

"That she cured him."

They stood looking at each other, then Judith hoisted the
handbag and clutched it under her arm. "I'm going to walk a bit.
Wait here in case he shows up." She went down the steps and
leisurely crossed the plaza, stopping near the middle to stand
gazing off into space. Linda watched curiously.

*There's something wrong here.   Did I hit a nerve asking
about her sex life with Paul? Probably. She's just discovered
what she's been living with. Naturally, she's touchy about it.
Walking around with one hell of an emotional burden, and a gun
in her handbag—*

The gun.

Why would Isaac give her a gun?

And would he really let her walk into danger alone?

Judith was still standing in the plaza. She glanced back at
Royce—and up—and Linda wondered what she was looking at.

The carillon sounded from the speakers atop Powell Library,
signaling the noon class break with a reverberating concert.
Linda cringed at the deafening notes. Behind her, doors slammed
and she heard scuffling feet from back in the hallway. Students
came pouring out, filling up Dickson Plaza, a milling mob on
their way to lunch, home, or the next class.

Linda scanned faces, craning her neck, wondering what was
keeping Paul, realizing he was probably waiting for this stam-
pede to provide cover. The crowd thinned.

And why are you here, dopey? You've got even less reason for

risking your life. At least Judith is in love with Paul. Or is she?
That doesn't ring true, either. She's not doing this out of love.
Oh, sure, she must feel something for him, but she's behaving
with cold logic. She lied to the police, so now she believes she
has to make up for it by handing over her boyfriend.

That's logical, isn't it?

But the gun. What if they have trouble with Paul? Would
she—?

Linda went out to join Judith, trying to recall something
important about the bells, something from the articles she'd read
this morning—no, from the tapes she'd heard in Dahlke's office.
Gary Steen had mentioned bells tolling the hours to dawn as he
waited, hidden— She looked up at the towers of Royce.

Suddenly she knew where Paul was.

And she didn't want to go up there with Judith.

Her heart began to pound. She decided to wait a few minutes,
then try to convince Judith that Paul was too scared to come out,
that he was hiding somewhere and they hadn't a hope of finding
him. She would make Judith see that they should go back to
Grodman's and wait for Paul to contact them again.

Judith's hand gripped her arm, her voice hard in Linda's ear.
"I know where he is."

Oh, no.

Judith pulled Linda down the hallway into Royce, and Linda
felt momentary relief as they headed for the back of the building,
away from the towers. Then Judith stopped to cross the hall and
examine a wall directory. "Third floor," she said, turning to the
stairs.

Linda protested. "Judith, do you know where you're going?"

She just kept moving. Linda followed. They came out on the
third floor and Linda saw with a sinking feeling that Judith had
changed direction again and was on her way down the hall to the
front of the building, where the towers were.

With Bass slumped in a chair, sipping coffee from a Styrofoam
cup, Brian dug frantically through the phone book. He found four
Grodmans—three women and Isaac . . . *Isaac Grodman.* He
grabbed the phone and punched out the numbers, then waited. It
was picked up on the second ring.

"Slade, homicide."

"Brian Hawthorn, L.A. *Times*."

"Ah—the media. Listen, Hawthorn, I'm not public affairs. You'll get your statement—"

"Slade, I'm a lot closer to this case than you think. Just answer one question. Was anybody else found in the apartment?"

"Who, for instance?"

"A woman."

"What woman?"

"Paul Mizzell's girl friend, Judith Berg."

There was a pause, then, "Go on, Hawthorn. I'm listening."

"Grodman got Mizzell released yesterday."

"We know that."

"Mizzell got home and argued with his girl friend. She walked out on him and stayed at Grodman's place last night."

Brian heard paper rustling on the other end, then Slade was asking for details: repeat the girl's name, spell it, describe her. "I can't," Brian said. "I've never met her."

"That's great. How do you know she was here?"

"She called me this morning."

"You—why?"

He explained his involvement with the Gary Steen case and his contact with Linda Sharman. Slade asked to speak with Linda. Brian stalled. "She's stepped out," he said. "What time do you figure Grodman was killed?"

"Early. Maybe six A.M. Any idea where Mizzell is?"

"No."

Slade didn't believe him. He asked Brian to wait, then cupped the phone and carried on a whispered conversation with someone else. "Where are you at the *Times*?" he said when he came back.

"Around."

"What floor? What office? Give me your number. I might have to call you back."

Sure he would. He was probably sending someone over right now. "Look," Brian said, "I don't know where Mizzell is. Believe me, if I did, I'd tell you."

"Glad to hear it. What office?"

"You'll find it." Brian said, and hung up.

Bass was staring at him with intense curiosity. "What did they say?" he croaked.

"The lawyer's still dead." Brian jumped up, knowing he had to do something, but what? Get out of the building first of all. Get Linda and leave. But how? Parker Center was two blocks away. The cops could be here before he reached the elevator.

Ah, but they don't know what you look like, Brian old boy.

"Stay here," he told Bass. "I'll be back in a few minutes."

He grabbed his coat and ran out. Leaving people in the lurch was getting to be a habit, but somebody had to be here when the police showed up. Bass would keep them very busy.

As he hurried down the halls, Brian tried to figure out how Paul had done it. Probably had Grodman's address, went to his apartment, surprised him with Judith, killed the lawyer, then dragged her off. . . . Why? Angry because she'd walked out on him? Whatever it was, he must have murdered Grodman, then taken the girl someplace to kill *her*. But where?

Brian cursed Linda for leading him astray. Of course Mizzell was the killer! He was the only one with a motive. Maybe Linda knew where Mizzell would go. Maybe Judith told her on the phone this morning—

Wait a minute. Wait a minute. That's wrong! He stopped at a bend in the hall and tried to remember what Judith had told Linda—that she was alone: Grodman had left early for Pasadena to see a client. But Slade had said Grodman died at six A.M.!

Was he lying in the bathtub with his guts hanging out while Judith was on the phone in another room?

Brian revised the scenario in his head: Mizzell got into the apartment, killed Grodman, held Judith till morning then forced her to call Linda. Why? To lure her someplace.

He was going to kill both women!

"Jesus Christ!" Brian shouted. He dashed to the library and threw open the door. Startled, Sally Beachman looked up, her Mickey Mouse T-shirt swinging around with her chest.

The door was closed. The number 320 was printed on the glass. Beneath it, the words "Germanic Studies." Judith paused to look at a small hand-printed sign that read, "Closed, 12–1."

"What are we doing?" Linda asked.

"Paul said if he didn't show up downstairs by noon to look for him here."

Linda glanced at the door anxiously. "Why didn't you tell me?"

Judith reached for the knob. "He said he'd leave the door unlatched as soon as everyone went to lunch."

"He's hiding in here? I don't believe it."

"Not in the office. In the tower."

Linda moved between her and the door. "Judith, let's think about this."

"Why—are you afraid?"

"Yes, damn it! Meeting him in the open is one thing, but we can't go up in that tower. That's where he hid out when he killed the Cornell girl. It's too dangerous. We don't know what's going through his head."

"I'll take care of him."

"With the gun?"

They stared at each other. Judith reached past Linda and opened the door. It swung back and she walked in. Reluctantly, Linda followed, looking around apprehensively. There was no one in the office. Empty desks were spaced back toward the south wall, covered with stacks of papers. A door on the left led to a large library. Judith paused at a staircase and looked up at the landing above.

Linda stood next to one of the desks. Determined to stop things before they went any further, she reached for a telephone.

Judith turned abruptly. "What are you doing?"

"Calling the police."

"I thought you wanted to help him."

"I do, but this isn't the way."

"Put the phone down, Linda."

She dialed "O," got the campus operator and asked for the police. Cupping the receiver in her hand, she said, "Leave the gun down here and I'll think about going up there."

Judith met her gaze then dug into the bag and pulled out the revolver. Instead of putting it down, she cocked the hammer and pointed it at Linda's breast. "Hang up."

Linda stared back in disbelief.

"I know what I'm doing, Linda. We're going to find Paul."

She moved closer, took the phone away and hung it up. "And we don't need any help." She motioned Linda to the stairs.

Linda shook her head. "I'm not going."

"You're not staying here."

"Judith, put the gun down."

"Up the stairs."

Judith closed the door, then backed Linda toward the stairs and made her start up.

The landing was bordered by a concrete ledge, and all Linda could think of was a maniac crouched on the other side with a knife and this woman behind her with a gun. She didn't know which frightened her more. She glanced back. With the gun still leveled at her, Judith was following. They reached the landing and Linda looked down an empty hall.

"No one here," she said.

"Quiet." Judith pressed the gun into Linda's back, forcing her on. In a corner alcove, they found a set of iron rungs bolted to the wall, ascending to a square opening in the ceiling.

Judith waved the gun. "Up."

"Judith, please . . ."

She shoved Linda to the wall. "Climb!"

Shaking, Linda reached for the first rung and looked up through the open hole into blackness. Her legs went rubbery.

What if he's there, right on the other side of that hole, waiting? You're the bait.

Somehow, she pulled herself up. The blackness got bigger, seducing her upward. She stopped with her head just below the opening.

Didn't Paul ask Judith to bring her along? He couldn't mean to harm you. No? Then who carved up your photograph last night? Who left the warning? Who came down to the Times *this morning and dragged you out here? Who is holding a gun on you right now and threatening your life—?*

Not Paul.

She couldn't bring herself to look back. She knew Judith was down there but she didn't dare do anything to provoke her. She wanted to stay right where she was and think it out, but Judith called from below, "Climb!"

Linda poked her head through the hole and looked around. The room was a square, gloomy box with a filthy cement floor and a single window covered with grime.

"Is he there?" Judith asked.

"No." She climbed out, her attention drawn to a ladder going up to the ceiling and disappearing into another hole. Before she could think to turn, Judith was through the hole and pointing the gun at her.

"This is insane," Linda said. "Let's go back."

Judith waved the gun at the ladder.

"No."

Without any emotion at all, as calmly as if she were inviting Linda to supper, Judith said, "Do you want me to kill you right here?"

"Come on, come on," Brian told the elevator. Why the goddamned hell hadn't Linda the sense to call him before leaving? Because she doesn't trust you, he growled to himself. The elevator doors opened and he leaped inside, jabbing the first floor button and stamping his foot repeatedly as if that would get the machine to hurry.

According to Sally Beachman, a dark-haired woman had been brought up by PR and had met with Linda. They talked quietly, then left together. It had to be Judith. But what the hell was going on? Were they going somewhere to meet Paul? But if Judith knew about Grodman's death, would she willingly return to that goofball? Alone in the elevator, he began to wonder if Paul was in the building, if Paul was after *him*.

The doors opened and he ran across the hall to the guard desk in the rotunda. Before George could object, he snatched up the visitors list and scanned it. "The woman I came in with this morning—did she leave, George?"

"Uh-huh."

"With another woman?"

"Uh-huh. Two of them." George stood up and his finger landed on Linda's name. "The other one came in later." He eased the board out of Brian's hand and flipped back to the front page. "Here she is. Wasn't here twenty minutes."

Brian stared at the name. Judith Berg. "Was there a man with her?"

"No, she was alone."

"Did Mrs. Sharman leave any message for me? Did she tell you where she was going?"

"No, sorry."

Brian saw the police car pull up outside and two plainclothes detectives get out. They came toward the door. He turned to the guard. "George, do me a favor. Those cops are looking for me. There's a story breaking and I can't talk to them right now. Tell them I left five minutes ago and you don't know where I've gone."

"Sure, Mr. Hawthorn."

Brian took the stairs three at a time, came out on the second floor and ran to the elevator. He got off on the fourth floor and sprinted all the way back to the newsroom. They might believe George; they might not. If they decided to search, he had bought some time. But they would come to the newsroom first. He thought fleetingly that he ought to turn right around and tell them that Judith was taking Linda to meet Paul, and they don't realize the danger they're in and somebody ought to go after them.

Go after them where?

He reached the newsroom out of breath, pausing to wonder again what Judith was doing. If she knew Grodman was dead—

The reporter who had given him the news about Grodman rushed past him, clutching a set of black and white glossies in his hand. "Jackpot!" he said. "Got a picture of the dead lawyer. Taken yesterday—everybody's in it!"

Brian grabbed his arm. "Can I see?" The reporter fumbled one free and thrust it at him, then shot through the door and headed for the city editor's cubicle. Brian studied the picture. There was Mizzell in the doorway of his house, shoving two people into a crowd of reporters—really *shoving*—and the expression on his face: pure anger. The man stumbling off the front step looked surprised—that had to be Grodman. And the girl was staring right into the camera, her arm a blur as she tried to cover her face. Brian stared hard at Judith Berg. Though they had never met, he was dead certain he'd seen her before.

Where?

CHAPTER 17

The second room was empty.

Linda could see worry starting to gnaw at Judith. She said nothing, hoping that whatever Judith intended had to include Paul and, if he wasn't here, maybe she wouldn't follow through with her threat.

Using the gun as a prod, Judith made her climb the next ladder. Halfway up, Linda wondered why the hell she was being so cooperative.

Let go. You'll come crashing down on her head. You might suffer a few cuts and bruises, but that's better than bulletholes.

Linda glanced down. Judith was climbing one-handed, keeping the gun pointed at her. All thoughts of heroism vanished. Cautiously, Linda stuck her head through the last hole and looked around. She saw no one. Relieved, she hauled herself through and fell on the concrete floor. It was filthier than the others, littered with bird-droppings and leaves. Looking around, she saw that each wall went up about three feet to a set of triple arches, separated by columns and open to the air.

Evidently, there was work being done on the tower: a pipe scaffolding on wheels rose from the floor to the ceiling. The base was square and ran about a third the length of one wall. Canvas dropcloths were draped over the top of the platform, twenty-five feet up.

"Where's Paul?" Linda said.

Judith came through the hole and looked around, surprised and confused.

Linda stood up. Judith hissed at her to stay crouched. Linda backed into a corner and watched Judith circle the room, absorbed in thinking something out. She set down her bag and switched the gun to her other hand. "He'll come back," she said. "We'll just wait."

"What if he doesn't?"

Judith didn't answer. She opened the bag and fumbled inside, pulling out a large thermos. Sitting on the floor, she gripped it between her knees and opened it with one hand. "Thirsty?" she asked.

Linda eyed the gun. "Are we having a tea party?"

Judith smiled. "You've got it all wrong."

"That is a gun, isn't it?"

"I had to get you up here. This won't work without you."

"I might believe that if you put the gun away."

Judith shrugged and set the gun down at her side, within reach. She poured a cupful of iced tea and placed it on the floor between them. Gesturing at it, she said, "Peace offering."

"Why did you threaten to kill me?"

"I couldn't let you leave."

What the hell is going on? Does she mean she won't use the gun? What'll happen if you try to go down that ladder right now? Want to gamble?

No way.

She slid to a squat in the corner and glanced at the cup.

Take the tea. Humor her.

She reached for the cup and brought it to her lap. Judith seemed pleased.

"Do you know how difficult it's been living with Paul?" Judith said. "You worked with him; you saw only one side. I got everything else."

"Nobody forced you."

"You're right. It was my choice. But it still wasn't easy. Are you going to drink that? I've only got one cup."

Linda raised it to her lips and tasted it. Too sweet, loaded with sugar. She forced herself to sip it slowly, then put the empty cup back on the floor. Judith poured some more.

Linda told herself to keep talking. "Why wasn't it easy?"

Judith swirled the liquid in the cup. "Did you go to college?"

"Yes."

"I didn't."

Congratulations. Now we're sitting here reminiscing.

"And that has something to do with Paul?"

"In a way. I didn't even like high school. I felt stifled. A misfit. You know what it's like to be misunderstood?"

Linda stared at her. "Yes, I was a teenager once. It's a disease we outgrow."

"Not all of us. Sometimes things happen that you never forget." She seemed far away. "They stay with you forever. Like . . ." She put the cup down. "Like first love."

Oh, dear God. She's still hung up on the first guy she fell for!

"All right. Go on, tell me. Who was it?"

"My cousin."

"Judith," Linda said impatiently, "have you dragged me up here at gunpoint to tell me about an incestuous affair with your cousin in high school?"

"We loved each other very much. We spent a whole summer together."

"Then what—your family stepped in?"

"They never found out about it. Somebody else got in the way.

Jesus Christ, Judith—at that age people fall in and out of love once a week!"

"This was different. I've never loved anyone else."

Linda frowned. "Not even Paul?"

Judith looked at her contemptuously. "Never."

"Really? You've been sleeping with him for almost a year! Was that a charade?"

"A necessity."

It didn't make sense. Linda grew restless. She tried to draw her legs up but the movement made her nauseous.

This is really getting to me. I'm going to be sick. . . .

"I had to let him use me. That was the only way to keep him. It was disgusting at first, but I learned how to fuck him and not think about it."

Again Linda tried to move. She leaned forward on her arms, but even that slight imbalance made her dizzy. She fell back and caught her breath.

What's wrong with me?

Judith had stopped talking and was looking at her curiously.

Linda fought a wave of nausea and said in a small voice, "If you didn't . . . didn't care for him . . . why did you . . . ?"

"I had to."

"*Why?*"

"Because of what he did to my cousin, *Lori Cornell*."

Clutching the photo, Brian hurried back to his desk. Bass was on his feet, mumbling that he had to leave, and if Brian didn't need him anymore . . .

"Sit down, Hugo."

Exasperated, Bass dropped back into the chair, watching curiously as Brian fished among the eight-by-tens he'd made earlier.

Brian found the shot he was looking for, one taken outside the courtroom right after the verdict was read, a picture he remembered as profoundly affecting him all those years ago. There was the Cornell clan, a collective portrait of shock and disbelief. Herbert and Lovita Cornell and a gaggle of good old churchgoing Americans. He searched among the faces of the kids—there were four teenagers, two of them girls. They were all in the row behind the grownups, where the focus was a bit soft, but there she was.

Different hair color and style, bushier eyebrows, plumper cheeks and a look of wide-eyed devastation. . . . Another picture, taken a few moments later, with the family huddled and in tears, except for the one girl sitting away from the others, her face frozen in outrage. Judith Berg wasn't her real name.

She was the cousin who had offered to sleep with Brian to keep him from smearing Lori's reputation—

"I know that woman," Bass said.

"What?" Brian looked up.

Bass was leaning over, looking at the other photo, the one of Judith and Grodman taken outside the Mizzell house. "I know her," he said again. "She was one of Gene's patients."

"That's Mizzell's girl, Judith Berg."

Bass shook his head. "No—her name is Marilyn Hanser. Gene worked with her for eight months—"

Brian stared at him.

The door to the newsroom opened and two men walked in.

Brian grabbed Bass's arm and pulled him away from the desk. "Don't say a word, Hugo." He snatched up the pictures. "We're getting out of here. Those are cops. Unless you feel like answering more questions, just keep walking."

Glancing back, Bass followed Brian quickly to the end of the newsroom, then into a hall and out to another elevator. As soon as the doors closed and they started down, Brian said, "Tell me more about Marilyn Hanser."

"She was a lesbian."

"Come on, Hugo, she's been living with Mizzell!"

"I'm not kidding. That was her problem when she came to Gene."

"When did he start treating her?"

"Two years ago."

Brian stared at the wall. "Son of a bitch, she used Dahlke to get a line on Mizzell!"

"Gene would never disclose anything about a patient—"

"No?" Brian spoke through his teeth. "He was such a pushover for a pair of legs that when Linda Sharman walked into his office to ask about Mizzell, he forgot all about patient confidentiality and threw his tapes at her. Why? Was he hoping to turn her on by letting her discover what a genius he was?"

Bass wiped his brow.

Brian paced the elevator, a plot unraveling in his mind. His findings about Lori Cornell's sex life had only scratched the surface. What if she had gone both ways? Could Lori and her mousey little cousin have been lovers? Was that why the cousin had offered to sleep with him? To keep him quiet, to stop him from finding out their sordid little secret? Maybe that's what she had meant about protecting Lori's name.

If he was right, then where in the scheme of things did that place Judith or Marilyn or whoever the hell she really was? She had been living with Mizzell. She *had* to know that he was Gary Steen. But did *he* know she was Lori Cornell's cousin? Doubtful. Unlikely. Impossible.

When Steen killed Lori, wouldn't the cousin have been crushed? And what must she have felt when he was sent to Camarillo

instead of the gas chamber? And when he was released . . . ?
Whatever was boiling inside this girl had found only one outlet,
hatred for Gary Steen. Over the years, that hatred had become a
passionate desire for revenge, and it must have driven her to
extreme, almost improbable lengths. . . .

She had planned it. She had stalked Paul Mizzell to avenge
Lori's murder. That's why she became involved with Dahlke—to
track down Paul. Once she found him, she became his lover and
gained his confidence. She was the one who sent him all those
things in the mail—Linda was right about that. But why? What
was she planning to do? Scare him to death? Torture him? Drive
him to commit murder? Or just make him *believe* that he was
killing again? She murdered Dahlke, knowing that the finger of
guilt would point to Paul, then she followed up with Grodman,
Paul's lawyer—

And now she's got Linda!

The elevator stopped in the basement, and Brian led Bass into
the printing room. They crossed an ink-coated catwalk overlooking the thundering presses then went through a door into a huge
storage area.

"Did Dahlke cure Marilyn Hanser?" Brian shouted over the
noise.

"Not on his own!" Bass hollered back. "He sent her to
Breakthrough."

"You're kidding."

"But she fell in love with a lesbian up there, one of the
surrogates—"

Brian grabbed Bass's arm again and swung him around, but he
didn't have to ask. He knew instinctively which lesbian Bass was
referring to. *Norma.*

Bass pulled his arm free. "They met one more time in the
office and had an argument. She walked out and disappeared.
Gene was very upset about it."

"Come on!" He pulled Bass to a door that opened onto a
loading dock. They went past a fleet of delivery trucks and out to
the street.

"Now what?" Bass asked as Brian paused at the curb, still
clutching the photographs.

"I'm thinking. We've got quite a responsibility here. That woman is crazy. Whatever Mizzell is, she's worse. I think she killed your partner and probably the lawyer too."

Bass stared at him.

"Now she's got Linda and I don't know where the hell they've gone. Think!" he shouted at himself.

"Why—why would she kill Gene?"

"Didn't want to be recognized. She was living with Mizzell as Judith Berg. As long as she could keep him happy in bed, he wouldn't go to his doctor, and she could continue to make him crazy. But Linda went to see Dahlke, and that must have renewed your partner's interest in Paul. Judith couldn't risk a meeting, so she killed him, implicating Paul. Then she did in Grodman to make it look even better. And ultimately, she'll get Paul—self-defense! What a fucking story!"

He turned and ran toward the corner of First and Spring.

"Where are you going?" Bass yelled.

"Parker Center—the police!"

"I thought you wanted to avoid them."

"Not anymore! Come on!"

The light changed and Brian sprinted across the street. Without knowing why, Bass jogged after him.

A weight like a mass of stone held Linda down to the floor, and a warm flush worked through her body. Judith squatted a few yards away, watching her. "I feel sick," Linda said.

"You're doing fine." Judith held the cup out again. "More?"

Linda tried to shake her head but it wobbled on her neck and made her feel even worse. Her heart pounded and her pulse was racing.

What's wrong with me?

Judith watched her without moving.

Linda tried to push herself up. Her elbow wouldn't lock. It kept collapsing and that started her laughing.

Nothing's working.

She gasped and her head lolled to one side. She saw Judith carefully pouring the tea back into the thermos then screwing the cap back on. Her mind tried to focus.

Judith and Lori Cornell, cousins. What does that mean? Cousins . . .

She closed her eyes and tried to concentrate, but giddiness invaded her stomach. Sweat broke out over her body. She wanted to get up, to stand on her feet and prove she still had control of herself, but her limbs wouldn't cooperate. Invisible hands held her down. She saw Judith move closer, dragging the handbag. Her face loomed up and eyes probed hers.

"How do you feel?"

I'm sick. . . . Help me up.

The words wouldn't come. Her mouth had a metallic taste.

What's wrong? What have you done to me?

Judith raised a hand. Strong fingers cupped Linda's face, moving it gently from side to side. Linda was overcome by dizziness.

Don't do that. Leave me alone. Please go away.

Judith's hand dropped to Linda's shoulder, lightly brushing strands of damp hair off her neck then, trailing downward, slid across Linda's breast.

Oh God, don't do that.

Judith's fingers tapping lightly on her breast felt like a series of hammer blows. Pain radiated outward and she tried pulling back to escape the hand. Judith looked at her sharply, then her fingers closed and squeezed. Pain exploded across Linda's chest and swept through her body. She gasped as it subsided to a fierce ache. Her mouth opened; she tried to form a protest. Judith had already released the breast. Her hand lay absently on Linda's leg. Heat spread from her touch.

Oh, please. Please let go of me—

Judith's eyes darted over Linda's body. "You look warm," she said. "Let's get you comfortable."

Just get me out—

Linda's head rolled again and her eyes settled on the thermos.

The tea. There was something in the tea!

"Acid," Judith said, seeing the look and anticipating Linda's question. "Ever had LSD before?"

Linda mouthed no and, almost detached, watched Judith's hands descend on her, parting her vest and sliding it down her shoulders, picking up her arms and pulling them through, throwing the vest into a corner of the tower then untying the scarf at her throat. She pulled the silk across the back of Linda's neck. The fabric scraping her skin felt like razor blades. She wanted to scream. Then Judith ripped her blouse open and pulled the tails out of her skirt. Pressing Linda's head to her chest, she worked the blouse off. Linda tried to pull away, but her muscles were useless. Judith popped the hooks of her bra.

Linda started to sob, panicked by her helplessness.

"Easy now," Judith said. "Let's just get these things off and you'll feel much better. You have to understand, Linda, there's nothing personal in any of this." She pushed, and Linda fell back against the wall, gasping as the rough mortar cut into her skin. "Nothing personal at all."

Judith propped her up and stared at her breasts. Linda wanted desperately to cover herself, to hide from those cold brown eyes. Then she felt fingers at her waist. Judith was unzipping her skirt. She was pulled forward again and everything swam crazily. Hands scrabbled at her back, pulling down her skirt and everything else in one movement. Then she was dropped hard on the floor, bits of gravel digging into her exposed buttocks.

She stared in disbelief as Judith worked the clothing down her legs. "Isn't that better?" Judith said. "It's much easier if you don't resist."

The words echoed in Linda's ears. She found it harder to focus now. Judith's face kept drifting to the right.

"Dahlke was easy. He thought I was back for more of his precious therapy. Was he surprised . . ." Her voice drifted, too, closed out momentarily by a high-pitched whistle that came from somewhere deep in Linda's protesting brain.

Judith lifted Linda's calves and pulled off her shoes, throwing them into the corner along with everything else. Linda slumped naked against the wall, her flesh clammy as Judith ran a hand up her leg.

It's not my body. It can't be mine. What would I be doing in this horrible place with no clothes on?

"Grodman was harder," Judith was saying. "I had to ball him, then I ran a bath and told him we'd go again in the tub. He

got in first, then I came in with the knife—Oh, I forgot!'' She
turned to the handbag, dug in it and hauled out a long-handled
kitchen blade.

What's happening to me?

The tower walls, the scaffolding, Judith—everything receded
but the cold metal blade growing larger in front of her.

Judith moved closer and laid the flat of the blade against
Linda's breast. Linda gasped.

Please don't. Please, please don't!

"Do you know what's amazing?" Judith's whisper in her ear
sounded like a roar. "The look of surprise when you stab someone. They know what's happening, but they can't believe it.
Grodman threw up his hands to protect his face, but I put it right
in here—''

The tip of the knife rested below Linda's breastbone, then
Judith drew the blade gently down her stomach to the thatch of
hair between her legs.

"And I pulled it all the way down to there. He didn't even
scream. He looked at me with big dumb eyes and groaned. Then
he saw the water change color and just couldn't believe it.''

She smiled and backed away, placing the knife on the floor
near the gun. Then she began to undress herself, neatly folding
her clothes and piling them into the corner with Linda's. "You
have to be methodical,'' she said. "You have to think of everything. I can't be found with blood on my clothes.''

Her voice became overlapping echoes, and Linda watched her
recede, shrinking. . . . Or was it the walls behind her growing
bigger? The arches thinned and lengthened like taffy, stretching
upward, pushing the cross-beamed ceiling above the scaffold
higher into the sky—

That's wrong. That's impossible. Your eyes are lying.

The tower wasn't stretching at all. The floor was dropping and
she was sinking with it. Her fingers scratched at the concrete as
her center of gravity lifted. She felt herself falling. It was like the
sudden plunge of an elevator. She wanted to reach up and grab
the scaffolding, let the floor and Judith fall away—Her chin
dropped to her chest and she forced her eyes shut.

When she opened them again, she was looking down along her

own bare legs. Her feet appeared to be growing longer; it felt as if bone and flesh were pulling apart. She tried to scream, but again nothing came out. She saw the knife shimmering on the floor. The blade began to lengthen and flow toward her from the handle like a flat silver snake, creeping between her legs, broadening until its edges touched the inside of her thighs. She felt a tingle, then a cutting sensation . . .

Her legs jerked up involuntarily.

Judith stepped into her line of sight, naked, her voice making the walls vibrate like the cone of a speaker—

". . . had to go through to get this far. My skin still crawls when he touches me. I have to tune him out and just think about doing this for Lori . . ." Judith squatted and fished in the handbag again. "Dahlke was my first step. If I could stand being pawed by him, I figured I could handle Paul. But it didn't work. I went cold when he touched me. So he sent me to that place you went to last night—you and your nosy reporter."

What are you talking about?

Judith pulled something out of the bag and moved closer, staring into Linda's eyes, reaching up and lifting her lids to examine her pupils. "I found someone at Breakthrough who understood. She taught me a lot. Not just how to fake doing it, but how to take liking it." She froze for a moment, thinking about it. Tears rolled down her cheeks. "I got her to tell me about Paul. She said he needed an aggressive woman, so I made her show me how. Then I went after him." She sucked in her breath and her face hardened. "Here, let's get this on you—"

She stood up, straddled Linda's legs and shook out a garment she was holding. Linda stared at it. Pink filled her vision. Judith turned it around. White letters. UCLA.

The sweat shirt.

Judith pushed it over Linda's head and pulled her arms through the sleeves. She drew it down until it bunched at the waist. Then she stood back and put her hands on her bare hips. "Oh, he'll like that," she purred. "It'll bring back everything."

Take it off. Please take it off.

Judith squatted again and looked Linda in the eye. Scratching her nose, she said, "As soon as I heard they let him out of the hospital, I knew I had to do *something*. Took me a while to find him, then I had to make him dependent on me. I had to make sure he wouldn't want any other friends. I had to keep him so involved in *us* that nobody else mattered. It wasn't so hard: he wanted to be dominated. Then I started my little mail campaign. He got scared, and that made him depend on me even more. That worked out fine. See, my first plan was to drive him crazy, then rig an accident that would kill him. I fixed the brakes on his car but he survived that. Then I got to thinking that was too good for him. I wanted him to suffer. I had such power over him, I decided to use it. When Dahlke stuck his nose in, I had to speed things up. And in deciding what to do about him, I hit on the idea of a few dead bodies pointing the finger at Paul. And it would be even better if I could make him believe *he* was doing the killing. I knew right away you would be one of his victims." She smiled as if it was a great honor.

Linda watched Judith's face grow into an immense white mask, her eyes deepening into seething brown pools.

"Nobody will question what happened. The police already think he killed Dahlke. And I'll retract my story about being at Sabato's with him. I'll tell them I was emotional and just trying to help Paul. When they find Isaac Grodman, they'll be sure Paul did that too. I'll tell them that he played on our sympathies to get us up here. He drugged both of us, killed you . . . but I had the gun." She grinned. "And no choice. I had to use it."

Linda's breath tightened in her chest. Her head lolled back and she stared up at the ceiling, at the crumpled drop cloths on top of the scaffolding. Was her mind playing tricks again—or did one of them move?

Lieutenant Eddie Vega lit another rum-soaked cigar, smoothed his black hair into place, and listened intently to what Brian and Bass were trying to tell him. He had long experience with Brian Hawthorn's theories and had learned over the years that it was best to let him finish, but finally he'd heard enough. He pushed the photographs back across the desk and said, "So she used two names. So what?"

"Jesus Christ, Eddie," said Brian, "will you get the tacos out of your ears? Mizzell was living with her and he didn't know she was the cousin of the girl he killed years ago! He's been set up right down the line! She's crazier than he ever was!"

"That's your opinion," said Vega. "We think otherwise."

"Of course you do—you're cops!" Brian snapped back. "According to you, Grodman was killed around six A.M., right?"

"Right."

"Judith Berg was staying with him. She called me from Grodman's home just after eight this morning, and she didn't say anything about a dead body in the bathtub. Little hard to overlook, especially since she had spent the night. Now, if Mizzell was standing there, forcing her to make the call, I could understand her silence. But when she showed up at the *Times*, she was alone. There was no one holding a gun on her!"

Vega shook his head. "If she's the killer, why did she come to the *Times*?"

"To convince Linda Sharman to leave with her and not tell me where they were going."

"Can't blame her for that."

"I think Judith told her they were going to meet Mizzell, and she's setting Linda up as victim number three. I also think she knows where Mizzell is. She's going to kill Linda and make it look like he did it!"

Vega was silent a moment, then said quietly, "She's not the only one who knows where he is. He left a message on Grodman's answering machine last night, which included a number where he could be reached. Turned out to be a pay phone at the UCLA Student Union."

Bass grunted. "That's very interesting."

"Very smart," countered Vega. "Easy to get lost. Lots of places to hide on that campus. But we'll find him. We've already got men over there looking for him."

"I meant interesting that he would go back *there*," said Bass.

"But you're hunting the wrong person!" Brian insisted. "Look, Eddie, how fast can we get out there?"

"Me—about fifteen minutes by chopper. You—take your chances on the freeway." Vega picked up his coat. "Now, if you don't mind—"

"We're going with you," Brian said.

"Uh-uh." Vega started out the door then looked back at Bass. "You could be some help. Mizzell might listen to you."

Bass hesitated. Catching Brian's desperate look, he said, "Only if he comes too."

Vega scowled, then pitched his cigar into an ashtray. Five minutes later, they piled into a helicopter on the roof of Parker Center and took off, heading west.

CHAPTER 18

He shifted position and inched his body across the platform, pulled back the edge of the tarp, and looked down at the floor twenty-five feet below. His mind swirled as he tried to understand what was happening. Even from this vantage point, he could see the glazed look in Linda's eyes, her body limp against the wall, with the sweat shirt covering her torso. Judith, nude, kneeling over her with the knife . . .

He had been here since shortly past noon, after spotting Linda outside and realizing that Judith had not come alone. Frightened, he had slipped through the throng of students, made his way back up to the roof and through the window he had been using to get in and out of the tower, then up to the first little room to wait.

A few minutes later, he had heard the door open downstairs, followed by hushed voices.

"What are you doing?"

"Calling the police."

"I thought you wanted to help him."

"I do, but this isn't the way."

"Put the phone down, Linda."

"Leave the gun down here and I'll think about going up there."

Hearing that, he had moved without stopping, reaching the top room with the open arches, realizing too late that if they came up here, he was trapped. He began to panic and couldn't understand why. Judith wouldn't—

Then he had heard her voice, loud: "Do you want me to kill you right here?"

Shrinking back, he had bumped into the scaffolding, then he had turned and looked up at the platform above, stacked with drop cloths. He had climbed quickly. Reaching the top, he had covered himself with the cloths and waited.

Now they were in the room, and he had listened to every word, his mind alternately resisting then accepting, drifting between past and present in a maze of confusing images. Judith Berg . . . The truth penetrated and began to clear his doubt.

It's not me! Gary Steen is dead and buried and I'm here in his place, but I'm not the killer!

Looking over the edge of the platform, he stared at Judith's naked body crouched before Linda, and he thought about going down there, about getting his hands on Judith.

You did it. You lied to me, took over my life.

Lori's cousin . . .

Paul's eyes locked on the knife blade and Judith's hand clutching it, knuckles white with tension.

Lori's cousin . . . Lori's cousin . . .

What was she going to do to Linda?

". . . *Police already think he killed Dahlke . . . retract my story . . . When they find Isaac Grodman . . . played on our sympathies . . . killed you . . . killed you . . . killed you . . .*"

All of it, from the packages in the mail—even further back, their first chance meeting—no accident at all. She had planned everything.

And now she's going to kill again.

He stared at Linda's legs. The whiteness of her flesh. The rumpled pink sweat shirt.

Blood again.

Arms jumping in the air as he stabbed repeatedly. Screams. Wiping his hands on the pink sweat shirt . . .

It's Lori down there. Lori's going to die again.

A sob caught in his throat. He wiped sweat from his eyes and tired to focus.

Linda—not Lori. That's Linda.

Linda's head fell back and she stared upward, her gaze connecting with Paul's. Sluggishly, only dimly aware, she watched him push the tarpaulin off, move to the edge of the platform, and sling a leg over.

*   *   *

The helicopter churned across Beverly Hills at fifteen hundred feet. Brian and Bass were in the back of the four-seater, Lieutenant Vega and a pilot in front. Responding to something coming in on his headset, Vega pressed it tighter to his ear and listened.

"Uh, repeat that, would you, Sergeant?" He listened again. "Thank you. Out." He turned and looked back at Brian. He had to shout to be heard. "They've just finished a search of the Student Union. No sign of Mizzell. Any idea where he might have gone?"

Brian thought for a moment. "He wouldn't risk staying in the open. He'd want to go someplace safe."

"Gee, that's a big help," said Vega.

"I mean someplace he *believes* is safe," added Brian.

"You got any ideas, Doc?"

Bass frowned. "That he went to the college is significant. Obviously, he feels comfortable there. It's possible he's regressing to when he killed the Cornell girl. He found a place to hide then; maybe he's gone back there."

Brian stared at him then shouted, "The tower at Royce Hall!"

"I think that's it," Bass agreed.

Vega was skeptical. "Hawthorn, I don't believe he's that dumb. Let us do our own work."

"Eddie, it's the only lead you've got!"

Vega thought about that, then flipped a switch on the communications panel and spoke into the mike. "This is Vega in Airborne Unit Four. Patch me through to SWAT."

Brian looked down at a broad green field, the Los Angeles Country Club, as Vega barked a series of orders calling for a SWAT team to descend on Royce Hall. Vega turned around suddenly—

"Can you see into that tower from the air?"

Brian leaned forward, trying to recall what Royce looked like. "I think so," he said. "It's got these large open arches—"

"You know how to get in?"

"Yeah, I went up there for a story. There are three little rooms—"

"All right," Vega interrupted. He passed Brian his headset. "Explain to these guys. And be specific."

*   *   *

Linda began to shake uncontrollably. She wanted to stop, but she couldn't make her body cooperate. Judith was leaning forward, lips stretched in a taut smile, eyes gleaming as she placed the point of the blade beneath Linda's breast and whispered, "Don't move . . ."

Linda winced and glanced at the blade. The point dug into the pink material and pricked her skin beneath. She threw her head back and stared up at the ceiling. A black shadow oozed over the platform. It flowed evenly, blotting out the scaffold. It seemed to take forever to descend only a few feet. Then she realized it wasn't a shadow. It was a moving figure. A man.

She was distracted by a sound coming from somewhere deep in her mind, a distant whirring like the beat of a large pair of wings. It grew in intensity. The figure stirred on the scaffold. The face stared down at her, vaguely familiar.

Linda gasped as the knife pricked her skin again, then pulled along the pink material.

The whirring came closer, filling the room. A blast of wind blew into the tower, raising eddies of dust and rattling the scaffold. One of the tarpaulins was blown off the top and flapped against an arch.

The man climbing down froze where he was, the breeze tugging at his trousers.

Judith sat up sharply and looked out. She saw the helicopter hovering outside, descending slowly, the letters LAPD stenciled in paint on its side. She rose in disbelief and glanced up at the scaffold. She saw the tarp fluttering to the floor—

And the man looking down at her.

Dropping the knife at Linda's feet, she scooped up the revolver and flung herself against the wall, out of sight of the chopper. She raised the gun and fired at Paul.

The bullet struck him in the arm near the left shoulder. He bellowed in pain, then lost his grip and dropped like a stone. He hit the floor and sprawled. Dazed, he stared at Judith. She fired again and missed. He scrambled up and threw himself at her, shoving her bare skin along the wall, scraping her back open. She screamed and grappled with him—

What's happening?

Linda stared up at the fight, her senses dulled, her reactions maddeningly slow—

Judith struggled to get the gun around for another shot and yelled at Paul, "Bastard! Murdering, fucking son of a bitch bastard!"

The wind from the hovering chopper pushed them off balance. Linda stared up at the fight, seeing two animals viciously clawing at each other, the female howling insanely. The male's teeth were bared in pain and anger, the back of his shoulder a gory mess.

He grabbed Judith by the wrist and threw her across the room. She crashed into the scaffolding and dropped the revolver.

Brian, Bass, and Eddie Vega watched, horrified. To them, it looked like a madman attacking a naked woman. Brian couldn't believe what he was seeing. Mizzell—no doubt about it. And his look of rage was unmistakable. Vega was already talking to the SWAT team. Brian glanced down and saw some of them, in black flak vests and carrying rifles, coming off the portico. Vega yelled at the pilot to land.

"What are you going to do?" Brian shouted.

"We need a marksman!"

The chopper set down. One of the SWAT men ran out and Vega opened the door. The SWAT man turned and sat on the floor. Vega grabbed his belt to hold him steady, then jerked his thumb at the pilot. The marksman unslung his rifle as the chopper rose.

Brian gripped the seat in front, a voice roaring in his ears: Where's Linda? What's happened to Linda?

They hovered as close as they could to the arches and Brian looked into the tower.

Paul leaped past Judith, trying to get the gun. She snatched up the tarp and flung it over him. He fell in a tangle and struggled to get free. Judith bent to get the knife. Her fingers closed on the handle, and when he came lurching to his feet, she drove the knife into his side with the full weight of her body.

Paul groaned and his eyes bulged.

No! Oh no! Leave him alone!

Linda shrieked to herself, the words still unable to come out.

Judith tried to get the knife out for another attack. Paul's good arm lashed out and clamped around her neck. He pulled her body tightly against his. She screamed, "Let go!" and beat him with her fist.

Linda saw blood pouring down Paul's trousers.

Oh God, she's killed him. Get away. Move. Come on, get to the hatch.

It was her only possible escape. She concentrated on forcing her body to function.

"You in the tower—freeze!"

Vega's voice thundered through the bullhorn but was drowned out by the rotors. From the chopper they watched the fight but couldn't be sure what was happening. The woman was pounding the man with her fist. He had one arm around her neck and was choking her.

"Put him down!" Vega yelled at the marksman.

"Can't get a clear shot! He's got to let the girl go!"

Bass peered over Brian's shoulder and both of them saw the knife buried in Paul's side when he moved around abruptly. Then Judith got free and shoved him clear.

For a split second, Paul was framed in the archway and Brian suddenly knew that they were going to make a horrible mistake. "Don't—!" he started to shout. Then it was too late.

The rifle crack was swallowed up by the sound of the rotors, but he saw Paul lifted up by an invisible hand and flung against the scaffolding, a look of astonishment on his face and a rose blooming in his chest. Then he slid to the floor.

Brian's mouth fell open.

What about Linda?

The helicopter dropped suddenly and he saw the ground rushing up. Vega was on the mike, calmly telling the SWAT team to get into the tower immediately. The skids hit grass and the marksman jumped clear.

Linda stared at Paul's body slumped against the scaffolding, at his dazed and dying eyes and the pulsing hole in his chest. Comprehension cut through her drugged haze. Judith was huddled in the corner, her flesh streaked and splattered with blood. Linda's jaw worked as she tried to get a scream out. Finally it came in a long, rising howl of horror. She turned and forced her hands to work. She began clawing across the floor to the open hatch.

Too stunned to move, Judith stayed in the corner while she told herself there was one more thing that had to be done. Linda could not be found alive. And it had to look like Paul had killed her.

Linda looked back at her legs. They still wouldn't work. She hammered at them.

Come on, damn you! Move! We can get killed here—

She heard voices below. Somebody was coming, somebody to help. She glanced back and saw Judith bent over near Paul, flipping the tarp aside.

The gun! She's looking for the gun!

Linda dropped to the floor and reached as far as she could, curling her fingers around the edge of the hatch, trying to pull herself along. She looked back and groaned.

Judith had the gun and was pointing it at her.

Oh, please don't do it—

Judith froze, listening.

Linda tried calling out to whoever was coming up from below. The words wouldn't come.

They're so close. If she fires now, they'll know she killed me. She's listening. She hears the voices too. She's not going to do anything. She's going to let me reach the hatch and get away. Please—just a few more inches!

Linda dragged herself along, then realized she wasn't getting closer. She was stopped. She looked back and discovered the sweatshirt hung up on a rusted steel rod sticking out of the wall.

No! Oh, God, please—

She fumbled with the material, then looked over her shoulder at Judith.

What's she doing—? The knife!

Judith bent over Paul, hesitating. Then her hand closed around the knife hilt and she jerked the blade out of his body. Blood spurted after it and splashed on her leg. Paul gasped and his body shuddered.

She's coming for you!

Judith grabbed Linda's foot and pulled her back from the hatch. Linda's nails scraped on the concrete as she clawed for the grip she'd lost.

Linda heard the chuck of the knife going into flesh. Pain exploded upward from her leg. She looked back and saw the blade buried in her thigh. She choked on a scream.

Don't let her do it again! Get her wrist!

She grabbed Judith's arm, and with every ounce of force left in her body, she held the knife where it was, ignoring the pain.

If she gets it out, the next stroke will kill you! Look at her eyes. She's—Ow!

Judith hammered Linda's leg with her free hand. "Let go, you bitch!" she said through her teeth.

Linda's strength ebbed. Numbness crept into her hands. Her grip softened. Judith ripped out the knife and raised her arm for another blow. Linda gasped at the pain and tried to fend her off. The knife dodged around her arm and came down between her legs.

"No!"

Her hand clamped on Judith's wrist, and even though she felt nothing in her fingers, her brain got the message and she tightened them into an iron grip and yelled as loud as she could, "No—no—no—!"

Judith howled with frustration.

A rifle barrel came through the open hatch, and a man in black followed.

Judith leaped up, the bloody knife in her upraised hand, insanity in her eyes. "Don't touch me!" she screamed. "Don't touch me don't touch me don't touch me—!" She backed to the archway.

The man with the rifle stared at Linda lying on the floor in front of him, her face controted in pain, then his gaze shifted to Paul's body at the foot of the scaffold. "Shit," he muttered and brought his legs through the hatch.

Judith knew it was too late. She turned, dropping the knife and making her last decision. She threw up her arms and pulled herself through the open archway, tumbling out of sight with a scream that was cut off abruptly when she hit the concrete below.

The man in black stared at the empty archway and swore.

Linda sank back with a relieved groan. Then her eyes went to Paul and she crawled toward him, vaguely conscious of other voices and orders and men coming through the hatch, filling the room. But she concentrated on Paul, on his barely moving lips. She reached him and pulled herself up to look at his face. A froth of red bubbles formed at the corner of his mouth and the breath rattled in his throat.

Linda's shaking hand went to his forehead and wiped away the perspiration running into his eyes. She looked up as men grouped around her, then caught sight of another figure coming through the hatch, eyes meeting hers. Then he was at her side, holding her.

"Brian," she said in a feeble croak. "Why did they kill him?"

Brian didn't answer. His face was an anguished mask.

She looked back at Paul and saw him droop sideways and breathe his last. Then she plunged down a long tunnel into darkness.

CHAPTER 19

Linda sat propped up in the hospital bed and sipped her orange juice. One good thing about being incapacitated: she was having the best rest of her life. Even the frequent fits of depression were tolerable when she compared them to what could have happened in that tower.

She glanced at the two bouquets of flowers on the window sill, both from Tony Benedict. What in the world had gotten into him? Calling every morning to be sure she was okay, refusing to discuss work except to say everything was well in hand. Was this the prelude to the big kissoff? The first time he had called, he had stumbled over his words and seemed in awe of her. What happened in the tower had been all over the news—which she had not read. She had refused all newspapers, especially the *Times*. She was afraid that if she saw Brian Hawthorn's byline she would sink into a depression and never come out. She got her information from TV, and there was plenty of that, at least the first couple of days. Then Tricia and Connie and Tom and all the other local newscasters had lost interest. The case was over, the killer was dead, back to more mundane news: the world in turmoil, a double suicide and triple murder in Rochester, New York . . . Paul Mizzell and Judith Berg were just a pair of statistics.

But Tony had become all warm and runny again, and she couldn't understand the change. She couldn't believe there was a genuine good side to that prick. He couldn't really be sweet even if he were dipped in chocolate.

She pondered on that, staring at her poor bruised leg, which was stretched out on the bed and strapped to a metal support to keep the stitches from tearing. Her thigh was covered with a dressing that was changed several times a day.

She closed her eyes and tried to remember the last man who had told her she had lovely legs. Brian? Nope. Tony? Nope. Rocky? Yeah, Rocky used to tell her she had gorgeous legs, but then he was a leg man and thought the slightest bit of exposed skin was worthy of praise. He didn't count.

Jennifer. That's right. Your own kid. Your precious teenaged pumpkin once watched you stepping out of the shower and said, "Hey, Mom, you know you've got great wheels?" Linda smiled: she had *meant* it. When a woman tells you you've got something great—

A chill crept up her neck as Judith's face flashed before her eyes. Never mind.

She sighed. Then her eyes filled with tears as she contemplated the black bruises surrounding the dressing. What would Jennifer think now? When she called, Linda had told her everything was fine: she had a slight wound, a little loss of blood, nothing to worry about. She'd said nothing about the doctor's warning that she might come out of this with a limp, that too much muscle tissue had been severed. She had kept her voice calm, assuring Jennifer there was no reason to interrupt school to come down and nurse poor old Mom. Jennifer had cried on the phone and insisted she would be down on the weekend. But who would pick her up? She'd drive down with her boyfriend. Oh. Linda had said "oh," flat like that.

They would probably get in late Friday night and come to see her Saturday morning. She hoped the bruises would be gone by then. *Oh, what the hell are you worrying about?* she snarled at herself. *Put a blanket over the goddamned thing and quit acting like a vain old lady.*

"I want to be pampered," she said aloud, and the tears came again. She drowned them in her orange juice.

Visiting hours started at 10 A.M. Brian had been pestering her from the moment she woke up the first day, but she had consistently and coldly told him she didn't want to see anyone. She was punishing him for some reason she didn't even understand herself. Maybe he was too closely linked with what had happened and she didn't want to think about that. Finally, last night, he had insisted on coming down this morning and she had told him flatly she didn't want to see him at all, and if he came, she would simply ignore him.

Now she heard footsteps in the hall. The morning parade. An elderly lady waddled past the door, carrying a load of flowers. She peeked in and smiled. Linda's lips crinkled wanly. The woman went past and into the next room, to be met by squeals of recognition and delight. Linda tried to imagine who was in there.

A few minutes later, there was a face at her door, an aging, ravaged-looking face with a spreading grin and an unruly mop of gray hair.

"Rocky," she said, then grinned and bit her lip.

"Hiya, sweetheart." He rolled in with an outrageous bouquet of flowers and a big box of candy. Miller, Rok's former chief attorney, was pushing the wheelchair. Miller wiggled his fingers and stood back out of the way.

"Would have made it up here sooner," Rocky said, leaning over to give her a loud kiss on the lips, "but my motor conked out halfway up from the desert. Miller had to push from Pomona on."

Linda blinked and laughed.

"So, how ya comin'?"

"Oh, fine." She waved a hand at her leg and his. "Now we're a matched pair."

"Sorry—I forgot your Purple Heart. How's the food?"

"Passable."

Rocky made a face. "I can send out for deli."

"No, thank you." She shook her orange juice at him. "I'm doing quite well."

Rocky rolled a bit closer and put his hand on her calf to massage it. "Like that?"

"Mmm. Feels nice. It won't get you anywhere, though," she kidded. "I'm out of commission for a while."

"That's okay. Me, too. Gotta go in for a prostate operation." His smile was more of a wince and she read fear in it. Miller was looking at the floor.

"How are you, Rocky?" she asked.

"Sick as a fucking dog. But the hell with that." He squeezed her ankle. "God, what a leg."

Linda's eyes rolled. "You didn't come up here to play with my body, I hope."

"No." He chuckled. "Actually, Miller and I have just finished reorganizing the company. Wanna hear about it?"

Her smile faded. She regarded him helplessly, dreading that the final curtain was about to drop. Her play was going to close, and here was the kindly old theater manager come to give her two weeks' notice. "Sure," she whispered.

"Don't look so grim."

"Well, if you're going to fire me, why should I look happy?"

"Fire you?" He blinked in shock.

She waved a hand at the flowers. "Roses and peonies from you, carnations and marigolds from Benedict. Where's my wreath?"

Rocky laughed, then choked on it, yanked out a handkerchief and spat into it. He folded it quickly, but not before she saw flecks of blood. His face was red and he had trouble getting the words out after that. "I'm not here to fire you."

She couldn't help herself. Despite his illness, he was making her mad. "You didn't come up from the desert to declare your love."

"Nope. I'm here to reaffirm my faith in you."

"What are you talking about?"

He took a few deep breaths and cleared his throat, hacking. "Jesus, I'm sorry. Don't let any nurses hear this. They'll probably declare me a germ and fumigate me. Listen . . . I had no idea what was going on over at the company with this Mizzell character. No idea how involved it was. I got some sort of crazy report from Tony, but it didn't make sense. Only when I saw it on the news and began reading about it—that was some holy shit you got put through, you know?"

"Thank you." She reached for the water pitcher and poured some into her orange juice, thinning it. Then she poured a glass and passed it wordlessly to Rocky. He drank gratefully.

"Tony was concerned about the company's image in all this and I had to tell him, Hey, Tony, that's *our* girl. She helped *make* our image. I'm not about to—You know what I mean?"

Linda nodded.

"But he got me thinking. Some of the complaints, some of the things I've noticed . . . It all sort of came together and cooked. Now, the main thing is you've got to get well. Then I want to take some of the pressure off you.''

Here it comes, she thought.

''I've noticed one thing, honey, and you'll have to promise to keep your mouth shut while I tell you this.'' She nodded, closing her mouth with a click of her teeth. ''Over the last year or so, you seem to have lost a lot of enthusiasm for what you're doing. You're not the same fire-breathing creative artist I hired sixteen years ago. You delegate almost everything. You don't design anymore, you just give orders. And you've done that very well. But it got me to thinking there's no longer any reason for you to be creative director. I think you and I have the same problem: neither of us has the drive anymore. And in our two positions— mine in running the company and yours in creative art—there's got to be drive. Now, I know you think Tony is a jerk.''

Linda nodded vigorously.

''Well, so do I.''

She stared at him.

''That's the truth. I thought so the first moment I met him. But then I think that about most of the young bucks I meet in this business. They're all drive and push and ambition and greed, but they're also tremendously talented, and that's what we need.'' He looked at her for comment.

Linda choked on her words. ''You—you want to make him creative director too?''

''No. But I want somebody else in that job. Somebody *like* a Tony Benedict. Another go-getter. Someone who'll take risks and bring in new blood and make mistakes and learn from them. You don't make mistakes, Linda, but you don't take risks anymore, and neither do I. Pop music is no longer a business of long-range trends. Everything is short-term. A trend is born and dies in less than six months. We've got to stay on top of that. Can't just ride on old, threadbare coattails.''

His hand was on her ankle again. She pulled her leg up slowly, freeing it. He glanced at the ankle and smiled. ''I don't blame you. I wouldn't want me touching me. That's a hell of a leg, though. Anyway, I got a problem. I can bring in another creative director, but what do I do with Tony?''

"Boil him in oil."

Rocky laughed again. "No, he's good—*when* he's good. But he has to be sat on. Now, I think you've done pretty well with him. You've hung in there when he's been at his worst, totally in control, literally answering to nobody. And you had no support from me. You were entirely at his mercy and you didn't let him get to you."

Oh, no? she wanted to say, then suddenly she went rigid. *Wait a minute. What is he telling me?* "You knew what was going on?" she blurted out. "You knew he was trying to drive me out, and you set me up! You tested me!"

He pursed his lips and glanced at Miller, who finally spoke. "Rocky wants to kick you upstairs, Linda. He thinks you're the only one in the company capable of supervising Tony. He'll run things, but you'll be approving everything he does."

"The voice of restraint," Rocky added.

"After sixteen years," Linda said slowly, ignoring what they were saying, "you still felt that you had to *test* me?"

Rocky fidgeted. "Now, Linda—"

She pointed to the two bouquets at the window. "Does Tony know about this? Is that why he sent the flowers?"

Rocky nodded.

"And what's his reaction?"

"So delighted he ate his Gucci loafers, brass buckle and all." She didn't laugh.

"He had one condition. He said that in order for him to remain effective, we ought to keep this quiet."

Linda frowned. "Why?"

Rocky glanced at Miller. "We figure it has to do with Tony's *image.*"

"And what about mine? You want me to call the shots in private but in public make it look like I'm still answering to him? Is that sort of a corporate walk-behind-me-three-paces-lady?"

Rocky shifted uncomfortably. "Listen, I don't intend you to be a rubber stamp for that son of a bitch. I just want a smooth transition."

She pulled the covers over her bare leg and fixed him with a cold stare. "I'll tell you how to make it smooth. Let me deal with Tony Benedict. I'll make him see the light, and I guarantee he won't walk away." She sat back and gave him a determined look.

At last, Rocky grinned and said, "Sharman, I always knew you had balls."

In the afternoon, Linda had a visit from Hugo Bass, offering his services as a courtesy, if she had any need for them. She admitted she was suffering depression but felt she could deal with it as long as she knew the cause. He told her she could expect some tough moments once she got out of the hospital and she wasn't being sedated at night anymore.

"Darkness, loneliness, sudden noises, strangers, nightmares—any of these things could set you off," he said cheerfully. "In your waking hours, the middle of the day, at work in your office, in a place as safe as you can imagine, you might suddenly experience severe depression, hysterics, paralyzing fear. Of course, I'm not trying to scare you," he added.

"What a relief."

"You've got to be in touch with your feelings. You can't just forget about what happened, because it won't go away like that. It'll burrow in and eat at you like—"

"All right, all right," she said. "Just leave your card. The minute I feel like killing myself, I'll call you."

Bass looked relieved. "Thank you. Makes me feel much better."

Strange, she thought: who was supposed to be helping whom?

"Another thing," he added. "I wouldn't advise being alone when you go home."

"I'll think about that."

She did too. As soon as Bass left, she began to think about who she could get to come and stay: Jennifer and her boyfriend? No—they wouldn't hang around more than a few days. A nurse? She couldn't bear the idea of a stranger in her home, telling her what to do. A dog? Don't be silly.

Brian?

Never.

She laughed, though. He would probably leap at the chance.

It was after six P.M. and dinner was late. Impatiently, she rang for the nurse and asked what was holding things up. The head nurse walked in and announced, "We're taking you for a little walk."

They helped her into a robe, then got her off the bed and into a wheelchair, bracing the leg on the extendable support. "Where are we going?" she said.

"Tests."

"But I'm hungry."

"In due time."

The head nurse took over, wheeling her into the hall and hurrying her past the nurses' station and around a corner and into a lounge. The light was low and the curtains were closed. In the corner, a table and chairs were set up with white linen and candles. And there was Brian Hawthorn in a clean pressed suit, getting to his feet and smiling hesitantly.

The nurse wheeled Linda over to the table. "There, now. Isn't this nice for a change? A lovely candlelight supper with an absolutely charming gentleman, lots of privacy, and my personal promise you won't be disturbed"—she checked her watch—"for at least an hour."

She shook the napkin out and spread it in Linda's lap, then she stood back, clasped her hands and surveyed the setting. "Very nice," she said, and hurried out.

Brian still stood. "Hope you don't mind if I join you," he said.

Linda took a deep breath and blew it out. "Of course not. Have a seat."

"Great. I'm starved." He plopped into his chair and loosened his tie. "They promised steak and baked potato. Can I butter a roll for you?"

"If you like."

"I do." There was silence as he broke open the roll and spread it with big pats of butter. Linda gritted her teeth. If he tried to feed her—

He put the roll down and looked at her. "If you don't want me here, I'll leave. I just thought I ought to have one chance to let you know—" He broke off.

"Let me know what?"

"God damn it, I saved your life. More or less. I never did that for anyone before. The least you can do is thank me."

"Thanks."

He frowned and passed her the roll. "Did you read my articles?"
She shook her head.

"You're kidding. Why not? They were good."

"I'm happy for you. I don't care to relive it."

"Oh, well, okay, I can understand that. Not important, anyway. I mean, I never asked to see any of your work."

"We're even."

He grunted in exasperation, then remembered something in his briefcase. He pulled out a bottle of wine and set it on the table.

"I can't have that," she said. "It won't mix with the sedatives I have to take later." She winced. Her leg was starting to hurt. It always happened in the early evening. By eight, she would need a pain killer.

Brian put the wine away. "Forget it. I wouldn't exactly call this a party anyway. What have you got against me?"

"Did anybody do anything about a funeral for Paul?"

"Yeah. We had it yesterday. Contributions from your record company and my newspaper."

"Did you go?"

"Yes."

She looked at the roll, conscious of his eyes trying to bore into her.

"My apologies for being human, Linda. But you can't blame what happened to him on me or yourself. I'm sorry for what I thought all along, but it just proved my point. Tragically."

"What point?"

"About being so damn sure that someone you know isn't capable of killing. You knew Judith. Did you guess?"

She shook her head.

His voice grew husky. "Don't make me get tough. I don't want to be right. I just want to be with you."

She looked at him and the tears came. When the hospital orderly entered with their food, she was still crying and Brian was sitting next to her, dabbing at her eyes with an old, used hanky. The orderly hesitated a moment, then began to whistle as he served the dinner.

Linda thought she recognized the tune, then realized he was improvising. So was Brian, as he murmured things in her ear.

The orderly left, and soon she couldn't remember why she had been so nasty to Brian. He ate like a pig and told her old newspaper stories all through dinner. Finally, he asked what she was planning to do when she got out of the hospital.

"Go home and rest."

"What about your job?"

She told him about Rocky's visit and her promotion. He was pleased and wished her well, but expressed hope that she would take time off to fully recover. Then he asked if she would be able to manage okay alone.

Linda sat back and gauged him soberly. *What was the point of holding him at arm's length? Just don't be too open with him. Be subtle. . . . Oh, what the hell.*

"Your friend Hugo Bass came in today," she said. "He suggested I find somebody to hold my hand when I have nightmares."

Brian's face split into a wide grin.

"Is that funny?"

He apologized. "I was just remembering a piece of advice my dad gave me. He said, 'Son, never volunteer for anything.' Boy, was he wrong."

Dell Bestsellers

- ☐ **QUINN** by Sally Mandel $3.50 (17176-8)
- ☐ **STILL THE MIGHTY WATERS**
  by Janice Young Brooks $3.95 (17630-1)
- ☐ **NORTH AND SOUTH** by John Jakes $4.95 (16204-1)
- ☐ **THE SEEDS OF SINGING**
  by Kay McGrath $3.95 (19120-3)
- ☐ **GO SLOWLY, COME BACK QUICKLY**
  by David Niven..$3.95 (13113-8)
- ☐ **SEIZE THE DAWN** by Vanessa Royal $3.50 (17788-X)
- ☐ **PALOMINO** by Danielle Steel $3.50 (16753-1)
- ☐ **BETTE: THE LIFE OF BETTE DAVIS**
  by Charles Higham $3.95 (10662-1)

At your local bookstore or use this handy coupon for ordering:

Dell   DELL BOOKS
P.O. BOX 1000, PINE BROOK, N.J. 07058-1000

Please send me the books I have checked above. I am enclosing $ _____ (please add 75c per copy to cover postage and handling). Send check or money order—no cash or C.O.D.'s. Please allow up to 8 weeks for shipment.

Name _____

Address _____

City_____ State/Zip _____

It can happen to anyone. Anywhere.
At any time. You could lose control.
And in that microsecond between thinking a thing and doing it, someone else
could take command, someone willing
to wreak havoc in a mad scheme to alter
the past and change the future, and who
will stop at nothing to take Control. "Intri-
guing. Engrossing. Fascinating."
—The Los Angeles Times

WILLIAM GOLDMAN

Bestselling author of
MAGIC and **TINSEL**

A DELL BOOK • 11464-0 • $3.95
CONTROL • 11464-0 • $3.95

Dell Bestsellers

☐ **ELIZABETH TAYLOR:** The Last Star
by Kitty Kelley.................................$3.95 (12410-7)

☐ **THE LEGACY** by Howard Fast.................$3.95 (14719-0)

☐ **LUCIANO'S LUCK** by Jack Higgins...........$3.50 (14321-7)

☐ **MAZES AND MONSTERS** by Rona Jaffe...$3.50 (15699-8)

☐ **TRIPLETS** by Joyce Rebeta-Burditt...........$3.95 (18943-8)

☐ **BABY** by Robert Lieberman.......................$3.50 (10432-7)

☐ **CIRCLES OF TIME** by Phillip Rock.............$3.50 (11320-2)

☐ **SWEET WILD WIND** by Joyce Verrette......$3.95 (17634-4)

☐ **BREAD UPON THE WATERS**
by Irwin Shaw....................................$3.95 (10845-4)

☐ **STILL MISSING** by Beth Gutcheon...........$3.50 (17864-9)

☐ **NOBLE HOUSE** by James Clavell.............$5.95 (16483-4)

☐ **THE BLUE AND THE GRAY**
by John Leekley...................................$3.50 (10631-1)